ME DEEP

An utterly gripping crime thriller with an epic twist

JANE ADAMS

Detective Rozlyn Priest Book 1

JOFFE BOOKS

Joffe Books, London
www.joffebooks.com

First published in Great Britain in 2021

Cover art by Dee Dee Book Covers

ISBN: 978-1-78931-659-9

PROLOGUE

PRESENT DAY

The kill had been a clean one. A swift shove and then a single strike, powerful and accurate, and it was all over. The dead man lay on his back, a look of profound surprise on his face. The knock on the door that followed shook him far more than the act of killing.

"I heard a crash, sir. Is everything all right?"

"I dropped something, Albert. That's all. Nothing for you to worry about."

He sensed the other hesitate. "Earlier today, there was a man hanging round, sir. He wanted to speak to you, but I sent him on his way."

He could hear the curiosity in Albert's voice. "Good, good. That will be all, thank you."

He waited until the footsteps had receded down the hall and sounded on the wooden stairs. Then, turning back to the dead man, he tried to pull the weapon from the body, but succeeded only in pulling the shaft free. The spearhead stuck fast. He glanced out of the window and noted that it was thickly dark. Hefting the body onto his shoulder, he opened the solid oak door and made his way in the opposite direction to Albert, down the narrow back stairs. There would be no one in the kitchen at this time of night, no one to see as he let himself out of the kitchen and crossed the stable yard. The body lay heavy on his shoulder and the socket of the spearhead dug into his back, bruising painfully.

It was only a short distance to where his car was parked but he felt every step of it. He bundled the body into the capacious boot then set off, finally, down the long drive and out into the night.

He had been relieved that there had been so little blood. Less to clean up.

Later, much later, he took the body from the boot. The sky was light now and he had grown cramped and chilled from half the night spent in his car. He carried the body down the roadside verge and in through the open five-bar gate. Portacabins stood on one side of the site, trenches open on the other. It pleased him that he could drop this body into an already open grave. It amused him that the site director, a man he did not like, would find this new death on an ancient site that had already witnessed many.

Dropping the body into the grave he leaned into arrange it neatly, arms by its side. Then he had another go at freeing the weapon from its comfortable wound. Rocking it back and forth he finally pulled it free.

He shoved the weapon almost carelessly into his pocket and then took off, pushing through trees and splashing through a little stream to take a more circuitous route back to his car. In his haste to pull the keys from his pocket, he did not realise that the weapon fell to the ground, coming to rest in a patch of nettles. It was not until he reached his car that he discovered its loss and by then it was too late to go back.

He drove home, cursing his luck. Cursed it further when he reached his house and found Albert waiting anxiously for him.

"That man who came to the house, that man I chased away, he must have found a way inside."

"What do you mean?" Had there been blood after all? Had Albert seen?

"A piece is missing from a cabinet. The brooch, shaped like a shield, boss. The one in the cabinet beside the window."

"What?" He went upstairs, satisfied himself that no trace on the carpet betrayed what he had done, but Albert was correct. In a side room, off the main gallery, there was an empty space where the brooch had been. Had he had it in on him, that little man? That little man who thought he could threaten him with blackmail? That little man that no one would miss.

Albert had followed him in. "Should we call the police?"

"No, we will not call the police."

"He was here, sir, yesterday afternoon. I saw him by the chantry. I chased him away. Cook says she saw him at the rear of the house. He must have found a way inside."

He must indeed. "You saw him yesterday afternoon, you say?" Meaning the visit close to midnight had been his second one.

"Yes sir, an hour before you came home. I threatened him with the dogs."

And yet he came back. "Thank you, Albert. That will be all."

He watched Albert leave, stiff backed and disapproving. So. That insignificant little man had taken the brooch away and then returned. There was no knowing what he'd done with it, though there was another who might know and someone else who would enjoy finding out.

* * *

From the writings of Abbot Kendryk of Storton Abbey, Year of Grace 878:

> *It is the land that best remembers. The earth that preserves, which holds and records each thought and action that humanity lets loose into the world. They are locked tight until such*

time, perhaps, when one comes who knows how to interpret the message. One who knows that the rivers of time do not flow only in the one direction.

Some memories have strength beyond others. Some last and breathe and haunt the living; perhaps, even, they torment the dead, nagging and tugging at them to put right the wrongs they committed or to preserve those loves they left behind. For the strongest of these memories proceed from love and from death and so often such emotions, such memories are bound as one, guiding and directing the works of those who were not even conceived of when those actions were laid down in the strata of earth.

* * *

THEADING. YEAR OF GRACE 878

He was relieved that there had been so little blood. He was not a fighting man, not even a farmer who needed to butcher his own cattle. Others did that for him, men working with knives and skill and calm focus. But their task was natural and necessary in such a community as theirs. However he looked upon it, what he had done this night could not be seen as natural, or lawful, either in the eyes of God or of his fellow man.

He had followed her when she slipped from the house, letting the latch down softly so that even the dogs barely stirred. Knowing her scent and her step they had merely whined in their sleep. The moon was full, sitting on the horizon, but still bright enough to make her easy to see as she slipped from one low, elongated shadow to the next. The trees seemed to bend to give her shelter, so dense and long did their darkness lie upon the grass as she circled the great pond marking the eastern bounds of their land.

Twice she had looked back and he fancied that she sensed him behind her. The first time, she merely glanced over her shoulder, but the second, pausing at the field's edge where it gave way to dense hedge and even denser woodland, she gazed long and hard at the steading and he breathed in relief, thinking that in that almost too-late instant she had changed her mind. That divining her impulse and the evil that would come from it, perhaps even sensing that he had followed her, she would turn about and creep home as silently as she had left, and this terrible thing would all be over. Unseen, and so, easily forgiven.

His heart almost stopped when she turned again, pushing her way through a narrow gap in the field hedge and slipping like a shade into the woods beyond. No doubt keeping her tryst with *him*, that stranger, that *waelas, w*hose arrival all those months before had led to this disaster.

He knew then that he had no choice. He had known before, he supposed, when their whispering in corners and their sneaking and deceit had first alerted him. Weeks ago he had made this weapon, a strong stave of ash whittled to a club, sensing that this night would come and he would have to act.

And so he followed her, time passing and the moon setting beyond the trees so that he lost her track in the dark woods, guessing more than knowing which way she would go. Then, when he had been certain he had lost them — certain and, almost, relieved — he caught the faint whisper of her voice some way ahead.

"What was that? I heard something."

"Night creatures, nothing more. Allis, you are certain? You know that we can never come back."

"I am certain. Never more so. I'm leaving nothing to regret. Owain, I would walk through the gates of Hell to be with you even should the angels try to hold me back." She paused, startled again by some half-heard sound. "But what was that? Owain, do you think . . . ?"

But Owain did not reply, the cudgel brought down upon his head made sure of that. The first blow fetching the *waelas* man to his knees, the second felling him like a butchered ox.

She screamed once, Allis. Backed away and tried to run, but the ash club caught her as she turned, smashing hard across her temple and crushing the fine bones of her cheek and when she fell, he brought the cudgel down again and again upon her head and neck, obliterating her smile, her soft grey eyes, the curl of hair that fell loose from her coif, trailing down onto that slender neck.

And then he ran, not thinking until he reached the steading to cast his weapon aside. He hurled it as far into the pond as the fast-failing strength of his arms would allow. Then he sank down and wept, tears of shock and anger, though not regret. What needed to be done had been achieved and when he had finished weeping, he told himself that he would think of it no more.

CHAPTER 1

THEADINGFORD. PRESENT DAY

Despite being partly raised in the heart of rural England, Rozlyn Priest was not and never had been a country girl. Her view of cows echoed that of her New York grandfather; that they should arrive medium rare on a large plate, preferably with fries or tiny new potatoes and a little salad on the side. These fully grown four-footed steaks, snuffling at her with moistly discharging noses and pressing their greasy hides against her freshly cleaned suit, were doing nothing to change her opinion. Their insistent, over-inquisitive crowding made her wonder vaguely about their propensity for revenge.

Constable Riba Mills, the uniformed officer who had met her at the gate, seemed to have no such worries.

"Git!" she said and accompanied the staccato word with a quick shove against the flank of the nearest beast. It moved, just enough for her to push through the herd and for Rozlyn, reluctantly, to follow through the gap before it closed behind.

Riba was, Rozlyn noticed, wearing Wellingtons. They were mired in filth; mud and shit from the curious, smelly, fly ridden cows.

"Bullocks," she said, as though hearing Rozlyn's thoughts and feeling the need to correct. "It's all bullocks in this field — not dairy cows like you'd think to look at them. But they're just youngsters, ma'am. They won't hurt you." She grinned. "I'll have a go at getting you a pair of wellies. There's spares down at the dig. What's your size?"

She was about to tell Riba that she didn't *do* Wellingtons. Particularly not dull green wellies with the kind of heavy tread on the soles that seemed designed for muck collection, but the sight of her polished leather shoes, now caked in the stuff and the spatter of mud — she hoped it was only mud — decorating her newly pressed trousers made her think again.

"Six," she told the officer. "Is it as filthy down there?"

PC Riba Mills grinned again. "Not so bad. It's the cows, they churn up the ground, especially near the gate."

Rozlyn sighed. "Bullocks," she corrected her.

* * *

She had never been to a dig before. The closest brush Rozlyn had with actual archaeology was reruns of *Time Team* on a friend's television. Her own set she regarded mainly as a conduit for her collection of vintage films, rarely watching anything that was actually broadcast. Lately, she had even taken to avoiding the news.

"What are they digging for?"

"It's an Anglo-Saxon site," the PC said. "Apparently that's before 1066 and all that."

"Oh." On the episode she had seen they had found a Roman villa. She recalled from school history and museum visits with her mother that the Anglo Saxons had invaded sometime after the Romans and before the Battle of Hastings, and she had a vague feeling it all had something to do with King Arthur.

"What have they found?" She asked, more to keep the conversation alive than that she really wished to know.

"Oh, right. Well, this was a farm, they reckon, but it must have been a rich bloke that owned it. The house — hall — is big for the time period and there are what they think are barns and outbuildings. There's another dig a couple of miles across those fields." She pointed back to where she could see the smog haze of the city on the horizon. "A village, probably."

"And where the body was found?"

"Well, that's what's upset them most, I think. Whoever dumped it there left it in a half-dug trench. One of the graves they'd just started to open."

"Graves?"

"Yeah, this place had its own little cemetery. They reckon on there being half a dozen graves but they don't think there'll be anything in them but skeletons. No jewellery or anything. I saw this documentary once about a grave with gold plates and swords and jewellery. The guy presenting it reckoned they used to bury the dead with all their stuff ready for the next life."

"Like they did in Egypt." That idea at least felt familiar. Rozlyn had always been more taken with the ancient Egyptians than the early British.

The PC laughed. "We'd need bloody big graves these days. Play stations, TV's, mobile phones, make-up bag . . ."

Rozlyn laughed with her. "Shower gel," she added. "I'd have to have my shower gel. I once heard of some woman being buried in her Cadillac. It seemed like such a waste. I'd've been more than willing to take care of it for her."

PC Mills nodded. "Oh, lord. Me too! You know when my nan died she had it put in her will that she should be buried wearing her best suit and favourite brooch. I remember her telling my mum, she didn't want to meet God unless she was looking her best. Nowt as funny as folk."

They had reached the edge of the bullock field and crossed the stile set between hawthorn bushes, their scarlet weight of autumn berries glowing in the afternoon sun. Rozlyn stepped carefully, keeping her suit sleeves clear of the thorns and scraping the worst of the mud from her shoes on the drier grass on the other side. She'd been in court when the call came. She'd just finished her stint of giving evidence and, as the court had risen early in preparation for the weekend, she'd been looking forward to sneaking back to the office to catch up on paperwork before mooching home. Then the usher came running out with the message.

The urgency of it left her no chance to change into anything more suitable and now her one really decent suit was getting crapped up like this and she wished that she'd just snatched the time anyway. After all, the dead man wasn't going anywhere. Finishing with her shoes she glanced around, wondering what the countryside might next have in store. She and PC Mills were standing on a grassy ledge, the ground dropping off quite steeply in front of them. A narrow but mercifully dry path followed the contours of the land and promised a fairly easy way down. Below them lay an open area, enclosed on three sides by dense hawthorn hedges and tall trees, while the fourth side, directly below them, was protected by a shallow but lively stream that disappeared from view here and there between high banks. A wooden bridge, little more than a plank with a broken handrail, crossed at a point where the banks fell away and the stream spread wider as though taking advantage of its sudden freedom. A ford, once upon a time, Rozlyn guessed.

In the centre of the open area she could see deep trenches, some of them covering quite an expanse of land and, seen from above, their positioning gave her a sense of the layout of the place as it must have been. Two corners and a section of wall had been defined of the main building. Others pegged and marked with red striped tape some way behind. Smaller trenches, ranging from a few feet long, right down to squares that could be little more than a foot wide showed her the locations of other sites of interest. The outbuildings, perhaps? To her unpractised eye they looked a little random and oddly placed for that.

"Over there," PC Mills was pointing to an area half hidden by an outgrowth of rowan trees, planted in a line, straight and defined as though to act as a deliberate screen or as boundary markers. Bright ruby berries glowed against leaves just touched with gold. "That's the grave site."

"Ah." That part of the scene at least she understood. Blue-and-white tape marked out the police line. Uniformed police in shirt sleeves stood around drinking tea and waiting for the white clad figures of the forensic team to finish so that they could have the body moved and take possession of the site. A small knot of people — staff from the dig, she assumed — stood or sat in front of a portacabin. She wondered briefly how they'd got it through the bullock field and felt a momentary surge of irritation that there might have been a cleaner, easier way of getting here that no one had told her about. From time to time the civilians who'd had their workplace so disrupted glanced across at the other group. She was too far away to see their faces but their body language spoke of anxiety and deep resentment and the usual upset that came with finding a freshly dead person where you had no reason to expect one to be.

"You say the body was found in an old grave?"

"Yes."

"Someone had a sense of the appropriate."

"Sure did. It's really pissed the diggers off though."

"Murderers are not the most considerate of social groups."

"No, I guess they're not. It isn't just that though. I mean, they're all upset by it, of course. I guess digging up old bones doesn't prepare you for having a corpse dumped in your back yard so to speak. One or two asked to leave the site but DCI Brook wouldn't have it, not 'til they'd all been interviewed. Wanted them around so they could explain exactly how and when the body was found."

"Brook?" Rozlyn interrupted her. "It was Martyn that called me. I thought he was the SIO."

"No. It's Brook." The PC flashed her a curious look.

Brook, Rozlyn thought. Her suspicion about there being an easier route began to gnaw again. Brook was the type who'd find it funny to see her gored by a ruddy bull. Not, she admitted, that their horns had been very much in evidence. Her companion, realising no doubt that her curiosity was not about to be satisfied, had continued with her train of thought as though Rozlyn had not interrupted.

"Originally it was rescue archaeology, you see." She spoke the words with the air of one who has discovered a new buzzword. "They'd only got a limited time to excavate before the work started. Apparently they've had two seasons here," she frowned. "They can't dig all year round, I suppose — just late spring into autumn and the dig leader called that a season. Anyway, there've been objections to the plans so he reckons they might even get another season after this and they've been able to extend their trenches. Though with a murder investigation going on . . . I think he's worried it's going to really slow things down."

"What are they planning? Another road?"

She shook her head. "The whole valley's going to be flooded. New reservoir."

Rozlyn looked at her in surprise. For some reason she had thought that sort of thing didn't happen anymore. She turned back to look down into the valley. Country lover that she wasn't, she still felt an unexpected and equally sharp stab of pain at the thought, and the sudden overwhelming sense of loss completely caught her off guard.

"That's a shame," she said softly, noting uncomfortably that her voice seemed to shake a little. "A real shame."

* * *

Brook hauled himself up from the side of the trench. At five feet seven, he was a good few inches shorter than Rozlyn, but he made up for the deficit in width and attitude. Rozlyn had never met another man with Brook's ability to make her seem so much smaller than she was.

"Someone's taken a dislike to one of your snouts," Brook said. "Go on, don't be shy, take a good look."

He stepped aside to allow Rozlyn access to the trench and then leaned over her shoulder, breathing heavily as Rozlyn crouched down.

"Charlie Higgins." Rozlyn said. "Yes, he's one of mine. What the hell's he doing out here?"

The dead man lay upon his back with his arms outstretched on either side. His position reminded Rozlyn of a game she used to play with her friends when they were all just little kids. Standing on the end of her mother's bed, they let themselves fall straight back, no hands, nothing to break their fall but the spring of the mattress and a puffy green quilt.

It was harder than it sounded, trusting yourself and the softness of the bed just to fall back straight and flat and not panic and bend in the middle before you hit bottom. If you managed to do it right, then you fell flat out like Charlie Higgins. On your back with your toes turned up and your limp arms straight out to either side.

His eyes were open and his mouth just slightly gaping. He looked shocked, Rozlyn thought. Death had taken Charlie Higgins by surprise.

"A single stab wound," the young woman in the white coverall told her. "We've not turned him yet, but we don't think there's more."

Rozlyn nodded. Charlie was dressed as he always was, in a cheap pinstriped suit and a white poly-cotton shirt. The cuffs were worn. Charlie's cuffs were always worn. The front of the shirt was drenched with blood.

Rozlyn bent closer, leaning down into the trench, examining the sides and what section of the base was visible around the body. The surrounding area was clean of blood.

"There are blood spots there and there." The SOCO pointed to where two of her colleagues cast about the open ground, carefully pegging any trace.

"So killed, then brought here?"

"That's what it looks like so far."

"But the body wasn't wrapped in anything. Just left here."

"Just as you see it. It was dry too and there was heavy dew this morning according to the diggers. Most likely scenario is someone came in here while they were all at breakfast, dumped him in the grave and then left."

Rozlyn raised an eyebrow.

"Cool customer," Brook said, from close beside her ear. "OK, let's take a look at the back of him, now Detective Inspector Priest has given him his last rites."

Rozlyn stepped back, watching as two of the SOCO eased the body over onto his side. The ground beneath was damp, bearing out the heavy dew fall. Blood had drizzled down the sides of Charlie Higgins' chest, seeping through the jacket, but there were no further wounds visible on the dead man's back.

"OK. He's all yours," Brook told the SOCO. "Your snitches often end up dead, don't they?" he commented, turning to Rozlyn. "There was that one a few months back, decided to top herself from what I remember."

Rozlyn ignored him. Jennis Morgan had been an addict. Heroin. A user since the age of seventeen, she'd died not of an overdose, as Brook well knew, but because some bastard had cut her drug of choice with rat poison.

"But why would anyone want to kill the likes of Charlie Higgins? He was such a harmless little man."

Brook shrugged. "Being harmless doesn't keep you out of harm's way, does it?"

"No," she agreed reluctantly. "I suppose not." She stared down at the body, trying to make some sense of it being here.

Charlie was a listener; he had ears that twitched like radar for a niblet of juicy gossip and a memory like an elephant's when it came to trivia. If there had been exams in useless facts, Charlie would have had a PhD. He'd been feeding Rozlyn dribs and drabs of information since just after she joined the force and Rozlyn kept him on more from habit than for the world-shattering importance of anything Charlie had revealed. Habit, and the memory of how once or twice Charlie had, in all innocence, provided the missing piece that linked two facts together. She could think of nothing Charlie could have done or known that would have made him worth killing and certainly not worth the effort of his body being shifted way out here. Charlie was the sort of man for whom a casual death in a back alley had been a possibility for years, but this was of a different order. It made no sense, Rozlyn thought as she watched them bag the body and lay it on a folding gurney ready to be wheeled away. She watched too in growing irritation as a mortuary ambulance drove into the site from a gate she could just see in the far corner of the field.

She scowled at Brook, who grinned back at her. "You made me come all the way through that field full of bloody cows when there was a way in from the road?"

"Just thought you might enjoy the country air," Brook said.

CHAPTER 2

From the writings of Abbot Kendryk of Storton Abbey:

> *Treven was a man who knew how to touch the earth and read what was written there. He knew how strong could be the memory of the land. He felt it often and knew in his heart that whatever new gods might be brought into a place, the blood and fear and love poured out for centuries into the blessed earth was still held captive, ready to feed the harvest, to nurture hope or to nourish much darker urges. And so it was that he recognised a certain wrongness in that place. A memory, a hunger buried deep and never assuaged. Evil that waited for the man without pure purpose to fall down into its grasp.*

* * *

THEADINGFORD. YEAR OF GRACE 878

At the foot of a low, tree-crowned hill, where the road was crossed by a shepherd's trail, there stood two indicators that people still lived here.

Treven was hard pressed to say which disturbed him more.

The first was a wheel-headed cross. Carved of ash, the roots of the tree from which it had been created still reached into the earth. A thing at once natural and made, Treven thought, as though the man that had formed it wished somehow to bridge that gap between the living and the dead.

It was crudely engraved with the image of a hanging man, his arms outstretched but uplifted and fastened to the arms of a cross. He was clothed like a warrior, a sword hanging from his side and a shield lying beneath his feet. A spear was being thrust by a second warrior to pierce just below his heart. The spear had been reddened with ochre, as had wounds on his hands and feet. But for that, Treven would have thought that it depicted Odin suffering for knowledge on the world tree, a thought borne out by the fact that the hanging figure only possessed a single eye. Wotan, All Father, had given an eye to Mimir in exchange for wisdom.

A loose and crudely wrought pattern of threads and knots decorated the cross's wheel and beneath the feet of the spear carrier stood an arc-backed boar, head down as though ready for the charge.

At the foot of the cross lay an offering of flowers and berries. Placed recently, Treven thought, for the fruit had not spoiled, despite the unexpected heat of the autumn sun. But beside that, its wings outstretched and pegged firmly to the hard-baked ground, lay a large black crow.

He had the strongest feeling, looking at the position of the creature, that it had been living when someone pinned it there. Blood on the ground gave testimony to its struggles and Treven was oddly sickened by it, almost more than by the nauseous odour emanating from the second thing that stood upon the rise.

He was not afraid of either death or the sight of it. He had seen too many fall, then pecked by battle scavengers and flesh bitten and wrenched by the carrion eaters, for death to evoke feelings other than that of pity and, when he could spare time for it, of loss. He had lived too long by the sword to have any doubt that one day he would die that way and had long since discovered that a man cannot live forever fearful. Dread is a life-destroying, strength-sapping emotion and cannot be sustained by those who are tired and hungry and exist in anticipation of the next sword blow, the next clash of shields. So it was not the sight of the hanging tree or what was left of a man after the crows had taken their fill that brought such a feeling of wrongness into Treven's thoughts. Rather it was something about the positioning of the cross and the gibbet, and the man and the great black bird. The corpse stank, poisoning the air, the stench settling in the sheltered stillness of a pathway trapped between rising land on either side. The corpse's belly swelled fit to burst with the rot and putrefaction the bag of skin contained. Maggots writhed beneath the muscles of his face as though they sought to create some last vestige of human expression before they spilled from the tongue-choked, partly opened mouth.

The sight and scent made their horses skittish, battle-trained beasts though they were and well used to the caustic stink of death. Their unease added to Treven's sense of wrongness, to his fleeting but insistent impression that there was something evil here, beyond what his eye could see, or which choked the breath from him. But what it was he could not say, only recall that he had felt this way before and that the consequences of such a feeling had not been good.

"Some rule of law exists here still," Hugh commented wryly, jerking Treven from his reverie.

"It would seem so. Though I would wish to know if the man's crime had been great enough to be deserving of death, or if it were only that he lacked wealth to pay the *wergild*."

"Or had not been strung up by some thief after the contents of his purse," Hugh shrugged. "To know that, you must ask the steward and the *tythingmen*."

"If such men still exist here." Treven paused a moment longer, half inclined to give the order to his servants to cut the man down. He disliked this practice of leaving the corpse to hang, as though death were not sufficient punishment. And in these days when the shire courts were so often bypassed and common law gave way to the wishes of the mob, it was not so strange to see the freshly dead strung up beside those whose flesh dropped from the bones.

These were brutal times, Treven thought. Though truthfully neither he nor his father or his grandsire could have recalled a place in memory when times had not been brutal. War and death seemed to cry out for more death until the ways of justice seemed often to be forgotten and swift vengeance the only thing that mattered. Treven gestured towards the cross. "The bird," he said. "Release it." Then as an afterthought, one that seemed to come from another's wishes and not his own, "Burn it."

"And then what, sir?"

Treven sighed, the impulse, the other voice having fled his mind as swiftly as it had come. He gestured impatiently at his servant. "Whatever seems fit to do," he said, then wheeled his horse and rode on, aware of the look his servants and even Hugh exchanged as he passed them by.

* * *

Treven had been told that his hall at Theadingford was some two miles from the village of Theading and that his new home was in need of some repair. However Treven's first sight of the ramshackle building brought to mind a saying of his grandfather's. "Beware the gifts of kings," the old man would say. "More often than not, they turn and bite."

"In times of war," Hugh observed, "I expect to sleep where sleep finds me. But when my old friend promises me a bed in his house, I expect there at least to be a house."

"There is a house . . . of sorts," Treven shrugged. "If you'd prefer a good hard bed in a Kentish Abbey I'm certain your sire would welcome you with joy."

Hugh grimaced. A younger son, destined for the church, his father had not been pleased when he chose a life of battle rather than one of contemplation. "I'll settle for your hovel," he said. "For tonight, anyway. There might be some young *wifmann*, lonely for company, who'll offer me a bed elsewhere. Favours from a Shire Reeve are not to be gainsaid lightly after all."

Treven snorted. "You're not yet Shire Reeve," he reminded Hugh. "There seems little yet to be Reeve of. And you'd do well to mend your thoughts. I recall the last time you sought a woman's favours you neglected to enquire how long her *weaponmann* would be from home."

He sniffed, the scent of wood smoke rising to them from the valley and with it the rich odour of roasting meat. "There is food at least," he said. "Pig, if I'm not mistook."

"Well, the Lord be blessed for his favours," Hugh replied. "Let's go down."

Theadingford lay in a sheltered valley. The manor had been surrounded by farmland, but the forest was encroaching once again after years of neglect, saplings of sycamore and birch marching past the line of rowan at the boundary and across strip-cultivated fields. It would need clearing before any crop was sown. Sheep — small, black-faced creatures, their fleeces almost re-grown ready for the coming winter — cropped amongst the dips and hollows and what looked like the remains of an apple orchard, overcrowded but well laden, stood to the west side of the Manor.

The house itself showed a generation of neglect. It had been close on a decade since its last habitation and Treven had known that he should have expected the worst, but after years of fighting and the loss of his father's land, he had hoped perhaps for something more. When the King had given him charter for Theadingford he had accepted gratefully, despite the fact that this was an effective frontier, the Great Heathen Army less than a day's march north. He had been pledged in battle to serve his lord and now that Aelfred was safely throned, he had pledged to keep the king's peace. If his somewhat dubious reward for this was to become master of Theadingford, then so be it.

Hugh had been his friend and comrade at arms these past five years. To look at, the contrast could not have been greater and should any onlooker be asked to point out which was *thegn* of this place, they would have indicated Hugh as their first choice. The Kentish man was dressed in style. A soft grey tunic of finest wool worn over a shirt of linen with braid-trimmed cuffs and metal closures. His cloak was dyed a rich, fresh blue and fastened with a finely worked brooch, shaped like a shield boss and inlaid with red enamel work that sparkled in the autumn sun. Hugh's fair hair had seen the recent services of a comb and lay neatly about his shoulders.

By contrast, Treven was travel stained. He wore no shirt and his tunic was sleeveless, overlaid by a jerkin of boiled leather plates. His cloak had once been red but had faded to a russet brown. Thick and much mended, it had seen him through three winters without benefit of more than a sound beating when the caked-on mud grew thick enough to cause him grief. He had combed his fox-coloured hair, but that had been four days before, when they had left Winchester. On leaving, he had changed back into his travelling clothes and tossed his comb into his pack, there to lie forgotten.

His horse was well cared for though, groomed, with its harness cleaned and greased to keep the leather supple and the fittings from rusting. And the sword he wore at his side was very fine, passed from father to son for generations and forged and pattern welded, so it was said, in Raedwald's time, when Treven's family on his father's side had been close kin to the Kings of Anglia. It lay in a sheath of finely worked leather, lined with fleece, and the wax from the wool kept the blade clean and clear of rust.

Treven, Hugh and their servants splashed through the shallow ford that gave Theadingford its name. Those he had sent ahead five days before stood in front of the ruined Hall tending to the fire and the pig spit roasting over it, coarse barley bread baked on hot stones resting close by. The three men tending to the food and fire looked far from happy. Osric, the elder of the three by a good many summers, stepped forward to take the reins of Treven's horse as he dismounted. Osric had served his lord since both of them were boys. He was generally a man of few words, all of them direct and to the point.

"I've turfed out the swine," he said, jerking his head back towards the house, "but the place still stinks like a midden. The walls are rotten and the Abbot's men have been here this morning. They say the land is now the property of the church and you have no rights here."

"Abbot?"

"Abbot Kendryk." Osric elaborated. "Abbey at Storton, an hour's ride that way," he nodded briefly to where Treven could see a trackway leading off into the wood. Having delivered all necessary information, Osric clucked his tongue and led the horse away.

"A fine welcome," Hugh commented sourly.

Treven nodded. "We've had worse. At least there's food at the end of this journey."

As Hugh fell hungrily upon the meat and bread, devouring both in great fistfuls, Treven glanced about with interest. Notwithstanding that the house leaned at an alarming angle and, if Osric was to be believed, was in a far worse state inside, Treven liked what he was seeing. Late afternoon sun slanted through oak and ash and thickets of hazel, set the rowan ablaze and bathed the valley in golden light, dancing and glancing off the stream. The manor itself had been built upon a slight rise in the land, keeping it safe from the winter floods. For the most part, the water coursed between steep banks, breaking out only at the shallow ford. There were signs of old defences — earth banks raised on the far side of the stream — though this was never designed to be a fortified manor. It was a farm, built, with unwarranted optimism, for times of peace. Perversely, man of war that he was, Treven liked the notion that he might settle in a place not designed for battle.

Hugh, mouth full of pig and barley bread, cut through his thoughts. "We should refortify those banks," he commented. "Build a palisade. And there's a natural rise to the land behind the house, I noticed as we came down from the road. It could be made defensible."

Treven felt a sudden surge of anger, irritation that Hugh should tread upon even these momentary imaginings. But it soon passed. He recognised that Hugh was right. Guthrum and his army might have signed Peace with Aelfred back at Eastertime, but here they were so close to the enemy — and treaty or not, Treven found it hard to think of them any other way — that to hope to live here in peace meant that they must be prepared for war.

Guthrum might have accepted his defeat, even accepted baptism, with King Aelfred as his godfather. He had taken a new name, a Christian name of Athelstan, but frankly Treven did not believe a word of it. Guthrum might now publicly address his prayers to Jesus Christ, but Treven would be willing to wager that any kill he made in battle would be dedicated still to Odin.

CHAPTER 3

BILLINGTON. PRESENT DAY

The Queen's Head on the corner of Mortimer Street and Cradely Road was packed by nine o'clock at night. It still carried the vestiges of its Victorian past; a glass divider set into wooden panelling that separated the public bar from the lounge and the marble-topped counters, complete with old fashioned beer pumps, long ago decommissioned but kept on for their looks. The Queen's Head, now simply 'the Queen's,' had supposedly become a theme pub. The "head" had been dropped from its title and a gaudily painted sign showing three drag artists in large blond wigs hung proudly over the entrance.

Not that it made a fig of difference to the clientele. Much to the discomfort of the new owners, hoping to turn the place into a trendy student dive — the University, one-time Billington Polytechnic, being a scant half mile away — the Queen's had stubbornly refused to be reformed and the new landlords seriously regretted not having done more on-the-spot market research. The students, knowing that the Queen's catered for a particular sector of the local community, still went a half a mile in the other direction, taking themselves off to the wine bars and nightclubs and converted banks in town; and the locals signed a petition against the flashing lights and equally flashy music and backed it by the threat of more direct action, as they informed the new landlord that if he didn't cut the bloody piped music and remove the glitter ball, he was likely to find it jammed somewhere it wouldn't glitter nearly so well.

Six months on, the only thing left of the hoped-for transformation was the coloured sign depicting the garishly clad impersonators, permitted to remain, so it was rumoured, because Big Frank Parker had a soft spot for Lily Savage on TV and nobody with an ounce of sense was going to argue with Big Frank.

Inside, the only remaining indicator of the change of management was the introduction of 'guest beers' — a move generally welcomed by the clientele.

The Queen's had been a favourite haunt of Charlie Higgins' and, being the venue of choice for a number of the local hard men, a verdant pasture for his intelligence gathering. It was the third watering hole that Rozlyn had entered that night, the first two being in the town centre, crowded early and more anonymous. Rozlyn had asked questions, received few useful answers and been unable to find the one man she had really hoped to see. She had no notion that her quarry might be here, for the Queen's was not the kind of stop in which the Mouse Man was likely to feel at home. It had *no* sense of anonymity. This was a venue in which everyone was either a regular or the guest of one and strangers stood out like . . . Rozlyn Priest.

Rozlyn knew that in this crowd — folk who could tell a copper by the scent of his aftershave or the size of her feet — the idea of anonymity was someone's idea of a tasteless joke. Hers was also the only non-white face in the place. She walked in feeling like a bit player in a bad Western, where the stranger enters and the room falls silent just a scant few seconds before the gunshots ring out.

She wasn't wrong about the silence.

Rozlyn glanced around looking for Big Frank. He was holding court in a corner of the lounge. Then Rozlyn crossed to the bar, and took her time surveying the list of specialty beers, settling finally on a Budwar. She was aware of Frank watching and the hum of expectancy in the crowded room. The murmur of conversation picked up again, only to drop as Rozlyn turned to look at Big Frank and gestured towards the bar and tilting her hand in a drinking gesture.

Momentarily put out, Frank hesitated before raising a half empty glass.

"Whatever he's drinking," Rozlyn told the barman and then crossed the lounge, stepping carefully between the stools and small round tables, carrying her own beer and a bottle of something called Speckled Hen.

"Give the lady a stool," Frank commanded, and a stool arrived and was squeezed into a narrow space between two of Frank's "boys". Rozlyn sat down and handed Frank his beer. No one spoke while Frank set about refilling his now drained glass, tilting it just so, allowing the gasses to escape and a level, half-inch head to form. Rozlyn admired his expertise.

"Charlie Higgins," she said. Frank's gaze flicked her way for the merest instant, then drifted back to his beer.

"Cheers," he said and lifted it to his lips, drinking deep before setting the once more half-empty vessel down on the cluttered table. The glass collectors weren't exactly respecting their calling in this corner, Rozlyn observed.

"He was murdered." Rozlyn said. "Early this morning as far as we can make out. We'll know more after the autopsy, of course, but it looks like a single stab wound straight into the heart."

Frank's gaze lifted again and this time he held Rozlyn's. Frank was as big as his nickname implied. Tall and stout and powerful, with cold grey eyes and a delicate little cupid's bow of a mouth that rightfully belonged on an advert for lipstick.

Holding his gaze was akin to trying to outstare a shark. Rozlyn didn't even try, she reached for her drink and took a sip of beer, a prissy little sip compared to Franks great thirsty gulps.

"I'll send flowers to his funeral."

"Kind of you. Who'd want to kill him, Frank? He was such a shrimp of a man, it hardly seems worth anybody's time to stab him then dump his body miles away from anywhere."

"I hear you had a use for him."

"A use for him! Frank, the man was a garbage pail of bits and scraps of useless information."

"For which you paid him," Frank observed.

"For which I paid him when it warranted and the only times it warranted were those times when you let slip a tasty bit of something, knowing he'd pass it on to me. Something that made *you* look good and made a few difficulties for your business rivals, shall we say."

"You think *I* had him killed?"

"No. No, actually, I don't. Charlie was occasionally useful to you, same way he was to me, but otherwise he wasn't big enough for you to notice. Charlie was a tick on a sheep's backside. A loser. Week on week I expected him to turn up dead in an alley somewhere because he'd hit on the wrong guy or been mugged for something he didn't have."

"If he was such a tick, why the interest?"

"It's *still* a murder." Rozlyn took another sip of beer. "Anyway, he may have been a tick, but he was *my* tick and I would hate to think that something he tried to find out on my behalf might have got him killed."

Frank smiled. It was not the most beautiful of sights. "The girl's got a conscience," he said, and his boys laughed at his joke.

Frank leaned forward and placed a great, meaty hand on Rozlyn's, his pasty white skin contrasting against the deep brown of hers. He patted her fingers with an almost avuncular air but then the hand was removed, the smile gone and the glass lifted again, this time drained to the bottom in a single gulp. He set it down again with a purposeful thud on the wooden table and Rozlyn knew that her audience was effectively at an end.

"I'll be in touch," Frank said. "If I hear anything about a murdered tick."

A ripple of appreciative laughter drifted around the table and Rozlyn reluctantly got to her feet. She would learn nothing more from Frank tonight, that much was clear, but she had the odd feeling that Frank would be true to his word.

* * *

Rozlyn stepped out into the rain, relieved to be out of the Queen's. Behind her the volume had picked up again.

The day had been warm and bright but the wind had risen in the early evening and the rain began while Rozlyn was bar hopping in town. It brought with it an almost winter chill and she was glad she'd had the foresight to wear a coat.

Pulling up her collar and tucking her hair inside, Rozlyn turned left into Mortimer Street and headed back towards the town centre. The streets were deserted and it wasn't just the rain keeping people inside. The area was not one for walking in at night. Streets of terraced houses were interspersed with waste ground where demolition had begun but the promised redevelopment had stalled. The little streets around the Queen's were not quite close enough to the newly fashionable canal basin to have benefited from the move towards Urban Living that the local council was doing its damnedest to promote. It was working after a fashion, Rozlyn had to admit. The area around the canal, between that and the university campus, had been planted with avenues of trees, had its old factories converted into ultra-expensive loft-style apartments with secure underground parking and was attracting the single professional types who made the most of the motorway links to work in London and could still commute to the less expensive hinterland.

The locals didn't stand a chance of affording these so-called New York-style des reses. It was a description that

Rozlyn took issue with, doubting that the designers had ever been anywhere near her beloved Manhattan, but it was better, she supposed, than the often-beautiful old buildings falling into the canal from pure neglect.

She wondered if the drive towards improvement would ever spread to Mortimer Street and if it did how many local councillors and builders Big Frank would buy off just to keep the Queen's intact.

She turned to cross Mortimer Street, planning on cutting down Hazel Street and then back across behind the University. Glancing sideways, more from habit than an expectation of traffic, she caught sight of movement, as though someone had dodged back into the shadow of a house wall.

Not breaking her stride, Rozlyn crossed the road and walked down into Hazel Street. The houses in these Victorian terraces had a common entryway leading to the back yards, one entry shared between two. Most had doors or locked gates blocking the way but a half dozen houses down, Rozlyn spotted an open door. Twice since leaving the Queen's she had sensed someone following but had ignored it. She had heard no footsteps bar her own echoing off the houses and sounds that might have carried had been distorted by the heavily falling rain.

Rozlyn waited now, breathing through her mouth the better to hear, back pressed tight against the entry wall, peering through the gap between gate and wall. Had Frank sent someone after her? She dismissed the thought at once. For one thing, Frank's men rarely travelled in less than pairs. For another, Rozlyn was sure she'd done nothing to rattle the big man's cage. Frank had been amused by her audacity, but nothing more.

She pressed closer to the wall changing the restricted view of the road end. A slight shuffling sound told her that there was someone out there, someone who paused before turning into the street and looked anxiously around. The figure that hove into view was small and slight, but it was the smell that Rozlyn recognised even before the light of a streetlamp confirmed the features.

"Hey, Mouse Man," Rozlyn called softly and was gratified to see the man leap what looked like a good three feet into the air and on landing stagger back, looking as though the devil himself had called his name.

Rozlyn stepped out from the entry. Mouse clutched at his heart, his face grey and pale in the light of the lamp.

"God, you could have killed me." He glanced nervously around, skittering back against the wall, away from the yellow light.

"What are you doing here, Mouse Man?"

"Looking for you. I saw you go into the Queen's and I waited outside, then when you left, that man came and stood outside and I daren't come after. Not 'til he'd gone away."

"What man? Who was he, Mouse?"

"Don't know, don't know. Big man, tall with long hair. I don't know where he went."

Mouse stared anxiously about once again and then looked back at Rozlyn. "We can't talk here. You shouldn't have come looking for me like that in town. You were asking around for me. That's not good news. Not good news."

Rozlyn frowned. The Mouse was always jumpy, but she'd never seen him quite like this.

"My place," Mouse said. "We'll go back to my place. Need to talk to you about Charlie. That's why you looked for me, wasn't it? Talk about Charlie?"

"Your place," Rozlyn groaned inwardly but the little man was practically wetting himself with fear. "Ok," she said. "We'll go back to yours, but you open the goddamned windows, you hear?"

* * *

Mouse Man derived his name from one of his varied occupations. He lived in a run-down terraced house about a mile from the Queen's, a couple of streets outside of Big Frank's territory. Downstairs in Mouse's domain was a front living room that Rozlyn had never actually entered, though she knew from peering through the door that it was stacked from floor to ceiling with stuff that Mouse bought at auctions when he had the funds. These were not everyday auctions, but sales of old computer stuff and office equipment. With so many local firms going bust in the past decade, the auction houses for this type of merchandise were doing a good trade. Mouse didn't bid. He went around afterwards, at the end of the business day, buying up for pence what no other purchaser had wanted. Mouse had got it into his head that this was the computer age and so anything that said computer on the box was bound to be a seller. It never seemed to occur to him that there might be a good reason for the stuff he bought to have remained unsold at the auction. That it might be obsolete, incomplete or simply busted and his failure to sell on didn't make an iota of difference to his optimism. He bought, he stored, he bought some more. When Rozlyn had once commented that he might get lucky one day and discover these were real museum pieces, Mouse's face had lit with such a pleased smile that Rozlyn had felt mean to have made a joke at Mouse's expense. Especially one that the man just did not understand.

There was a second room downstairs which housed a couple of chairs and a television and from which could be seen a filthy kitchen. Rozlyn as usual declined the offer of refreshment. This room might have been almost liveable if it hadn't been for the smell. It was a musky, musty, sour and choking odour that Rozlyn knew from experience she'd be hours getting out of her nose and clothes. The same smell clung to Mouse Man himself, emanating from him in waves of body heat.

Rozlyn stood in the middle of the room, trying not to touch anything, while all around in cages, stacked three high, squeaked and scrambled and stank a load of tiny, long-tailed, big-eared rodents, breeding and scrapping and squealing and now chewing on the handfuls of grains that Mouse man tipped into their cages.

"Look," he said. "More little ones."

He pulled his hand from the nearest cage and held it out to Rozlyn. His palm was filled with pink, writhing, grub-like creatures, naked and almost tailless.

"Nice," Rozlyn said briefly, then regretted the need to speak as the foul air flooded into her lungs. "Mouse, this place stinks even on the outside. Don't your neighbours complain?"

Mouse shrugged. "It's my house," he said defensively. "My mother left it to me, nothing owing. Nothing. Anyway, there's no one lived next door, they moved out, told the landlord his drains must be blocked. And the old woman on the other side, she's deaf as a post, so she never complains."

He slipped the grub-like mouse pups back to their now frantic mother, leaving Rozlyn, her eyes watering, to wonder what being deaf had to do with a sense of smell. She had asked once what Mouse did with his charges when there were simply too many to fit in the cages. "Oh," he had told Rozlyn happily. "I take them to the waste ground and I let them go."

"You were going to tell me about Charlie," she said.

"Oh. Oh yes."

Mouse sighed, his now empty hands dropped to his sides and he stood quite still, looking lost and dejected as though now he had Rozlyn here he'd quite forgotten what to tell her. Their walk back to his house had been filled with Mouse jumping at every shadow and whittering about the big man following them, though Rozlyn had seen no sign. He had refused to talk about Charlie 'til they were 'safe', but now that they were, presumably, safe, he seemed at a loss.

"Charlie," Rozlyn prompted him. "Charlie Higgins is dead, Mouse. Can you tell me anything about why that might be?" She paused, waiting. "Or am I wasting my time?"

The sharpness in Rozlyn's voice seemed to jerk Mouse out of his reverie. "Oh no, Inspector Priest, I wouldn't dream of wasting your time." He seemed to gather his thoughts, then glanced around again as he had done on the street as though afraid that someone might be listening. Then he moved closer to Rozlyn, his voice dropping to a confidential whisper. Rozlyn almost choked at the stench which seemed to emanate from the man like a dense cotton wool textured cloud, wrapping about her nose and mouth and amplified by the room full of rodents with whom he shared his pungency.

"They've got no bladders, you know," he whispered and it took Rozlyn a moment to realise that he was talking about his mice and not Charlie. "So they're . . . doing their little business all the time. People don't understand that it's not their fault, they pick them up and the poor little things dribble all over and they don't seem to understand it's not their fault."

Rozlyn closed her eyes and sighed in exasperation. "Well don't you learn something new every day." she said. "Now what about Charlie. What did you want to tell me about Charlie?"

That seemed to agitate Mouse even more. He stepped away from Rozlyn and thrust his grubby hands deep into the pockets of his greasy trousers. "He knew what you thought about him," Mouse Man said. "Charlie knew you didn't think he was capable of nothing but he respected you, Inspector Priest, he really did. He reckoned you been good to him over the years, slipping him a fiver here and there, even when he didn't have much to tell you. That counted for a man like Charlie. But he reckoned he got something really big to tell you this time, that he'd got an *in*." He paused. Halted his pacing and swivelled round to face Rozlyn.

"An in?" Rozlyn prompted him.

"An in," Mouse confirmed looking suddenly triumphant. "On a job. He was going to be a mole, he said and give you the deal. The whole deal, right up to the when."

"He told you this?"

"Oh yes, he told me. He was proud of it. This was something he could give that would be worth more than the odd fiver. Charlie reckoned he'd get rich out of it."

Instead of which he'd got himself murdered. Rozlyn frowned wondering what the hell Charlie might have been up to. Charlie hadn't had two brain cells to rub together and had had the subtlety of the average concrete block. The idea of him infiltrating anything but the nearest whisky bottle was one that Rozlyn found absolutely absurd. Absurd and pathetically sad.

But it explained, perhaps, why he'd wound up dead.

"What was going on, Mouse Man? Charlie tell you that?"

Mouse shook his head. "Something big, he said and something about stuff that was very old and very rare."

"Antiques?" Rozlyn asked. "Some kind of antiques?"

Mouse shrugged. "*Old* antiques, Charlie said, like they have in the museums. Something really, really old."

Antiquities, Rozlyn thought. The dig? Did this have something to do with the dig? She remembered what the constable had told her that the archaeologists didn't expect to find anything valuable in the graves.

Had someone thought different and been wrong? Or had there been something there valuable enough to get Charlie Higgins killed?

CHAPTER 4

YEAR OF GRACE 878

Theading was about two miles ride from the manor by the ford, along a narrow track that led first through woodland and then onto a ridge of land forming the backbone of gentle hills.

This too was his land. On this eastern side of the manor there were fifteen hides between Boden's wood and the river Pearce which marked the boundary of Abbey lands. Theading was his, as was the *tun* of Bearwell and the homesteads that lay between.

"Your first task," he said to Hugh "will be a survey of the land and the appointment of *tythingmen*."

"For that I'll have need of local knowledge. I hope there are men you can trust in this *vill* of yours."

"As do I . . . it's likely the abbey has already done the work for you if the abbot is intent on claiming the land for himself. I'll not believe that any of his kind would miss the chance to take a *tything*." He said sourly. "No doubt Abbot Kendryk will be most upset to find us come just as the harvest is brought home."

"And no doubt the villagers and *ceorls* will feel the same way," Hugh warned him, "if the abbot has demanded a *tything* already in work done on the abbey fields, you'll find men reluctant to give yet another to a Lord they do not even know."

"Whichever season saw our coming would be difficult for some. Had we come *Aerra Litha* or *Aefterra Litha*, we would have been a far greater burden. That, I would have been loath to be." June and July, those times just before and after midsummer, were the hungry months among the poor. The winter store had dwindled almost to nothing, the first harvest not due until Lammas, the loaf mass. It was a time of year when the Thegn's duty would have been to support his people, not, as Hugh was pledged to do on the King's behalf and Treven bound to support, to assess them for taxes.

The people of Theading had been aware of their coming. They came out of their houses to stare at the strangers, Hugh in his rich clothes, Treven, a linen shirt added to his outfit and his hair showing some effort with the comb and now accompanied by his three armed and mounted servants.

The *vill* consisted of a dozen houses scattered either side of the dusty road. Timber framed and thatched, many of the houses looked new and here and there were visible the burnt timbers and scorched land left from the earlier burning by the raiding army.

Pigs snuffed and chickens and geese clucked and hissed between the buildings where small children tumbled and played. For the most part they looked well enough fed, Treven noted, though their parents were poorly clad and looked worn and tired. They had just completed the busiest time of their farming year and the long hours of work, beginning when the sun first broke over the horizon and continuing well into the night if the moon was bright, had clearly taken a heavy toll.

Women called their children back from the road. Some of the adults murmured greeting, but it was clear to both Hugh and Treven that these people were wary, untrusting of this stranger appointed by a king whose name they recognised but who had been so often in battle that they as yet knew nothing of him as a ruler, only as a warrior.

There were remnants of palisade surrounding the *vill*, close up against the forest edge, though much of it was broken down and also showed clear signs of burning. In places this gave way to bramble thickets and mixed hedging. The Hall stood beside a great pond. It had been a natural feature, Treven guessed, and a small stream on the forest side could be seen emptying itself into a natural dip in the landscape, but he guessed also that it had been deepened and widened by generations of owners and stocked, most likely, with food fish, as the abbeys did. It was a feature that spoke of a time of prosperity and labour to spare. Treven wondered idly how long ago that had been and if the large building standing by the water had once been the Manor of Theading before the now ramshackle but more substantial house had been built closer to the ford. The hall was old and strongly built, though the rear of the building showed signs of new lime wash that did not quite conceal the repaired timbers. The thatch too had been patched, new straws showing golden against the grey aged bundles. That it had survived at all told Treven that it had been in use, perhaps as a base or storehouse for the Heathen army before being reclaimed and repaired by its owners. At the rear stood a new building, long and low with smoke indicating hearths at either end. The cookhouse, Treven guessed. Another sign of hoped-for prosperity, that this should be housed in a separate building. Other small outbuildings close beside the palisade suggested privies and stores and a half dozen fattened pigs grunted happily in a wooden pen.

The doors of the great hall stood wide atop three wooden steps.

Two men and a woman emerged and came down the steps to greet Treven and his company. The men looked alike enough to be brothers, dark haired and heavily built, their shoulders and arms muscled and the close fit of the woollen *breeks* showing well-formed thighs and calves. Men used to hard work, though not fighting men, Treven thought; they were built for the plough rather than the sword.

The woman was of a different order. Dark also, but more delicately made and with bright blue eyes. Her undershirt was of good linen cloth and the russet of her dress was meant to be that colour, not faded from red like Treven's cloak. A leather thong hung about her neck from which was suspended a shallow, pierced spoon designed for straining beer as it was poured from jug to drinking vessel. A symbol of her position in the household, she touched this lightly with her fingertips, as though it were an unfamiliar object.

Beside him Hugh drew a swift breath. "Things improve by the moment," he whispered. Treven cast him a disapproving look but had time for no more as the older of the two men stepped forward.

"Lord, my name is Edmund Scrivener. We had letters concerning your arrival, but my servants tell me you came last evening to Theadingford. Had I known, you would have had better welcome."

"We made faster time than I had hoped," Treven told him. "My servants had the camp prepared. It is of little matter."

Edmund bowed his head slightly in acknowledgement. "This is my brother, Eldred," he said, "and his wife, Cate."

Cate smiled shyly, but Eldred, Treven noted, was tight faced and his eyes held no greeting.

"This is Hugh de Vries," Treven told him. "The King, in his wisdom, has appointed him Shire Reeve for this Hundred and those bordering on it . . ."

"Shire Reeve?" Eldred sounded outraged. "My father has served these past five years as Steward and as Shire Reeve. What justice appoints another over him?"

Treven looked sharply at the younger man. "The king's justice," he told him. "Your father will be paid his dues."

"Dues!" Eldred began, but his brother silenced him.

"Eldred. Enough. These men are guests in our father's house. Would you shame him?"

His brother fell into a reluctant silence and Edmund continued. "Our father is unwell. He gave word that you should be welcomed as if he were able to do so himself. Come inside. If your men take themselves to the cookhouse out back, they will be fed and watered."

Treven and Hugh followed the brothers into the hall. The interior was dim, with narrow windows, covered with oiled and scraped vellum only at the farthest end and even those were set high into the wall so that shafts of filtered light fell, sharply angled, into the room.

A loom had been set close to the doors to take advantage of the morning brightness. On it was a length of half-worked cloth, the threads stretched tight with weights of baked clay. Beside that a carved chest acted as shelf for rush baskets of wool, skeined ready for plying, dyed the same shade as the green of the woven cloth. It was intended for winter wear, Treven guessed. A mantle for one or other of the men. Treven remembered the long hours he spent as a child, sitting at his mother's feet, his hands outstretched until they ached, as though he'd spent all day handling his wooden sword, while she wound skeins of wool into balls and then plied the yarn ready for the winter weaving. A single winter cloak took the wool of a half dozen sheep and many hours of women's work.

Beside the left-hand wall was propped a trestle table, dismantled until required and a long oak bench. A second bench rested against the opposite wall. A small table stood just inside the doorway, laden with cold meats and apples, a flagon of ale and — an especial treat for men used to coarse fare — a loaf of wheaten bread with dishes of preserves and honey.

Cate poured weak ale into leather flagons. It was the small beer from the third brewing, suitable for drinking throughout the day whereas the stronger ale was kept for the evening meal. She strained the residue from the dark liquid with the pierced spoon and wiped it clean on a piece of old linen. She then lifted the cup to her lips before giving it to Treven.

"A health to you," she said. She spoke softly and found it hard to meet his eyes.

"And to you, lady," Treven told her. "I thank you for your hospitality." Though it was, if he were to be honest, of the bare minimum that courtesy allowed. And he sensed that Cate thought this also, that their welcome, although polite, was frosted with suspicion.

Hugh seemed beset by no such thoughts. He made a point of brushing, as though by accident, the slender fingers of the lady as she handed him the cup. The touch might well have gone unnoticed, but she flinched away as though his fingers stung and Eldred bridled like a badly handled horse. He would have spoken, Treven thought, but Edmund caught his look, warning him off with a stare that would have frozen all but the most foolhardy of men.

"Eat, please," Edmund urged them. "Sit, there are chairs set beside."

Treven sat down in one of the two carved chairs that were more usually for the brothers' use. Edmund pulled up a tall three-legged stool and began to carve the meat. Cate stood hesitantly for a further moment and then with a word that might have been excuse, slipped off to her weaving. She stood side on to the group of men and Hugh's gaze strayed her way far more often than could be considered proper. Eldred paced restlessly, like a man whose energies are too pent up for rest.

A chamber with a curtained door occupied one end of the hall, divided, Treven assumed, by a partition of wood to give some semblance of privacy to the married couple. He wondered about Edmund. Strange that the younger son should have a wife and yet there be no evidence of Edmund being wed. The straining of the ale was something the lady of the Hall would do, the wife of Edmund's father, or of the eldest son. Cate, wed to the younger and, now he had looked at her more closely Treven had seen her to be barely more than a girl, seemed young to have such responsibility.

"Your father has been Steward to my estates?" Treven asked, when he had eaten enough for courtesy and conversation could be allowed to turn to business.

"Steward, yes, though he's had no time to maintain the hall at Theadingford. The *vill* has twice been burned. It seemed more fitting to house those who'd lost homes than upkeep a building with no master and no use."

"I've no argument with that," Treven told him, "though I'll need men now at least to make it safe and weatherproof before winter. Come spring it can be taken down. I've plans for the rebuilding of it."

Edmund hesitated before he spoke again. "We've few young men," he said. "Not enough to spare for work that doesn't bring in food for their families or fodder for the kine."

Treven's eyes narrowed. "I could order it," he said. "Edmund, whatever position your father and your kin hold here, I'll not be gainsaid if I require a thing done."

"And I've not gainsaid you," Edmund's voice raised in mild annoyance. Then he recovered himself. "Forgive me, it's long since any assumed control over this land and, though my brother put it ungraciously, he was right in that if my father had not taken power and led our people through these times, many would have died and the land been ruined into the bargain."

"What my brother refrains from saying," Eldred interrupted, "is that we have little faith in any king's peace or any king's men. Where was the king when our *vill* was razed, not once, but twice in the space of as many years? When our women were raped and the old folk forced to flee with the children into the woods. The winter was bitter that year and they dared not return. There were men camped here, in this house until past the Christmastide. We buried five out in the woods. Cate's mother among them and children too. Cold and sick with no shelter and fire only when we dared to risk."

"I lost my family to these invaders," Treven replied with equal heat. "Father, wife and son and the lands my family held.

You have returned. Your children are fed, your harvest brought home. There has been peace here since the Eastertime and this peace will be kept. My king pledges this and I, as his servant, pledge it too."

"And does Guthrum pledge it? Or are these just words he saw fit to say, knowing that for one battle he had been defeated? And what of those that Guthrum does not control? How many in that Great Army only a dozen miles away agree with Guthrum, or Athelstan or whatever his name should be, that they will keep the peace because he bids them do so. Will the pledge he made to king and Christ outweigh the pledges he has made, lifelong to his own kings and his own gods? I've known men boast that they've gathered as many as thirty Baptismal shirts; one for each time they've made a promise to the church."

Treven said nothing for a moment. Eldred's words were so like his own thoughts — the ones that came when he was at his weakest — that he did not know the way to reply. Finally, he said, "I have fought beside my king when things had grown so sour that all he had to claim as his was a scant half mile of land. He never admitted, not even to himself, that he might not win out against the foe. That this time the battle would see him utterly defeated. I rode with messages to men who might have doubted him had they seen in what dire straits he had landed himself. Holed up in marshland so treacherous it could be navigated only by flat boat. He sent messages, bidding those that might lose heart to come and fight with him because he would never surrender the government of our land. That there would be no defeat, only victory and the rule of law. Our king is a warrior. Guthrum is a warrior. Guthrum knows when he looks into Aelfred's eyes that the thoughts behind his gaze are the same thoughts, the same courage, the same resolve as Guthrum himself carried into battle. Aelfred could have shamed his enemy. He chose not to shame him but to welcome him into the Church and give him land and a place where his own laws and judgments would be kept."

"And how is that different from the blood gold that his kinsmen paid? How is it changed? Once they said, 'here, have gold and horses and then leave us,' and the Danes would leave for a time until the gold ran out and they needed new brood mares to improve their stock and more slaves to sell in Paris and the Eastern lands beyond. Then they came back and attacked again, knowing they would be paid well for their warfare. How is this different? Instead of gold, we now give land. Instead of horses, cattle for them to farm. How long before they will encroach upon our land by a mile, or a field or a hide? Before these strangers take our women as wives or slaves?"

"My brother speaks as many feel," Edmund said and Treven could hear the impatience in his voice.

"As many have a right to feel," Hugh told him. "But we must face the times as they are made. Treven here does not come to strip the land. He looks for a place of peace in which to remarry and raise his children."

I do? Treven wondered. The thought of wife and children was not an idea which had previously occurred.

"I too have served King Aelfred since boyhood," Hugh said. "And his brothers before him. I know him to be an honest man and a wise ruler. He places men like Treven at his frontiers knowing that they will brook no trouble and no encroachment. Men whose hunger for their own land is as great as the hunger you and your folk endured in that bloody winter."

"Fine words," Eldred interrupted.

"Words that will be backed by action," Treven informed him angrily. He took a deep frustrated breath. "I have endured talk which another would have maintained was treason. I have allowed you to question my words, to doubt the King's intent because I know what the land has suffered. The bloodshed and the pain. I know that you and your men must have gathered at the weapontake knowing that the most you could achieve would be to fight until your women and children and old people were in hiding and how much that must have chafed against men like yourselves, who, I don't doubt, have hearts as strong as any warriors that met full battle. And I know too the anger that you must have felt when the king's demand for foot soldiers stripped your lands of the youngest and fittest of men and forced one of you to leave when you would fain have stayed and protected your own."

He intercepted Eldred's quick and anxious glance towards his brother and knew his guess had hit the mark. One of these brothers could justifiably have remained to assist an ageing father and lead a community, but not both. Had they served the king's demands then one at least would have led men from their lands to join the king's foot. They would not, Treven knew, be the first *vill* who had ignored the king's command to send at least a tithe of men. He knew how dreadfully painful this could be for a small community then left, perhaps, without sufficient defence. Treven himself had been away from his own home fighting for Aelfred's elder brother when his family had been killed. In his more clear-sighted moments, Treven would not have wished such pain on any, but there was a part of his soul that had hardened against what he saw as such cowardice and asked what gave other men the right to shirk their duty when his own sense of honour had brought such terrible consequences.

He had no idea if Hild, his wife, and their son Hlisa would have lived had he been there, but his heart always wondered, teased and worried at the thought and gave him little peace.

He was about to challenge them when the noise of shouting from outside drew his attention back towards the door. He saw Cate raise her hands to her face as though in shock or fear and cast an anxious glance back towards the brothers. She then fled towards the door and Treven could hear her remonstrating with someone outside. Edmund and Eldred exchanged looks that Treven could not fully interpret, but Eldred's face was dark with fury and Treven sensed that much of his anger was directed towards his wife.

Treven rose to his feet and strode towards the door giving the brothers little option but to follow.

Outside an old man, dishevelled and only partly clothed, capered about with a leather flask clasped tightly in one hand and a child's wooden sword in the other. Two men, serfs, from their dress and demeanour stood back, clearly apologising to their young mistress for something while Cate herself sought to catch the old man's arms and calm him. He was laughing like an idiot, waving his arms and spilling his drink over himself and the girl.

"Father," Cate pleaded with him, "please be calm. Please."

Beside him, Treven heard Edmund curse.

"Father?" Treven questioned. "Your father was *unwell*, you said . . ."

Eldred stormed down the steps and grabbed his young wife. He shook her angrily. "You were told to see that he was kept away," he shouted. "Now look what you have done. The man is shamed before his lord and a laughingstock among his servants."

"The woman cannot be blamed for the actions of a grown man," Treven remonstrated. He turned sharply on Edmund. "And how long has he been like this? Is the steward of my lands nothing more than a drunken sot? It is not yet midday and the man can barely stand."

"Our father is a troubled man," Edmund told him, his teeth gritted against the words that he would like to say, for Treven's criticisms had stung the worse because of the truth in them. "And as for how long? Until a month since, he was as able a man as any you could find among the King's counsellors. Grief has done this to him, the loss of his child . . ."

Treven turned on him, eyes narrowed. "Many have lost children," he said softly, "and I know that grief can drive a man to strong drink. But did none of you seek to mend this? Put him aside, you say, hide him away, nothing more than that?" He looked back at the old man and shook his head. "And I do not see only drunkenness here, Edmund. I see in those eyes a madness of more than a single month or even a single season. What goes on here?"

Edmund sighed and looked away, the muscles in his jaw working to keep the emotions in check and the words where they were. Eldred had no such reserve.

"So you'll blame our father for the run-down lands and the house about to fall. Had he been the strongest, the fittest of men with all of his faculties as sharp as when his mind was young we could have done no more." He turned once more on his wife. She shied away from him as he gestured toward her.

"Get him inside," he told her, "give him something to calm his mood. Poppy or white bryony, whatever you have."

Cate looked at Treven with apology in her eyes and tried hard to avoid Hugh's gaze, though the man was obvious in his attempts to make her look his way.

"Might I help you?" he asked her as she passed him to reach out once more for the old man's arm. He had grown quiet now, standing with a foolish look upon his face and humming softly to himself.

"There is nothing you can do," she whispered and Treven felt a jolt go through him, knowing she did not speak only of the old man and that Hugh's interest attracted her far more than she dared show. She loosened her father's hold on the bottle and this time he gave it up easily. Then, without a backward look, her shoulders squared against Hugh's gaze, she led him inside.

CHAPTER 5

Treven had been deep in thought since they had left Theading. Hugh had not seemed to notice his silence and had, in any case talked enough for both of them, in turn berating the insolent attitude of the two men and singing the praises of the young woman.

Surprised, eventually, by Treven's silence, his thoughts concerning Cate had become more and more elaborate until at the last they verged on the obscene. Only then did Treven quiet him.

"Leave her be, Hugh. She's a countrywoman with nowhere to go and nowhere to hide if you shame her. You want a woman, go find the nearest whore house and take your pick. Lord knows you can afford it now."

"Time was you'd have been of my mind," Hugh returned irritably. "Since when did your view of women become any more considered than mine."

Treven scowled but didn't answer. It was true, he acknowledged, that when the first grief of losing his wife and son had subsided, Treven had promised himself he'd never become so entangled with any woman again. The pain of losing Hild and Hlisa had burned worse and for longer than any battle wound. Afterwards, he'd been as careless of the women he took to his bed as had Hugh — though he'd never had his friend's appetites and neither had he had Hugh's success. But that feeling had passed. He'd woken one morning beside some unknown, unnamed female and it seemed to him that while he slept he must have dreamed of Hild. She'd been standing in the doorway of their old home, watching their son play with the other lads and as he'd come near to her, she'd smiled at him and held out her hand.

There had been, he thought, no blame in her eyes, no recrimination, though he felt she had seen everything and known all he'd done since the day she died.

Since then, there'd been no women, though perhaps Hugh was right in what he'd said earlier. The time had come to settle and to find a wife. Aelfred had spoken of this also and made it plain that the king's peace needed families as much as it required fighting men. So many deaths called for children to replace them.

It was late afternoon by the time they returned to Theadingford and the dilapidated Hall, its state seeming worse now he had the steading at Theading village to compare it with. Treven wandered away from Hugh and, despite Osric's warning, went inside to have a proper look at what was left of the building.

Unlike that at Theadingford, the doorway here was placed centrally on the longest side and, amongst the rubble of the part-fallen building and filth left by the swine Treven could make out two hearths, one set at either end of the main room. Beyond that on the right, as he stood in the doorway, what was left of a wooden partition and beyond that again, visible through the part broken wattle of the wall, a second room. This puzzled him at first until, peering through the gap, he realised this must be the cattle shed. It was a good thought, Treven acknowledged. This smaller chamber would be warmed by the hearth fire on the one side and by the body heat of the animals in the shed on the other.

He studied the design of the hall more carefully. The evening light slanted through the partly missing roof and the gaps in the end wall. It revealed a sophisticated construction, the like of which Treven had seen only in the King's hall at Winchester and in one other. The hall was not a simple A-frame but was cruik built at either end, a stronger and more elegant design, which if handled well allowed for a gallery to be stretched above the main room. Peering closely, Treven could just make out the supports for this, set high in the wall, though the gallery itself was long gone.

The thought pleased him. He wondered if there were carpenters and woodworkers in Theading capable of understanding the structure and of replicating it, or if outside labour had created it and he would be forced to send elsewhere for skilled men.

His thoughts were interrupted by Osric calling to him from the doorway that food was ready.

"It's built like the King's house," he said as he wandered over to where his servant stood.

"I seen it," Osric told him. "I asked about it today. The father of the local smith saw a house like this and carried the way of making home. His grandson reckons he was told how."

Treven nodded, satisfied. "I'll talk with them," he said. "And what of the Scriveners, what did you find out?"

Osric shrugged. "The father of the two women owns the land. He married them to the men, the brothers, to unite their land with his and treated them like sons. They took his name. Scrivener, since the land was his. There's talk the women have lost their right to inherit and the old servants think that's wrong. The steading has been passed through the female line these past five generations, or so they reckon. They got their name, Scrivener, from being scribes to the Thegns that held this land before."

Treven nodded and made a mental note that he should find out more about his. Conflicts over land were best resolved at root and not left to infect the branch. "Two women?" He asked.

"Cate Scrivener had a sister. Wife to the older brother, Edmund. Her name was Allis."

"Was?"

He shrugged again. "Word is she's either run off with a *Waelas* man, in which case she's good as dead so far as her kin are concerned, or her husband got wind of her plans and done away with them both."

Treven raised an eyebrow. "Is that likely? I could believe that of Eldred, but Edmund seemed the more reasoned of the two." He sensed that there was more. Osric was always wont to stretch his stories out, doling them out in episodes as rewards for patience. It annoyed Hugh; Treven was simply so used to it he gave it little thought.

"Other word is he might have let the woman go with his blessing."

"Oh?" That was stranger news.

"Three years and no sign of offspring, when it's known he's fathered at least two elsewhere. They say he dealt fairly with both the women. Paid a good bride price and found them sound husbands to marry, but no son or child from Allis Scrivener."

"And what of Cate? Is she happy in her marriage?"

Osric spat, to show his displeasure. "Eldred beats her," he said. "She was a lass of fifteen when he married her at Christmastide. If she looks elsewhere for comfort, it'll be others to blame." He glanced through the doorway at Hugh and Treven was painfully aware that Osric would have heard every word Hugh uttered on the journey home. He should have silenced him earlier, as Osric was now pointing out in his own inimitable fashion. Osric himself was true and loyal as day, but the others would gossip, Treven was in no doubt of that, and it wasn't seemly for the new Shire Reeve to be speaking so openly of cuckolding another man and even less seemly for the new Thegn to be tacitly encouraging this by his silence. He had, he acknowledged, a good deal to learn about the management of his new position.

"When did Allis Scrivener disappear?" he asked.

"Six weeks since, they said. Reckoned it drove the old man mad with grieving, though some say he was heading there long before, since after his wife died."

Treven nodded, recalling what he had been told about the winter deaths and Cate's mother being buried out in the woods. He was not surprised there had been no mention of her elder sister and this, perhaps, explained much about the state of the father. He wondered, though, if it were true that Tilian Scrivener had not been in his right mind since his wife's death, who had, in reality been managing the estates. He found it hard to cast either of the brothers in the role of steward. His thoughts were interrupted by Hugh shouting at him from his place beside the fire.

"Will you come out and eat, man? I'm half starved."

Treven glanced in his direction, then patted Osric on the shoulder. "See what else you can discover," he said, "and be sure you and the others have your fill of the food."

Osric jerked his head in what might have been acknowledgement and took himself away to eat with the other servants. Treven, his thoughts now filled with Osric's revelations, joined Hugh by the fire.

* * *

Cate had come outside to catch the last of the evening light. She had her spindle with her and stood on the steps of the hall, spinning the last of the wool she'd combed earlier in the day.

Cate didn't need to think about her task. She'd learnt to spin so long ago she could no longer recall a time when her fingers had not known how to twist the thread and draw the staple from the combed wool. Her yarn was smooth and even and the cloth she wove hard-wearing and warm and Cate was proud of her skills. Allis had never had the patience for it. She could use the spindle adequately enough — what woman couldn't? — but Cate despaired of the knots and slubs Allis managed to catch in her work, though she was, Cate owned, an even better weaver than Cate herself.

Cate blinked aside the tears that threatened whenever she thought of Allis. She missed her so much she felt almost split in two. The two of them might have been different in temperament and four years apart in age, but they had been very close, especially after their mother had died and so much more of the responsibility fallen on their shoulders. Their mother, Aeldryn, had been at the heart of their small community. Her knowledge of herbs and healing salves and the best plants for dyeing cloth were unchallenged in the neighbourhood. Her death had left a hole that the two girls together had tried hard to fill. Now Allis was gone too and Cate knew herself to be incapable of plugging such a gap. Sometimes the responsibility felt overwhelming for a woman of just sixteen years. Sometimes, she felt such rage at Allis for choosing to go when she, Cate, had no option but to stay. Other times, most times, her grief at her sister's loss was far greater than her anger.

She looked round at the sound of feet on the steps behind her. Edmund came out and stood, as she had done, staring towards the wood and the path that led towards Theadingford. Golden, autumnal light was giving way now to a blazing red that filled the sky as the sun set beyond the line of trees and flushed the few white clouds with rose.

"What do you think of him?" Edmund asked.

"Treven or Hugh?" she asked.

Edmund snorted. "I don't need to ask what you made of Hugh de Vries," he said harshly. "Or what he thought of you. Have a care, little sister. You may not like my brother overmuch, but he's still your husband. He'd not take kindly to his wife following the way of mine."

"And what way's that?" Cate demanded. Then she sighed. "I'm sorry, Edmund. I'd not cause you pain for anything. Allis was strong minded and wrong-headed all lifelong. She'd ever have her own way, no matter who or what stood between."

"I know it," Edmund said. "Cate, I think, truly, that she and Eldred would have been better matched."

"Lord, no. Can you imagine the storms? Each as determined as the other to get their way?" She laughed briefly at the thought of it, but the laughter choked and diminished into sobs that she tried hard to contain.

Edmund reached out and patted her hand. "Her going has caused you great pain, I know. Truth is I miss her too, Cate. While I can't say with honesty that she was a good wife, she was a good companion when the mood took her. And a more knowledgeable, sharper-minded woman I never met."

"Nor sharper tongued!" Cate managed a smile. "I know you love her, Edmund."

"Yes," he agreed. "I do and, Cate, if she stumbled back here tomorrow or in a year from now and asked me to take her in, I would and I'd face down any man or woman that even suggested I should be shamed to do it."

"She won't come back," Cate said softly.

"Can you be so sure? That . . . man . . . she left me for, you think he'll give her the life she hopes for?" He shook his head. "No, Cate, I'd see him dead and pay what blood price his kin thought him worth, but I'd have her back."

Cate didn't reply, she pretended to busy herself with some invisible tangle in her thread and Edmund chose not to press the point further. Instead, he turned and went back inside.

"She won't be coming back," Cate whispered. She bowed her head and the tears fell onto her hands as she wound the remaining twine back onto the spindle. Cate had heard her leave that night and had almost called out to her, begged her not to go. But she'd resisted the temptation to keep her sister there on her own account. She'd seen how happy Allis had been those past months, falling in love with Owain, stealing time with him, fearful of being caught but utterly unable to desist. Cate envied her that passion, that intensity of love that made her risk everything, be willing to leave all she knew behind — including Cate herself — and there was a small part of the younger sister that found that hard to forgive. Cate longed for such devotion.

But in the end, it had all been lost. Cate knew that as surely as she knew, watching the red and gold of the evening sky, that tomorrow would be a bright, fine day. She knew because she had seen another figure leave that night and, much later on, return. She'd seen him throw something the thickness of a man's arm into the deepest part of the pond and then fall to his knees, weeping, soundless sobs that wracked his body. And Cate had known then that Allis had lost her dream.

Allis was gone. Dead and gone and Cate, even knowing who had been responsible, could tell no-one what she had seen.

CHAPTER 6

PRESENT DAY

Although Rozlyn had known Charlie Higgins for almost seven years, she had never been to his tiny flat on the sixth floor of Haywood House, one of the few remaining tower blocks in that part of town.

Haywood wasn't bad, as such things went, Rozlyn mused. Sure, there was graffiti in the stairwell and the lift smelt of piss and drunks, but usually it worked, which was a definite plus in a twelve-storey building. The tower had been taken over by a private housing association the previous year and they'd put security locks on the main doors and provided a man and dog to do evening patrols. They'd also formed a tenants' association in an attempt to deal with the problems of rowdy teens with nowhere to go and had provided play facilities for their younger siblings. Rozlyn had attended one of their earlier meetings, directed to do so by DCI Brook, who informed her that this month's buzz was the importance of community policing. To Rozlyn's reply that community policing was the domain of uniform, she was further informed that the directive from on high was to improve community relations between the police and the ethnic minorities and as one of the few representatives of such they had handy, she'd better get herself down there and show just how inclusive modern policing could be. Rozlyn gathered from this that 'inclusive' was another of the latest buzzwords that Brook had finally decided he ought to use.

She went to the meeting.

Charlie Higgins had been there with a handful of other tenants, mainly pensioners, Rozlyn noted. They sat around, staring uncomfortably at the representative from the housing association as she tried hard to find out what it was that they wanted for their community and, more importantly, what was actually possible given a distinct lack of budget.

At the time, Rozlyn had put the presence of Charlie Higgins down to his wanting to impress his pet police officer, but, looking round the flat, Rozlyn began to think there might have been far more to it than that. That Charlie Higgins might genuinely have cared what happened to the place in which he lived.

There were three flats per landing, and two landings per floor, branching off from the staircase. The landings, being communal, depended for their upkeep on the willingness of tenants. Charlie's landing was spotless. There were even plastic tubs of flowers placed outside the doors, a rarity in Haywood House, where anything not nailed down was likely to be nicked or tossed over the balcony, despite the improved security. The entrance door to Charlie's flat was painted in a vivid red and the brass letterbox gleamed as though recently polished. The door was open, left ajar by the search team already inside. Rozlyn could hear them chatting and was glad to recognise the voice of DC Jenny Harper. If there was anything to find in Charlie's flat, Jenny would make certain it surfaced; she had a bloodhound instinct for the relevant. Rozlyn pushed the door open and went inside.

There were three in the search team. SOCO had already done their thing and here and there doorframes and shelves were mired with fine, silver grey powder but, Rozlyn noted, there were remarkably few prints in Charlie's apartment and, apart from that which the fingerprint officer had left, remarkably little dust. Charlie's place was beyond clean; well past being tidy. Despite the careful ravages of the search crew, Charlie's flat was immaculately organised and precisely ordered.

Rozlyn stood on the threshold to the living room and stared about. The walls were magnolia and there was no carpet. The parts that showed revealed the vinyl tiling that the local council used in all its buildings. Most of this was covered by four matching red rugs, precisely placed so that their edges lined up with the squares of tiling. One had already been rolled back and the floor beneath checked, but Rozlyn guessed the others had been left in place precisely so that she could get the best impression of the room as it had been.

Charlie's furniture was old and worn. A three-seater sofa, upholstered in the kind of sage green moquette that Rozlyn would always associate with nursing homes and two mis-matched armchairs; one blue, the other a dark shade of green.

"He'd covered them with throws," Jenny told her, holding up a length of cream fabric.

Red cushions, Rozlyn noted, matching the rugs on the vinyl covered floor. The team had removed the covers and examined them before stacking them back on the sofa, covers folded on the arm; cushions on the seat. Rozlyn could almost feel Charlie's anguish at this disorder and it was all she could do not to begin posting the plump cushion pads back into their velvet envelopes.

"Found anything?"

Jenny shrugged. "We only got here half an hour ago. Place was neat and tidy. No signs of anything untoward. SOCO was right, he wasn't killed here. He took care of his place anyway and from what we've found so far, all his personal stuff is in those drawers over there. We thought we'd wait for you. Stan's in the kitchen and I've sent Andy into the bedroom, but it won't take either of them long."

Rozlyn nodded thanks and went over to the sideboard Jenny had indicated. It was large, 1930s by the design, with art-deco carving running across the front of the two drawers and trimming the lower border of the cupboards beneath. It had been lovingly polished and cared for. A linen runner, crudely embroidered with flowers, protected the dull sheen of the unfashionably dark wood. A glass tray sat on top of this with matching moulded-glass candlesticks set with great precision on either side.

Charlie had a thing for charity shops, Rozlyn remembered. She wondered if this nasty little runner and cheap glass had been amongst his finds.

Rozlyn opened the cupboards first and peered inside. Crockery and glass, stacked with care on shelves lined with newspaper. Rozlyn bent her head round to see the date. Three months before and taken from a copy of the *Sun*. Charlie habitually read the *Guardian* in Rozlyn's presence or scrounged Rozlyn's copy of the *Guardian*, but he always made a point of reading a tabloid as well. He said he'd seen in some film or other that this was the only way to keep up with the news properly. Read a broadsheet and a tabloid every day and what one missed the other got. Charlie had no internet and so had never bothered with online news, as far as Rozlyn knew.

Rozlyn couldn't recall which film he'd said it was.

"Check underneath the papers," she reminded Jenny.

"Of course."

She grinned at her and turned back to look at the drawers.

"Don't know if you noticed," Jenny commented. "Nothing in the cupboards match. He'd got a cheap dinner service in the kitchen, half a dozen mugs and the same of glasses, all from the same range, but those things in there . . . mostly thirties, I'd guess. There's even the odd bit of Claris Cliff."

Rozlyn looked again at the mix of glass and crockery in the sideboard and saw that Jenny was right. She took out a stack of plates and shuffled through them. "He liked charity shops and flea markets," she said. "I remember him mentioning it a time or two, telling me what he found." She remembered tuning him out, too, switching off what she saw as Charlie's irrelevant chattering and was suddenly struck by a sharp and unexpected stab of regret. What had she really known about this lonely middle-aged man? She recalled Mouse Man's declaration that Charlie had got into whatever it was that killed him to prove himself to Rozlyn and the shame that she'd taken so little notice of someone that clearly hung on her every word, deepened.

She frowned and mentally shook herself. Charlie was an informant. A tick of a man, just as she'd told Big Frank Parker. But, as she'd also told Big Frank, Charlie had been Rozlyn's tick and, more and more, Rozlyn was feeling his death as a personal affront.

Charlie had made some cardboard dividers for the drawers. Each one was separated into four sections. Letters, bills and personal documents were filed like with like.

"You seen this?"

Jenny nodded, coming over to stand beside her. "Puts me to shame," she said. "I just chuck everything in a pile. What was he like, this Charlie Higgins?"

Good question, Rozlyn thought.

"Middle aged. I'd have said fairly well educated, though he never had a proper job that I knew about. Did a lot of little backhanders. A bit of cleaning here and there . . ."

Jenny laughed. "Cleaning! He could have headed up one of those reality TV shows. You know where those two women tell you how filthy your house is?"

Rozlyn shook her head. "Can't say I do."

"Oh, I forgot. You don't watch television."

"Not often. No."

Jenny laughed again. "Can't imagine life without my telly," she said. "Only thing I feel like doing when I get home. Glass of wine, ready meal, telly."

"Oh, the sophistication! Left drawer or right?"

"Left. So, what else. You knew him what . . . ?"

"Seven years or so. But I wouldn't say I knew him. Not as such. He was . . . part of the scenery, I suppose. Just . . . well, just there."

"Hmmm," Jenny slid her selected drawer from its space and paused to feel around inside the sideboard before carrying it over to the sofa and placing it carefully on the floor. Rozlyn followed her.

"Anyone to miss him?" Jenny asked.

"I really don't know." Mouse Man. Mouse would miss him. Rozlyn too, in an odd sort of way. Like she'd said, Charlie had been part of the scenery. Now there'd be a piece missing. A small piece, granted. So small as to be almost unnoticed — until it wasn't there.

"Sad, that," Jenny commented. "Living fifty-odd years and no one to care when you're gone. Not much of a footprint to leave behind."

"Footprint?"

"Oh," she grinned. "I had this boyfriend once, into all this eco stuff. He had this poster, said something like 'leave only footprints and take only photographs.' We had this big argument over how much damage you could do if you left too many footprints. Silly really, but I got this idea afterwards, that some people leave the buggers all over the place. Others, there's not even a single one."

Rozlyn nodded. It was a sad thought. She allowed herself a brief moment of self-pity as she wondered who'd be there to miss her should she depart this life as unexpectedly as Charlie Higgins had. Apart from her grandfather, a man now so sick that he could not even recall Rozlyn's existence, never mind notice her absence, there was no one really. Mouse would notice, she thought, and her colleagues, but would she really leave much more of a footprint than Charlie Higgins?

"What have you got?" Rozlyn asked, concentrating on the matter in hand and telling herself firmly not to be so maudlin.

"Bills, in date order. Look, he's written down the date he paid them. Telephone, utilities . . ." She paused and looked around. "Funny . . ."

"What?"

“There are phone bills, but no phone.”

“For a landline? I only ever knew him to use a mobile. Before that, he’d call me from pay phones.” Rozlyn took the bills and examined them. The latest was for two months previously. “No,” she said. “Look, they’re not for this address. They’re for a flat on . . . well must be on the third floor, I guess, number 303. What’s all that about, then?”

Jenny shrugged. “Want me to go down and knock on the door?”

“Later. Finish up here, see if we have any other anomalies, then I’ll tag along.” She looked at the bills more closely. They seemed to be for some kind of low-user tariff and, in all, recorded maybe a dozen calls per quarter, most of which were to Charlie’s mobile phone. Scanning them, Rozlyn could see only two other numbers recorded.

She handed them back to Jenny and returned to her own search. “Personal documents,” she said. “Birth certificate, medical card. I don’t think I even know where mine is. Marriage certificate! Charlie was married?”

“So there might be next of kin after all. That looks like an address book.” Jenny fished in the bottom of her own drawer and withdrew a black bound book. “Yep, telephone numbers, mostly, but it’s a start. Hang on, there’s another one here. You think he ran out of space?”

Rozlyn frowned suddenly recalling something she should have noted at the crime scene. “He had his wallet on him,” she mused. “The body had been dumped and the wallet chucked away a few feet from the body. They’d left his wristwatch — not that it was worth anything — but no mobile and no address book . . . no keys either. Jenny, was there anything to suggest you weren’t the first to get in here?”

She shook her head. “Nothing, but we’d a man on the door from an hour after the body was found, I believe. Of course, they might have come here straight after they killed him but if they searched this place they must have been super careful. Like you say, his wallet was found same time as the body, but there was no address book in the inventory,

I'm sure of that. Did he always have it on him? What about these?"

Rozlyn frowned, trying to remember. Charlie was meticulous about his phone numbers, both those in his phone and those in his little black books. Rozlyn would never have noticed him changing them had Charlie not pointed it out. It was a regular habit to update his book every six months or so, copying his numbers with care into an identical new book, leaving out anything not current. He hated anything to be out of date.

Rozlyn picked up the collection of books and skimmed through until she had the most recent. She knew it had to be this one because her own new mobile number was listed with her old one crossed out. Three or four such amendments would have been enough for Charlie to have abandoned this little book and start another. Charlie hated disorder and crossings out were disorder in Charlie's mind. Rozlyn found she had absorbed all of this without being aware of it. Evidently, more of Charlie Higgins' ramblings had permeated her brain than she had initially thought.

"Someone knew he'd have recorded their number?" Jenny guessed. "Didn't like the idea of it getting into the wrong hands?"

Rozlyn nodded. "This book must have been replaced recently," she explained, showing her the change in telephone number. "I bought my new phone three months ago."

"So, if whoever killed Charlie took the book and the mobile, they'd probably assume they'd covered their tracks. Probably wouldn't have bothered coming here. Or maybe the body was found before they were ready?"

"Maybe, though the timing was so precise . . . they had a window of maybe half an hour to dump Charlie's body while everyone on site was eating breakfast. They must have known what went on at the dig site well enough to realise that. Given that, they must have been aware that the diggers would have reported it quickly and they made no attempt to hide Charlie's identity."

"The dig site's pretty remote," Jenny observed. "You think it must have been someone local? For them to know how the place is run, I mean?"

"Maybe. What I don't get is why take him out there anyway. Charlie wasn't killed there and he wasn't killed here, so why not just leave him where he died?"

"Because that would tell us something about the murderer or the motive," Jenny guessed.

Rozlyn nodded slowly. "So we need to know where. It's not unreasonable to assume that the dig site is somewhere en route from the crime scene," she added.

"En route to where?" Jenny asked. "And does that help us?"

"Not a whole lot." Rozlyn took the more recent address book and sealed it in an evidence bag, then slipped it into her pocket. "Don't forget to log that one with the others."

"As if I would."

"Personal letters?"

"Nothing so far."

Rozlyn's phone began to ring. She answered it and listened, then got to her feet. "Won't be coming with you to check out the other flat," she told Jenny. "Take Stan or Andy if you want some company and let me know when I get back."

"Will do. Developments?"

Rozlyn nodded. "They've found the murder weapon," she said.

CHAPTER 7

Rozlyn arrived by road this time, a winding single track that took its route along the ridge of a hill, between cultivated fields before falling sharply into the wooded valley.

The entrance to the site gave Rozlyn a moment's pause. She'd expected a farm gate, but instead, the entrance way was flanked by stone gateposts and the driveway leading to the dig was lined by a double row of small rowan trees. In the September sun they hung bright with crimson berries. She parked her car beside a half dozen others and checked herself in the rear-view mirror, tucking an errant strand of hair back behind her ear and checking that the rest was still held in place by the bright red band.

Her mother always told her fondly that she had *exuberant* hair.

She walked the remainder of the way onto the dig. She could see the rising land beyond the stream and the hedge that bounded the bullock field and, from where she now stood, could tell that the path she'd followed down to the plank bridge was well established, dug deep into the side of the steep bank as though through long usage it had eaten its way into the landscape. The day was warm; here in this sheltered valley, it had become more than warm. A heat haze rose from the higher ground and, just for a brief moment, Rozlyn fancied she saw something ranged up there on the hill. A tall, but simple structure. A building, she thought, or the memory of one . . . Of course, with sudden clarity she realised that this little valley would be a perfect place to live, but you'd need to defend it as well.

Perhaps they'd had a watchtower of some kind up there on that ridge. From there, as she now knew, you could see for miles across the escarpment. How heavily wooded would it have been, back then? A sudden image of dense, wild woodland interspersed with avenues of coppiced trees filled her mind. She shook herself abruptly, irritated that she'd given in to fantasy when there was a job to do, but she couldn't completely chase the memory away, for such it was, Rozlyn was sure. Neither could she dispel the sudden vision of an imperious, strongly built man, overseeing the building of the hill tower and gazing down proudly onto his land. It was there and then gone, but, like a dream that arrives almost on waking, it sat at the edge of her consciousness and would not be swept away.

She frowned irritably. All her life she had seen things that might have been there, or might once have been there, and that no one else seemed to be aware of. Her mother always said she had an exuberant imagination too.

"Inspector. Over here." A uniformed officer, white shirt sleeves rolled back in the heat, was waving to her from the entrance to one of the porta-cabins. Rozlyn became suddenly aware of the lack of activity on the site. She'd expected to catch glimpses of search teams moving though the undergrowth. To see the diggers, still redundant and increasingly irritated, sitting, drinking tea outside. But the whole place, apart from the waving policeman, looked deserted.

Approaching the portacabin, she realised why. About twenty odd people were all packed inside and the feeling of excitement, coupled with an odd air of bewilderment was palpable.

"What's going on?"

"We think we've got the murder weapon," the constable informed her. "But it's not . . . well, it's not exactly what we expected."

* * *

The diggers had been helping with the search, PC Patel told her. It had seemed like a good idea, since they were used to looking for stuff and bored stupid with sitting around. They'd been clearing the undergrowth from the west side of the dig, close beside the ford, where the stream turned back into the forest, when they'd seen it in the mud.

"It looked like it'd been thrown there, but, fortunately, it'd landed haft side down with the pointed end clear of the mud." He grinned at her. "The diggers have been teaching me all the technical terms. Scientific support was still here and we got it photographed in situ." He paused, pointing to the dozen or so images pinned to the board. "We took these as well. I thought you'd like to see something straight away. The diggers printed them out for us."

Rozlyn nodded. "Good thinking," she said. Then frowned. "It's a bloody spear!"

"Quite."

Rozlyn turned to look at this new speaker and found herself confronted by the dig director, Emlyn Reece. He'd been introduced briefly on her earlier visit.

"Come and look, Inspector. You won't see many of these in a lifetime."

Rozlyn looked. Even to her unpractised eye, it was obvious that this was something special. There was no shaft fitted into the socket, but the socket itself was decorated with a twisting, writhing pattern that shone dully in the strong sunlight, which poured through the cabin windows. It was evidently very old, though the metal didn't seem rusted or decayed. More inlay embroidered the neck, where the end of the haft would have been fitted and, as Rozlyn moved to look more closely and the reflected light shifted across the surface, a pattern emerged, faint but clearly there. It looked for all the world like watered silk. Watered silk, now heavily stained with darkened blood.

She looked sharply at Reece, her expression asking all the questions for her.

"Your experts have confirmed that's blood," Reece said. "The object itself is indeed a spearhead and it's either a fantastic replica or it's at a guess ninth, tenth century."

"You're kidding me?"

Reece shook his head. The suppressed excitement caused his short, slight body to tremble. "I've never seen anything more perfect. If it is a replica, then whoever made it is a craftsman. A true artist."

"Do you think it is a replica?"

"I can think, offhand, of three people in the country capable of it, so it shouldn't take much checking, but no. I know their work. This . . . this is something else."

"It didn't come from here? From the dig, I mean. Isn't this supposed to be a ninth-century site?"

Reece laughed. "Your constable asked the same question, Inspector, so we showed him this." He gestured at one of his assistants who produced a large plastic box and laid it on the table. Inside was a lump of what looked to Rozlyn like rusted metal and dark red clay studded with the odd stone.

"This is the state in which metal comes out of the ground. It's probably a knife. Too short for a sword and, even in Christian burial, we do sometimes find knives. Believe me, Inspector, if I found something like this in a dig, I'd be dancing naked in the streets of Stamford."

Rozlyn studied both finds again. "I've seen stuff in museums," she said. "I mean, recognisable swords and the like. So, how do you get from that lump of crud, to something like this?"

"This 'lump of crud' will go to be cleaned and conserved and probably end up in storage somewhere. It will be recognisable as a knife, by the time our experts have done with it, but it won't look anything like this. This spear was buried in what must have been ideal conditions. If it was buried at all, and frankly, I have my doubts. Grave sites have been found in which metals have been discovered in an amazing state of preservation, but this . . . this is so rare, so unusual . . . and it didn't come from here. That, regretfully, I can attest and affirm."

Rozlyn looked at the photographs ranged on the cabin wall, frowning as she took this all in. Aw, come on! She thought. This was just too crazy for words. A Dark Age spear used to kill Charlie Higgins was bad enough, but for him then to be dumped on a dig site contemporaneous with the murder weapon. That was all too much.

"We're sure this is the murder weapon?" she asked Patel.

"The post-mortem will confirm it, ma'am, but there doesn't seem to be any doubt. The victim was killed by a single stab wound, it'd be a bit much to find two bloody weapons on site. We'd have to find ourselves another body."

A ripple of laughter greeted Patel's comments and Rozlyn allowed herself a wry smile. Patel was enjoying himself, she thought. An appreciative audience and the knowledge that, not only had he done a good job, but he'd unearthed a bloody good mystery into the bargain.

"You'd better show me the site," Rozlyn said. Everyone around her moved and Rozlyn got the impression they intended to follow. "If you don't mind, I'd rather you all stayed put." She saw the disappointment on Reece's face and relented slightly. "Apart from Doctor Reece, of course. You could, maybe, give me an insight into the lay of the land. And PC Patel, naturally. You can talk me through how the spearhead was discovered."

Reece nodded enthusiastically and the others subsided with a collective sigh of disappointment. Odd, Rozlyn thought, now that the body was safely out of the way and they could detach themselves slightly from the fact that a man's life was ended, this event was transformed into a bit of excitement that no doubt they'd be dining out on for months to come.

* * *

Almost dancing at her side in a mood of puppylike excitement, Reece led them around the perimeter of the dig. Despite his exuberance he was as careful of preserving his domain as Rozlyn would have been in guarding the integrity of a crime scene. He pointed out the areas of greatest interest as they passed.

"The main house would have been there. It's an unusual structure, stone foundations and walls, we think to about two feet in height, then wattle and daub and also some planking. Thatched roof, presumably. We've found a number of post holes and the remains of two hearths."

"Two?" Something leapt in Rozlyn's memory, but she could not place the reference. "Isn't that unusual?"

"It is, yes. Generally, there'd have been a central hearth used for heating and cooking, but this one seems to have had a doorway at the midpoint of the long wall, there, look. Hearths at either end. Stone built, too, not a scraping in the ground lined with rock. Whoever owned this place knew what they wanted and went for it."

Rozlyn nodded slowly, her gaze drawn back towards the bank above the stream. "Anything up there?" She asked.

"I don't know. We did a general survey, but our time is so limited. We've got to push on here, find out as much as we can before we lose the site."

"That definite, is it? I was told this area will be flooded."

Reece shrugged. "There's a final appeal. If that's successful, there'll be a public inquiry and that might reverse the decision. From our point of view, it's bloody disastrous. This valley is so rich in Dark Age finds. We lost God knows what when Rutland Water was created. The teams working on that barely scratched the surface. If you ever find yourself in Oakham, you can get a flavour of what they uncovered in the museum, but they knew there was a mountain of stuff they didn't have time to reach and, of course, that's gone for ever now. I'm still hopeful we may at least get a further stay of execution. If there was some way of convincing the authorities that this spear head came from here we'd be laughing."

"I went to school in Oakham," Rozlyn mused. "I know the museum. Where do you think it came from?"

Reece shrugged. "Private collection somewhere, probably. Of course, if it is a replica, that changes things. If it's the real thing — and I'd stake my reputation that it is — then there are collectors out there . . . It's not been catalogued, at least not that I could see. No mark on it."

"Catalogued?"

"A piece like that, you'd need to know where it was found, the circumstances, the context. That way, it becomes part of the overall picture of the community. Who made it, where? How the community lived. It would have belonged to an important man. Or possibly a woman, that's a little more unusual, but as we're beginning to discover, it's definitely a possibility. A museum or a serious collector would have painted a reference number on it and that reference would have led us to a catalogue and all the rest of the information."

Rozlyn nodded, recalling that she'd seen such numbers on museum objects. "I thought, if it was ninth or tenth century, then . . . I guess what I'm asking is, they didn't bury grave goods then, did they? At least not in a Christian burial."

"Generally, no. It could be earlier, but the pattern around the haft . . . I'd say later. It's less fine, looser, somehow. There are subtle differences, but you'd need someone with a more detailed knowledge than me to fill you in on that. Look, that's where it was found." He pointed and PC Patel took over, moving them forward carefully on a track designated with blue-and-white tape, between tall trees, until they stood on the bank of the stream some six feet or so from where the spear had been recovered.

"No footprints."

Patel shook his head. "The little path we came on is baked hard. But I'll bet you could stand on the edge of the grave and chuck the thing and it'd end up here."

Rozlyn turned and looked back through the trees. From where she stood, she could make out the portacabins and the tape marking the hall and, yes, the grave in which Charlie's body had been dumped. "It'd take a good throw," she said, "but it's possible." She turned back to Reece. "You mentioned collectors and catalogues . . ."

Reece nodded. "A piece of that importance would normally end up in a museum," he said. "But there are private collectors, some more legitimate than others."

"Would it be valuable? I mean in monetary terms?"

Reece nodded. "Things are better now than they were. The government brought in the portable antiquities scheme, you see, so it's in everybody's interest to report finds. Before that, you'd get metal detectorists, for instance, just keeping what they found, or selling it on. Oh, not all of course. Most have always been aware that archaeology is as much about context as it is about finds. We've had a local group working with us here, for instance, going through the spoil heaps and surveying the area. They've been terrific and most of them know nearly as much as our diggers do," he laughed. "Puts the odd nose out of joint, that does. But there's a lot of stuff out there unrecorded and uncatalogued and so, however beautiful it might be, it's almost useless from an archaeological perspective. Of course, to the people who pay big money to collect on the black market, that doesn't matter a damn."

"And, if they acquired this illegally, they're not going to report it stolen now," Patel filled in.

"Shouldn't think so. No."

"Anyone local?" Rozlyn asked

Emlyn Reece shrugged again. "I wouldn't know. I'm not from round here, but the man to ask is Ethan Merril. Lives in Stamford, runs a little shop there now and writes the occasional book. He retired from academia two or three years back, but he's the man to ask. Irascible old sod, mind you. He'll only talk to you if he's a mind to."

Ethan Merril, Rozlyn thought, wondering where she'd heard that name before.

CHAPTER 8

There had been a message waiting for her on the answerphone when she got back home. It was from PC Jenny Harper, about the phone bills found in Charlie's flat. If anything, it deepened the sense of mystery that now surrounded him.

"They're for a Mrs Chinowski," Jenny said. "She's ancient, practically housebound. Charlie looked after her, she says. He paid her phone bill and sorted out someone from the social to come in five days a week to do her shopping and cleaning. She was absolutely devastated when I told her Charlie was gone. I sat with her as long as I could, then tried to get a neighbour to come in. Mrs C wouldn't have it. Said they were all no-goods and thieves, but I think this needs a follow-up call at the very least."

Listening to the message, Rozlyn nodded in agreement. It seemed that Charlie Higgins had left a bigger footprint on the world than anyone would have guessed . . . or maybe Rozlyn would have known, had she listened properly.

Rozlyn dumped her keys in the blue and white dish that sat next to the phone. It was chipped and cracked, mended with an ugly rivet and she probably wasn't helping its survival by using it as a key depository. It had been her mother's, one of the few things of hers that Rozlyn retained and, though she hated the look of the thing, she couldn't quite bear to let it go. When she touched it, it was as if a memory had been triggered in her brain. No, not quite a memory . . . it was as if she were seeing it through her mother's eyes, feeling her affection for its chipped and battered self.

The feeling was similar to the one she'd had at the dig site; that moment that was almost like remembering and too vivid for imagination. Her grandfather had always suggested it was a kind of expanded intuition. There had been a time when Rozlyn had thought that believing in or following your intuition was a phony kind of thing to do, until she'd realised that to a greater or lesser extent all of her colleagues seemed to do so. Some called it copper's nose. Others suggested this was all that was going on with so-called profiling. Whatever, it seemed born of some blend of instinct and knowledge and Rozlyn had come to accept her own experiences as simply a rather odd manifestation of this same phenomenon.

Sighing, Rozlyn dragged the red band from her hair and shook it loose. Curls fell about her face, sprang, halo like to frame her head, softening Rozlyn's habitually stern expression. Softer than her Nigerian father's hair, more tightly sprung than her mother's blonde waves, she wore it always as long as it would grow, which was just past her shoulders. Then she ruthlessly confined it. No one, but no one, ever saw it loose.

Aside from the small oak table, the phone and the dish, the hall was empty. Cream walls, bare of pictures, original Victorian tiles covering the floor in a red, black and white mosaic. She went through to the kitchen. Pale, limed wood and a lot of chrome, out of keeping with the rest of the house. It had been like that when Rozlyn moved in three years before. It was functional and she liked the range-style oven, so she left it alone.

Rozlyn filled the kettle, then shrugged out of her jacket. She hung it on the back of a dining chair and extracted Charlie's address book from the pocket. It smelt of Charlie. Peppermints and the faintest whiff of cigarette smoke. Charlie smoked rollups. Or, at least, he made rollups, carefully and precisely, with one of those little machines that looked like a wide rubber band wrapped round rollers. More often than not, he'd then leave them to go out in the ashtray; hands too busy gesticulating to hold a cigarette.

The only time Charlie's hands were still or quiet was when he rolled his skinny little smokes.

Rozlyn made a pot of tea. Earl Grey, tonight, because she could drink that black, a swift check of the fridge having informed her she'd run out of milk again. She drank her coffee black too but had long ago adopted her mother's habit of never drinking coffee after six at night. And she thought about food. Hungry, but not sure she could be bothered to cook; knowing she'd regret it later if she didn't eat. She never could sleep hungry. Water on to boil for the pasta, she blanched, peeled and chopped tomatoes, crushed garlic and sliced olives, drinking her tea as she cooked, remembering she had half a bottle of wine from the night before to go with her meal. The capers had hidden at the back of the cupboard again. She dragged them out, adding a scant teaspoon, stirred anchovies into the mix and finished with fresh torn basil. Never touch it with a blade, her mother had told her, and she smiled at the memory.

She grew salad leaves, along with herbs in the tiny conservatory — more of a lean-to really, but as it was big enough to hold a chair, she'd decided it deserved the promotion. She dressed the salad in the bowl, drizzling it with olive oil, lemon juice and more fresh herbs. Satisfied with the result, she put the cooking pots in the dishwasher before sitting down to eat. Then, fork poised in hand, she opened Charlie's little book. Mindful of her grandfather's prohibition on reading at the table, she mentally apologised to the old man and began to do just that.

An hour later found her still sitting at the table. The crockery had joined the rest of the cooking things in the washer and only the bottle and glass remained. Charlie had been meticulous. Of the two dozen or so numbers listed, most had an explanation beside. J.D, for instance, was his bookmaker and three of the numbers were the pubs he cleaned for — usefully listed as work one, two and three. Thanks to Jenny's call, Rozlyn could now identify 'Mrs C, Downstairs' and there were a half dozen others that she could guess at, being acquaintances Charlie had mentioned. She could follow those up in the morning.

Four numbers puzzled her. One had no name next to it and when Rozlyn tried it, she just got a ring tone, then an automated message telling her that this number was no longer in use but that A1 Taxis could be reached on . . . She hung up and tried the next. That had the initials C.T. next to it and proved to be a Chinese takeaway. C.T. Fair enough, Rozlyn thought, and Mr T. Thompson wasn't available on his mobile. Then there was the one marked Donovan. Rozlyn tried this too, but again there was no reply. An answerphone clicked in after a half-dozen rings and a man's voice instructed her to leave a message. Rozlyn was about to comply, explain who she was and about Charlie Higgins, when some instinct warned her off. She put the phone down and stared hard. If her guess was right then someone had wanted their name erased from Charlie's records and, so far, Donovan and Mr Thompson were the only contacts for which Rozlyn could not account.

She glanced at her watch. Almost nine, too late to do anything tonight. She'd need a warrant to trace the number and chances were, she wouldn't get hold of anyone now that would be willing to give her one until Monday. She couldn't, off hand, think of any weight of evidence that would convince a magistrate this was worth bothering with on a Saturday night.

Mouse Man would know who Mr Thompson was and probably Donovan too. Rozlyn looked at her watch again, trying to think where Mouse would likely be at 9 p.m. on a Saturday. She drew a blank. She could go and look, she supposed, but the idea of tramping the streets searching for Mouse as she had on the previous evening held little appeal, especially as she could make a good guess where Mouse would be the following morning.

Rozlyn went back into the kitchen to retrieve her wine and carried what remained of the bottle through to the living room. The walls were lined with videos and music and DVDs. Above the fireplace was a framed poster; The Ramones, posed carelessly with their instruments in front of CBGB, beneath the sign for Bowery and Bleecker. She had a second version of this poster hanging on her bedroom wall. An image of a very young Rozlyn, posing alone and nervous, beneath the same Manhattan sign.

In the living room, a leather sofa nestled in the bay window, ready for the occasional guest; a matching chair had been positioned centre stage, in the sweet spot where the sound from the speakers converged and the music was at its most potent. She selected a Wynton Marsalis CD and sat back in the chair, cueing 'Angel Eyes', hoping that the light, fast intro, sensuous melody and insistent percussion that followed would conspire to purge her thoughts of the day's rudeness. Marsalis, she had found, was not a musician that left you with any space for thinking.

But tonight, even this familiar remedy refused to help. The events she had witnessed kept on intruding. The spear, the names in the address book. The clinical tidiness of Charlie's flat that reminded her so much of her own home and that brief image of the watchtower, if that's what it was, up on that damned hill. That and the odd familiarity of the man who stood beside it, gazing down into the valley as though master of it all.

CHAPTER 9

THEADING. YEAR OF GRACE 878

"I should not be here."

She stood, nervous, not quite willing to enter the birch grove.

"I'll not seek to stop you should you wish to go." He took a small step closer to her, noting the way the autumn sun caught the loose strands of hair that blew about her face, the low, bright rays finding the red that glowed among the brown.

"Cate." He spoke her name softly. Almost within reach now, he raised a hand towards her, beckoning her on; then dropped it to his side as she skittered back. "I would not hurt you. How could I hurt you?"

"I don't know." She met his gaze, briefly, and then looked away, gazing down at the grassy, leaf-littered ground. At the birch leaves scattered like gold coins beneath her feet. Autumn had arrived in a mood of spectacular glee and had, with a sweep of her hand, turned the whole world red and gold.

"Cate," Hugh said again. "Come here to me." He spoke with an insistent softness that he knew instinctively she could not resist and so indeed did not. She stepped forward into the birch grove, laying one hand on the white barked tree beside her and extending the other towards Hugh as though to have him share in this so momentous decision.

Hugh took her hand and drew her to him and she stood still, eyes downcast, as he loosed her hair and only then, shy and uncertain and yet, he saw in her eyes, oh so eager, did she lift her face to receive his kiss.

* * *

BILLINGTON. PRESENT DAY

"Hey! Mouse Man!" Rozlyn watched him skittering down the street after emerging from the little chapel he attended every Sunday. Mouse kept close to the house walls, running nervously on tippy toe with many an anxious glance from side to side, looking for all the world like one of the small rodents he so adored. Rozlyn had been surprised at Mouse's religious leanings, but knew he attended chapel for the ten o'clock service almost weekly, staying to drink coffee with the other parishioners. Rozlyn had often wondered what they thought of the smell he carried with him and if the bill for air freshener outweighed that of communion wine.

Mouse started, hearing Rozlyn call. He swung around to face her, feet square planted on the floor, head down and hands raised as though poised for flight.

"Oh, it's you." He composed himself, the drop in his tension reflected in a small relaxation of the hands as he trotted across the road. "What are you doing here?"

"I came to see you."

"How did you know where to find me?"

"You told me you came here on a Sunday. Hey, what's with you? You're jumpy as one of those little animals of yours."

"They have a right to be jumpy. The whole world is out to get them."

"Well, that may be, but that's not exactly true for you, is it?" She studied Mouse's reaction closely. The man was even more on edge than usual. "Well? Is it?"

"How should I know?" Mouse man replied. "But it's best to be careful, that's what I always say."

Rozlyn shrugged and began to walk, Mouse falling into step beside her.

"Why did you want to see me?"

"I've been looking at Charlie's flat. His address books in particular."

"Books? He had more than one?"

Rozlyn paused and stared at him. "That significant, Mouse Man?"

"I don't know enough people to fill even the one, that's all." Mouse shrugged and moved on and Rozlyn let it lie.

"I found a few names I've not managed to follow up. I figured you might be able to help me out."

"What makes you think that?"

"You knew Charlie better than most. He might have mentioned something."

"Charlie liked to talk. I like to listen," he said.

"Meaning, I didn't."

Mouse shrugged again but didn't deny it. "So," he said. "What names?"

"There are two," Rozlyn told him. "One is someone called Mr T. Thompson. Mean anything to you?"

Mouse nodded enthusiastically. "Thomas Thompson," he said. "Parents with no imagination. He runs a house business."

"House business?"

"Yes, you know, people rent them, then they go away again. Move out, move on. He rents them out again."

"Oh, so he's a landlord?"

"Landlords run pubs, he has a house business."

Rozlyn decided not to split hairs. Mouse Man definitions were frequently a little contrary. "And what connection did Charlie have with him?"

"Charlie cleaned. When the people moved out and moved on, Charlie cleaned ready for the next. Thomas Thompson knew he could trust Charlie to clean. He let Charlie keep anything that got left behind and he paid him over a hundred pounds every time he did it."

Judging by Charlie's flat it was probably worth every penny, Rozlyn thought. "Charlie listed his work numbers as work numbers, Mouse. Works one, two and three in his book. You got any idea why he'd not list Mr T that way?"

Mouse man nodded. "Sure," he said. "Because it wasn't like other work he did. He did work for two pubs, the Queen's, the Ship and a working man's club. He paid taxes on those."

Mouse Man sounded impressed at the idea of paying tax. "Mr Thomas Thompson gave him money in an envelope. That's why he didn't put it in his book as a work number. Charlie wasn't stupid."

"How often did he clean for Mr T?"

"Two, three times a month, I think."

"You're sure? That's a lot of moving on for people to be doing."

Mouse Man shrugged again, this time with an injured air as though hurt that Rozlyn expressed such disbelief. "Like I told you, people come, then they go somewhere else. Charlie cleaned and kept anything they left behind."

Alarm bells were ringing in Rozlyn's head. Maybe Mouse Man's insistence that this man was not a landlord meant more than just his off-kilter way of defining things. "Do you know where any of these houses were, Mouse, and what sort of things got left behind? Things that Charlie kept?"

Mouse had to stand still to think about that one, unable to process complex information and walk at the same time. "Charlie wanted to tell you about it," he said, "but if he had done, he would have lost the work and he had dependants, you see?"

"Dependants? I know about the old lady on the third floor, Charlie paid her phone bills."

"Yes, she was one. But Charlie couldn't tell you about the houses. He said there was something funny about the way people came and then went on somewhere else. He said he had to clean really well in these houses and sometimes he found things that had been left behind that people wouldn't usually leave behind."

"Like what, Mouse?"

Mouse Man's face grew anxious. "He didn't tell me." Then he brightened. "He gave me a radio once. A little radio. I've still got it if you want to see? It had writing on it in a funny language, Charlie told me it was Chinese. But I can still get Radio Two in the morning, so I don't mind if it's a foreign radio."

Rozlyn was momentarily distracted. "Radio Two?"

"Terry Wogan," Mouse told her as though it was such an obvious thing it didn't need explaining. "We both like Terry Wogan, Charlie and me. Listen every day. My radio broke and then Charlie gave me this little one with the foreign writing on it." He turned fully to look at Rozlyn, a sudden cloud of anxiety darkening his pale blue eyes. "If I showed you the radio, you'd take it away from me, wouldn't you? You'd say it was evidence?"

"I thought Terry Wogan was dead," Rozlyn said.

Mouse shook his head emphatically. "I know that's what people say," he told her. "But it isn't true."

Rozlyn thought it best to let that one go. "Mouse," Rozlyn found herself saying. "If, for any reason, I had to take your radio away, I'd give you a new one to take its place. I wouldn't leave you without your music, or your Terry Wogan. I promise. Now, these houses, Charlie cleaned. You can tell me where?"

Mouse studied her for a moment as though to make certain she was telling the truth, then he nodded and the shadow passed from his watery eyes. "I can show you one," he said. "Maybe two. I don't know the others. Charlie said there were more than two."

"Near here?"

"Two near here. I don't know about the rest. But I wouldn't go too close, Inspector Priest. Charlie said it was OK for him to go and clean, but only when the places were empty. If they had people there, before they went on somewhere else, he had to stay off from them."

I'll bet he did, Rozlyn thought. "Mouse, did Charlie ever mention someone called Donovan to you?"

Mouse Man halted again and began to turn away.

"Hey, where are you going?"

"I told you enough, Inspector Priest. I don't want any trouble."

"Has this Donovan got anything to do with the houses Charlie cleaned?"

Mouse shook his head.

"Then what? Hey, Mouse Man, don't run out on me now. I'm trying to find who killed our Charlie. You want to help me do that, don't you?"

Reluctantly, Mouse turned back. He seemed to brace himself as though expecting a physical blow. He stepped closer to Rozlyn, so close that the smell of him overwhelmed Rozlyn's senses and brought tears to her eyes. "I'll show you the houses," he said. "I'll tell you everything Charlie told me about Mr Thomas Thompson, and I'll let you take my little radio with the foreign letters on it, so long as you give me another one. But I don't know nothing about Donovan. And I won't tell nothing neither. Donovan is a bad man and Charlie said I didn't want to know about him. He was going to tell you when he knew enough, he said. It was a big thing he could tell you about old antique things. The things Donovan does are about old antique things, selling old antique things, not about the people that go to the houses. Charlie said this Donovan knew about the houses but he didn't bring the people there. Charlie didn't clean for Donovan. He said that Donovan was a bad man and I didn't want to know no more."

He was shaking in his boots, quite literally. Rozlyn, though always reluctant to touch the Mouse Man, laid a soothing hand on his greasy arm. "It's OK, Mouse," she said. "I won't ask you more about him. You just show me the houses, all right? Then you can go off home and feed your friends. Listen to your radio."

Mouse Man nodded rapidly, then took a deep breath. "If I knew any more, I'd tell you, Inspector Priest," he said. "Charlie was my friend. I want you to get who killed him. But be careful. Donovan's a bad man. You're not careful enough, he might get you too."

* * *

From the writings of Abbot Kendryk of Storton Abbey, Year of Grace 878:

> *I had been disturbed by the rumours that were spread abroad from the vill of Theading and the gossip that inevitably reached my ears regarding the new lord of Theadingford. To be more exact, it was gossip regarding the man he had appointed Shire Reeve that troubled me. Treven himself was already, in those first days, gaining a reputation for fair dealing and it seemed this was a man who understood the needs of both land and the people thereon and sought approval from his community. But the same could not be said of the man Hugh de Vries. His scions looked towards Frankish ancestry and tradition and had the wealth and power, even in those straitened times, to satisfy their own wishes and desires, regardless and uncaring of what damage that might do to reputation. Hugh de Vries, in short, was a selfish man. I am myself a son of Frankish lords. I have been always conscious of the power such families wield and what rights they see as theirs to take without thought of consequence.*
>
> *I felt most greatly troubled that this man should have turned his attention to the Scrivener girl. The women of that family have long been the wealth of this land, with knowledge and skill passed from mother to daughter such that some men looked askance. It has always seemed to me*

that the strength and knowledge of men and women both are needed for the health of any community. That the strength of both should be valued. At that time winter and war had both lately taken their tribute and strength of either sort had been diminished.

This man, this Hugh, such men need firm handling, especially firm should they be placed in position of influence and power and it seemed to me that though the heart of this new lord, this Treven, was reported by so many to be sound, his judgement was not. When the Shire Reeve shows so little concern for those that they are meant to serve, what hope can there be of protection from the evil that waits at every false turn? Such ill consideration feeds the hunger of that which waits for evil to be done. The hunger buried deep within the land, long fed on blood and need and want and desire and waiting always for the careless step.

CHAPTER 10

Mrs Chinowski had the chain on the door and peered out cautiously, one pale blue eye framed in the opening. She was a tiny woman, Rozlyn having to stoop so that she could see her face and the I.D. card she held.

"Can I talk to you?" Rozlyn asked gently. "It's about Charlie Higgins from upstairs."

To her surprise and some alarm she saw the one eye fill with tears. They overflowed and ran down the pale, wrinkled skin of the old lady's face.

"He was good to me, was Charlie. Why would anyone want to hurt him?" Her voice was heavily accented and now, thickened by tears.

"I don't know, Mrs Chinowski. That's what I'm trying to find out. Can I come inside?"

She nodded, then closed the door so she could release the chain. Rozlyn got the impression she was in two minds whether or not to open it again and wished she'd had the foresight to bring Jenny as Mrs Chinowski had already deigned to speak with her. Not that Jenny'd have been too happy about that on a Sunday, she reminded herself. She'd probably have told Rozlyn that some people have a life and would rather spend their Sundays participating in it.

The door was opened just enough for Rozlyn to slide through. Mrs Chinowski closed it behind her and then stood on the threshold, wringing her hands as though the distress caused by Charlie's death had been compounded by her having to let this stranger into her home.

"I don't have strangers coming in here," she whispered.

"Do you mind if we sit down? My colleague, Jenny Harper, she told me you were very upset to hear about Charlie. That he was a good friend to you? Did he come to visit you here?"

"I only let him in the hall," she said defensively. "He never asked to come further than that." She seemed affronted that Rozlyn would want to sit down. "He got that lady in to clean for me. I had forms to fill in. I told him, Charlie, I can't fill in forms. Not at my age. He did it for me. He stood here in the hall and asked me what he needed to know and I told him and he wrote it down. Then that woman came from Hibbert House."

"Hibbert House? Oh, social services."

Mrs Chinowski hissed at her. It was a startling sound. Aggressive and surprisingly loud to be emitted from her frail old lady's body. Rozlyn gathered she had said the wrong thing.

"No," she told her stoutly. "Not social services." She spat the words out as though they tasted bad. "I told Charlie, I wouldn't have no busy body from there, so he got that woman from Hibbert House. I paid her," she added proudly. "Out of my pension each week. She did shopping for me and she put the Hoover over and did bits for me. Then she went and that other one came." She sighed and gestured irritation. "I had to train this new one all over again. Young thing, she is. Young things are so . . ." she sought the word, clawing at the air with bone thin fingers; finally found it. "Deficient." She concluded triumphantly, closing her hand upon the word so it couldn't escape. Rozlyn shuddered, momentarily enthralled by the grasp of that fleshed-out skeleton.

She recovered herself enough to ask how long Mrs Chinowski had known Charlie.

She shrugged. "Three years perhaps."

"How often did he visit you?"

"When I called him on the phone and said I needed him."

So, not often then, Rozlyn thought, casting her mind back to the light use evidenced by the phone bills. "What things did you need him for, Mrs Chinowski?"

It was clear by now that she wasn't about to let Rozlyn go further into the flat, so she leaned back against the wall and earned herself another displeasured hiss. Rozlyn ignored it. "Mrs Chinowski?" She prompted. "What kind of things did you need Charlie for?"

"He helped me," she snapped. "When that one woman didn't come any more and the new one came, Charlie talked to her and then when I got this other new one, well, Charlie arranged it all." She shrugged. "She wasn't as good, of course, but Charlie said they were short staffed over there at Hibbert House so . . ." She allowed her disapproval to hang between them. Rozlyn could feel it, curdling the air. Then, suddenly, the old lady was crying again. "What will I do now Charlie's gone? He was like a son to me." She covered her eyes with her bone white hands. Somehow, she seemed to get smaller, shrinking into herself, diminishing until Rozlyn was possessed of the quite irrational anxiety that, if she looked long enough, Mrs Chinowski would disappear altogether.

"Can I make you a cup of tea?" Rozlyn asked quietly.

"What? You mean, in my kitchen?"

"I won't make a mess. I'm pretty good with the tea pot."

Mrs Chinowski wiped her eyes and sniffed, then felt in her sleeve for a hankie. "That girl. Jennifer, she said you were Charlie's friend. That's why I let you in. She was nice to me and she said you'd be calling. A tall lady, she said and she told me you were a black lady so I wasn't worried."

"Would you have been?"

Mrs Chinowski nodded solemnly. "It's not your fault," she told her. Rozlyn refrained from asking if Mrs Chinowski meant that she was black. "You see, when I went out to the shops. To do my own shopping. The last time I went out to do my own shopping. I was robbed."

"You had your bag stolen?"

"I've been frightened ever since then."

Rozlyn nodded. "Did we catch him?"

A shake of the head. "He rode a bicycle and he got away. He was laughing at me. I lay there on the ground and he was laughing at me."

"Let me make you that tea," Rozlyn coaxed and Mrs Chinowski nodded finally, pointed a shaking hand towards a door at the end of the hall, then followed her nervously as she went through. Silently, Rozlyn celebrated that small success. The effort it took to be nice to people who were so obviously uncomfortable with your very existence was exhausting, even when that person was an obviously frightened elderly lady. "*Connections are what matter*," her grandfather always told her. "*Make that connection, build that bridge. You are capable of doing that when sometimes other people just can't see the way. You are the strong one here.*"

Living in a rural town in England meant that Rozlyn had to be 'strong' a lot. Sometimes, Rozlyn thought, being the strong one just stank. It was something she was getting really sick of having to do.

Mrs Chinowski's kitchen was, for the most part, clean and neat, though the units were old and battered and the small table had a folded postcard wedged under one leg to stop it from tipping. From the colour of the card and the evidence of dust trapped beneath, Rozlyn figured it had been there for a long, long time. Evidently, her cleaning lady didn't trouble too much about the kitchen floor. A quick vacuum and the occasional mop would be about the limit.

The counters were in a better state; though stained here and there they had been wiped and scrubbed. Rozlyn detected the smell of bleach emanating from the sink and the white plastic of the kettle was spotless. She filled it from a polished tap and followed the old lady's instructions for the teapot and cups.

"How did you get to know Charlie?" She asked as they waited for the kettle to boil.

"It was after I had my bag stolen. He saw it in the papers. He brought me money and I let him into my hall. He was a gentleman, was Charlie Higgins. Never presumed."

"Not like me?" Rozlyn couldn't resist.

The old lady didn't rise to the bait. Instead, she regarded Rozlyn thoughtfully. The pale eyes still watered when she talked of Charlie but she seemed more composed. "I'm sure your manners are well enough for a policewoman," she said. "A policewoman is used to dealing with people who have none, I suppose."

Rozlyn made the tea and carried the pot over to the table. The tea bags were some economy supermarket brand, she noted. She wondered if they were Mrs Chinowski's choice or if they'd been selected by a thrifty home help.

"Did Charlie ever talk about himself?"

"He talked. We talked about people who had died and gone. About the old days."

"The old days?" Charlie was only fifty-odd, Rozlyn thought. Mrs Chinowski was in her mid-eighties.

"When we were both young," she said as though that were obvious.

"What about when you were young?"

"Oh, leaving my home, coming over here. Knowing that the family I left behind might not live to see the end of the war." She shook her head. "It was a dreadful time."

"Forgive me, Mrs Chinowski, but Charlie wasn't old enough to remember that."

She hissed again and reached for the teapot. "That didn't mean he couldn't listen," she told Rozlyn acerbically. "Charlie *knew* how to listen."

Did he listen standing in the hall, Rozlyn wondered. But she said nothing, still not certain what to make of this old lady. Instead, she drank her supermarket tea, hating the sweetened taste of it — the old lady had added sugar without asking — and listened as Mrs Chinowski spoke about her childhood in

Poland. The family had crossed the sea to England in 1940, when she was just a tiny child. Even so, she could remember her first night on UK soil, sleeping on the floor of a hostel with her brother and sister, and how glad they'd been of the shelter because, despite the bombings, they really believed that they were safe at last. Rozlyn listened as she told how her parents had died and how she'd married and eventually come to live here when the flats were new. She elaborated on how things had changed. She spoke as though recounting a story so often relived she did not even have to think of the words anymore. A story that could only be partly hers; more likely one handed down to her by older siblings because she had been too young to remember much about their journey. A story so threadbare with use that the emotion had long been wrung from the fabric of it because there were only so many times your heart could cry. But when Mrs Chinowski told Rozlyn about Charlie and the small kindnesses of this man she hardly knew, she wept again and, when Rozlyn finally left her, having eventually wrested from her the names of her cleaning lady and a Mr Bishopson — who, it seemed was another beneficiary of Charlie's kindness — Rozlyn felt exhausted, worn out by Mrs Chinowski's life.

It was six fifteen and her route home took her past the Queen's. She stopped off for a drink, but Big Frank Parker had not yet arrived. Tearing a page from her notebook, Rozlyn wrote a message for him, thinking how to phrase it while she drank her beer, trying Speckled Hen purely because she'd seen Frank Parker drinking it.

The note she finally left with the barman was cryptic, but she figured Big Frank would get the gist. She left the name of Thomas Thompson and the addresses of the two houses Mouse Man had shown her that day. One was definitely on Big Frank's patch and the other only a street or so beyond his domain. Beneath that, she drew a large question mark.

The bar man, recalling Rozlyn from her previous visit, looked over at what she'd written. "You want to leave a number with that?" he asked.

Rozlyn shook her head. "He'll know how to get in touch if he needs me," she said, and the bar man nodded. Big Frank was not known to be big on phone calls. If he wanted someone, he sent someone else to fetch them.

"He'll definitely be in later?"

The barman nodded again and slid the note behind one of the optics. "He likes to watch the *Antiques Roadshow* first, then have a spot of supper before he comes over here."

"The *Antiques Roadshow*?" Rozlyn laughed. It didn't quite fit with her take on Big Frank Parker. Rozlyn's grandfather had liked to watch that, seeing it when he had stayed in England with his granddaughter. Later, Rozlyn recorded episodes for him and sent them over to the States. Later still, her granddad had rung to say he could get it on BBC America or some such. He'd been bugged about that. Rozlyn doubted he watched it now. He watched nothing, just stared into the middle distance at some world no one else could see and sometimes, just sometimes, he would smile as though glimpsing the face of an old friend through that mist of ruined memory.

Rozlyn, deciding that Speckled Hen was the dry white of beers, finished her drink and took herself off home.

* * *

THEADING, YEAR OF GRACE 878

All night Cate had sat with their neighbour, Aedra. Her son and daughter-in-law had been nursing her for weeks and were worn out with the grief of it. Alwyn was awaiting the birth of their first child and was now heavy and uncomfortable and very much in need of rest. Her man was exhausted by the harvest and the task of rebuilding not only their own home but assisting others before the autumn gave way to winter.

So Cate, knowing that the old woman had little time left on this earth, had taken on the task of keeping vigil while they both slept.

Home was a single room, a box bed at one end for the married couple and a heap of bracken and pine at the other on which the old woman lay. A central hearth, the smoke from which lifted into the rafters and filtered out through the thatch, keeping the mice and vermin at bay. The miasma of rot and death rose from the body of the old woman. That Aedra had lingered for so long was, Cate thought, because she had received such love and such care from her family. Though it might have been better for all if she had been allowed to slip from their grasp sooner. It was time for her to be released from the pain of the mass that bulged her stomach and the second that broke the skin of her breast and for which Cate had no remedy. It was time as well for the couple to turn their thoughts and energy to the new life soon to come.

Aedra roused with a little gasp of pain and Cate knelt down beside her, slipping an arm behind frail shoulders, holding the fragile body close to her own and pressing a cup to cracked lips. "Drink, sweetness, drink and lose the pain for a while. There, that's good."

The lips parted and the woman did her best to swallow the infusion of honey, white bryony and other herbs. It was moot, Cate thought, which would kill her first — the remedy or the sickness — but at least she would pass with less pain.

Settling her gently, Cate fetched the water she had left to keep warm beside the fire, infused with more herbs to both sweeten the air and soothe the broken skin. Carefully she drew back the rags that absorbed Aedra's urine, washed her carefully and placed fresh rags beneath her and between the stick like legs. Then she covered her warmly once more.

Stepping outside to place the soiled cloths in a bucket ready for washing, Cate stood for a while in the cold and the dark and gazed up at the stars. She doubted Aedra would live to see another dawn and she could not regret that. All life ended and Aedra had enjoyed her full season.

Tears sprang unbidden, but they were not for Aedra. Cate lay a hand on her still flat belly. She had not bled this month, she who was regular as the moon and whose blood kept pace with its waxing and waning could not yet be positive, but she knew her own body and had always had the facility for recognising early pregnancy in others. She was with child and, despite being married, she knew that the child could not be that of her husband.

CHAPTER 11

Vivid dreams had been something Rozlyn had endured in childhood but as she'd grown older, their richness of colour and intimidating reality had paled until her dreams were merely pastel-shaded imitations. This one was different.

A cool breeze blew past her cheeks, cold enough to nip the lobes of her ears, though a warm sun shone on her back and the sky was polished Delft, the exact shade of the blue on her mother's little bowl.

They had come to Charlie's funeral; Rozlyn, Mouse and Mrs Chinowski, the latter dressed from head to foot in deepest black, the depth of mourning relieved only by the dyed purple of the poppies decorating her wide brimmed hat.

Charlie himself lay uncovered in the grave, still dressed in his pinstriped suit and blood-stained shirt with its frayed cuffs and worn collar.

As Rozlyn watched, a stranger stepped forward, face hidden from Rozlyn's view, screened out by a series of blocked pixels, like those used on television to hide someone's identity. The stranger held the spear that had killed Charlie Higgins. He bent down and placed it carefully, close beside Charlie's left hand and then, beside his right, a full glass of beer. Rozlyn knew the heavy mug — Charlie favoured glasses with handles — had come from the Queen's and was filled with Speckled Hen.

She watched, sadly, as the diggers from the archaeological site gathered silently around and slowly began to fill the grave, shovelling the fine red earth to cover Charlie's face and suit and stained white shirt.

Beside her, Mrs Chinowski began to cry; to wail, her body shaking until the poppies on the wide brimmed hat waved and stuttered and Rozlyn was forced to reach out her hand and hold them still.

"It's all right, Inspector Priest. You'll get the bastard."

Startled, Rozlyn looked towards the line of rowan. Charlie Higgins stood, smiling at her. In his hand he held a long, green staff and, for some reason that Rozlyn could not fathom, his feet were bare. In an instance of that strange empathy that comes in dreams, Rozlyn could feel the chill as Charlie walked on dew-drenched grass and, as she looked, she saw that the early morning sun illuminated a myriad of spider webs, strung out across the grass and silvered in the early light.

Dazzled by the sight, Rozlyn blinked hard and, as she raised her eyes again, looking back to where the ghost of Charlie stood, it seemed that some persistence of vision carried the pattern of bejewelled webs far up into the open sky.

Rozlyn woke with a startled cry, hands brushing frantically across her face. She sat up and glanced urgently around. The room was just as clean and ordered and as normal as ever, no sign of webs or ghosts or other disturbance. But even so, she had to get out of bed and hurry to the bathroom where, gazing into the mirror, she was finally able to shake off the feeling of chill, sticky web, spun out across her face.

* * *

Monday morning briefing. Rozlyn had arrived early, typing up her report ready for when the shift arrived.

It had been a sad, oddly disturbing dream and Rozlyn could not fully shake the effects of it. The irritating part was, she'd been involved in many murder investigations, seen bodies battered and burned and mutilated beyond belief but she'd rarely dreamed about them, always managing to file her work away when she got home. To shut out the horror and let go of the anger, at least for a little time. She knew that this ability had earned her a reputation for coldness, for inhumanity. That and the fact that she never seemed to share her life outside of work with anyone when the norm was to gather with your peers at least a couple of times a week and chew the fat over a pint or three.

So why was Charlie's death so difficult to shake?

She copied the report, setting the machine to collate and staple then made her way down to the briefing. The team had started to arrive, helping themselves to coffee, complaining about the football match the night before — the locals had lost, again. At home. The photos from the crime scene had already been pinned to the wall and Rozlyn added the images of the spear and some contextual shots of where it had been found. She also added the names of Thomas Thompson and Donovan and the two addresses Mouse Man had provided.

"What's all this, then?" DCI Brook peered at the names and addresses. He was slurping thick black coffee from a plastic cup. Coffee so strong that the fumes invaded Rozlyn's eyes and nose as she moved close.

Briefly, Rozlyn filled him in, drawing his attention to the houses where Charlie cleaned and the transient nature of those staying there. Could this indicate people trafficking, she suggested. Brook raised an eyebrow but made no comment about the information. Instead he said, "Jenny tells me you've been visiting old ladies?"

"Mrs Chinowski from the third floor. Charlie paid her phone bill, helped her out in other ways. There's an old guy called Mr Bishopson, too, lives in a residential home. I want someone to go and talk to him today. Mrs C reckoned Charlie helped him out too and that fits with what Mouse

Man told me. He said Charlie had dependants. I'm guessing there could be more."

"Proper little public servant, our Charlie," Brook commented. "Snitching to you and helping old ladies with their little problems." He shrugged. "His cleaning jobs are interesting, though I'd like to check it out before we get immigration involved. You might be right and this might well involve people trafficking . . . but we don't want egg on our faces, do we?"

We want to get the arrests on our tally and not theirs, more like, Rozlyn thought. "If it checks out, it could be that Charlie saw something he shouldn't have," she said. "Then there's what Mouse said about antiquities. That would fit with where he was found and with the murder weapon."

Brook didn't look impressed. "What would the likes of Charlie Higgins know about antiquities?"

"About as much as he'd know about illegal immigrants but Charlie was no idiot and he kept his eyes and ears open."

"And came up with naff all. When was the last time anything Higgins told you led to an arrest?"

Rozlyn didn't reply. She didn't want to admit out loud that Brook had a point.

"But you still kept paying the stupid old bugger."

"Charlie wasn't old. For that matter, he wasn't stupid. Look, I reckon he was on to something and that something got him killed. Now, whether it was bodies coming into the country or antiques going out, he still got killed for it. I say we have to follow both leads."

Brook shrugged and turned back to the room, now full and buzzing with conversation. He set his coffee on the edge of a desk and clapped his hands together. "Morning, children."

"Morning, sir." The usual giggles from the probationers.

Rozlyn watched. Brook commanded attention. Effortlessly. He'd commanded Rozlyn's even when she hated the man, instead of, as now, merely disliking him. Swiftly and concisely, he briefed the team, bringing them up to speed on the events since Friday and surprising Rozlyn by showing he'd already read the report she'd prepared that morning. Despite his sneering attitude in their private conversation, he seemed to give equal weight now to the two leads on Charlie's death. Rozlyn took over, fielding the more detailed questions and assigning tasks. The two addresses were to be kept under surveillance. Jenny Harper was to talk to Mr Bishopson and track down the cleaning lady — the address was vague; they had the street name but no number and Clara Buranou, the woman Charlie had found to clean for Mrs Chinowski, didn't show up on the electoral register. "See if social services can get you an address," Rozlyn told her, "but something Mrs C said makes me think she wasn't on their books. I reckon Charlie fixed things up, so you may just have to knock on doors."

"And what's DI Priest going to be doing?" Brook asked as the meeting broke up.

"DI Priest," Rozlyn told him, unpinning two of the photos from the board so that she could copy them, "is going to see a man about a spear."

* * *

The address she had for Ethan Merrill was in Stamford, about an hour's drive away and on the other side of the dig site. Sir Walter Scott had apparently declared the place to be "*the finest stone town in England*." Rozlyn had no idea what other delights Sir Walter had available by way of comparison, but she had to admit that the little town, with its winding streets lined with shops and pubs and a proliferation of churches built either of soft golden ironstone or the cooler, gull grey limestone was an attractive one. Rozlyn had been to Stamford only a few times. Twice for the music festival and once to visit Burghley House. She'd taken her grandfather there, knowing the old man's love of history. The Elizabethan mansion had enchanted him with its sparkling, mullioned windows and odd little towers and cupolas perched high on the roof line which they'd only belatedly realised were elaborate chimneys. She had spent a good hour telling her grandfather about the landscaping of the park by the famous Capability Brown, only to have the old man turn to her with a look of vague disgust and comment "this place was mine, I'd fill this garden with every flower you could think of and a few more besides." Recalling the overcrowded yard, so full of vegetation it was barely possible to walk from back door to gate without ending up entwined and pollinated, Rozlyn could well believe he'd do just that.

Not sure where she had to go, she decided to park next to the George Hotel and then make her way on foot. She hadn't recognised the address but Cheyne Lane turned out to be a narrow and ancient pedestrian thoroughfare, lined with small shops and even smaller eateries. Entering from the main street, Rozlyn instinctively ducked, the upper storeys of the houses jutting out so far that they almost met what seemed like only inches over Rozlyn's head.

She almost missed the place she wanted. Having been told that Ethan Merrill now ran a shop she'd therefore been looking for a shop front, but Merrill's, as it was simply known, hardly qualified for that kind of status. The door was set back from the lane and the shop windows restricted to narrow, angled panes forming a porch on either side. Rozlyn peered through dusty glass at vague shapes of vases and clocks and trays of jumble. Perhaps, she thought, if you came to see Ethan Merrill it was because you knew what you were looking for and such wares as he sold didn't require anything so obvious as display or advertising. Rozlyn pushed the door and eased inside, startled by the jangling of a brass bell fixed to a spring above the entrance.

Inside was as uninspiring at first glance as the window display, though the room was wider than she would have guessed from the poky little entrance. Inside, the shop smelt of old books and bees-wax polish, though there was no evidence of the latter being recently applied if the layer of dust was anything to go by. A cat, stretched out on a table close to the door, turned to stare, then arched its back and hissed at her. It sounded like Mrs Chinowski. Rozlyn ignored it and looked around.

The shop was dimly lit. The lane being narrow and the windows small and filthy, not much light filtered inside. Dust motes swam in the single beam that fought through the glass panelled door and illuminated a space of some two feet wide and three feet long. Small wall lights, of a kind more at home in a living room than a shop, created tiny pools of radiance high up on the walls and revealed shelves of objects too deep in shadow for Rozlyn to properly define. The light lacked the energy to reach the floor.

Warily, she took a further step and called out Ethan Merrill's name. Hadn't he heard the bell? Did he always leave this place unattended? Anyone could walk in off the street and help themselves. Or maybe that was what the cat was for. It watched her still, no longer hissing, but the back arched and the amber eyes glittered. Rozlyn raised her hands to where it could see. "Look. Nothing," she said. "You can relax, go back to sleep."

"He won't sleep until you've gone," a soft voice said. Rozlyn nearly jumped out of her skin. She'd heard no one and yet, when she turned, the old man who'd spoken was almost at her elbow.

"Shhi— Sorry. You scared the hell out of me."

"An American?" The man raised a quizzical brow. "Or no. Something between. The accent is an odd mix. New York . . . Brooklyn, perhaps . . . meets Louisiana and a little home counties English thrown in for good measure."

Rozlyn laughed uneasily. "Not a bad guess," she admitted. "Um, I'm looking for Mr Ethan Merrill. I'm Inspector Priest, I was told that Mr Merrill might be the man to give me some information I need."

"Oh, and what information would that be?"

"Are you Ethan Merrill?"

"So they tell me. Jasper, you've already met."

"Who?" Rozlyn glanced around. "Oh, the guard cat. Right." She looked curiously at Ethan Merrill. It was hard to guess the man's age. His hair was white, hanging past his collar in a thick mane that waved at the tip and showed no sign of thinning on top. His skin looked dark in the dim light, but smooth too. There were lines around the eyes, which spoke of good humour, but the rest was soft and clear. He was a tall man, almost matching Rozlyn's six feet. Straight backed, he looked strong and fit. The hand that reached out to fondle the ears of the brindled cat, transforming the almost subliminal hiss into a purr, was broad at the palm, tapering at the fingers, capable looking and, like the face, tanned nut brown. The rest of Ethan Merrill was covered by a suit. Not quite black, Rozlyn noted, her eyes having adjusted to the low levels of light. The shirt was grey, open at the neck and Rozlyn caught a glimpse of gold as though he wore a chain concealed beneath his clothes.

"I want to ask you about a spear," she said. "It was used to kill someone."

"They often were."

"What? Oh, I suppose so. But this was used to kill a man just a few days ago. His body was dumped at the dig site out at Theadingford. The spear was chucked in bushes close by. We're almost certain it was the murder weapon."

"Almost?"

"We're just waiting for forensics to confirm it. I'm told you're the man to ask about Dark Age weapons."

Ethan Merrill looked amused. "I'm probably *one* of them," he agreed. "You've brought it with you, this murder weapon?"

"Forensics have it. I've brought some pictures for you to see. I was hoping you could tell me something from those."

"Hmm. It would be easier with the real thing, but I'll do my best." He reached out his hand again. "Some light, I think."

Rozlyn blinked. "Yow. You could have warned me." Three fluorescent tubes burst into life at Ethan's bidding. Eyes that had become accustomed to twilight now watered painfully in light that would have outshone the average noon.

Merrill chuckled, the old man seemingly unaffected by the transition.

"You have the pictures?"

"Yeah, right here." Rozlyn slid them from her inside pocket. "I've brought some context shots, too, so you could see where and how it landed after the killer chucked it away. I did wonder if it might be a replica and if so, who'd have made it? If it's real, could you give me some idea where it might have come from? They're adamant it didn't come from the dig."

Ethan Merrill shuffled through the pictures and then laid them out on Jasper's table. The cat sniffed at the images, then moved aside, seating himself on one corner and tucking his tail neatly out of the way. Merrill produced a hand lens from the table drawer and peered more closely. He was silent for so long that Rozlyn felt she had almost been forgotten.

"If you could tell me anything, I'd be grateful," she said, to remind the old man of her presence.

Merrill straightened and turned to look at her. "If it's a copy I'd be amazed," he said thoughtfully. "I suppose you'll be running tests? Dating it?"

"I suppose," Rozlyn said doubtfully. "I really don't know. Our main concern is to verify that it's the murder weapon and figure out where the killer got it from and why use that anyway. It seems . . ." Rozlyn felt for the words "I don't know. Kind of pretentious, I guess."

Merrill laughed. "I suppose it is unusual as murder weapons go. In this context, I mean. Frankly, I doubt whether this particular spear ever saw action, as it were. My guess is that it was a status symbol, though, of course, I could be wrong. The Anglo Saxons made the most beautiful swords. Works of art, woven from strands of tempered metal, and yet they were designed to kill in battle and very efficient they were too."

"Woven?" Rozlyn was confused.

Ethan smiled. "I'm using poetic metaphor, I suppose," he said. "You see, steel was an unpredictable metal back then. You needed a sharp, tempered edge. Something hard enough to cut, but not so brittle that the sword would shatter. They achieved their aims by a process called pattern welding. You'd begin with many layers of metal, laid together and then heated in the forge. The strands would then be twisted and drawn out to form the shape of the sword. Sometimes there'd be several layers of these twists, elaborate patterns that would show up on the sword blade once it had been finished and treated with acid. A good swordsmith would actually be able to replicate a particular pattern of twists. Some patterns even had names. Weavers of metal, Inspector Priest. Swords that had flex and spring at the heart and tempered steel at the edge. It's a wondrous art."

"But this is a spear. You're saying that was made in the same way?"

Merrill nodded. "It's unusual, but not unknown. Ceremonial spears of this type have been found, though the condition of this one is little short of miraculous. If it's been in the ground, then conditions must have been very unusual. If it's a replica, it's still a major work. I'd need to see the real thing to tell you. I would date it to perhaps the seventh or eighth century, but I'd need to see the item to tell you more accurately." He gathered the photographs and handed them back to Rozlyn. Rozlyn felt that she was being dismissed, no longer of interest.

"Where would this have come from?" she persisted. "If I'm right and this was stolen . . ."

"By rights it should be in a museum," Ethan Merrill told her sternly. "A find like this should be recorded, researched."

"But there are collectors out there who don't care about provenance?"

Merrill frowned. "There are," he acknowledged.

"Local collectors?"

Merrill considered. Rozlyn felt that not only was he considering the question, he was weighing Rozlyn as being worthy, or not, of an answer.

"Two that I can think of," Merrill said at last.

"Names? Addresses?"

Merrill sighed. Jasper stretched himself and arched his back again. Rozlyn guessed that the hiss was imminent. She took out her notebook and stood with pen poised. Finally, Ethan gave her two names and she wrote them down.

"The second is the man to look at," he said finally, turning away and switching off the main lights. Rozlyn's eyes protested at the adjustment. It was like being plunged into utter blackness. She blinked rapidly, trying to get her eyes to adapt.

"Mark Richards," Ethan told her from the darkness. "The man has money to burn and an absence of any sort of conscience. Be careful, Inspector Priest."

* * *

THEADINGFORD. YEAR OF GRACE 878

Sitting in the afternoon sun, sharpening his knife, Treven's thoughts strayed to that last battle. The one that had finally turned the tide against Guthrum and had, eventually, brought him to this place. This place he had already begun to think of as home.

The night before they fought he had dreamed the battle at Eddington. Perhaps it was the memory of so many skirmishes, so many death fights that caused him to see so clearly, but whatever the cause, Treven knew even before waking how the day would go.

The previous night they had left their stronghold and travelled by flat boat across the marshes. Then the forced march through ankle-deep mire, the stink of rotting vegetation choking as they disturbed the stagnant water.

"They'll smell us coming," Hugh had whispered. "We will not need to fight, the stench will choke the air from their lungs even before we begin."

They had halted an hour or so before dawn. Treven, standing blind in the deep shadows of their encampment, ears straining to catch the night sounds, had heard but not seen the arrival of the others. Men summoned from their fields, from their boats, from their hiding places. Treven himself had gone out as messenger in the days before, calling to the broken stone cross all those who still held to Aelfred's cause. Praying, even as he spread the word, that those who heard it would come faithfully, praying even harder that they would not betray their king, not at this late time.

Aelfred had been king of very little on that day. He could claim ownership of only a short stretch of land that had once housed a hunting lodge and been a playground for he and his elder brothers in time of peace. If they had failed on that day, Treven knew that there would be no hope of regrouping. The line of Aelfred's kin would be finished and men like Treven good as dead.

A woman's voice, very soft but clear on the cold air reminded him of his duties should they fail. Aelfred's children would wait here, beside this once holy place and, should their father fail, then Treven and Hugh and a trusted handful of others would have been responsible for ensuring their escape.

If they survived,

If they could make their way back here.

If . . .

The night before that final battle Treven had fallen into an uneasy sleep with those thoughts on his mind but when he had roused a scant two hours later, he had woken with a sense of certainty.

They would succeed. He knew it. Guthrum would fail and Aelfred win out against him.

Treven had dreamed of the half-blind god. Seen him as he strode across the land of Treven's birth, his twin ravens flying high above his head and crying back the news to their master's ears and, as Treven watched, half afraid that Wotan would see him, half afraid that he would not, he heard the sound of a horn and, suddenly, as it often is in dreams, the scene was changed and Wotan no longer walked. He rode astride a powerful, coal-black horse. His battle axe was raised as he charged full pelt across the field of battle and behind him streamed the hunt, gathering the souls of the fallen as the blood soaked and seeped into the land.

"What do you see?" Hugh had asked him softly.

"See?"

"Since we broke camp, your eyes have been everywhere but on the path we walk. What do you see, Treven?"

Treven had shrugged but glanced again at the line of trees that ran parallel to the track they were taking. He had been aware of them since waking, those others that recalled the nature of his dream. The movement, caught out of the tail of his eye, gone when he looked direct. The soft sound of leather against leather, metal catching against metal, shield scraping against shield and the shush of drawn sword and the creaking of tired bones. Could he hear all of that?

Treven looked back at Hugh. "I see nothing," he said.

"But," Hugh persisted. "You sense something?"

Treven could see the unease, the questioning in his friend's eyes. This otherness of Treven disturbed and troubled him.

"Sometimes," Hugh said, as lightly as he could, "I think you have more kinship with the spirits and magic of our enemy than that of Christ."

Treven made no reply. He glanced back at the line of trees. Friend or enemy, he wondered, then knew the question to be a worthless, meaningless one. The ones who marched and watched and sometimes ran beside them, half seen, half felt beneath the trees no longer troubled themselves with the rights and wrongs of men, they just *were*. They waited, they watched, they gathered the dead, trampled the blood-soaked earth beneath their booted feet, but left no track or sign that a living man could follow.

Treven had shuddered and caught the fear and alarm in Hugh's eyes. "This day will go well for us," he had said. "On that score, you should have no fear."

Hugh had relaxed, his shoulders losing their tension and his eyes became less troubled. Treven shifted his attention to the road ahead. What was it he was seeing? What was it that had caused him to see? Sometimes he thought that Hugh must indeed be right. He had been baptised into the religion his father served, but at times the faith and beliefs of his pagan mother seemed more fiercely burned into his soul.

Now, sitting beside his own Hall, the land that was now in his care stretching out in all directions, Treven breathed deep of the cool, fragrant air and gave thanks. This would be home, this was where he would begin again and, he promised himself, none would stand in the way of that.

CHAPTER 12

Rozlyn drew a blank with the first contact, Mr Ed Foulks being away for the summer according to his housekeeper. She seemed deeply affronted at the idea he might have had any part of his collection stolen without her knowledge.

Rozlyn left, Foulks's name on her reserve list should she be unsuccessful elsewhere, but if the housekeeper was to be believed, the man hadn't even been in the county for the past six weeks. It was always possible, of course, that a theft and murder had taken place on his property and that the housekeeper had merely tidied up after it, so as not to inconvenience her employer . . . somehow, Rozlyn couldn't see it.

Besides, she had the feeling that Ethan Merrill fancied Mark Richards for ownership of the spear and, having nothing to contradict that, Rozlyn was prepared to give that notion its head.

She was within a half mile of Richards' place when Jenny called her on the mobile. Irritated at having forgotten, she groped about on the passenger seat for her headset, her attempts to position it almost landing her in the hedge as the car swerved on the narrow road. She was still cursing and muttering as she pressed the button to take the call.

"You OK?" Jenny asked. "You sound out of breath."

"Yes, I'm fine. What've you got for me?"

"Well, I found the old man. Mr Bishopson."

"And?"

"He's in a home over on Westbury Close. The Larks, they call the place. Local authority, but it seems nice enough. Old Mr Bishopson won't be much help to us, I'm afraid."

"Why's that then?"

"Gone gaga," Jenny told her. Rozlyn winced. "Senile dementia. Tends to wander off if they don't watch him. That's how Charlie got to know him, apparently. The old boy'd got out one day and Charlie Higgins found him wandering, brought him back. He's been visiting about once a week ever since. Brings little bits in for him; apparently the old man likes chocolate and lemonade and he's no family to provide the extras."

Extras. Chocolate and lemonade. Rozlyn shook her head at how pathetic that sounded, thinking about the extras she had provided for her grandfather; wondering if he actually noticed them anyway. "OK, so what about the cleaning lady. Any joy on that front?"

"Um, sort of. You were right, she's not from social services. They knew nothing about her. They remembered Mrs C, though. The home help they appointed refused to go back after the first couple of months. They sent another and she lasted a week."

"Don't tell me, she kept them in the hall?"

"At first. Yes. Then when they got into the flat, she stood over them and nagged. Nothing was right. She managed to reduce the first one to tears three times before she finally threw in the towel and the second just decided she wasn't going to be . . . what was it . . . oh yes, treated like a skivvy."

"Rings sort of true, from what I've seen of Mrs C," Rozlyn mused. "Did they remember Charlie?"

"Um, yes. Said he came around to discuss things after the second home help struck out. He tried to persuade them to try again, but, no go. The woman I spoke to . . . Mrs Marriot, one of the supervisors, she said what a nice man

Charlie was and she was sorry they couldn't help. That was three, nearly four months ago."

"So, this Clara Buranou?"

"Was definitely someone Charlie found."

"You have an address?"

"Not on the electoral register, so, like you said, I had to knock on a few doors. I found her eventually. Mrs C was right, she's in a bedsit on Mortimer Street but there was no one home when I called."

Mortimer, Rozlyn thought. A mile, maybe, from the Queen's. Close to the University and, until the Uni had instituted its latest building program, known for its cheap student lets. "Well, I think we'll have another go later." She was pulling up outside Mark Richards' place. *Estate*, she thought. That was probably the word for it, rather than mere house, or even residence. "Thanks, Jenny," Rozlyn said. "I'll get back to you on Clara Buranou." She signed off, tucked the phone into her pocket and removed the headset then sat for a moment surveying Mark Richards' domain.

High walls surrounded what must be a substantial chunk of land. Rozlyn had followed the wall for the last several minutes until she'd reached the gates. The iron gates were closed and an intercom on the wall indicated that she would have to request entry.

"Rich bugger, aren't we?"

Rozlyn drove the car as close as she could to the gates, but still had to get out of the car to use the intercom. She buzzed three times before getting a reply.

"Yes?"

"I'm here to see Mr Mark Richards."

"You have an appointment?"

"No. I'm a police officer. Detective Inspector Priest. I'd appreciate a few minutes of his time." She was aware as she spoke that cameras mounted on the high gate posts swivelled to stare down. Rozlyn resisted the impulse to wave.

"One moment."

Somewhat more than a moment passed before the voice returned. "You have identification, I take it?"

"Of course."

"Then you may enter."

"Well, whoop de do," Rozlyn muttered beneath her breath, her paternal grandmother's favourite indicator of annoyance coming naturally to her lips. She returned to the car and drove through before the guardian of Mark Richards' privacy changed his mind, then followed a long, tree-lined drive up to the house. It took a full five minutes. Rozlyn was suitably impressed.

The house itself was neo-Georgian, the gold of local stone, visible as she glimpsed the side view of the house, faced at the front with smooth, pale limestone. A man stood at the head of a flight of steps. He was dressed in knife-creased grey flannels and a dark blazer. His well-trimmed hair was white and sparse on top and Rozlyn placed him in his sixties or even a little older. Could this be Mark Richards?

As Rozlyn approached, the man held out his hand, but not to shake. Rozlyn recognised the voice of the gate keeper as he asked formally to see her identification and he studied it carefully, glancing several times from Rozlyn to the photograph as though hoping to find something amiss.

Finally, he handed it back and turned towards the double doors. "This way," he said and Rozlyn followed obediently, leaving the autumn sun behind and passing through the shadowed door. She found herself in a tall, square hall, the floor of which was tiled with coloured marble. An impressive staircase leading to a double landing lay straight ahead. Her guide led the way upstairs and to the left, finally pausing at the third identical wooden door and knocking lightly. He went inside leaving Rozlyn out in the cold. Rozlyn was getting heartily tired of this. Grasping the smooth brass handle, she pushed the door open and followed the gatekeeper. The man in the black blazer was standing by a desk talking to a younger man. They both looked up as Rozlyn made her entrance, the older one frowning in annoyance and making to move towards her, hand outstretched again, this time to chide and then dismiss.

"It's all right," the younger man rose and came around to the front of the desk. "You must forgive Albert," he apologised. "He knows how much I hate being disturbed when I'm working. You must be Inspector Priest?"

"Working?" Rozlyn queried. This man actually *did* something to earn all this.

"Yes," Richards indicated a laptop sitting atop the desk. Open but with the screen turned away from Rozlyn. He didn't elaborate. "What can I do for you, Inspector."

"I was given your name as someone who might be able to help me with a little information."

"Oh?" Mark Richards raised an eyebrow. "Always glad to help the police, of course, but what kind of information?"

"I understand you're a collector of antiquities. Dark Age antiquities?"

Mark Richards frowned. It didn't suit him, Rozlyn thought. He was the sort of man that relied upon good humour for his looks. Though, maybe with his money, that didn't matter. "I collect many things. Why?"

"Items like this?" Rozlyn withdrew the printouts of the spear from her pocket and laid them on the table. She got the feeling that neither Mark Richards nor his guardian appreciated her getting that close . . . to them? To the laptop?

Richards picked up the images and skimmed through.

He laughed. "I'd love to own a piece like that," he said with feeling. "I take it that's a replica?"

"What makes you think so?"

"Well, the condition, for one thing." He lifted the pictures closer to his eyes and peered at them, then reached onto the desk for his glasses before holding the pictures away and studying them again. "It's too good," he said. "Nothing stays in that condition after a thousand years or so."

"Unless it was never in the ground?"

Richards looked up sharply, then laughed. "Not very likely, Inspector. This isn't the kind of thing people keep in their ancestral attics."

"Was it in yours?" Rozlyn couldn't be bothered to pussyfoot.

Again, that sharp look and, she sensed, a sharper intake of breath — albeit metaphorical — from Albert. Disapprobation at her unrefined manners, Rozlyn wondered, or something more?

"Why would you think that?"

"It was found not far from here. You'll agree it's an uncommon item. You're known to be a collector." Rozlyn shrugged. "So, logic dictates it might be yours. I've heard there've been a number of thefts in the area. Unusual stuff taken."

This last was a pure fiction so far as Rozlyn knew but Mark Richards nodded slowly. "I understand that's so," he conceded. "Which is why I have a very expensive security system here, Inspector. I like to protect my interests . . . and my privacy."

"That, I can understand," Rozlyn told him. "May I ask what kind of security system you have in place. Aside from the walls and fence, of course." And Albert, she added silently. The man was watching her with predatory attention.

"No doubt you noted the cameras?"

"Outside, yes. What about in the house itself? Perhaps I could get one of the crime prevention team to come and give you some advice?"

Albert straightened and began to move towards the door. Clearly, he felt it time for Rozlyn to leave. "I really don't think that's anyone's concern but Mr Richards'," he said. "You may be assured that it is more than adequate."

Mark Richards was still examining the pictures. "What's the staining on the tip," he asked. "It's a shame when the rest is so pristine."

Rozlyn took the picture from him and looked at it as though for the first time. "Oh," she said. "That would be blood. The spear was used to kill a man."

CHAPTER 13

Rozlyn left after another half hour. She had finally been granted reluctant access to Richards' collection, housed in a first-floor room that extended practically the width of the house and whose tall sash windows gave views out onto rolling grassland and aged stands of trees. At some distance away, Rozlyn could just glimpse the wall that she had followed along the road.

Richards' collection gave the impression of being a private museum, glass cased and catalogued. Albert, acting as escort, pointed out the items from the period Rozlyn was interested in and stood over Rozlyn as though afraid she might touch. Rozlyn found herself putting her hands behind her back in unconscious response as she admired the pot shards and mangled metalwork. It reminded her of the stuff she had seen at the dig site but there was nothing even remotely like the spearhead.

Rozlyn glanced about, hoping to see something in the room that might look as if it were worth stealing. "Any of this stuff actually worth anything?"

Albert bristled. "To an educated individual, yes." He avowed. "These pieces are of great historical significance."

"I'm sure they are, but I'm talking commercial value. Are these cabinets alarmed?"

"Presently, no."

"Presently? Are there plans then?"

"I wouldn't know," Albert told her. Rozlyn waited for more, knowing that Albert had just caught himself saying the wrong thing.

"Maybe I should ask your boss?" She sensed Albert wince.

"It has been discussed," he admitted reluctantly. "As you reminded us, there have been robberies in the area."

"Have there?" Rozlyn mused. "Oh yes. I did say that, didn't I?" she could almost feel the waves of irritation and dislike rolling from the older man. She glanced around again, noting the Egyptian antiquities. Shabti, she recognised, and seal stones and faience jewellery. Roman mosaic and pottery too, were familiar, recalling their cousins seen on museum trips with her mother and grandfather. From the number of cabinets dedicated to it, it was clear that Anglo Saxon was Richards' period of choice. In a small display by the window was a selection of jewellery. Amber and glass beads, laid out to give the impression of being strung and a pair of cruciform brooches, one set on either side. There were rings, too and small fragments of enamel work placed carefully in position on a slab of rusted metal that Rozlyn presumed must be a sword.

She felt Albert shift as though suddenly uncomfortable. A small movement, but enough for Rozlyn to be aware of. Rozlyn looked more closely at the exhibits.

"What else was in here, Albert?"

"What else? I'm sure I . . ."

"You really shouldn't put dark colours near the window. Light fades them, you know." Rozlyn pointed to where a disk of richer blue showed the pattern of something that had been there for some time, but which was now missing.

"Oh." Albert told her. "That's gone for restoration. Conservation."

"Oh, really? What was it before it was sent away?"

"A brooch," Albert sounded dismissive. "Just a brooch."

Rozlyn left soon after that, Albert's impatience showing to the extent that Rozlyn wondered if he'd be calling on reinforcements should Rozlyn not shift. She discovered one more interesting thing though. On leaving she asked. "Anyone coming out of there, would they have to go down via the main stairs? I've heard there are servants' stairs in a house this size."

"There are two flights, yes. One each end of the house."

"Care to show me?"

Albert sighed elaborately, but Rozlyn got the impression that he was almost pleased. That servants' stairs were exactly what he felt Rozlyn should be using. He led her along the main corridor and through a small door at the end, then down the back stairs and into the scullery. "You go out through the kitchen," he told Rozlyn, pointing to a door that stood open and led out onto a green space beyond. "I'm sure you can find your own way. You'll have to walk back round to your car."

"Will do. It's been nice meeting you, Albert. This is a magnificent place."

"Quite," Albert returned. He stood at the foot of the stairs. Watching. The three members of staff in the kitchen glanced curiously at Rozlyn.

"Something smells good," Rozlyn commented as she wandered through, suddenly aware that she'd not eaten since very early that morning. Out of the corner of her eye she saw Albert look at his watch. But she'd be back. Rozlyn knew beyond doubt that she'd be coming back. She left through the kitchen door and ascended three steps into a courtyard. Tall shrubs in massive pots screened the kitchen entrance and it was this that had given her the initial impression of there being a green space outside. A stable block extended on the right-hand side back from the house and a further wing that Rozlyn guessed might be servant's quarters bounded the other. The fourth was open, leading back into woods. Glancing up, Rozlyn glimpsed Albert watching from a first-floor window. Rozlyn waved and smiled. "See you later, Albert."

Ethan Merill, she thought, may well have been on to something when he'd directed Rozlyn here.

* * *

She'd driven from the house to the dig site, not quite sure what drew her back there, but feeling the compulsion nonetheless. She approached the site from the field crossing as she had done on that first day. The bullocks were no longer there — she spied them in an adjacent field and the previous dryish days had allowed the worst of the mud to set. She didn't exactly cross the field unscathed but arrived at the other side without a second trip to the dry cleaners becoming necessary.

Once she had reached the escarpment, she looked down onto the site laid out below. She had far more of a feel for the layout now and could imagine the hall and the barn and the other buildings that made up the steading. She saw it busy with people, smoke rising from the chimneys and the golden sunlight gleaming on the stream.

She moved across to the point where she fancied she had seen that elusive watchtower and scrubbed about in the long grass with the toes of her shoes looking for sign of it. Of course, she thought, there would be nothing. The wooden structure long gone. She knew now, from conversation with the diggers, that any wooden structure would possibly leave dark staining in the ground from the post holes and framing, but that wouldn't be visible on the surface. There would be nothing obvious to see.

She wished she'd had the foresight to pack a picnic. When was the last time she'd been on a picnic? Probably, she thought, it had been with her grandfather when he had come to live here for a while with Rozlyn. She had grown up not a dozen miles from the dig site and it seemed odd now, that so much history had been going on and Rozlyn unaware of it. Grandad had enjoyed picnics, loved the countryside and the little villages and the fishing . . .

Did he remember any of that now? Were the memories still in there, somewhere? Or had they been wiped completely as the old man's mind decayed?

Rozlyn preferred to remember him in younger, stronger, wiser times.

She settled down on the long grass and stared down into the valley. The afternoon sun was warm on her back. She felt too hot, but at the same time, too lazy to shrug out of her blue cord jacket. Her mind nagging at the twin problems of Charlie Higgins and Mark Richards, Rozlyn slid into that state between reverie and dream where the mind is free to wander. In this state, it seemed that the day became warmer, though, when the wind blew across her cheek, it carried with it the promise of chill days to come. Looking towards the trees, she saw, or half dreamed she saw, Ethan Merrill standing there. He was dressed in grey and almost-black as he had been in the shop, and his thick white hair lay upon his shoulders and lifted in the breeze. Rozlyn shivered, despite the fact that she felt unusually warm. Ethan Merrill pointed. Following the direction of the gesture to that place just in front of the Great Hall, where a fire burned and a man lay dozing on the ground while another, resting on his side, but with his head propped on his hand talked to or at him.

Rozlyn caught the aroma of roasting meat and the distinctive scent of wood smoke drifting from the valley. This man, lying on his back, one arm thrown carelessly behind his head, the other hand resting lightly on the hilt of his sword, was the tall, thick-set man that Rozlyn had noticed that last time, standing on the hill. She felt a sudden thrill of excitement at the realisation and looked back towards where Ethan stood, the urge to share this with him overwhelming.

Ethan wasn't there. Rozlyn jerked into wakefulness and looked guiltily about, suddenly concerned that someone would have noticed this moment of weakness and be about to censure her for it.

She shook herself, laughing uneasily, the taste of the dream, the essence of it, still clinging in her mouth and nostrils and, like wood smoke, to her clothes.

"Christ," she muttered. "You've got to get a life."

* * *

THEADINGFORD. YEAR OF GRACE 878

Treven woke, jerking out of a dream that had come unbidden almost before sleep. Through it all, he could hear Hugh's voice, his friend telling him something inconsequential that Treven could not quite recall. But the dream, if that's all it was, had shaken him enough to pull him from the fringes of sleep and leave him trembling.

"What is it?" Hugh's voice was light and unconcerned. "Did you remember something else you need to do today? You should take your rest while the fine days last."

Treven muttered something vague, enough to satisfy Hugh, and made his way from the fire to the rear of the house. Then, away from Hugh's sight, he turned back to face the wood. He had seen him there, that old man dressed in the colours of twilight, with the mane of white hair and the one missing eye. Christian he might be, but Treven knew the Old Ones when he saw them and that figure was a familiar one. He could name him Odin, as Guthrum did, or in his father's tongue . . .

"Wotan," Treven whispered, then looked round in case the servants should overhear. But it was the one who had stood beside him that gave Treven more pause. Skin that was richly brown and strange clothes and a bearing that spoke of nobility and power.

What the vision meant, Treven could not fully guess, but that Wotan and this stranger should appear in land so newly claimed for the king's peace could not be good.

CHAPTER 14

Late afternoon Rozlyn and DC Jenny Harper visited Clara Buranou. Clara's bedsit was right at the top of a converted house. The attic might once have been a good place for storage, but Rozlyn could not believe it had ever been intended as a living space. It was cramped and damp and, despite the late afternoon sun streaming in through the roof lights, dark and cold. A single mattress had been placed in the space beneath the eaves and her clothes packed into cardboard boxes beside it. One chair occupied a corner space opposite a battered television, which had been placed precariously on a plastic stool. The room was L-shaped and the short end of the L, separated off by a plastic curtain, housed the two-ring cooker and the single cupboard. There was no comfort here. It called to mind the student digs she'd shared with a friend in their second year at university. It had been their first taste of independent living — moving out of the halls of residence and the semi-protection that they offered. Cold, damp and dingy as this, their attic flat had been the scene for some major parties — friends spilling out onto the fire escape and taking over all available space on the stairs — but even they had tired of the sordid little flat in a couple of terms and by the end of the year they had settled into a shared house. A move that at least allowed Rozlyn to stand upright anywhere without risk of concussion.

Clara Buranou had little problem with the ceiling height. She was small and slight with a sallow complexion not helped by the mass of dark hair that tumbled across her forehead and threatened to drown her rather delicate features. She would have been pretty, Rozlyn thought, if she'd smiled occasionally, tied back her hair and let the sun get to her skin. She wondered how on earth Clara and Mrs Chinowski coped. She could just imagine the old lady criticising out loud what Rozlyn silently observed.

She'd have been prettier anyway, Rozlyn thought, if she could manage to look less scared.

She left the single chair for Jenny on the grounds that she was wearing a skirt and seated herself on the edge of Clara's bed. Clara sat down too, moving to the end, as far from her visitors as the cramped space and skinny mattress allowed. She wrapped her arms around her knees and peered at them through a curtain of heavy, wavy hair. Rozlyn resisted the impulse to push it back from her face and to dig in her pocket for a spare hair band.

"You heard about Charlie Higgins. About him being killed?"

She nodded, a quick upward jerk of her head. "I saw it in the paper. I cannot believe it. Charlie was a good man."

Her accent, Rozlyn noted, was heavy and her English, though essentially sound, was spoken with the hesitation of someone searching for the next word. Rather like Rozlyn herself attempting to converse in her schoolgirl German. "How did you get to know Charlie?"

Clara shrugged and looked away. "I do not remember."

"How long have you known him, then?"

She shrugged again. "A year. Maybe more."

"But you can't remember."

"No," she shook her head. "I can't remember."

"But Charlie must have felt he knew you well enough to suggest you to Mrs Chinowski."

"I don't know. She is difficult. No one stay. I need the job, she need the cleaning. Charlie arrange for me to go."

"Do you get on OK with Mrs Chinowski?"

Clara pulled a face which made her look very young, like a child anticipating a bad taste. "It is money," she said. "I need to earn money."

"And how long have you been here?" Jenny asked.

Rozlyn could have kicked her. At this stage it was the last question she wanted to ask. She noted the fear in Clara's eyes and changed the subject swiftly. "Do you clean anywhere else or work at any other jobs?"

She looked uncomfortable, but she answered these questions. "I work for old people, at the Larks. In the kitchen. I go to college to get my better English, then they will send me on a hygiene course for the kitchen."

"That's good, Clara," Rozlyn approved. "Can you think of anyone who'd want to hurt Charlie?"

This time the headshake was emphatic. "Charlie is a good man," she insisted, as though Rozlyn might dare to disagree. "He would hurt no one."

Rozlyn hesitated about the next question. Finally, she asked, "Clara, Charlie cleaned houses for a man called Thomas Thompson. Did you know him, or did you ever help Charlie clean for him?"

Her blank look was, Rozlyn decided, genuine. The name meant nothing to her, but then, it was unlikely she knew who had owned the safe house she must first have been taken to. She knew that most of the illegal immigrants coming into the country were let loose to fend for themselves pretty soon after their arrival. The lucky ones might be given some form of new identity; some degree of support or, if they were truly fortunate, have friends and family in the community to take them in.

"Do you have family in the UK, Clara?"

She hesitated and then shook her head. "I work," she said. "Then I come back here. One day I will go back home."

Her lips tightened on the word as though it was not something she generally allowed herself to say.

"And where is home, Clara? Croatia?"

It was a guess, but she nodded. Rozlyn wondered if she was telling the truth or if it had just been easier to agree.

She could feel Jenny's impatience and, glancing up, saw her about to pursue this line. Rozlyn warned her off with a look and took a business card from the pocket of her coat. "I know you want us to get the person that killed Charlie," she told Clara. "If you think of anything, this is how you can contact me. Understand?"

Clara's hand closed over it. Tightly. Rozlyn saw the card fold in her palm, crease unevenly in her grip. She's really scared, she thought. "Clara, did Charlie ever mention someone called Donovan?"

She shook her head, that rapid jerk. Her eyes said no, she had never heard of Donovan. Charlie had not spoken of such a man.

Rozlyn got to her feet, carefully avoiding the sloping ceiling and gestured to Jenny to follow. "Remember. Call me," she said.

* * *

Outside, Jenny was bristling with annoyance. "You know she's an illegal. We should be taking her in."

Rozlyn nodded. "I don't doubt it," she said. "I'll try and organise some surveillance, see if she contacts anyone else and we'll get someone over to the Larks — check their records or lack of." She frowned. "That's where that old man lives. The one Charlie befriended?"

Jenny nodded. "God," she said. "Living like that. I'd pack my bags and be off home to Croatia or wherever she came from."

"To do that you need money and a passport. I doubt she's got either." Rozlyn shrugged. "We'd probably be doing her a favour getting her deported."

Jenny glanced up at the house. "What a dump," she said. "It's a fire trap too. No escape from Clara's room. Did you notice?"

Rozlyn hadn't. She figured that the landlord failed to declare rental on the attic space.

"And you'll be lucky to get surveillance," Jenny went on.

"Oh?"

"Brook's got every available body watching those addresses you gave him. He's out to make good on that before we have to hand it on to immigration."

"I'd figured that one," Rozlyn said wryly. She frowned, wondering. If they were so short of officers, she should bring Clara in for questioning now. She decided to talk to Brook first.

She opened the car door and slid into her seat then closed her eyes, feeling the slight rock of the vehicle as Jenny got in the other side. "You ever have those dreams where everything is just too real?" she asked. Then. "Forget it." Rozlyn opened her eyes and turned the key, aware that Jenny was regarding her quizzically.

"Long day?" she asked.

"Not over yet."

"Did you get lunch or did you forget again?"

"Guilty." Rozlyn admitted.

Jenny shook her head. "I'm not your mother so I'm not going to lecture you, but you know what I'd have to say if I did?"

"Yes ma'am," Rozlyn drawled. She smiled back then allowed her thoughts to drift back to Clara Buranou and her tawdry little bedsit. "You think she had any idea she'd end up in a place like that?"

"No. How could she? What are you going to do about her?"

Rozlyn sighed, knowing Jenny was right. She couldn't just leave this. "Talk to Brook when we get back. Uniform can have her. But if Brook thinks he's got bigger fish to fry, he'll probably want us to hold off anyway. Taking Clara might alert others."

"I suppose so. Any joy with the spear expert?"

"Couple of leads. Two collectors of antiquities, both of whom deny having anything stolen."

"You don't believe them?"

"I don't believe *one* of them. There's . . . something. I can't get a handle on it yet."

She thought about Ethan Merrill. Try as she might, she still could not shake the emotional impact of that dream or the feeling that it had some obscure significance.

* * *

Brook was getting ready to leave when Rozlyn arrived. Rozlyn briefed him quickly as to the progress of the day and their visit to Clara Buranou. Brook re-emphasised what Jenny had told her. They were shorthanded; Rozlyn would have to make her own arrangements. It was clear that Brook had his eye on the bigger prize and one insignificant little girl that could easily be picked up later was of little interest to him. After all, even if she decided to run away, just how far could she get with no friends and little money?

It was not a satisfactory argument, but Rozlyn was oddly relieved to have had that decision taken away, at least for now. Brooks' suggestion that she organise something was an ill-disguised hint that if she wanted watch kept, she'd have to do it herself. Rozlyn knew from experience that trying to find unassigned officers at this time of the evening, for what was likely to be a really small return, was not on the cards.

* * *

In the briefing room, she added Clara Buranou's name and address to the board and took her time to write a report on the girl and on Mark Richards. Translated into official language, there was little to tell. Most of what she thought or felt was mere speculation and therefore not the sort of thing that needed typing up. When she glanced at her watch she saw that it was five past seven. One more thing she wanted to do. Logging onto the Intranet, she ran Donovan's name, cross-referenced to people smuggling and then to antiquities, unsure of which part of the picture she should be looking at. Half a dozen hits in all. Two in prison, one deceased. The imprisoned pair she checked for dates, but in neither case was their incarceration recent. She logged the three remaining and put in a request for files, then, unable to get any further, took herself off home.

* * *

That night she dreamed of Ethan Merrill. They were walking through a mist-covered landscape. A soft light illuminated both mist and dew-damp grass. As Rozlyn looked more closely, it seemed that the webs of a thousand spiders spread out across the landscape, their silvered filaments shining and shimmering in the diffused light, linking and spreading their delicate tracery as far in every direction as Rozlyn could see. She was reminded of the dream she'd had of Charlie's funeral. Ethan Merrill spoke to her, his words only half heard and incomprehensible. There seemed to be a rhythm to the words, almost, but not quite, like poetry, and the language he used was sonorous and rich. And it occurred to Rozlyn, even though the words were strange, that the old man talked about the web spread wide beneath their feet and the vaster web that linked all things alive and dead and yet to be.

Rozlyn found herself straining to hear more. To understand the way of the *wyrd* described in the old man's words. In her dream she wept with frustration at her lack of understanding; at the complexity of it all and at the strange and magical simplicity.

Rozlyn woke, bathed in sweat, the cold morning light just breaking through the gap in the curtained window, her body aching as though, in her sleep, she'd walked for miles.

CHAPTER 15

A car had followed Rozlyn back to Clara Buranou's flat. When she pulled in at the side of the road, it passed her and the driver eased into an almost-too-small parking spot a hundred yards further on.

"Looks like we've got company?"

There were two men in the car. The passenger got out and leaned against the wing, glancing along the length of the thoroughfare before allowing his gaze finally to rest upon Rozlyn's vehicle.

Rozlyn glanced at the female uniform seated in the passenger seat. "Quality of the car and cut of the suit, I'd say he's one of Big Frank Parker's minions. Frank likes his boys to be well dressed."

The policewoman laughed, then asked. "Think it has anything to do with the Buranou woman?"

The Buranou woman, Rozlyn thought. She was used to the way her fellow officers depersonalised those they were involved with but, although she understood their reasons, she still didn't like it. "I doubt it," she said. "Whatever it is can wait until we've seen her anyway."

She led the way into the house, aware that the man watched, but made no move, almost as though he expected Rozlyn to attend to business first.

"Bit of a dive, this, isn't it?"

Rozlyn nodded. The odour that rose up from the carpet and peeled from the walls, bringing paint and paper with it, spoke of damp and long-term decay, and the stair carpet was so old and rotten that in places it had frayed to holes at the edge of the tread. Very safety conscious landlord, Rozlyn thought, reminded of what Jenny had said about the lack of fire escape.

"You know she won't be here."

Rozlyn nodded. "I know she won't be here."

Clara's door stood open. Her keys hung from a nail beside it. The boxes that had contained her clothes were empty. Left behind was only the scant furnishing that came with the flat, the television and a few groceries in the kitchen cupboard.

Rozlyn listed them. Flour, sugar, instant coffee and the same brand of cheap tea bag she had seen at Mrs Chinowski's. The tiny fridge, on the floor behind the curtain, was empty. What did Clara eat? Was she given her meals at the Larks, or had she taken the rest with her? Did she even use the fridge?

Opening it, she felt a blast of cold, so supposed Clara must have done, and a patch that looked like desiccated milk on the lower shelf indicated that she had stored something inside. She could hear her colleague moving furniture, searching for traces of the missing girl. Rozlyn straightened up, shutting the fridge door with her foot, and went to join her. There was little to examine and her colleague had already completed the task.

"Anything?"

"A magazine, couple of newspapers and a till receipt for milk and chicken breast." She showed Rozlyn her finds. The receipt was from the local Co-op, the magazine a back issue of *Cosmopolitan*. The newspapers, dated from just the day before were a copy of the *Sun* and a broadsheet, which, when Rozlyn unfolded it, turned out to be the *Guardian*. Rozlyn smiled wryly. Shades of Charlie Higgins, she thought, remembering the man's insistence that you had to read both types of paper to fully cover the news.

Was it a habit of Clara's, adopted from Charlie? In which case, did she know him far better than she'd been letting on? Or was that reading too much into such a random find?

"OK," she said. "Call it in and notify the landlord. Oh, and get Health and Safety and the buildings inspector in on the act."

"Why?"

"Third floor and no fire escape. I'll make a bet he's not declaring income from this excuse for a slum, to say nothing of the state of the rest of the building. It's rotten through, "

"Oh. Right," her colleague said. She neither looked nor sounded convinced that this was her responsibility. "Shouldn't we be out searching for her?" She quailed under Rozlyn's gaze but then shrugged her shoulders as though to feign indifference. "Don't suppose she'll get far anyway." She sounded satisfied with that conclusion.

"Hard to say." Rozlyn went to the door, reflecting that in terms of distance, Clara had come right the way across Europe and that had to mean something though in all other respects, she wondered if that distance could be measured in terms of miles northward or a precipitous southward slide.

She paused at the head of the stairs, looking down into the dim, dusty emptiness. After a dozen steps down, the staircase dog-legged at a small landing and turned away, invisible from where she stood. It was an oddly vertiginous feeling, looking down into an empty pit of stairs and landing and then bleak wall, as though Clara's world had been separated and dissociated from the rest of the house and, by extension, the remainder of humanity.

Did Charlie come and visit her here? How did they meet? She should have pressed Clara about that yesterday.

Why hadn't she? Why had she left time for Clara to pack her stuff and run without Rozlyn learning anything more about Charlie, or how she had come to be here or her association — and there must, surely, be an association — with the mysterious Thomas Thompson?

Had Charlie met her on one of his cleaning jobs? Had he, despite his warnings to Mouse, gone to one of the houses when there were people there? People like Clara Buranou? Rozlyn reached out for the handrail and then, almost unconsciously, to rest her other hand against the wall.

What, she asked herself, constituted the set or subset of people like Clara Buranou and why would their kind entice the likes of Charlie Higgins to become involved?

With a sudden flash of pained insight she knew what Charlie Higgins had seen in Clara Buranou and in Mrs Chinowski and probably also in the old man he'd visited in the Larks. He'd *recognised* them. Recognised that *something* in them that was also at the heart of his own self and, though Rozlyn instantly tried to force the analogy away, saw the same thing reflected in Rozlyn. The shocked realisation dawned that Charlie's continued association with her had been because Charlie had understood Rozlyn's need. Her loneliness, her sense of being somehow dispossessed. *That* was what kept Charlie Higgins coming back to her. Kept feeding her the scraps and shreds of information for the small bills with which Rozlyn had rewarded him.

She'd told herself that Charlie Higgins needed the money. *That*, Rozlyn knew now, was little more than a convenient fiction. Charlie worked three jobs plus his cleaning for Mr T. Charlie didn't need Rozlyn's handouts. It went much deeper than that and the knowledge that Charlie Higgins had pitied her, had sought to make her, Rozlyn Priest, one of his dependants, shocked Rozlyn to the very core.

How dare the likes of Charlie Higgins pity her?

"Ma'am?"

"What?"

"We going or what?"

She'd been standing at the head of the stairs, buried so deep in her shocked response that she'd all but forgotten about the uniformed officer. Rozlyn scowled and then continued down the stairs, her hand still touching the sticky dampness of the shedding paper, needing something at least seemingly solid against her palm as though that would help to regain her equilibrium. Once outside, she sent her colleague back to the car to report Clara's disappearance and summon the authorities to inspect the building.

Rozlyn was aware that her colleague watched as she stood and waited for the man in the suit to cross the road and saunter along the pavement towards her. The constable was miffed at being kept out of the loop; Rozlyn could see it in the sour look on her face.

"You've got a message for me?" Rozlyn prompted the big man, a handspan taller than Rozlyn, but also outhouse broad.

"Big Frank wants to see you, Inspector Priest. Eight o'clock, tonight. In the Queen's. Says *he's* buying."

Rozlyn raised an eyebrow. "Tell him, in that case, I'll be sure not to be late."

The man nodded approval. "Big Frank likes people to be punctual."

"I'll not be late, unless it's unavoidable. Criminals don't keep regular hours, in my experience."

The big man said nothing. He raised his chin, staring, for several seconds, beneath half-closed lids at the top floor of the house and then fixing his gaze back upon Rozlyn. "Someone done a runner, have they?"

"What makes you think that?"

He shrugged and turned away. "Eight o'clock, remember."

"How could I forget?"

Walking back to the car, Rozlyn could feel the constable's eyes on her, see the woman's mouth still fixed in its stiff, disapproving line — which, Rozlyn figured, was quite a feat, considering she was talking on her mobile at the same time. Rozlyn wondered if the lack of movement clipped her words or sharpened them, or made her more difficult to understand, the stiff upper lip extending to her entire jaw.

“What was all that about?” the constable asked as Rozlyn returned to the car.

“Just a message.” Had it been Jenny, or Constable Patel she’d have explained, Rozlyn realised. She wasn’t certain what made it different with this woman. Perhaps her lack of interest in the person of Clara Buranou. The implied lack of compassion.

She turned the key in the ignition, wondering at her own despairing mood and aware that it extended, probably unfairly, to the rest of the human race.

CHAPTER 16

He had fallen asleep reading from the *Heliand*; the God Spell given to him by his father and one of Treven's most treasured possessions. Before battle, when — however brave the man, however tried and tested the warrior — strange thoughts and doubts would creep unbidden into the mind, Treven would read the words of the Good Thegn Thomas and draw strength from the knowledge that to serve your Lord was the only option of an honourable man.

Thomas gimalda — uuas im githugan mann,
Diulic drohtines thegan -: 'ne sculun uui . . .

Thomas, one of the Twelve and a man worthy of his Lord's praise then spoke.

We should not argue with our Lord's will, he said. Rather we should endure with him, our Lord and ruler. For this is a Thegn's free choice, that we stand fast beside him and there die with him. For we all must die.

We will follow him wherever he goes and not count ourselves worthy of life, except that we, his people, live and die beside our leader. Upon this act will lie the judgement of God and of those who will come after us.

Treven had followed and Treven had endured and it seemed strange to him now that this should be his reward. A lifetime's worth of troubled sleep and evil dreams.

Once again, he dreamed of Wotan and now the dark-skinned woman walked beside him. The stranger had loosed her hair. It curled and waved and writhed about her face and shoulders like a dark and living halo. She moved as though in a dream of her own, staring in wonder and stepping cautiously as one who wakes and finds themselves sleepwalking and standing on unfamiliar, dangerous ground.

In his dream Treven had found himself on the rise, between the banks and trees where the hanged man had dropped flesh on that first day he had come to Theadingford. He gagged on the stench of rotting meat, more noisome in his dream than it had been in reality. It was as though the corpses of all those slain in battle, the battles of years and the bodies of his lost friends and fallen enemies had been stacked high in this one place and the stench of them thickened the air so that he could hardly draw breath.

Even in his dream, Treven was choking, his lungs filled up with the stink of blood and shit and sweat that had filled his nostrils so often in battle. Even as he struggled for air he felt strong hands grasping at his ankles and, looking down, the faces of fallen warriors stared up at him, mouths open, silently screaming, their last breath rising up to block his lungs and their hands, so many hands, clasping at his ankles and threatening to drag him down.

He could not pull free.

Again and again he strove and struggled, heaving himself this way and that until at last, he drew his sword and cut downwards, slicing through the faces of the dead, slashing at the sinew through wrists and the iron fingers of his fallen comrades. In his dream he could name each one. In his dream he breathed the last agonies of their death. In his dream he fought them, terrified that he would die in his sleep and be trapped forever in their death throes.

Somehow he fought free. He struggled to the rising land where he had seen that carved wooden cross with its ambiguous figure. The Christ or the Lord Wotan? Treven could no longer tell, but the black woman stood there, staring up in wonder at the hanging figure and as her hand reached out to touch, Treven felt as though the woman reached into his very heart and soul and tore them from him. The pain in his gut ripped through his consciousness and for a time he could hear only his own screams as the fire in his bowels threatened to rip him apart.

Then, as the pain subsided, he heard a hammer striking wood. He was lying on the ground now, at the foot of the cross, gazing up at that scarred, carved face with its wise and missing eye.

Painfully, Treven turned his head towards the rhythm of the hammer blows, seeing, as he did, the bird with its spread wings pegged fast to the ground. Its cries of pain pierced him, as the hammer fell, metal on wood, as a man — Treven could not make out his features– drove the wooden spikes deep into the earth. The crow pecked and tore at the hand that held it down and, as the man stepped away, Treven saw his shadow, hammer still gripped in its fist, raise the blooded knuckles to his lips and lick them clean.

Treven woke with a stone in his stomach, cold as ice that chilled him through and did not thaw even when he broke his fast with meat and warm bread. Gratefully, but none the less impatient, he drank the herb concoction that Osric had brewed for him these past five mornings. Since that day he had first dreamed of the white-haired, one-eyed man the sickness in his stomach had begun to disturb almost his every meal. Osric's potion worked, but it was hard pressed. Treven, unused to sickness of any kind, bore the whole thing grudgingly and allowed his temper to fray at both ends. His servants kept their distance from his outbursts and even Hugh made himself scarce, though Treven knew that his moods were simply an additional excuse for his Shire Reeve to absent himself.

Knowing that Hugh sought the company of Cate Scrivener did nothing to soothe him. Treven had grown tired of the arguments between them. Treven's urging that Hugh should leave the girl alone and his empty threats to send Hugh away should he not comply. Empty, because Hugh had been appointed at the king's command and not Treven's own and, though Hugh never pressed the point, that knowledge lay heavy between them. For the first time, their friendship was strained. Friendship forged in battle was struggling for life in times of peace as Treven slowly realised just how little they now shared in common.

Trying hard to be hopeful, Treven acknowledged that in the past month, something at least had been achieved. The hall had been re-roofed and the walls shored up sound enough to last out the winter. The earth floor had been cleared and re-packed and strewn with hay and sweet herbs and a trestle table and benches crafted of green wood by the local carpenter, there being no seasoned timber available sufficient to the task. He'd cut the planks and laid then alternately face up and face down to minimise the warp and braced the underside with four straight bands, pegged solidly to the top. It would still twist a little as it dried, he reckoned, but there was little could be done to help that. The carpenter and his son had braced the walls, again with green timber, which would tighten about the pegs as it dried and strengthen the whole and reinforced them with new wattle hurdles, daubed well with river clay and dung mixed in with crushed reed and straw. The hall now windproof and, lit with tallow and rush lights, was a pleasing enough dwelling to spend the winter — though Hugh, used to better lodging in time of peace, had not yet ceased to complain.

The carpenter had made also two box beds, with close slats that lifted the sleeper clear of the floor. Bracken, dried and spread with a coarse blanket, gave some degree of comfort and Treven was not displeased with the arrangement. For a man who had spent more years than he cared to count sleeping where he fell, this was close to luxury, which was not to say he did not have plans for an increase of comfort given a little time.

"You were late last night," Treven said as Hugh joined him by the fire.

Hugh shrugged. "You were snoring when I returned. How would you know?"

"I woke when you near fell on top of me. I could smell the ale on your breath and when I went outside to piss, the moon had almost set. You were late enough almost to be early."

Hugh laughed. "What of it?" he asked lightly.

"Were you with Cate?"

Hugh sighed, impatient with this ongoing refrain. "For some time I was with Cate," he acknowledged. "We argued about that husband of hers. She said she must return home before he missed her, so I found someone more willing."

"Hugh, this will not do. Leave the lass alone, for the love of Christ."

Hugh cut himself another chunk of mutton and folded it inside his bread. "Ay, well, on that score, you'll be getting your wish. She told me last night, she'd not see me again."

"She's said that before."

"She has, but last night she meant it and I must respect her word, though it grieves me to think of her in Eldred's bed. The man is an oaf and an ingrate. If you'd any sense, my friend, you'd be rid of him."

"And what good would that do any of us? Eldred is coming to see I have the best interest of the community at heart. You can't expect change overnight, Hugh. The man and his brother have been effective lords here these past years. To them, I am a usurper." And you even more so, he thought, but he chose not to say this aloud. "I'm glad the girl has seen sense, though," he added with feeling. "Your relations with her could only lead to grief."

"She's with child," Hugh blurted suddenly.

Treven stared at him. "Yours or his? Or don't you know?"

Hugh didn't answer at first. "It could be either," he admitted finally. "She had to tell him. She told him also she'd done nothing with me to be shamed of and she thinks he believes her, or, at least, chooses to seem to."

"God above, Hugh. When will you learn?"

"The man is an animal, Treven."

"And you're not? You rut like one. You yourself told me you went from this lass to another's bed." He shook his head and then rubbed hard at his belly as it cramped painfully. "Christ curse it!" He poured more of Osric's mint fragrant potion into his cup and drank, fighting the urge to vomit.

Hugh watched him with narrowed gaze. "If this continues, you should return to Winchester and seek help," he said. "I do not trust Osric's skills. Treven, I've not seen you cramped like this, even when we've been forced to eat rotten food and carrion leavings."

Treven waved his concern away. "It will pass," he told Hugh. "It is better than it was." He had not told Hugh about his dream or the sense that it was the omen of something so very wrong. Hugh's way of thinking was not like Treven's. He would either laugh at his imaginings or tell him to see a priest.

And thinking of priests . . . Reaching for his pack, Treven withdrew the leather wallet that had been sent by the King. Inside were the deeds to this land and a command signed by Aelfred himself that Abbot Kendryk of Storton Abbey should respect Treven as King's Thegn and leave off troubling him. It was an honour Treven had never looked for, that the King should name him as one under his direct command and he had read the words practically off the page in the days since the messenger had arrived bearing it. There was a sanction attached, of course. Treven, as King's Thegn, would have to spend each third month in his Lord's house, but Aelfred had put off this demand until Eastertime the following year, to give Treven time to settle affairs on his lands and for this, Treven was doubly grateful. He recalled the words of the *Heliand* that he had read the night before and felt a moment of exaltation. Perhaps, after all, the reward for service was not only night terrors.

Kendryk was due today. He'd lodge at the Scrivener's home, it still being more fitting to his status and comfort than Treven's half-finished hall. There were grievances to be heard, disputes held over from the Shire Court and directed to Treven's judgement and Treven was glad that Kendryk had come to observe the proceedings. Not only was it good timing for Treven to show this new covenant, but Kendryk would see, also, that Aelfred's newly drafted laws were to be implemented without delay.

Glancing up as a shadow blocked the light from the door, he saw Osric standing in readiness.

"It's time we were on our way," he told Hugh. "It wouldn't do to keep the Abbot waiting on us. At least, not for too long."

* * *

Abbot Kendryk had set up court in the Scrivener's yard. A massive oak chair, carried from the abbey, had been set atop the steps and from this vantage point, Kendryk surveyed his subjects. He lifted his gaze to observe Treven and Hugh and their little entourage as they trotted into the yard and Treven was struck by the political play in which this man of God involved himself.

"He seeks to lord it over you," Hugh commented.

"He *requires* the trappings of authority," Treven said simply. "I do not. He must bring twenty monks plus their servants and lay brothers with him to make a point of his own importance. He's welcome to them. I hold power here, Hugh, and the Abbot knows it."

He was conscious of Hugh's sideways look. Of the little doubt in his friend's mind. Treven had not been one for such game play, but he had observed it at close enough quarters to understand it. Kendryk had his entourage; Treven had the authority of the King. Both Abbot and Thegn were required if the peace was to be kept and the region prosper and the two were equally aware of that.

Hugh laughed briefly and softly. "Since when were you a reader of men's minds?"

"Since I had reason to be. Come, let us get to business."

They dismounted and crossed the open space. Kendryk did not move to greet them. Hugh, raised with customs that Treven saw as Frankish and demeaning, knelt to receive his blessing while Treven looked on, meeting Kendryk's gaze; the man's attention on Treven even while he murmured the *Benedictus* over his companion.

Kendryk was an old man but he had lost nothing of his strength or sinew. His grey hair curled softly about his tonsure, but that was the only moderated aspect. His skin, stretched tight enough to outline his skull, was tanned as dark as that of a farmer, the sharp planes of his cheek bones jutting and cadaverous and his hands, leathery on their backs, scuffed and calloused at the palm like a pair of well-worn gloves that fitted tight to the bone.

He motioned to one of his followers. "Bring seats for their lordships," he said, and it was done in the next instant. Two monks returning with the carved chairs belonging to the brothers. They set them beside Kendryk on the topmost step and Treven sat, then looked about him wondering where the Scriveners could be.

"Edmund and his brother will return presently," Kendryk told him, noting his interest. "There was some disturbance they were called to investigate."

"Oh?"

Kendryk shrugged, a tiny lifting of one shoulder, though Treven noted also the fractional irritation that flitted across his death's-head features.

"They were not here to greet you?" Treven guessed.

"They left instructions for our comfort with their serving men."

"And Cate. She was absent also?"

Kendryk turned his head to look at Treven. He registered faint surprise, as though the woman's nonattendance had not registered with him before. "Yes," he said. "She too was gone." He frowned. "Let us hope that her disappearance is a temporary one. One woman missing from the Scrivener household is misfortune enough."

"You heard of that?" Treven was not surprised. "They say she fled with her lover?" He made a question of the comment and Kendryk thought before replying.

"Some say that."

"And what do you say?"

Kendryk held Treven's gaze for a moment more, then he turned his head slowly away and scanned the scene before him as though considering. "I say that it was Allis Scrivener's skill that kept this land intact and this *vill* from suffering." He registered Treven's surprise without turning back to him. "You don't think those two oafs have the slightest notion, do you? Or the father, for that matter. He's been sick with grief since his wife was taken from him."

"So Allis ran the estate?"

"Allis and her sister. Their mother before that. The land came down from the female line and the women had sense to keep it that way."

"You knew the mother?"

"I have been here for many seasons, King's Thegn. Oh yes," he replied to Treven's unspoken question. "Aelfred sent a copy of your deeds to lodge in the Abbey library. For safekeeping, so he told me, but also, I am sure, to emphasise his reckoning of your territories. But to return to our discussion. I knew the mother while she was still a child and watched the girls grow into women. Had Edmund sense, he would have clung and cloven to his woman like a limpet to a rock. She was the wealth of this land, the knowledge, the healer and the wise woman after her mother went. The man was a fool not to take note of another's interest or to give Allis reason enough to remain."

"It's rumoured she was barren." It was the first contribution Hugh had made to the conversation.

"It is rumoured, also, that she chose not to encumber herself with an infant until she was certain that the peace would be lasting."

"She chose?" Treven was confused. "How can a woman choose?"

Hugh laughed aloud. "I'm told there are ways," he said. "Certain herbs. A sponge soaked in oil or honey. I've never encountered such," he added quickly, his face and mood growing solemn as though suddenly recalling that he was discussing such matters with an Abbot.

Treven looked to Kendryk for confirmation.

"Allis once told me that she'd seen too many babes die of lack of milk when their mothers starved and too many infants perish with the cold," he said. "She told me she would choose a time to bear Edmund's children, when she could be certain there was a future for them in which to grow."

"And you condoned this?" Treven was not sure what to think. "Surely, the gods . . ." He broke off and began again. "Surely," he repeated. "God grants the right to have a child."

Kendryk's lips tightened, though whether in disapproval at his slip or in amusement Treven could not quite decide. He suspected the latter and was irritated with himself that the beliefs of his pagan mother could still insinuate when he least expected.

"Perhaps another time might be better in pursuit of this," Kendryk said. "Since the brothers have not returned, we should proceed without them and hear the disputes we came here to judge."

Treven nodded. Kendryk was right, the morning was well advanced and the string of petitioners reached now back almost to the forest fence. Kendryk spoke to one of his entourage and the monk went down into the crowd and brought a man forward to speak.

* * *

It was almost noon when a shout from somewhere in the crowd distracted them. Treven rose to his feet and laid a hand on the pommel of his sword, looking towards the cause of the disturbance.

Along the path from the wood came a bullock cart, the animals urged forward by a frantic Edmund. Eldred could be seen, bending over something or someone in the pit of the cart and following on behind a straggled knot of villagers.

Treven ran down the steps and went swiftly to meet them on the path.

Hugh, on his feet now, remained beside Kendryk atop the steps. The abbot himself did not move but gestured to two of his monks to follow Treven.

"What is it?" Treven demanded.

Edmund turned to him, his face stricken and pale. "It's Cate," he said. "She's badly hurt." He lowered his voice. "I don't give much for her chances, but Eldred will hear none of that. Gwan!" he urged the cattle forward, the hazel rod across their flanks prompting greater speed, though Treven could see that the animals were at full pace. He came around the back of the cart and looked down on the flat bed to see what Eldred was tending. Cate Scrivener, pretty, neat little Cate, lay like a bundle of blooded rags across her husband's legs. He clasped her close to him and Treven could see from his face that he had been weeping. Now, though, that grief had transmuted into slow burning and dangerous rage.

"Where did you find her?"

"Ranuf found her beside the trackway this dawn." He jerked his chin towards those following the cart. "She'd been all night in the open. Her clothes were wet with dew and the ground soaked in blood. Ranuf carried her home and send the boy to fetch me."

"At dawn?" It was now almost noon. Why had this taken so long? "How far away was this?"

"The place is not easy. Ranuf burns charcoal. He and his son had been watching the clamp all night. When his brother came to relieve him, he found her, close by the main track.

We had to send to fetch the cart." He took a deep uneven breath. "This is your doing, Treven."

"Mine?"

"You brought him here. He used her, discarded her, left her like this to die and lie like wolf bait."

"Hugh. You're accusing Hugh of doing this. On what grounds?"

Eldred laughed wildly. "Are you blind and stupid? You know his interest in her. I know she's crept out at night to lie with him. She roused once, when we came to her. She spoke his name."

The cart had halted now and Edmund come round the back to help lift Cate. "This is true," Treven questioned. "She accused Hugh?"

Edmund hesitated. "As my brother said. She spoke his name. Gently now, let us get her inside. Gently brother. Tend to your wife first . . ." But Eldred had seen his enemy and was out of the cart and running for the steps. Treven leapt after him, grabbing him by the arm and then wrestling him to the ground before he reached his goal.

"Let me be!"

"So you can cut him down and have your own life forfeit?" Treven whispered furiously. "Eldred, think on, just for an instant." He hesitated. There was no kind way to say this. "What if her speaking of his name was not in accusation. What if . . .Eldred, if as you say they were lovers . . . is it not possible she roused and hoped to find him there?"

It was a painful, terrible question and he saw in Eldred's eyes that it was one he had already asked himself. So much easier to believe Cate spoke of guilt.

Treven looked towards the steps where Hugh still waited, uncertain. His eyes widened as he saw the bundle lifted from the cart. "Cate? Cate! Oh Sweet Jesus. What have you done to her?" This last was aimed at Eldred and he leaped for the man much as the brother had leaped towards Hugh. Treven was forced to release Eldred. He grabbed at Hugh, calling to Osric and his servants for aid. Osric seized Eldred's wrists and held them fast behind his back while Treven took charge of his recalcitrant friend. “There is nothing to be gained by this! Now calm, both of you, or I’ll have you bound and set under guard.”

“I want to go to my wife.”

“Then go. Peaceful!”

Osric released him reluctantly but followed close behind as Eldred mounted the steps and followed his brother into the hall. “Osric is skilled with herbs and healing,” Treven told him. “Let him see.”

Eldred looked back, his face dark and closed and his eyes cold as though he might refuse. The he nodded and gestured Treven’s man inside. “If she dies,” he told Hugh. “I’ll see you pay with your life, law or no law to back me.”

CHAPTER 17

Rozlyn arrived at the Queen's just before eight o'clock. It had begun to rain, a light, soaking drizzle fine as yellow mist in the sodium light. She paused outside to switch off her mobile. She didn't think it would improve relations should it ring during her audience with the king of Queens.

This time the silence on her entering the pub was only momentary; a mere dip in volume as she was assessed and recognised. Big Frank was seated in his accustomed place and he raised a bottle of beer in welcome as Rozlyn came in. He was pouring it by the time Rozlyn reached the table, tilting the glass with that skill Rozlyn had never quite mastered so that the head floated light and even. Whenever Rozlyn tried she had to pause to let it settle first before she could fill the glass. Usually, she just drank from the bottle, but didn't think Big Frank would approve of such uncouth behaviour.

No one spoke until Frank had placed the glass in front of Rozlyn and raised his own.

"Cheers," Rozlyn said.

Big Frank acknowledged with a slight inclination of his head before drinking deep. "Did you find that girl?" Frank asked when at last he came up for air.

"Girl?"

"The one who lived in that shit hole of a flat."

"Oh. Clara. No, not yet." She took another sip of her drink and then asked, "How did your boys know I'd be there today?"

"I put out word to keep an eye open for you, so they could tell you that I expected you here at eight."

Ah, Rozlyn thought. Well that was comforting — that Big Frank's boys were keeping an eye open for her. She merely nodded, as though this was expected and changed the subject.

"This Thomas Thompson you wanted to know about. Talk to me."

Rozlyn considered. She had an inkling that Frank already knew as much as she did and that this was as much a test of honest intent as it was a need to know. In truth, Rozlyn thought, there wasn't much to tell, and she didn't see harm in letting Frank know what they had. There would be far more harm in withholding.

"He owns at least two houses, probably more. He uses them to house illegal immigrants. We think. And there's precious little proof. We know that Charlie Higgins cleaned for him and that Thompson paid him well and used him regularly. I've got reason to believe that Clara Buranou was one who came into the country with the aid or otherwise of this Thomas Thompson. That Charlie got involved with her somehow because of that. I figure he felt sorry for her. Whatever, he helped her find work."

"And where did she work?"

Rozlyn hesitated, then said. "She cleaned for an old lady Charlie knew, lived in the same block of flats as him. And she worked in the kitchen of an old folks home. The Larks. You know it?"

"I know it. Do you think they know she's an illegal?"

Rozlyn shrugged. "I've yet to have the pleasure of asking," she said. "I'd be surprised if they asked. References might have been a problem, but I'm sure Charlie would have figured something out."

Big Frank smiled, briefly. "I thought you rated him as a useless tick," he said.

"Oh, that's not changed, not entirely, anyway, but now I figure him for a resourceful tick at any rate." More than that, Rozlyn thought. She'd actually begun to engender a grudging respect for Charlie Higgins, but she thought that was one scrap of information that Big Frank could go without.

"And these . . . people this Thompson smuggled in. Where are they from?"

"Eastern Europe, we think. Clara Buranou said she was Croatian." Not true, she thought. Rozlyn had said she was Croatian; she had simply not denied it. "Frank, there are people on the move everywhere, could be that Thompson varies his cargo." She remembered the little radio with the Chinese writing Mouse had told her about. "The two houses we know about, we've got under surveillance, but that's about the sum of it, I'm afraid."

Frank Parker took another large swallow of his pint. Rozlyn watched with interest. It was now a good two thirds down and she figured she had until Frank finished before her interview terminated. Frank lowered his glass and snapped his fingers. As if by magic a folded sheet of paper appeared in his hand. He held it thoughtfully, gazing at Rozlyn as though trying to figure something out. It was not a comfortable expression to be on the receiving end of.

"You know where to find this Thomas Thompson, do you?"

Rozlyn shook her head.

"Well, Inspector Priest, for the sake of his health, I suggest you find him before any of my people do. This bloke's been running a scam on my patch and I'd have appreciated knowing about it a good bit sooner than I did, if you get my meaning?"

Rozlyn nodded. Oh, you're sore because you didn't get your cut, she thought. "Yes. I get your meaning."

"Business," Frank told her. He slid the paper across the table, no easy task as it was crowded with bottles and empty glasses.

Rozlyn left it where it lay, noting that the corner of it had landed in a little puddle of spilt beer and was slowly soaking it up. "What I don't get," she said, "is how this could be happening so close to home, so to speak, and you not know." She looked up into Big Frank's face, eyes wide and childlike in their innocence.

"Oh, you can be sure that's also my concern," Big Frank told her. "You'll know when I've found out."

"I'm sure I will."

Big Frank drained his glass and Rozlyn took her cue. She reached for the paper and stood, careful not to crash the stool into those others packed so close around the table.

"Be seeing you," she said, then remembered something else. "Oh, I meant to ask. You heard of someone by the name of Donovan?"

There was a perceptible shift of mood. The man sitting to the right of Frank stood up and another moved as though about to. Frank waved them down. He looked Rozlyn in the eye, leaning as far forward across the table as his bulk would allow. "Donovan is not a nice man," he warned softly. "You leave well alone. Now, get off home."

Brook would have pressed the point, Rozlyn thought, as she nodded and then turned away. Brook would have sat himself down again and refused to shift until he'd got whatever point Big Frank wanted to make explained in triplicate — or he'd have tried to. Rozlyn had learned early on that the way to deal with Frank was to at least appear to do so on his terms. That way, you got pretty much what you needed to know and you didn't so much run the risk of winding up beaten or dead in some back alley.

Frank knew that, given the opportunity, Rozlyn would put him inside as soon as blink, but he also knew that Rozlyn was willing to play the game with Frank's ball and some of Frank's rules.

"See you, Frank," Rozlyn said as though nothing untoward had passed between them.

Big Frank nodded and Rozlyn made her way back across the bar. As she reached the door she turned and glanced back. Big Frank was pouring the remainder of Rozlyn's beer into his glass. Rozlyn laughed softly and let herself out. Waste not want not, I suppose, she thought. Now, what the hell was that all about? She tucked the mystery paper into the pocket of her coat and ran for her car.

Once in shelter, she reached into her pocket for paper and phone, switching on the interior light so she could read the message Big Frank had given her. The phone bleeped into life, then sounded a cheerful message to tell her she'd missed a call. She studied the number. No name attached, so no one she had in her speed dial list. Not a number she recognised either, though whoever it was seemed to have tried to reach her twice.

Figuring that if it was anything important, they'd ring back, she turned her attention to the sheet of lined paper, now stained at the corner with Big Frank's beer.

"Addresses?" The other houses. Had to be. Mouse said he thought Thompson owned four or five properties in all and here were two more. They were across town, quite a way from Big Frank's patch. Briefly, Rozlyn wondered where he'd got the information from; then decided she probably wouldn't like the answer. For this operation to have been kept from the boss man for so long — and she got the impression that Thompson had been operating for a while — there'd have to have been someone inside Frank's organisation giving him cover . . . and taking a cut.

Rozlyn didn't give much for their chances now. She recalled what Frank had said about Rozlyn knowing when Frank had found out how Thompson had kept his secret. No doubt there'd be another body in the canal sometime in the near future. Assisted suicide was rumoured to be one of Frank's specialties. Rozlyn shuddered. If even Frank considered Donovan a dangerous man, what the hell was he actually like? It was not a pleasant thought.

She returned to her more immediate concern.

“Well, Mr Thomas Thompson — and who the hell would call their kid that? It has to be a made-up name. I mean, come on! Anyway, whatever your name is, you’d better pray I’m the one that finds you first and not our beer-drinking friend back there.”

CHAPTER 18

Home before nine, entering an empty house, no lights, no heat — she'd forgotten to set the timer again. In the hall the red glow of the answerphone light told her she had a message. It solved the mystery of the missed calls.

"Rozlyn, this is Jenny, I'm at the General Hospital. It's your Mouse Man. Someone tried very hard to kill him and he's asking for you."

She added the ward number and the fact that she'd tried her mobile. Rozlyn retrieved her keys from the blue dish and left home a scant two minutes after walking in.

* * *

Rozlyn hated hospitals. She stepped reluctantly from the dark into the brightly lit world of medics and sickness and squeaky floors. That smell of death and disinfectant. Rozlyn had hated hospitals since she had watched her parents die in one. She had been just sixteen years old.

Mouse was propped in a clean white bed. His hands lay trembling on the coverlet, twitching like the whiskers of his pets. A tube ran into his left arm from a bag supported by a drip stand. Mouse, it seemed, was blood group O positive.

The right side of his face was almost black with bruising and the one visible eye was swollen closed.

"What the hell happened?"

Jenny shrugged, then got up and came over to Rozlyn, leading her away from the bed. "He's asked for you but he keeps drifting in and out of consciousness. Someone came to his house, wrecked the place and beat him to a pulp. Somehow, he managed to crawl out into the street and a passer-by, chap walking his dog, found him and called an ambulance. Other than that, we don't know much."

"Who the hell would want to hurt Mouse? How bad is he?"

"Broken ribs, internal bleeding and he's lost an eye. They thought at first he might have a ruptured liver. There was talk of him bleeding out, but they've managed to stabilise and they hope he'll pull through." She smiled, trying to reassure. "He's made it this far. He's tougher than he looks."

Rozlyn nodded, looking at the Mouse Man. He'd always struck Rozlyn as being as fragile and vulnerable as one of his small charges. Short and skinny, he gave no impression of durability. Rozlyn hoped that this appearance would indeed prove to be deceptive. "When did they bring him in?"

"About four this afternoon. They took him straight into theatre. He was asking for you then," she chuckled, "but they thought he wanted a vicar."

Rozlyn laughed. "Oh boy." She glanced at her watch. It was close to ten. "Had he been lying there for long?"

"Maybe. It began to rain at about half three. When they found him, Mouse was soaked through. The guy with the dog thought he'd been mugged but the police officers that arrived just after the ambulance crew noticed the open door and took a look. When they saw the blood in the hall, they realised he'd been attacked inside and think he might have interrupted a thief. I think that's the way it's gone down on the initial report. The place has been sealed and secured, but SOCO can't get there 'til tomorrow, they're stretched."

Rozlyn nodded. “Any idea when he’ll wake up?” If he’ll wake up.

Jenny shook her head. “No, but they think he’ll be OK. The Houseman’s still around somewhere. I told him you’d be here; he might be able to tell you more. I’ve supposedly got someone from uniform coming to sit with him. God knows when they’ll get here.”

If they get here. An old man, little better than a down and out, who’d been processed as a victim of an aggravated burglary wasn’t going to be a priority when it came to expenditure of police time, at least, until he either died — in which case it would be elevated to murder — or he could tell them something about his assailant.

Rozlyn nodded. “You get off home,” she said. “I’ll stay awhile.”

“Right you are, but look, there’s not much you can do here. You’d be better grabbing some sleep. I only called you out because I knew you’d never speak to me again if I hadn’t.” She grinned. “At least he’s a bit cleaner.”

“Yeah, right. He was attacked because he’d refused to take a bath. Anywhere I can get some coffee?”

“There’s a café on the ground floor and a machine at the end of that corridor,” Jenny pointed. ”Both equally vile.”

“Thanks. OK, I’ll see you in the morning.”

She nodded, snatched her coat from the back of the chair and made her exit. Rozlyn drew a deep and what she hoped would be a calming breath, then sat down in the chair that Jenny’s coat had vacated. “God, Mouse, what the hell have they done to you?” The side of his face was pulped and swollen and Rozlyn wondered if anything was broken. His nose was so inflamed and bloated that there was barely room for the tubes feeding him oxygen. His lips, split and puffy, drooled a faint trace of pink spittle.

Rozlyn leaned back in the chair and tried not to remember that other time. The crash she’d avoided because she’d been late getting to her grandparents’ house and her parents, due somewhere else, had left without her. Had she made them late? Had they been rushing because of her and taken a risk, despite the poor visibility in the pouring rain, maybe driven that bit too fast?

Rozlyn would never know. They'd both been taken to the same hospital, placed in different wards. She'd drifted from one to the other all night long, trying to work it so that her time at each bedside was roughly equal as though they might be offended should she show any kind of favouritism.

Then it was just her dad, her mom passing at the dawn of that first terrible morning. Her dad had lingered for two more days until Rozlyn, her body aching with tension and grief and lack of sleep, had almost wished it could be over so that she could let go and rest.

That had been a random thought. One among many, but the guilt that had smothered her because of that casual emotion had haunted her since her father died. Somewhere in her consciousness, Rozlyn was aware that she had tried to make recompense for that momentary lapse ever since.

As she watched, Mouse moved. A mere twitch of the hands that then extrapolated to the rest of his body and he whimpered in his sleep, a wordless, despairing sound that had Rozlyn leaning towards him and touching his hands. Stilling them.

"Hey, Mouse Man. It's OK. Nothing's going to hurt you now."

He was dreaming, Rozlyn realised. Maybe seeing in his nightmare what had hurt him so much in real life.

"Who did this to you? Was it this Donovan fella no one wants to talk about? Or someone sent by our Mr Thompson?"

Mouse relaxed and Rozlyn leaned back in the uncomfortable chair. First Charlie and now Mouse. Individuals for whom life was a big enough challenge without someone sticking the boot in. Or in Charlie's case, something far more deadly.

Had they wanted Mouse dead? No, Rozlyn thought, not dead. They'd just wanted him to talk. What did they think he knew that they had to beat him for, and with such brutality?

What could someone like Mouse Man possibly know or have that would trigger such a frenzied attack?

* * *

They had laid Cate down close to the hearth and Osric had taken charge, ordering more light so he could clean and tend her wounds, plundering Allis's careful stock of herbs to find what he required. Treven watched as he pounded herb with honey and made a paste to spread on those terrible wounds, gently turning Cate's head so that he could clean the blood from her hair and skin. He met Treven's eyes and shook his head. There was nothing he could do. Gaping through the ragged edges of her flesh and bone, Treven could distinguish blood and brain. That she still lingered was miracle enough — or cruelty? Treven could not decide. That she had lived long enough to have spoken any words, never mind Hugh's name, struck him as extraordinary enough to have divine purpose behind it and the thought of that filled him with revulsion and with dread. She had neither spoken nor even moved since they had brought her here and Edmund admitted that she had said nothing on the journey. Treven knew in his heart that she would not last the night.

Could Hugh have inflicted these injuries? He thought not. Hugh could be violent when the rage took him and in battle Treven would as soon have him at his side as a half dozen others, however well trained and brave. But that Hugh could attack a girl he claimed to have feelings for, attack her in such a brutal and personal way, Treven doubted. Whoever had struck Cate had done so from close quarters, though, and had come at her from front and side — he could only guess which blow had landed first. It pointed, in Treven's mind, to her knowing her assailant. Had she turned to run, the blow would have felled her from behind, or at an oblique angle, not as this had done, smashing the temple and the socket of the eye. The right-hand side of her face was practically untouched. Blood and a little bruising, but nothing more.

Kendryk caught his eye and motioned him away.

"Your thoughts, King's Thegn?"

Treven ignored the mockery. "The blows were hard and from the front. She saw who attacked her. I cannot be sure, but my guess is the second was struck after she had hit the ground. I've been witness to many such actions in time of battle. One blow to bring your foe down, a second to be sure they'll not stand again."

"I bow to your knowledge," Kendryk said dryly, then nodded. "You may be right, though the instrument here was blunt, the wound not made with a sword."

"Wood or stone would do just as well. She was found in woodland, the weapon could be one of chance. The impulse of a moment."

"You suspect her husband?"

Treven looked back at Eldred, the man still kneeling at her side, the expression on his face unreadable in the firelight, shadows passing over his features as the flames licked wood.

"He knew about Hugh. What man would know and do nothing?"

"Would you have killed your wife for lying with another?"

"My wife would not."

"But if she had?"

Treven eyed him warily, not sure where this was leading. He thought about Hild, remembered her laughter, the warmth of her skin as she lay beside him in their bed and he closed his eyes.

"I would have killed the man, as would have been my right. Sent her away . . . for a time. I might have beaten her." He shrugged and turned away. "I loved my wife. I do not know if Eldred loved his."

* * *

Tuesday night became Wednesday morning. The promised officer had failed to arrive and when Rozlyn called in to find out what had happened was told that there'd been trouble in town at one of the clubs and there'd been no one to spare.

"On a Tuesday? Sorry, I suppose it's Wednesday. We don't usually get problems until the weekend."

Private party that got out of hand, she was told. A fight had broken out, someone glassed and another with a broken arm. Mouse took a back seat to drunken brawls.

The junior doctor came at one o'clock. He looked as exhausted as Rozlyn felt and could tell her little more than Jenny already had.

"You should go home," he said. "Get some sleep. He's stable and we'll call you when he wakes."

Reluctantly, Rozlyn had to accept that this was good sense. "Tell him I came and that I'll be coming back."

"Will do. Or, rather, I'll pass the message on. My shift ends at six."

"Think you'll make it until then?"

The man smiled wearily. "I'm mainlining caffeine," he joked. "He hasn't any family?"

"Not that I know. His mother died a few years back. He still lived in the same house, but I've never heard him talk about other family."

The doctor nodded. "Go home," he said. "We'll let you know."

Rozlyn went, relieved to be out of the place but guilty about leaving. She stood in the car park, looking back towards the illuminated windows of the ward and slipping back in memory to that other time. Leaving her father there. Dead. She'd stood outside of the hospital then. That other place. Trying to recall her father's face from that time only a few days before when he'd been alive and happy and so full of living there could never have been enough time to do it all. And she thought about what she'd just told the doctor about Mouse, how she'd never heard him talk of family and she knew that, should their roles have been reversed, Mouse or Jenny or even Brook would have told him just the same about Rozlyn.

* * *

Cate gave up on life just before dawn. Treven watched her face and saw that momentary transition that told him that her spirit had fled and the body was now empty of that which made it human in his eyes.

He sighed and let his head drop into his hands.

"Oh God," Eldred whispered. "Oh sweet Jesus, no. He's killed her!"

"Hush man, you don't know that." Edmund's voice, though reasonable, held no conviction.

"Don't I? Cate is dead and he was with her the night she died. I know that much, brother."

Edmund looked at Treven. "Can you account for his movements?" he asked. "Was he within your hall?"

Treven would have liked to lie, but he could not. "Hugh returned late," he said. "He told me he had been with Cate, but that she left him swiftly and vowed never to take time with him again."

"And he returned to you? At what hour?"

Treven shook his head. "Late. Early. Not long before dawn. He said he had gone from Cate to . . . another. He did not name her."

"You should keep your reeve on a tighter leash," Edmund said angrily. "Is this a taste of the King's law? The King's peace?"

"It was my doing, not the Lord Aelfred's," Treven exploded angrily. "And you are right. I should have bound him tighter, even sent him from me, and I swear this to you, if Hugh is guilty he'll be punished according to the law. *If* Hugh is guilty."

"Punished!" Eldred exploded. "So he'll pay me gold in compensation? Cate paid with her life for her foolishness. Aye, and for mine in letting it pass without greater punishment."

"I've heard tell you punished her enough."

"What does that mean?"

"You beat the girl. It's common knowledge. Small wonder she fell in with the likes of Hugh."

Eldred turned, fists raised and Edmund moved to intervene. Kendryk, sitting silent in his corner roused himself. "Is this a way to behave? Grown men, fighting over the body of one newly dead. Eldred, if you would accuse Hugh de Vries, then do so and we will have judgement over him, but you'll not raise fists or brawl in my presence or in that of your dead wife. And you, Lord, you think any of this is seemly?"

Treven shook his head. "None of it," he said. "Hugh and I will face your judgement, but it is in my heart to ask, why, if you knew your woman was lying with another, why you did nothing?"

"And what should I do? Kill her? Take his life?"

"Had you discovered them and killed Hugh, I would have heard your plea and demanded recompense, but no law would have condemned you utterly. You should and could have made complaint. To me, to Abbot Kendryk here. To the shire courts." He took a deep breath and asked. "You knew she was with child?"

From his reaction it was clear that Edmund did not, but Eldred nodded.

"And that the child, most like, was Hugh's?"

"It could have been mine."

"Could it?" Treven was not sure what moved him to ask that question, but it hit the mark. Eldred flushed scarlet and turned away.

"Eldred?" Edmund was clearly not privy to this secret either.

"You'd have welcomed the child as your own," Treven said softly. He reached a hand towards the other man, then let it fall. "Eldred, you would not be the first to foster and love another man's son when you could not make your own. Forgive me, I would have willingly left this unsaid, but it is pertinent in this instance."

"How so?" Edmund demanded. He was watching his brother's face. Comprehension and pity now dawning on his own.

"Because if your brother turned a blind eye to this, hoping that his wife would gain that which he could not provide, then he is complicit, if not in her death, then certainly in her infidelity." He paused thoughtfully. "Cate told Hugh that the child could be his or yours. She gave no one reason to doubt you."

Eldred's jaw worked, but no words came out. Finally, he managed. "I had regard and respect for my wife. Cate . . . riled me often, but the fault was not hers. I had no wish for a wife and if the choice had to be made, would have chosen some woman who could fend for herself. Someone older, wiser. I had little to offer Cate and she soon learned that. For all that I respected her . . . I could not feel desire. I *tried*, Edmund, I tried and I consummated my marriage, but the victory of that was hollow. If she ran to Hugh de Vries, then Treven is right, I must take part of the blame. But I hold that he killed her and the child she carried gave him the more purpose and reason."

"How so?" Treven questioned.

"She could have threatened to name him. Eldred could have demanded compensation." Edmund suggested

"And had she done so, Eldred's secret would be exposed. Hugh had . . . has no reason to suppose a more than half likelihood of the child being his and, if anything, knowing that she was pregnant would have given him further pause." Treven shook his head. "I cannot see Hugh striking down any woman he knew was with child."

"Was he so careful in battle?" Kendryk asked with seeming innocence.

"That question isn't worthy of you," Treven told him sharply. "A man might commit in time of war many acts that haunt him. I do not believe that Hugh, in cold blood, could kill a woman and her unborn child."

"But you admit that my brother is within rights to call him to account?" Edmund demanded.

"I will admit that," Treven agreed. "But I warn you, both of you. Should Hugh see fit to make counter accusation against you, Eldred, then that too must be heard."

"And I will find oath takers enough to confirm my innocence," Eldred replied with equal heat. "Can he expect the same. This stranger?"

Treven scowled at him, but he said nothing more. He turned to Kendryk. "You had better come with me," he said. "Be witness to this."

Kendryk rose and went with Treven to formally inform Hugh de Vries that he had been charged with murder.

CHAPTER 19

BILLINGTON. PRESENT DAY

"Do you know who it was?"

Mouse shook his head painfully. "He came out of the dark," he explained.

"Dark? Mouse you were attacked at three in the afternoon . . ."

"I keep the curtains closed in the back room. He was waiting in the kitchen. The blind was down. I don't like the neighbours peering in."

Rozlyn sighed. "OK, Mouse, so he came out of the kitchen. You were in the back room?" She'd been about to say the mouse room.

"I'd just come in, see. I'd been out to the Co-op and when I got back I could hear them soon as I came in through the door. I knew something were wrong."

"Hear them?"

"My pets. Scared they were, all squealing and squeaking and I felt one run past my foot so I hurried into them and he was there. Waiting."

"Did he say anything? Did you get a look at him?"

"I told you, it was dark. He was big, that's all I can tell. Bigger than me. Tall and wide and his hands . . . he squeezed my arms, picked me right up off the floor like I was a rag doll. Then he chucked me back against the wall. I hit the cages. The cages fell and the poor little blighters, they were everywhere, all over the floor and running around the walls trying to get away. He were bigger than me."

Most people, Rozlyn reflected, were bigger than the Mouse Man. "Did he say anything?" Rozlyn asked again.

Mouse thought about it and then he nodded, wincing in pain. "He were asking about Charlie."

"Charlie?"

"'Where did he put it,' he kept saying. 'Where's Charlie hidden it?'"

"Did he say what Charlie had hidden?"

"No. He seemed to think I knew what he were on about, but I didn't, I swear I never knew."

"It's OK, Mouse. I believe you." Rozlyn thought for a minute. "There's no way Charlie could have hidden anything at your place without you knowing about it? Did he visit often?"

Mouse looked away as though suddenly troubled. Finally, he confessed. "Charlie didn't like to come on account of my little pets. He said the way they smelt made him feel bad. So he never came. We was friends though," he added emphatically, turning to look at Rozlyn once again, peering at her though his half-closed swollen eye. Even through the slits in the bruising Rozlyn could feel the intensity of his gaze.

"I know you were friends," she pacified. "Charlie thought a lot of you, Mouse. He really did."

"He told you that, Inspector Priest?"

Charlie had said no such thing, but he'd always talked about Mouse with a kind of concerned, big brotherly affection — despite the fact that Mouse was probably ten or twenty years his senior.

Rozlyn realised she had no idea how old Mouse Man was. She didn't even know his proper name. She wondered how he'd been registered at the hospital. Jenny had left the ward number in her message, so Rozlyn hadn't had to ask, but surely, he must have another moniker as well as just the Mouse Man?

She made a mental note to ask before she left. Somehow, asking Mouse about his regular name seemed almost insulting.

"Go and see to my pets," Mouse begged her. "They were so scared, like, and the cages were bust open and there's been no one to feed them either."

"I'll see what I can do," Rozlyn soothed him. She'd had the first reports from the SOCO team that morning. They'd talked about a lot of dead mice strewn amongst the outfall from a very untidy search. Rozlyn thought she'd better wait until she'd assessed the situation before telling Mouse any of that. "Look," she said. "I've got to be going. Your house is first stop on my list. I promise."

Mouse looked satisfied and relaxed into the pillows. "I feel so tired, Inspector Priest."

"You get some sleep. I'll be back to talk to you later. See if you can remember anything more about the man that attacked you." She hesitated for a moment. Talking had clearly exhausted the old man and she didn't want to disturb him anymore. Not yet. The ward sister was hovering and Rozlyn didn't think she was above calling security to turf her out if she upset the patient. "Mouse, d'you think this was anything to do with Donovan?"

Mouse's eye flew open and he lifted himself off the pillow with a gasp. "Donovan's a bad man, Inspector Priest. You stay away from him."

"Mouse, I'd stand a better chance of keeping out of his way if I knew where he could be found."

Mouse said nothing, but his pallor had increased and the sister was moving towards him about to shoo Rozlyn away. "Where can I find him, Mouse? Where would I start looking for this Donovan?"

Mouse shook his head as violently as the pain in his head would allow. "I wouldn't know," he said, so fervently that Rozlyn was inclined to believe him. "Charlie warned me about him. Said he was an evil man to rile, but I don't know where to find him out."

"You'd better go," the sister told Rozlyn.

"Yeah, OK, but Mouse, think about anything Charlie said about this Donovan. You think of anything he said, you be sure and tell me."

"I said you'd better go."

Rozlyn held up her hands in mock submission. "I'm going," she said.

The sister escorted her to the ward door just to be sure. "Is there anything he needs?"

"Well, I'd say pyjamas, but if you do decide to bring them, do us all a favour and buy new. I've sealed the clothes he was wearing in double bags. Oh, and toilet articles would be helpful, and magazines and bottled water. He doesn't like the taste of it from the taps."

"Bottled . . . OK, OK, I'll make myself a list. Oh, by the way, I meant to ask. I've only ever known him by his nickname. Does he have a proper one?"

The sister looked vaguely disapproving. "His name," she said, "is Arnold Simmonds and I'm sure Mr Simmonds will be very grateful when you bring those things in."

The sister turned her back on Rozlyn then and let the door close with a thud. Rozlyn found herself on the outside, peering in, watching as she crossed back to Mouse and checked his pulse and his drip stand.

"Arnold Simmonds," she mused. "Ok, Arnold, I wonder what magazines you like to read and if there are any out there on fancy mice."

* * *

The house, never tidy, was now a scene of absolute devastation.

Mouse Man's collection of obsolete electronics had been smashed to small pieces and lay shard sharp across the front-room floor. What hadn't been smashed was toppled sideways in a dangerous-looking pile that threatened any moment to fall on the SOCO working below it.

Blood was smeared across the walls in the doorway of the middle room, pooling on the floor where Mouse had fallen, trailed down the hall floor where he'd dragged himself along. A smeared handprint wrapped around the lower section of the door told Rozlyn that he had pulled it open from there. He must have been attacked even before he'd had time to close the front door, Rozlyn thought. Though that was probably just as well. He'd never have made it to his feet in order to undo the latch. He would have died inside and probably lay undiscovered until someone noticed he'd not been to church or until Rozlyn had another question for him.

She checked with the SOCO that it was OK, then went through into the second room. "Bloody hell!"

"Mess, isn't it. I've counted fifty of them so far. That's the dead ones."

"Any left alive?"

"That cage over there. Another in the kitchen. We fed them. There's a bag of grain and stuff." Rozlyn nodded. The second SOCO was a young woman. Rozlyn had met her a couple of times before and knew she was about halfway through her training.

"Were they killed in the struggle?" she asked. "Or . . ."

She shook her head. "Look at this one. There are more like it all over. Can't say I'm that fond of mice, myself, but whoever did this really had something against the little critters."

Rozlyn crouched down to look at the tiny body and saw what she meant. "Jesus." It had been squashed flat and the remains spread, like road kill across the carpet. The tread from the sole of someone's boot was clearly visible in the blood and flesh that remained.

"Mouse said he nearly trod on one when he came in . . ."

"Mouse?"

"Oh. Arnold Simmonds, the guy who owns this place."

She shook her head. "This wasn't trodden on. This was stomped, then spread around like it was some sort of game."

* * *

Treven had ridden out to the place where Cate's body was found. The sun was coming up, now, reaching that point in the sky where it had strength enough to burn off the heaviest of the dew and was visible above the line of trees. It was hot for the time of year, welcome heat on Treven's back as he crouched beside the track looking at the sign. It eased the knot between his shoulders and the pain lower down from his night of watching, seated in the hard, wooden chair.

The fire in his gut was back and he wished he'd had the foresight to ask Osric for his potion before leaving. The pain was made worse when he did not eat and he had not waited to break his fast, eager, instead to see the place as soon as it was light. Treven knew that a full day had passed since Cate had been found and that any sign he might have found to help him unravel this tangle would be stale or even gone. It had not rained now for three nights, but the dew lay heavy on cold ground and the yellow sky and band of bruised grey cloud he had seen at dawn, caused him to expect rain before the day was out.

The grass had been flattened where Cate had fallen and her blood, moistened again by the dew fall, stained brown when Treven touched it with his fingers. There was a great deal of blood.

"You saw her lying here?"

Ranuf, the charcoal burner, nodded. "I thought she was already dead. Then I saw her breath. The air was cold and her breath misted. I ran for help and brought my brother back with me to carry her home."

"Why delay?" Treven demanded. "The lady was of no weight. You could have carried her home yourself."

The man cast his eyes down. "I should have done, Lord. The truth is, I was so frighted by the scene, I did not think clearly. I thought . . . I thought that the one who'd harmed her would still be close by."

"So you left him to finish her?" Treven snorted his disgust, but the matter would have to wait. He didn't think the fellow's tardiness made much difference to the outcome — Cate would have died anyway — but it seemed unconscionable to have left her lying in the open longer than necessary.

Treven got to his feet and scanned the area. The narrow trackway led off the main path from Theading towards Theadingford. It was about two miles distant from the village, Treven guessed, but the going was rough once the main path had been left behind and could be reached only on foot or by horseback.

Woodland surrounded them. On one side of the trackway it had been cleared and coppiced. Hazel and ash thickets of some three years growth showed careful tending. They would be cut back again next spring and for a season or two the increase in light would allow bramble and nettles to thrive if the woodsman did not keep the ground free. Further back, beyond the stand of birch that stood white in the autumn sun, this year's growth of coppiced wood waved slender branches in the little breeze. The wood was golden, sunlit, tamed, unlike that which stood to Treven's back.

Here, was wild wood. Thickset oak and slender birch. Hazel, grown into a tangle through the branches of the larger trees. Late woodbind filled the air with a heady fragrance and the fierce thorns of brambles guarded the last of the shining berries. At his right hand, where a spring rose and trickled into a shallow stream, the track was lined with *withys* and a single, ancient crack willow, hollow hearted but still full of life. Treven had a deep affection for such trees and was glad that this one, though of no practical use, had been allowed to stand. He knew from boyhood conversations that the withymen often left an old guardian tree like this out of some ancient respect and belief long past words or stories and, Pagan though he supposed this was, Treven was glad the custom seemed to have been followed here.

To his left, the land rose a little and the path curved out of sight beyond the thickness of hedge and tree.

"That way leads only to your home?"

"Mine and my brother's. With our wives and children. Go on further and it leads to Bearwell, though the way is not passable in winter. It crosses a stream which is low enough to ford in summer, but much past *Winterfilleth*, it is impassable."

Treven nodded. It was close to that date now, though the month had been unusually dry. According to his calculations it wanted only three more days to the full moon that marked the beginning of winter.

He stepped away from them and once more scanned the area for sign of what had happened, not easy when the dozen people who had followed him here crowded his every move. Impatiently he waved them back and ordered them to be still. So many trampling feet could blur any rune that might remain. Treven was aware that he was being tried here, as thoroughly as Hugh would be when his turn came. They did not fully understand what it was he did, Treven, king's scout and battle-hardened warrior, used to reading that which might be invisible to others. But they respected the fact that he was here, even though they had heard some whisper that what he sought to do was magic.

"Someone walked there," he pointed and Edmund, standing beside him, followed where he indicated. "The grass is parted and the long reeds beside the withys broken. See?"

Edmund frowned and then nodded. He followed as Treven went to look more closely. "Look," Treven said. "Someone waited here, crouched in the damp. Shod feet and handprints where they leaned down and took their weight."

"They must have crouched low as she passed by," Edmund agreed. "A grown man might just be hidden if he kept his head low." He glanced about, puzzled. "But if it was concealment they sought, why not hide there, among the reeds. They are high as a man's head and dense too. This . . . it looks like something a child might do."

Treven strode over to where he indicated. He lifted a branch from the trackside and prodded the ground.

"Ah," Edmund agreed. "Wet enough to sink to the ankles at least."

"From the point he chose, he could move swiftly," Treven commented. "See her, wait for her to pass, then run out after. She would have heard him and turned."

"So," Edmund seemed reluctant, but perhaps felt he had to be fair minded, "the one who struck her need not have been known to her after all. She would have heard him, turned, and been struck down."

"Possibly," Treven was not convinced. "Look, the ground close to where she fell is wet. Her footprint is there, both pointing up the track towards the cottage and there see, she turns and stands. Both feet set square but facing back towards us."

"Which means she turned and faced her attacker."

"Which means she did not try to run."

"It would have been dark," Edmund mused.

"The moon is close to full, the nights have been clear and her eyes would have been accustomed to the dark, but even so . . . it must have been someone she would recognise at once, otherwise, startled, she would have taken at least a backward step."

He frowned. "It is almost as if she paused and waited. As though she expected someone to be behind her."

Hugh? Had she expected Hugh? Treven walked back down the path and called to the horsemen to come forward. He'd put Orsic and the younger, stronger servant, Strachen in charge of Hugh. They'd not bound him, but Osric had fixed a leading rein to the bridle of Hugh's horse and wrapped it firmly about his wrist. Hugh chafed at such treatment, but Treven had insisted. He could not afford to be seen to show favour, not when he'd declared his interest only in justice.

Hugh dismounted.

"Where did you meet the girl?"

"I told you. I met her there, in that stand of birch. The trees meet well enough to give some shelter and we were screened from the path and the main track."

"You'd met her there before. How many times?"

Hugh sighed heavily. "Five or six." He looked uncomfortable speaking before Edmund and the others. "Treven, for pity's sake, the girl is dead; must you drag her name through the mud, questioning me here before such witnesses?

"Her name was soiled long ago. You think it a secret, Hugh? Now, tell me, did you see anyone. Hear anything?"

Hugh shook his head. "I had hoped . . . she would have nothing to do with me. Struck my hand down when I tried to touch her. She said she would have no more to do with me. Told me about the child she carried and that she had informed her husband that he would be a father before *Litha* came next year. I was angry with her but I let her go. I returned to Theading and spent my night elsewhere. She was whole and unharmed when she left my side."

"It did not seem right that you take her back to Theading? You say you spent time after with another woman, you must have passed Cate's home, yet you left her here to find her own way back?"

Hugh was furious. "She swore she would not let me accompany her. That she had promised Eldred it was over between us and that if we were witnessed together it could be seen as her breaking that vow." He stepped forward, hands outstretched, voice pleading. "Treven, what else could I do? She went from me, I untied my horse and went on my way."

"Did you not pass her on the road?" Edmund asked.

Hugh hesitated, then shook his head. "No, but you are right, I should have done. God, had I realised then the significance of that, I might have found her."

Treven watched his friend with narrowed eyes. There was much here that Hugh had not told, but for the moment Treven could not fathom the truth from the lies. The cramp in his gut had receded a little but it returned now and it was all he could do to stay upright and not double in pain. He caught his breath, hoping no one had noticed, but was aware of Hugh watching him closely.

"Come," Treven said. "We will return to the Theading. I wish to examine the body now there is light enough to see."

* * *

Treven had Cate's body carried outside so that the full light of the sun could illuminate his search. He had the villagers assembled and with them but kept Hugh and Eldred well apart. Eldred was distressed. The women waited to prepare his wife for burial, but Treven had forbidden this until he returned. Eldred could not understand his reasons and it had been left to Kendryk to convince him that Treven must have good cause.

"At least, I hope you have," the Abbot told him sternly. "It's enough the poor child was killed so brutally, but for you to delay the proper rights becomes less and less forgivable the longer you take."

"I know, I know," Treven waved his protests away, "but when Osric tended her last night I glimpsed something I could not understand. I will hide nothing, Kendryk, which is why I call for this public display, distasteful though I know it is. In truth, I hope to shock some kind of response from one or other of them. I doubt either is telling the full truth."

Kendryk looked displeased but nodded assent. "I've told her father," he said. "Though I doubt the poor fool understood a word. I think we should spare him this exhibition, unless you have some purpose in his being here?"

Treven could not think of one. He came down the steps with Kendryk at his side and stood by Cate. She had been laid out on the trestle table brought from the hall. Her limbs had begun to stiffen and Treven knew that he would have to be swift so that the women could do their work before her body became too rigid to move. Her long dark hair was loose and Edmund stood at her head, his fingers straying through the long strands, his face empty of all thought. Treven observed him for a moment, thinking it strange that it should be the older brother and not the husband who stood like this, stroking the woman's hair. He recalled the rumours concerning Allis and wondered if there might be another reason Edmund was glad to be rid of her. Did he love his brother's wife?

Glancing at Eldred he saw that his gaze too was fixed upon his brother's hands, but there was no question in his eyes, just a deep and utter sadness.

Gently, Treven tilted Cate's chin and turned her head. Beside him, he heard Kendryk draw sharp breath. To confirm what he saw he moved her head again, this time exposing the neck on the other side, then he looked sideways to where Hugh and Eldred stood watching. On Eldred's face was a look of anger, incomprehension. But Hugh . . . as Hugh met his eyes, Treven realised that his friend knew exactly what he saw.

Treven snapped his gaze away and moved his hands onto Cate's arms. Her clothes were grimed with blood and earth but untorn. He lifted her hands, examining the nails. They were trimmed short. Ragged nails caught on the spindle thread and snagged the yarn, so she had kept them well. But beneath the middle and first fingers of her right hand was a rime of dirt.

Treven drew his knife and with the tip, scraped beneath Cate's fingernails, then wiped the stuff he found there on his palm. He spat, watching the red brown seep from the grime. Lifting his palm to his lips, he tasted it, his gaze fixed now on the two men he judged.

Eldred registered puzzlement and disgust. Hugh jerked his head, then returned Treven's gaze with a steadiness forced by sheer will.

Treven spat upon the ground.

"Blood?" Kendryk asked, curiosity fighting mild distaste.

"Is it blood, Hugh? Did she do more than slap your hands away?"

The crowd moved restlessly and Hugh took an instinctive step towards Treven and where Cate's body lay.

"I did not kill her." He spoke slowly as though trying to convince a child. "And look, no marks on my hands or my face and, should you find marks on my back, they come not from Cate but from the other one."

"The other one that you have yet to name."

"You'd have me do that here? In the face of her neighbours, kinsmen. *Weaponmann*?"

"So, another married woman," Treven said. Kendryk laid a hand upon his arm.

"I think," he said, "that in this Hugh has the right. The woman should not be publicly named. Hugh may name her privately and we will call each woman in this community to the hall and speak with them, so she not be singled out."

Treven scowled. "A priest that condones adultery!"

"A priest that puts the health of a community before need for vengeance," Kendryk told him sharply. "As well you should."

Treven made some small gesture of disgust, but he nodded assent. "If that is your guidance," he said. "I will accept it. Tell the women they can prepare the body." He made as though to go inside, then turned again and strode over to where Hugh stood. He laid hold of Hugh's hair and tugged his head forward, turning it left and right so that he could see his neck then pulled the tunic aside to expose his shoulders.

"I told you," Hugh was panicked now and the crowd about him moved restlessly. "It was the other one."

"She marked him!" Eldred sounded triumphant. He lunged forward. Treven wheeled, blocked him, knocking him off his feet.

"Stay down!" He let his gaze rove across the crowd. He could both see and feel their anger. This stranger had killed one of their own and they wanted nothing more or less than vengeance. Osric had drawn his seax and came to stand beside Treven, the long knife raised in his hand. Treven closed his fist over his servant's hand. "Put it away," he said softly. "I'll see justice and law served here, not the rule of the mob. Now, go to your homes. Hugh, go inside and Osric, keep him close confined."

"Confined! Treven, I swear, I did not kill her!"

"It will take more than *your* oath to prove innocence," Eldred growled.

Hugh swung about. "You had more reason to see her dead than I ever could or did," he whispered furiously. He faced the crowd, his face white with panic and distress. "I did not take her life. You seek a murderer? Look no further than a man deceived by his wife. I accuse you, Eldred. Accuse you before all witnessed here present. I accuse you of Cate's murder and that of her unborn child."

Treven looked from one to the other, a small doubt creeping back into his mind. "Go inside," he said softly. "Your accusation has been made and both will be answered." He gestured once again towards the crowd. "Now get you gone. You've work to do and families to care for. Go now!"

He waited until they had dispersed — all but the small knot of hovering women waiting to prepare their dead one. He looked one last time at Cate, remembering her as she had been on that first day. Bright, hopeful, nervous as a new-born deer. Treven stared at her until the image of Cate, living and breathing, shyly smiling and beautiful, replaced that of the corpse with smashed face and gaping wounds, then he left the women to their work.

CHAPTER 20

Rozlyn knew officers who enjoyed post-mortems. Their reasons were many and varied. Some were simply curious; some awed by the complexity of the process and the insight it afforded into the act of death and dying. Others — and Brook fell into this category — saw them as a rite of passage to be gone through as soon as possible on joining the force and repeated as often as necessary as a sort of system check to make sure you weren't going soft.

Rozlyn fell into none of those categories. Mortality was not something she required any reminder of and the methodical invasion of the human body was not something she ever could enjoy, even as an intellectual exercise.

She made herself attend because it was necessary to the efficiency of the job and because she didn't think she could cope with Brooke's jibes should she cop out.

Unlike those situations depicted in fiction it was quite rare for a body to jump the queue and be examined in the first hours after its discovery. While every effort was made to bump the victims of violence up the list, sometimes, especially when the cause of death was so evident, it was impossible. There were only so many hours in the day and so many pathologists to carry out the work. So, Charlie had to wait his turn.

This PM was one Rozlyn had dreaded. Charlie Higgins laid out on the stainless-steel table, naked and defenceless and with a large wound in the centre of his chest that shook Rozlyn badly. She leaned nonchalantly against the row of cupboards that ran the length of the room and watched from a respectable distance, coming closer only when directed by the man in charge.

"There's not a doubt about the murder weapon, then?"

"Not a dicky bird of doubt. Want to see? There's been some tissue shrinkage, of course, but . . ."

Before Rozlyn could protest that, no, she'd take the word of the expert, Chitall, the pathologist, had seized the weapon and begun its slow and careful insertion into the wound in Charlie's chest.

"Come closer. You can't see a damn thing from there. Now, look at the angle."

With the utmost care, Chitall pushed the spear head home, sheathing it for a second time in Charlie's flesh. "Of course, the force would have been greater than I'm applying. A single thrust, that was all it took, nicked the sternum and penetrated the heart. The cartilage attaching the rib did nothing to impede the progress. Whoever made this knew what they were doing, all right." He eased it home, then stood back, triumphant. "Look, do you see it now?" He ran a finger along the haft that still protruded from the wound. "See it, see the angle?"

Rozlyn hadn't taken it in. She'd been too busy feeling nauseous, fighting the red mist that blurred her vision and trying to swallow the bile rising in her throat. Then she saw what Chitall was getting at. The angle of attack didn't make sense unless . . . "He was on the ground. He was already down."

Chitall beamed at her.

"But how? I mean, his assailant would practically have had to be sitting on him. That would have been such an awkward strike."

Chitall was shaking his head.

"What am I missing?"

"The shaft."

"Shaft? There is no shaft."

"No, but there was."

"How do you know? If there was a shaft, why didn't it break off inside the neck of the spear."

"I know because I've found traces of it inside the neck, here," He pointed. "And it didn't break because when whoever did this tried to pull it out, it came away clean."

"How? Why?"

At that Chitall shrugged. "Speculation only," he said. "But the wood was common or garden stuff. Heavy dowel, probably. The kind you can find in any DIY superstore. I'm guessing it was used just for display. It'd been stained, there were fragments of that present too, and it probably looked good enough for show. It wasn't intended to stay in place well enough for you to stick someone, just to look pretty when its owner hung it on the wall, or however you'd display such an object."

That made a kind of sense. "Any other injury? Was he punched, kicked? How did he end up on the ground?"

Chitall shrugged again. "Anybody's guess," he said. "But he's not exactly a big fellow. A good push would have done as well as anything and there's micro bruising on the shoulders that might indicate that. But however he ended up on the floor, there's no doubt what stopped him getting up again."

Rozlyn nodded, her gaze fixed on that obscene conjunction between flesh and metal. "Would there have been much blood?"

"Depends if the assailant tried to pull the spear out at once or some time after and I'd go for the latter option. There's evidence . . . don't worry, I can show you that on the X-ray, you don't have to look inside. Here, evidence of a second, shorter strike. The bone carries a second, much smaller notch, see?"

Rozlyn nodded. "So, you're saying . . . you're speculating that his killer stabbed him then when he tried to pull the thing out, he only got the wooden handle. So, he, maybe, tried to get it out by hand . . ."

"And the rocking motion of either attempt would have notched the sternum for a second time, yes."

"So, it would have made sense to leave it in place until the body had been dumped." She frowned. "What I don't get is, if you go to the trouble of stealing an object like this, then to the further trouble of pulling it out of the wound, why chuck it away?"

"Why indeed? Sorry, I can't help you there. People, as you know, do some strange things under stress. It could be that the assailant suddenly realised how unique this is and that it could be identified."

"Then why dump it where it's sure to be found? No, that doesn't work." She considered for a moment. "So. How much blood?"

"No exit wound," Chitall told her, "so very little mess. The weapon itself would have plugged the hole, so to speak."

"So," Rozlyn was thinking aloud now. "At the murder scene, there'd have been very little cleaning up to do."

"Trace, of course, but if you're looking for puddles of blood you'll be unlucky." He went over to Charlie's body and withdrew the spearhead. Rozlyn winced. "I'll give it a wash for you and you'll have to sign the book. Where are you taking it anyway?"

"To show a man called Ethan Merrill in Stamford. He's an expert." She winced again as Chitall cleaned the object down with soap and a nail brush. She wasn't sure what the procedure was for cleaning ancient weaponry but was pretty sure that wasn't it.

"Don't worry," Chitall told her, misinterpreting her reaction. "I'm not destroying evidence. We've got everything we can from the little beauty."

Beauty, Rozlyn thought as Chitall dried it with paper towels and stuffed it into a plastic bag. She felt the weight of it in her hands as Chitall handed it to her and looked closely at the intricate patterns weaving across the surface. Yes, she supposed it was beautiful. Exquisite and deadly . . . and now smelling of anti-bacterial hand cleaner. Ethan Merrill would have a fit.

"Ok, then, thanks," she said. Steeling herself, she went back to stand beside Charlie's corpse and gently, touched the dead man's hand.

"I'll take good care of your friend," Chitall said. "Any idea who'll be claiming the body or is it a social security job?"

Rozlyn hadn't thought about it. She shook her head. "I really don't know," she said. "Just hold fire until you hear from me, OK?"

Chitall shrugged once more. Left shoulder slightly higher than right this time. "Plenty of room at the inn," he said. She left, thinking that Mouse would want to come to the funeral and Mrs Chinowski and maybe that old man at the Larks too, if they thought he was OK to go out . . . and Mrs C would need a new cleaner now Clara had disappeared and . . .

Laughing, Rozlyn shook her head, reminding herself that these people were not her responsibility. She could inform social services and let them take over.

The laughter died almost before it reached her lips and she glanced back towards the building where Charlie's body now lay. "It's OK," she told him softly. "I'll see they're taken care of. Promise."

CHAPTER 21

Treven sat close to the doorway and watched as Kendryk read through the documents his scribe handed to him. They appeared to be deeds of land; bequests left to the Abbey and features of land, left idle after too many battles, that Kendryk had adjoined to Abbey lands. It was not lost on Treven that he had applied for the same rights over his land at Theadingford and been denied.

Was Kendryk making a point? Treven was unsure but listening to the quiet conversation between Kendryk and his scribe, Treven was struck by the man's knowledge of the district and his understanding of land use. His questions were detailed and precise and twice now Treven had noted that sharp look when his scribe failed to give an adequate response and had seen the man quail beneath it.

"That land floods come winter. Come *Blotmonath* it is beneath water, often until the time of *Eastermonath*. Should Nerian be sincere in his desire to gift, then he should gift land that can be of use."

"Should I return his promise to him?" the scribe asked.

Kendryk considered the matter. "No," he said. "Amend the promise. Tell him that I accept his gift to Christ of fertile land, and of the labour required to dig drainage. We can use it then for winter grazing."

Treven chuckled softly, wondering if he should feel pity for the unfortunate Nerian or if such punishment was deserved.

"And this, the land named as belonging to Renweard. The man stood surety for his brother?"

The scribe nodded. "His brother was accused of theft. Renweard stood as surety until he should repay the amount claimed."

"As I recall, the theft was in question. Some said it was a debt from gambling."

"That was said, but Renweard held that it should be paid if owed, despite it being owed to one, Odi, known to have default of character. The brother has now fled, leaving Renweard with both debt and his brother's son to raise. He had appealed to Odi for time to pay, but Odi will have none of it. The Shire Courts have sent the matter to you, Lord Abbot, as the original surety was witnessed by the Abbey."

"Then my judgement is this," Kendryk said. "That the land thus indebted should be created *Fosterlean*, property held in trust, and given back to Redweard in return for the raising of his brother's child. On Redweard's death it shall be counted *Mortmain*, Dead Man's Land and given to the child in full. Should any child remain of Odi's line, then a tithe should be paid to them until the debt is serviced — and be sure it is noted what this comprises, we will suffer no arguments at some later date. This way, the debt will be honoured but the innocent should have no need to suffer for another's fault."

He got up from his chair and strode towards the flagon of small beer set out on the chest beside Cate's baskets of yarn.

"That will do for now. Have that written, then return to me with the scrip. If I am satisfied, you can have the copies made."

The other bowed his head and left. The hall was now empty of all but Treven and Kendryk.

"You are an unusual man," Treven noted.

"Unusual for a churchman or just unusual?"

"Both, I would say."

Kendryk drank deep and refreshed Treven's cup before refilling his own. "The day trails towards dusk," he commented. "I think it time to change to stronger ale."

He went to the steps and gave an order to one outside. "It is time for food, also," he said. "A man cannot think well on an empty stomach."

"What happens when you fast?" Treven asked. "Do your thoughts fail you then?"

"*My* thoughts," Kendryk told him, "never fail me. Others are not so fortunate. Most men require a nourished body to think clearly and it is not my belief that God wished any man to starve." This last was said softly and with a feeling that had nothing, Treven felt, to do with the present conversation.

"And now," Kendryk settled himself in the throne-like chair once more. "How are we to resolve this? You have spent the afternoon in thought, what conclusions have you come to?"

"That there was another reason for Eldred wishing Cate dead, once her sister was gone."

"The land," Kendryk confirmed. "He and Edmund will inherit, of course. Add this estate to their own, such as it is."

"Tell me."

"The land the brothers own is fertile but takes more skill at management than either of them has. In these past years much more has been brought under cultivation, but that was Allis's doing. She divided it into small parcels, a hide or so in each and set cottagers to live thereon and work the land. They pay their tithe, but thereafter, for the most part, need little from their lord in order to survive which, as you must know, takes strain from the shoulders in lean times. Wisely, she has set the tithe in terms of labour. The ditches she had dug have drained the fields and brought more into use and at the eastern end of their property, she had planted hedge and tree to break the wind from the fenlands. You remember, I am sure, how the North wind strikes cold when it blows across the water. We feel its force even this far inland."

"And how did the brothers react to this management?"

"Edmund was wise enough to welcome it. The mother, Allis and Cate's mother, was a woman of great wisdom and immense strength of will. She raised her children in the same mould, though little Cate was not by nature like to her mother and sister. She favoured the father, may the good Lord bless him."

"And Eldred, did he take this calmly?"

"Eldred rages against the slightest restraint, but he had sense enough to accept what must be done and the brothers have prospered by it. You know that the brothers took the women's name of Scrivener when they married. Tillian insisted upon that before agreeing to the marriage of Aliss. He wished his name preserved. He drew up a will that ensured their direct inheritance."

"A reason, perhaps, for the brothers to want rid of their women?"

Kendryk shook his head. "Less, in fact," he said. "There is another child. A third sister."

"A third? I have heard no mention of this."

"She is a mere babe," Kendryk told him. "Fathered by Tillian just after his wife's death. He confessed it and his family knew though the knowledge is not widely spread abroad. The woman is widowed, as was Tillian I believe at the time of the babe's conception. He has directed that she should have her share of the inheritance."

"And was he in his right mind when this child was conceived?" Treven enquired.

Kendryk pursed his thin lips. "That point is moot," he said. "Aliss doubted." He looked shrewdly at Treven. "Do not fear, King's Thegn. I will see that the child is kept safe. Whatever the matter of her conception, she is still entitled to her land."

Treven frowned but let the matter pass. There were more pressing needs to deal with. "And Aliss was unhappy enough to run away," Treven mused.

"So it seems. Even wise women can be foolish in matters of the heart. Men too for that matter."

They fell silent for a moment, waiting while food and drink were brought and Kendryk bade the servants depart. Treven pulled his chair closer to the fire and table.

"The marks on Cate's neck. They showed the grip of strong fingers, Treven. Is your Reeve capable of strangling a woman?"

Treven carved meat before replying. "Hugh left those marks," he said slowly. "Of that, I am certain. I watched his face and his eyes betrayed him. He knew what I would find."

"You think they quarrelled and he tried to kill her?"

"Had Hugh sincerely meant her death, she would have died, I think." He took a bite of meat and bread and then shook his head. "But no. There is a reverse of that argument. Had Hugh held back, realised she still lived; he must have known she would name him. He could have fled, instead he returned to his bed."

"Perhaps he thought he had done enough. In panic mistakes are made and Hugh could well have believed that he had killed her. To flee would have been to admit his guilt. So, he lay down to sleep then showed surprise at the manner of her death."

Treven nodded. "If she recovered consciousness and found him gone . . . she must have known that the charcoal burner lived but a little further on the path. If Hugh then saw her, living, about to raise the cry, he would have had no choice."

"He had choice," Kendryk argued. "Had he pleaded that his passion got the better of him. That she angered him and he did not know what he did, he could have pled manslaughter. He is a man of rank, and, one presumes, by those trinkets he wears, of wealth. He could have paid her blood price and be done with it. For that matter, he still could.

Eldred is out for vengeance, but the court could uphold Hugh's right to pay *Ficht-wite* and the matter be ended. You would, of course, have to send him from you and appoint another in his place."

Treven nodded slowly. "There are two men here accused according to *Folkright*," he reminded Kendryk, "and, according to that common law, both must answer charges."

"Eldred will swear his oath," Kendryk shrugged. "He will have no trouble finding a dozen men to be his oath helpers. Could Hugh find the same?"

"It could be done. We would have to send to his kin folk, or to the King. Enough still serve him that knew Hugh in times of war. They would swear an oath for him."

"But you are reluctant to have that done?"

Treven did not reply at once, he tore chunks from the bread and chewed slowly. Staring into the fire, he sought inspiration and clarity in the licking, leaping flames. Finally, he said. "I am reluctant on two counts. The first is that it would look to the King and to Hugh's kin that I cannot manage my own affairs here and must appeal for help. *You* might welcome that, but I would not. For the second; words are cheap. It has been known even for a man of honour to perjure himself on oath."

"But such instances are rare," Kendryk pointed out. "Most men believe their oath to be sworn before God. It is more than their honour or their soul is worth to swear false."

"And if I sent for Hugh's kinsmen or battle companions, they could swear with clear conscience that they'd know him to be brave and true and honourable. In battle, in all of those aspects of his life that they would deem precious, he has done no wrong. They would swear to his good character, not to the fact that he did not kill Cate."

"Is that all your reason?" Kendryk pushed him.

Treven shook his head. "No," he admitted. "I believe that at least the marks on her throat are Hugh's doing. If he did *not* kill her then it was by default."

"And the blows to the head?"

"If we see guilt in the one action, then the other has to follow." He pushed his food away and pressed a hand hard against the fierce pain in his belly.

"What ails you?" Kendryk asked him.

"Pain in the gut. It is nothing. Osric has made a potion for me."

Kendryk said nothing but continued to watch as Treven tried to ease his discomfort. "So," he said finally. "You will persuade him to pay the blood price and then send him packing?"

"I will try. I will stand surety for him until such funds can be raised."

Kendryk laughed aloud. Treven glared at him, irritated by his contempt but the sight was also a disturbing one, that skeletal face, split-mouthed as though a death's head cackled.

"I have said something to amuse you?"

"Eldred will want gold, not surety. And you, Lord Treven, King's Thegn, what do you own?"

"I have my land," Treven told him heatedly "and my sword and horse and sheep and cattle too. I own a hall and two books . . ."

"Two? Riches indeed. Maybe I misjudge you." He dropped the mocking tone and leaned forward across the table. "Treven, you hold land at the King's discretion and we all know the moods of kings are fickle. The sheep, I believe are strays from my Abbey farm . . ."

"Which strayed onto my land. They were there when I found them and no mark to say otherwise."

"We will let the sheep pass. The cattle, I grant you were bought free and fair and the farmer is gleeful that he will neither have to fodder them through winter nor have the trouble of salting their meat and, come Litha, when the poor of the district come to their lord for extra bread and apportion of meat, he too will be there with his hand held out for his share of those cattle you paid him for. The man stands to benefit twice. And as to your horse, he's seen more winters than that threadbare cloak of yours. Your horse keeps his feet by sheer force of will, love of his master and, no doubt, the herbs Osric adds to his feed that make him feel he is a colt again."

"The King has promised me two brood mares come *Eostre* time."

"You think your horse will have the strength to cover them? Osric will need to dose him well. Your sword, I grant, is a worthwhile thing. A swordsmith of great craft and worth made that, but I know too you'd as soon lose your life or that of Hugh de Vries as give that up." He sat back in his seat. "Send to his kinsmen, have them pay Cate's blood price or make Hugh sacrifice some of that finery he wears. The brooch with which he fastens his cloak, alone would come close to fulfilling his pledge."

"Whatever happens," Treven said slowly, "Hugh must leave this place."

"Too true. He has kinsmen in the south that will welcome him back?"

"They will welcome him, but I doubt he'd want to return."

"How so?"

Treven couldn't help but laugh at the absurdity. "They wish him to enter the Church," he said. "As a younger son he was destined always for the Abbey. He could rise high in the ranks there, his family are wealthy and have powerful friends."

"The Lord preserve us," Kendryk said fervently. "Still, at least he'd be in the right place to repent." He didn't sound hopeful of that happening. "Go to Hugh, tell him to confess his guilt. I will ensure that Eldred waits until the gelt can be raised and then I'll arrange for escort home to Kent. I do not trust Eldred or his friends not to look for vengeance, even after the blood price is paid."

CHAPTER 22

Rozlyn was half an hour from her destination when her phone rang. It was Brook.

"Where the hell are you?"

"I'm . . ."

"Never mind, Get your arse back here, pronto."

"Why?"

"Apart from the fact that I said so? We're raiding the house on Curzon Street. One of those your friend told you about."

"What! Now?"

"Yes, Now. One of those fancy people carriers turned up an hour ago, crammed to the gunnels. We want them before they've a chance to scarper. Meet me there."

He rang off leaving Rozlyn to wonder if you could really cram a people carrier to the gunnels and what gunnels were anyway?

On a country road the task was now to find a place to turn around. A farm gate a mile further on afforded the opportunity if not quite the space. She dived in and then wriggled the car into a reasonable position for take-off. The farm gate was just past a bend in the road, she'd have to make the turn in one or risk something coming around the bend and broadsiding her. Reversing until her back bumper touched the gate, she made ready to be off, glancing, more from habit than fear of anything behind, into the rear view.

"What the hell?" She blinked and looked again, then got out of her car and stared hard across the broad, stubble field.

There was no one and yet, just for that instant she had been certain. She had seen Ethan Merrill together with that tall, red-haired man she had dreamed about at the dig site.

Rozlyn got back into the car, unable to shake off the feeling of disorientation. On impulse, she pulled a road map out from beneath the seat and traced with her finger the road she had just travelled, then, as best she could, tracked across country towards the dig site. A mile, maybe two across the fields, that was it. With all the bends and twists in the rural road, she had lost touch with its proximity. Could Ethan have gone there? Could he then have walked across that particular field just in time for Rozlyn to see him and with that other one too . . . the odds would have taken Douglas Adams to calculate.

"You need a holiday," Rozlyn told herself. She had plenty of time owing that she never seemed to take and it was well overdue for her to go back across the pond to see her grandfather. Leave it too long, she reminded herself, and it might well be too late.

Impatient now with these imaginings, she swung the car back onto the road, cursing the inadequate lock that meant, despite her misgivings, she had to reverse and take a second bite. Rozlyn checked the road and glanced again into the rear-view mirror, then yelped in shock.

Turning to look into the back seat, she reassured herself that it was empty, but in that instant she had glanced into the mirror it had seemed that deep blue eyes had been staring back.

She'd stalled the car and was half blocking the carriageway. A horn blared loud and painful as a 4x4 hurtling round the bend had to track onto the verge to get around.

"What the fuck?" Rozlyn's hands were shaking and her breathing ragged and painful. She managed to restart the car and complete the manoeuvre, driving away slowly until she regained control, her entire body shaking as though she had a fever.

The phone rang again. It was Brook, demanding to know how long she was going to be.

"As long as it bloody takes," Rozlyn told him angrily and rang off before Brook could say another word.

* * *

As it happened, Rozlyn arrived in time to see Brook and a dozen other officers escort a group of frightened people from the Curzon Street house.

"Oh, turned up at last, have we? Get in there and give Jenny a hand. Second floor."

With what? Rozlyn wanted to ask, but Brook was already yelling at someone else, so she decided not to bother. The house was cold: the radiator in the hall freezing to the touch, the stairs uncarpeted. Her footsteps echoed.

Jenny was in a second-floor bedroom with another officer, trying to make a young woman understand that they did not intend to hurt her. Crouched in a corner, she clutched something tightly to her chest refusing to move. Jenny knelt facing her. The bare boards were scuffed and worn, badly laid where they'd been lifted at some time for plumbing or wiring to be installed and the wood beneath Jenny's knees was sharply splintered. Thread from her black trousers had caught, Rozlyn noticed, and the edges of the board made a hole in the knee. As she shifted position to get closer to the woman, she noted too the smear of blood she left behind.

"You've hurt yourself."

"It's these bloody boards. It doesn't matter, but these were a good pair of trousers."

"Send the bill to Brook. What's going on here?"

"We got the rest out. This one panicked and ran back upstairs. I don't know what she thinks we're going to do."

"We're police," Rozlyn said. "Who the hell knows what that means wherever she came from. She looks frozen."

"Not surprised. It's colder in here than outside. God knows when this place last had the heating on."

"Obviously, our mysterious Mr T is a thrifty bastard."

She moved forward and dropped down beside Jenny so she too was eye level with the woman and extended her hands slowly thinking that if Jenny couldn't get through to her, she very much doubted her own chances. "It's OK," she said softly. "No one will hurt you. No one will do anything you don't want them to."

"Except send her back," Jenny muttered beneath her breath.

"Except that," Rozlyn agreed. "Come on now, let's go somewhere warm. Are we getting a translator sent?"

"If we can figure out what language she speaks."

"Good point. I'm surprised Brook didn't just drag her out."

"The press have been tipped off. One of the neighbours spotted us when we came in. Hard not to, we made enough noise. Brook is of the opinion that a photographer is bound to show up the moment we appear on the steps carrying our unwilling victim here. Wouldn't look good. Even Brook gets a bit sensitive these days."

"Brook, sensitive!"

"Wants his full pension in three years' time, doesn't he? Anything untoward that could force early retirement and Brook wicks off and leaves someone else, namely us, to take the flak."

"I have to say, your opinion of our beloved leader leaves something to be desired."

Jenny grinned, then turned back to the woman. "Come on," she gestured, shifting just a little closer. "Let's get somewhere warm, get some food." She gestured eating and drinking and the woman moaned as though she were in pain.

"You think she's all right?

"I think she's just scared."

The bundle in her arms moved.

"Oh my God, she's got a baby." Jenny leaned towards her and the woman edged away crying out in panic.

"Hush now," Rozlyn spoke softly. She moved sideways, blocking the woman in case she should make a sudden break for the door. She couldn't get far but she'd rather not have to chase this frightened woman carrying her tiny child down those godawful steep stairs. "Hush now," she said again. "Shhh. Don't cry." Her voice had taken on an almost sing-song quality, like a parent comforting a child woken with nightmares. She inched forward. "Hush now, sweet, nothin's goin' to harm you." The words were her grandmother's, the rhythm too. "Nothin' bad. You come with me."

The woman was watching, but she was silent now, observing Rozlyn with wide, round, brown eyes. She clasped the baby closer, pulling the blanket round it when it moved again. Rozlyn was so close now she could feel the nervous, half-drawn breath upon her own skin. She leaned in and looked down at the baby. "Oh, she's so sweet. Does she have a name?" She reached out and, with one finger, stroked the baby's cheek. The woman whimpered, shifted even further into her corner.

"Hush, now," Rozlyn told her again. "Let's go somewhere we can both get warm."

She extended one hand and, reluctantly, the woman took it and permitted Rozlyn to raise her to her feet and lead her towards the door. They took the stairs slowly, Jenny bringing up the rear, Rozlyn leading, still holding the woman's hand. Now that she'd allowed that touch, she didn't seem ready to let go.

The cameras, as Brook predicted, were on hand when they reached the front door. Brook would be proud, Rozlyn reflected as she helped the woman into the car, Jenny beside her. The human, multi-ethnic side of policing would make it onto the front page and earn him a few brownie points.

She stepped back onto the pavement and watched the car drive away, then faced the chilly representatives of the local press ranged before her. She knew them all, greeted them by name. Carl from the *Mail* and Rob from the *Rutland and District*. "You got a new photographer, Rob?"

"Yes, Frankie, joined us a month ago. Got a statement Inspector?"

"Hi Frankie. Pleased to meet you. Be sure and get my best side now. Not much to tell, I'm afraid. I arrived late and missed most of it."

"Ooh, you'll be getting a tardy mark for that."

Rozlyn laughed. "OK, we think we have a network bringing illegal immigrants into the country. We think they're from Eastern Europe, presumably some country not yet part of the EU or they could apply for work visas and come here legitimately." She shrugged. "Until we've interviewed them, I can't even tell you their nationality. That's about it really. I'm as ignorant as you lot."

There was a murmur of good-natured grumbling, but they'd got their pictures and their statements and Rozlyn knew they were perfectly capable of building the rest of the story for themselves. In fact, she suspected there might even be resentment if she didn't confer that opportunity.

Rozlyn allowed one more photo and then made her way back to the car, hoping no one noticed that she checked the back seat before getting inside.

CHAPTER 23

"I had a wife and son," Treven was not drunk, exactly, but was certainly well on the road to that destination. Kendryk, though he'd matched him cup for cup, showed no sign.

"What happened to them?"

"Raiders came, wiped out my family, drove off the livestock. Took over my land."

"Where were you?"

"Away on the King's business. They died in springtime. It was near winter before I knew of it."

"And what pains you most, that you did not know or that you were absent from them when they needed you?"

"Both," Treven said shortly. He drank deep, first of the mead and then from the jug of steeped herbs Osric had placed beside him. The two battled, both in his mouth and his belly. "We should summon Hugh," he said.

"You stated such an hour ago. Two hours ago."

"Which?"

"Both."

"Oh." Treven fell silent. They had argued the matter from all angles and Kendryk had finally delivered a solution, though it was not one Treven liked. "My Grandsire traced his lineage back to Wotan himself. My mother too, kept faith with his gods, though she said the prayers of Christ also, to honour my father's wishes."

"As does Guthrum no doubt."

"He is no longer Guthrum. You should know that, Priest. He took another name. A Christian name."

"So he did," Kendryk leaned forward and refilled both their cups. He lifted the jug containing Osric's stomach medicine and sniffed. "Water mint, vervain. I cannot tell what else."

Treven shrugged. "Ask him. His mother taught him the skill. She died also when the invaders came. Do you believe in Guthrum's conversion?"

"It is not my place to believe, only to accept," Kendryk told him sententiously.

Treven eyed him with suspicion "And that means?"

"It means that the King was wise to give a cornered beast a way of escape. He avoided Guthrum's teeth and Guthrum avoided dishonour."

"Or death. Aelfred would have killed him."

"Would that have troubled Guthrum? I think not. He is a man raised in the shadow of death. For that matter, so is Aelfred. If either feared it even for a moment they would crush such thoughts beneath a shoe heel, but both he and Aelfred knew that to kill Guthrum would give only reason and space for another to rise in his place. Conversion was convenient. Guthrum will say the words that he must say and keep his own counsel in his heart."

"And you approve of that?"

"I see the expediency of it. In the end, God will judge. Thankfully, we can offer up that final responsibility to him."

Treven fell silent. To offer final judgement of Hugh to the Almighty was exactly what Kendryk had earlier proposed. All Father, Treven breathed, not knowing at that moment which version of God he addressed, should I permit this? Guide me now.

"I measure the man by his strength in battle and his courage," Treven said slowly. "Twice my life has been saved by Hugh's skill and three times I have kept him from death. Many others, too numerous to count, have we watched the other's back and fought odds I choose not to remember."

"Then you are an unusual man," Kendryk returned Treven's earlier observation to him.

"How so?"

"Most men choose not only to recall the odds, but to double those they met in battle."

Treven snorted. "When I am certain that the land is at peace and I have solved this dilemma with Hugh, then I will find a *scop* worthy of the name who can sing of my glory in battle, and he may raise the odds to suit his song. You'll forgive me if I wait a season or two meantime."

"I will forgive you that. But I must insist on an invitation to your new built hall and a place of honour at your feast. I would hear the lay of Treven of Theadingford."

"You can mock, Priest."

"Indeed I can. It is a skill I seek, daily, to perfect."

Treven's laughter exploded, disturbing the peace of the monks who slept beside the door. "How did you become a man of God?" he demanded. "You are as unsuited to the task as Hugh would be."

Kendryk nodded slowly. "I have learnt to make the best of it," he said. "Something I believe Hugh could never do. As to how? The way is similar. I am a younger son of a Frankish father. To avoid conversion by the sword at the hands of the Holy Emperor, his father, my grandsire, spoke the words of conversion and promised a son to the church. The first of each generation were kept, to be heir to their lands. The second they gave to God. I was a boy of six when I left my home. I've seen nothing of it since."

Treven stared at him. "I hope you have no such children at that Abbey of yours. A *man* may choose to make peace and settle to the holy life, but a child or a boy should be allowed to grow as the gods intended."

Kendryk raised an eyebrow, but Treven seemed unaware or uncaring of his slip. "Sometimes," he said softly, "it is better for a child to be homed with the brothers than unwanted and ill fed. You and I must disagree on this, King's Thegn."

Treven frowned but let it pass, another thought had drifted into his inebriated brain and he felt inclined to speak of it. "Do you believe the land has spirits in it?"

"Reluctantly. But, yes."

"What sway do the old gods have when the new ones come to take their place?"

"As much as they ever did, which is why we should be always on our guard. Why?"

"Because when I first came to this place it seemed to me I saw evil omens at every turn and since then . . . I have had strange dreams, Priest. Have you the skill of Joseph to interpret them?" He tried to keep his voice light and his mood seemingly untroubled, but the mead and the memory of these visions conspired to put a tremor in his voice. He drank again to steady his nerve.

"Tell me of these dreams and I will aspire, at least, to Joseph's virtues."

"You mock me again?"

"Sometimes it is easier to reply to mockery than to sincerity. Tell me anyway since you've a mind to?"

Treven drew a deep breath and held it before he began. "I saw two omens. On the day I came here there was a man hanged facing a wooden cross up on the hill above my home."

"I know the place."

"I looked at the figure on the cross and it seemed to me I could not tell clearly if it was an image of the Christ or of the All Father, but that was not the thing . . . the thing that troubled me."

"What then?"

"The bird. It was the bird, pegged down. Its wings fastened to the ground. A great black thing like a battle crow. It sickened me to see it captured and I cannot yet tell you why, though I've given so much thought to the matter . . ."

"What did you do about it?"

Treven looked uneasily at Kendryk, still not certain about the man; he was, nonetheless, drawn to him. "I set it free," he said.

"It was still living? Treven you'd have done better to put the poor creature from its misery."

"No, it was dead. I . . . had my men pull it free and ordered it burned."

"Burned? Why?"

Treven sighed. "I followed my mother's teaching," he confessed.

"The Christian or Heathen side of her?"

"The Heathen, I suppose. My mother was a woman of great wisdom and learning. She could read the Latin text and the Runic and Frisian script of her ancestors. She had us all, her children, taught to do the same. I knew what she would have done in this instance, a creature of the air should be set free into the air and the swiftest way to do this was with fire."

"So that its spirit could rise with the smoke towards the gods," Kendryk nodded. "I have heard of such customs. Treven, I will not blame you for this. The sight upset you and you sought remedy. But you spoke of two omens; what was the second?"

Treven hesitated, he still failed to understand his dream and it troubled him more than he liked to think. He was shamed by it. He'd woken in panic. Treven, a warrior, battle hardened and blooded more times than he could count with the gore of his enemies. "I had a dream," he said softly. "In my dream I saw the All Father."

"You saw Odin?"

"Wotan, yes. He walked in the guise of an old man with flowing silver hair. But I knew him by his blind eye and . . . and the power within him. Kendryk, I could sense his strength. I saw him walking from the woodland beside my hall and walking with him was a stranger from the far south. Her skin almost black and her hair loose and curling all about her head. Her clothes were strange and she looked bewildered as though finding herself in an unfamiliar place. I knew the

Lord Wotan had brought her here and I knew the reason must be a warning."

"You dreamed of this only once?"

Treven shook his head. "The first time was a brief matter. I had fallen asleep beside the fire. Hugh was talking to me but his words failed to hold my interest and I dozed. In my dream I saw them walking. Then the second time was the night before Cate was found. I saw them again and this time I saw other things. Faces of dead comrades, and worse, their hands reached out to me as thought to pull me down. Kendryk, if I had not woken . . ."

"Men have died of dreams," Kendryk confirmed thoughtfully. He fell silent for so long that Treven wondered if he slept, with his eyes still open.

"So, Priest," he said, feeling uncomfortable with the silence. "How do you interpret my dreams and what should I do to set this straight?"

"I interpret your visions as you do yourself. Images of ill omen. Treven, build a chapel on your land, build it close beside that wooden cross, sanctify it to the Christ and I will send a monk to reside there."

"A spy on my land, Priest?"

Kendryk smiled. "We could negotiate an exchange of hostages if you so wished. My man to live on your land and . . . say . . . Osric to be spy in my Abbey."

"I'd sooner send you Hugh!"

"Osric or nothing."

"Then nothing."

Kendryk laughed softly. "You are wise not to part with him," he said softly, "But, heed my advice, Treven. This is an ancient land and it does not forget. The forests and groves saw sacrifice to other gods long before the Christ was brought here, perhaps even before the All Father was worshipped in the ash grove close beside the place the wooden cross was carved." He noted Treven's surprise. "Go and look for yourself. Left to my wishes, the trees would be felled and the ground burned, but it does not lie on my land."

Treven shuddered. "I would not feel easy with your committing such an act," he confessed. He reached down to where his pack lay beside his chair and drew from it an object wrapped in bright red cloth. Kendryk leaned forward to see as he unwrapped it and laid between them on the table a spear head, the length of a man's hand, but slender and graceful. Beautifully wrought, the intricate serpents of its pattern welded surface writhing in the light from the fire.

"Wondrous," Kendryk murmured, "You carry this and yet you do not use it?"

Treven shook his head. "I brought it with me from my home and it has remained with me since. It is an heirloom of my house for many generations. When my grandsire of my father's kin, two, three sires ago, I do not know, when he converted to the Christian way, his priest took the spear and threw it into the sanctuary. The old gods fled, they say, but their power remained in this piece. While it hung in my hall, it kept the land safe and my kin protected."

"That is close to blasphemy, Treven," Kendryk said gently.

"Many things have been said this night that are close to blasphemy," Treven returned. "I speak as I find, Kendryk. Would you have me spout falsehoods just to satisfy you?"

"If it were expedient, then I would wish it." Kendryk told him. "And you believe that in taking this heirloom for your own protection, you deprived those left behind?"

Treven nodded. "I do believe that."

"What a weight of guilt you carry. And now there is Hugh. How simple life must have been when you needed only to survive each day. Kill or die. A simple enough choice."

"You mock me again, Priest?"

"Of course. What else would I do?" He pushed himself to his feet and Treven was relieved to see he swayed slightly and rested one hand on the back of the chair.

"You've drunk too much."

"As have you. The more have you. I'll see *you* try to stand before you insult my capacity to do so. Treven, it grows late and this is not the time for decisions to be carried through. Let Hugh sweat for the remainder of the night and think upon his sins. Tomorrow noon we will pronounce our judgement. Now we will sleep. May you fail to dream."

Treven watched him as he walked slowly and with care towards the rear of the hall and the curtained alcove that contained the brothers' beds, Kendryk having laid claim to one, leaving the other to Treven. He refilled his cup with more of Osric's medicine, grown cold now and bitter, reflecting that he should have told him to add valerian root to the mix, the herb that assured deep sleep and fended off the terrors of the night.

CHAPTER 24

Rozlyn had very little sleep. Interviews of those found in the house had gone on throughout the afternoon and into the night. The interviewees might be entitled to proper meal breaks and be subject to regulations defining the length and intensity of their questioning, but the interviewers were not; at least under Brook's regulations. Though, to give the man his due, he'd worked harder than all the rest of them put together, Rozlyn reckoned. Everywhere she'd looked, Brook seemed to be until Rozlyn began to wonder about the efficacy of human cloning. Rozlyn sat in on several interviews and in between acted as liaison between her section and others still searching the house and with immigration, preparing for the handover. She gathered mental snapshots of these eight people; their distress and exhaustion. The conditions under which they had travelled, crammed, with others into the back of a lorry with little food and almost no water, barely seeing light or breathing fresh air until finally, somewhere in a lay-by in the south of England, they had been transferred to two MPVs. No one seemed to know where the others had gone, only that they had been promised work.

At two o'clock that morning, after ten hours in the police station, they had been moved on again. Preliminary interviews over, Brook and his people had done with them and the folk from immigration taken over. Rozlyn had helped to load the cardboard boxes filled with their belongings into the boot of a car. She'd been touched by the ordinariness of them. The family photos, combs and lipsticks, matches and foreign cigarettes. A key ring in the shape of a teddy bear with one key, small and old fashioned of the sort that might open a jewellery box or even wind a clock. She couldn't help but wonder where the box was and what might have been inside. Gently, she ran her fingers over the pathetic little objects. She glanced over her shoulder, checking that she was alone and then picked up the key, held it self-consciously in the palm of her hand. The impressions seemed to rise up, flutter and flicker before her. *A woman, holding the key, an old man, threading it onto a velvet ribbon. A little box, carved wood, something precious inside.* Rozlyn smiled. The 'precious' objects contained within were a broken watch, a cheap ring and a bundle of pressed flowers and a photograph . . . a picture of a small child.

Reluctantly, she put the key back into the box and allowed the noise and bustle of her surroundings to break through into her thoughts.

What had she just felt now? Was that real? Or was it just a wishful projection? Induced by lack of sleep and a healthy dose of pity.

Rozlyn sighed. She leaned back against the wall and closed her eyes, just for a second. As kids, they, she and her friends, had played a game. Just imagine, just try and imagine who had owned something before, what they had been like. Try to guess, try to see. Rozlyn had been good at it. Too good. Good enough to scare herself stupid. For the most part, she had pushed the skill away. Rozlyn had learned to filter out the more intense experiences or pass them off as mere imagination, though sometimes the impressions she first received on arriving at the scene of some violent crime or other were overwhelming.

* * *

Rozlyn drove home and grabbed a couple of hours sleep, then early on the Friday morning, a week after Charlie Higgins had been found dead, Rozlyn returned to see Ethan Merrill.

A dank, drizzly night had given way to a bright, if still misty morning. This, Rozlyn thought, had been a magnificent autumn; the red earth of the newly ploughed fields almost matched the hawthorn for brilliance. The gold of the field maples caught the early sun as it broke through the mist and set light to the hips and haws of the hedgerows. There seemed more than usual this year. More berries and seeds and she wondered if her grandfather was right and this presaged a hard winter. The old man reckoned that the land always knew these things, anticipated the cold harshness of the coming season. Though, in her grandfather's case, Rozlyn thought, this feeling, this knowing, was probably merely a reaction to having moved from the mild south to the cold of New York winters and his observations of nature limited, in reality, to his regular walks in Central Park and the note he took of changes in his tiny, heavily planted yard.

Stamford was still closed when Rozlyn arrived and parked close to the George Hotel as she'd done that last time. She paid for a couple of hours and then set off on a slow walk to Ethan's shop, realising that she'd misjudged the time and it was only just gone nine in the morning. She noted, glancing at closed doors as she passed, that many of the more tourist-oriented stores didn't open until ten and wondered if Ethan's poky little place went by that timing. After all, it was hard to see what anyone would buy there anyway, never mind what anyone would want at nine in the morning.

The shop bell jangled as she pushed the door. Jasper, sprawled out on the table, taking advantage of the only patch of sun, roused and arched. But it was a half-hearted spat, the feline not bothering even to get to his feet. Rozlyn felt herself recognised and, it seemed, accepted by the guard cat. The thought pleased her and, almost, she reached out to fondle the animal's pricked ears. Then thought better of it. Maybe not wise to play on such a short acquaintance.

"Next time, he'll let you stroke him."

Ethan Merrill seemed to specialise in this appearing from nowhere thing.

"Don't you ever make a noise?"

"I don't know. I prefer soft shoes. Less jarring on old bones, I find."

Rozlyn glanced down at the other's feet. Ethan Merrill, epitome of sartorial elegance, wore crepe-soled shoes. "Brothel creepers! Oh my God. I didn't think you could even get those anymore."

Ethan Merrill smiled. He seemed pleased to be different. "You've brought the spear head this time? Good. Then come on back. I'm having breakfast."

Rozlyn followed him, struggling through the crowded little shop — how did he get this past fire regs? — and to a door she'd not seen on her first visit. Ethan held it open and gestured for her to pass. Rozlyn found herself in the small but fascinating space beyond. The layout of the premises was, Rozlyn now realised, similar to the rows of terraced houses like that inhabited by Mouse Man, albeit on a larger scale. The shop, then this room behind and a door probably leading to the stairs, another to the kitchen, this extending, as Rozlyn could see through the large sash window, into the enclosed yard.

One wall was lined, floor to ceiling, with books. Most were leather bound, though a shelf of modern hardbacks, their dust wrappers adding an oddly garish note, told her that Ethan kept up to date with his subject. Antiques guides and reference works sat beside learned-looking treatises on the worlds of art and archaeology. Beneath the window were further shelves, covered with bits of broken pot and fossils while the remaining walls were almost invisible behind a gallery of paintings and yellowed maps and postcards and play bills. Rozlyn supposed it must save on the decorating.

The room was warm; a fire had been lit in a cast-iron grate. The hearth and surround were decorated with Minton tiles in shades of green and sea blue. The fire crackled happily and Rozlyn couldn't blame it. This, for all its clutter — or maybe even because of it — was a friendly room. A calm and pleasant place to be. Ethan waved her into one of three old leather wing chairs. Two matched, their deep red brown, soft, well fed and warm, denoting them a pair. The smaller of the three was darker in colour and newer, though not by much. She sat in one of the pair, her hands moving to caress the smooth, well-worn leather of the arms. These were chairs made for reading or dozing or chatting by the fire. Firm enough to support the back, but with just enough give that they moulded to the individual. Rozlyn realised suddenly how tired she was.

"Would you like tea?" Without waiting for a reply Ethan opened the kitchen door and took a mug from the dresser. A pot of tea and the remains of toast stood on a small table beside the fire. Ethan refreshed his own mug and poured Rozlyn's drink before sitting down. "You look weary," he observed.

Weary, not tired or worn out. Weary. It was, Rozlyn realised, a perfect word, describing as it did that state which has gone beyond tired but instead, developed into a bone ache, heart ache, mind-numbing exhaustion.

"Late night," she said. It sounded so prosaic she wanted to add more. Instead, she delved into the pocket of her coat and withdrew the spearhead. "I tried to get this to you yesterday, but, well, things came up." She held it out but Ethan shook his head and pointed to a small desk standing in the alcove between the fireplace and the shop door. "Open the flap, the struts come out automatically, that's it. There's a blotter tucked inside, see it? Good, lay it down on that for me, will you. You know, you shouldn't keep it in a plastic bag, especially not if it's been allowed to get wet."

You probably shouldn't scrub it with a nailbrush and anti-bacterial soap, either, Rozlyn added silently, glad, when she took the object from the evidence bag, that none of the antiseptic smell lingered.

She stood back, but Ethan didn't move. Instead, he sat sipping his tea and gazing at the spear across the width of the room as though trying to see it in some kind of context that Rozlyn could not fathom.

"Sit down," Ethan said. "Drink your tea; give yourself a few minutes to take stock of the day while you have the chance. Then we'll both take a proper look." His eyes, bright blue and oddly youthful, fixed Rozlyn with their gentle amusement. For a mere instant she felt irritated and then, the spell cast by Ethan Merrill and his cosy room took hold and she thought, yes, what's the rush, five minutes either way won't do any harm and if Brook wants me, he can sing. She sat back down in the easy chair — never had the name seemed more appropriate — and rescued her mug from where she'd placed it on the floor and waited.

"How long have you had the shop?"

"Oh, eight, nearly nine years."

"Do you actually do any business? I mean, I don't mean to be rude, but . . ."

Ethan laughed. "I run a mail order company and most of my work comes via the internet. Oh yes, I'm actually quite twentieth century."

"Twentieth? Don't you mean twenty-first?"

"No. I don't believe in rushing into things."

"Ok." Rozlyn laughed. "What kind of things do you sell?"

"Oh, antiques, antiquities, I find rare books. Whatever is required."

"And that pays? Sorry. I'm being rude."

Ethan smiled. "I made some wise investments a few years ago when the stock market was worthy of the name. My work here keeps things topped up nicely." He got up and went over to where Rozlyn had laid the spear but still made no move to touch it. Instead, he remained standing with his hands clasped behind his back, gazing down as though almost afraid to make contact.

Rozlyn watched for a moment, impatience rising and then ebbing. Distracted, she glanced about the room, noting that, unlike the heavily clad walls of the rest, the chimney breast was remarkably bare. One single picture hung there, black ink on foxed paper. She got up to take a closer look. It looked like an etching, the lines finely wrought, spoiled somewhat by the brown spots of the foxing. The image portrayed, though, was crude. A cross, standing on a hillock with a man beside it. The man held a spear and, as Rozlyn examined it more closely, she realised that the spear carrier was actually part of the structure, enclosed within the outer boundaries of the carved cross and encompassed within a pattern of curving, interlacing lines which continued over the rounded head of the cross and down to the other side. A second figure balanced the spearman. A large bird, angled so that the wings fitted the shape, the spike of its beak pointing upward to echo the line of the spear on the other side.

The man on the cross had been nailed at the wrists and ankles, not at the palms and that struck Rozlyn as odd, so too were the ropes at his neck and knees and elbows. His naked feet touched the back of a wild boar, tusked and arch backed, which trampled leaves and berries beneath its feet. Rozlyn looked again at the face of the crucified man and was aware that Ethan watched her, his attention drawn from the spear back to Rozlyn.

"How come he only has one eye?" One eye was open, the other gouged and empty.

"The picture is a seventeenth-century copy of a stone cross said to stand out at Theadingford."

"Theadingford? The dig site?"

Ethan nodded. "I did some work out there years ago. The stone cross was long gone by then, but the tradition of it being there remained even into this century."

"Are we talking twentieth or twenty-first here?"

"Ah. I suppose I *should* catch up, shouldn't I? The drawing, from which the etching was taken, was made by a student of Stukeleys, but he was copying what was left of the cross, and, apparently, an earlier drawing. It's likely that the original was of wood and very old. If you look at the etching, it seems as though the cross has roots. See?"

Rozlyn peered at the writhing patterns. They did seem to go down into the earth, but roots? "Why would it have roots? And who was Stukeley?"

"He was an antiquarian who travelled the country recording ancient sites. Created a fad for Druidomania. Look him up. Interesting man. I have a theory that the original was carved directly onto a living tree. The tree eventually died, the cross remained until eventually it was replaced by stone and the design simply copied." He shrugged. "Only speculation, of course. And the one eye? Sometimes Pagan and Christian traditions mirrored one another closely. The figure could be Jesus of Nazareth; it could equally well have been the god Odin."

A movement out in the yard caught Rozlyn's eye. A girl stood looking in at them, slender and small, mid-teens, Rozlyn guessed, with short dark hair and the most wonderful violet eyes. Rozlyn caught her breath. The girl returned her interested gaze and then smiled and turned away. Rozlyn saw her go through a door into the kitchen and wondered if that meant she would be coming in.

"Her name is Cassandra," Ethan said. "Like the seer-ess."

"The one no one believed?"

Ethan laughed. "I hope I have more sense than the poor benighted inhabitants of Troy," he said.

"And is she a seer-ess?"

"No," Ethan shook his head sadly. "She's a child. Cassie has a mental age of about nine or ten." He turned back to the spear and added. "You can see how that might be a problem."

Rozlyn tried to hide her shock. The girl was strikingly beautiful. Her own reaction to Cassandra, though innocent, had been precisely the sort that Ethan must worry about. "Is she your daughter?"

"No, not mine. The child of an old friend. When he died, Cassie came to live with me.

"Now, about this spear."

"We know it was definitely the murder weapon," Rozlyn said, the image of it being refitted into Charlie's wounds causing a shudder to pass through her. "What I'm most concerned with now, is where it might have come from."

"You paid visits to the names I gave you."

"I did, yes. One was abroad, but Mr Mark Richards gave me a little of his precious time."

"And?"

"And what?"

"How did you find him?"

"Obnoxious. Rich. Uncooperative. I'm pretty sure he's had something stolen, though he denies it, which makes me think that whatever was stolen wasn't legit. Had it been, he'd have been tormenting the lives out of his insurers by now, not denying all knowledge."

"You've shown him the spear?"

"No, only photographs. I only got it back yesterday, after the PM. Post-mortem, that is."

"I know what it is. His reaction?"

"I asked him if it came from his collection and he said unfortunately not. He seemed to think it was a replica, he said on account of the condition. We know it's been on display somewhere and that it had a shaft fitted to it."

"Oh?"

"Um, forensics turned up fragments of paint and wood inside the socket. There'd be enough to get a match if the rest turns up. Until then . . ."

"Can't you get a warrant for Richard's house?"

Rozlyn laughed. "On what grounds?"

"I suppose you have a point." Ethan reached out and touched the spearhead. He moved his hand so suddenly that Rozlyn jumped. "It's older," Ethan said softly. "Far older than the dig site out at Theadingford. And now I look at the real thing instead of those tacky little pictures, I can see just how fine the workmanship really is. That's what fooled me, you see. In the pictures, you lose the detail but this really is exquisite."

"I'm sorry to sound crass," Rozlyn said. "But would it be worth stealing? In monetary terms, I mean."

"Oh yes, but you'd have to convince the buyer of its authenticity. To get the best price for this, you'd need the provenance."

"I thought black market dealers weren't too bothered about that sort of thing?"

"To get the best price for anything you need its story, Inspector Priest. The story is what separates the good from the wonderful. Without that provenance, most buyers would think as you did, that this has to be a copy. A wonderful piece of work, but nevertheless, not the real thing. With provenance, this is not only wonderful it is close to unique. You're looking at something as precious as any object that came out of Sutton Hoo and, I'd place it at a similar date. Sixth, Seventh century, perhaps."

"You're kidding me?" Rozlyn had been certain that this was a fake. "Pity in a way, I'd been looking forward to meeting the guy that made it. He sure knew his stuff."

Ethan nodded. "He did indeed. The devil of it is, though, we have no context. No idea where it came from or what else lay with it."

"You mean, there could have been more objects like this?"

Ethan frowned, but avoided the question. "Your murder victim. It was a single stab wound, to the chest?" He asked as if it was a question but Rozlyn had the odd sensation that he merely sought verification.

"Why do you ask?"

"And . . ." Ethan closed his eyes and lifted the spear from the blotter. "He was lying on the ground."

"How do you know that?"

Ethan smiled. "Sometimes," he said, "when I touch an object, I can . . . sense things. Know things about it."

"Right." Rozlyn said. She stared at Ethan for a moment, somewhat taken aback, shaken by the reference to the very skill Rozlyn tried to hide. "Look," she said. "I have to be going now. Thanks for your help, I'll be in touch and maybe you'd like to tell me where you were . . ."

"When your Charlie Higgins was killed? In Edinburgh, I'm afraid. I spent three days there last week and returned last Saturday morning. Don't worry, Inspector, I'll give you a list of names and addresses, you can check my story."

"I'll be doing that."

They both turned as the door opened and Cassie entered carrying more tea.

"You'll stay?"

"No, I'm sorry, I have to be getting back."

"Oh. But we've got biscuits?" Cassie said.

She sounded so disappointed that Rozlyn had to smile. "Sorry," she said. "Maybe another time." She took the spear from Ethan's hands and packed it back into the evidence bag and then her pocket. It dragged at her coat, felt heavy and hard as it swung against her leg. Heavier than she recalled it being. "I can see myself out."

Jasper hissed as she passed but Rozlyn barely heard him. Her brain buzzed and her fingers fizzed with something like a static charge. She felt cold inside.

Recovering the spear head, she had touched Ethan's hand and, just for the merest instant, her mind had been flooded with the image of Charlie's death. She had seen it; been it. Had been both Charlie lying there on the ground anticipating the blow a split second before it hit and the other, that invisible assailant, thrusting down at the helpless man. And Rozlyn had felt it, the flood of anger surging through the assailant's mind until it was all he could conceive and, still cramping her ribs so that she could not breath without the fire of it in her lungs, the pain as the spearhead pierced her flesh and touched her heart.

CHAPTER 25

By the time she got back to base Rozlyn had recovered enough to tell herself it was just imagination. Her own tiredness had led her to give in to the suggestions that Ethan had made so that she had taken those thoughts on board without really . . . without really what?

In the end she pushed the memory aside, decided that the ache in her ribs was due to indigestion and that Jenny was right when she said Rozlyn should eat more regularly. She was probably a prime candidate for an ulcer — yes that was it — and this was all down to stress and not taking better care of herself. If she didn't watch it she'd be swilling beers like Brook and have the belly to go with the haggard expression.

In the incident room she noticed that a description had been added to Clara Buranou's, together with a description and a possible link back to Thomas Thompson. As yet there seemed to be no response to the enquiry she'd made about Donovan with her contact in Art and Antiques.

She was reading the description of Clara and wondering if there was anything to add when Brook came in.

"Any trace yet of our mysterious landlord?" Rozlyn asked.

Brook shook his head. “Our Mr T. Thompson is still elusive,” he said. “We’ll see what immigration come up with and meantime keep digging locally.”

Rozlyn nodded wondering what, if anything, she should tell Big Frank. “You ever come across anyone called Donovan?” she asked Brook.

“Yeah,” Brook told her. “Folk singer or summat, isn’t he?” He grinned, wolf-like. “Never figured you for one of the finger-in-the-ear crowd.”

“The what?”

“You know. Singing through your nose with one finger in your ear?” He laughed at Rozlyn’s expression, then demonstrated for her benefit, inserting one fat digit into his left ear and droning loudly through his nose.

Jenny, just entering the room, gave him a slow handclap. “Very nice, boss. Missed your calling.”

“Less cheek from you. Our clerical inspector here wanted to know if I’d heard of Donovan. I was just giving her my best impression.”

Rozlyn, looking at Jenny, had the satisfaction of realising that the joke was lost on her.

“Right,” she said doubtfully. Then, “I think we’ve got a lead on Clara Buranou. And who’s this Donovan anyway?” She glanced back at Brook who was preparing once more to wedge his finger in his ear. “Never mind, boss, you can enlighten me another time.”

“Clara Buranou,” Rozlyn prompted her.

“Got a call, Mr Anonymous, reckoned she was at the bus station. I’ve got someone keeping an eye.”

“Anonymous? Who the hell else knows we’re looking for her?” Big Frank, she replied to her own question the moment it was out. Big Frank knew. She frowned, wondering what the man was playing at.

“You two getting off then?” Brook demanded. “Stand around here and she’ll have skipped it again.”

“You had a call about ten minutes ago,” Jenny told her as they got in the car. “I didn’t know you were back.

Someone called Stevens in Art and Antiques, reckoned he'd got something on that Donovan character."

Rozlyn smiled. "Not the folk singer, I take it?"

"Not unless he leads a double life. Stevens wants you to phone back, but he's emailing anyway. Sounds like Donovan is someone they've been after for a while."

"Oh?"

"Sorry, can't tell you more, he was about to go into a meeting. He just called to let you know he was onto it and would you call him back later."

That sounded important, Rozlyn thought. She nodded. "Good. Ok, let's see if we can round up Clara Buranou."

CHAPTER 26

Morning, chill enough to cut to the bone. The rain had passed in the late afternoon of the day before and the clouds fled, leaving open skies that had brought frost. Morning had dawned bright and treacherous and frozen. Two nights ago, the moon had been full and winter had begun and in his bones, Treven knew that the kindness of the softest autumn he could recall in many years had passed and winter would breathe harsh words.

Treven shivered despite the thick cloak pulled tight around him. Smoke rose from the roof of the smith's forge and the fierce hot glow of the fire bellowed his and Hugh's reason for standing there. Hugh, clad only in linen shirt and sleeveless tunic, held himself so stiffly he looked carved in stone, only the blue of his lips betraying his chilled body. He had said nothing all morning. Nothing either, so Osric told him, since Treven had left him last night. Now it was all in the hands of God. "All Father," Treven breathed. "If he is truly innocent then aid him now. If he is guilty, let him die swiftly."

Kendryk, three of his senior monks beside him, observed closely as the bar was heated in the fire. Treven watched him, studying his face. He too was pale and tense, the death mask features accentuated as he leaned in towards the fire. Hugh had claimed judgement by the church and, that being done, Treven could only look on, helpless and useless.

The tramp of feet behind him caused him to turn. The brothers arrived, accompanied by the twelve who would be oath keepers beside Eldred. They had come from Theading and others from Bearwell, still others from the lands the brothers had inherited from their kin, bringing their wives and children to witness this ritual of law in which Eldred would swear oaths to clear his name and Hugh would risk his life in pursuit of the same end.

"Hugh," Treven had begged, "let me pay the blood price. My land will serve as promise. Or allow me to send word to your kinsmen so that oath takers can be found. They would come . . ."

"And take me back to worse? No, Treven, I will not permit it. They would come to see me shamed, then take me home like a badly behaved child. And as for payment, as you've said yourself, if I'd a mind I could give my brooch and other jewels from my father's house. The *geld* could be raised, but I'll have none of that either. I'll walk from here a free man, clear in conscience and unstained by guilt. I will endure this, Treven, and I will be victorious."

After that no more could be said and Treven had spent a sleepless night waiting for the dawn.

"Come forward, Eldred and declare your purpose here," Kendryk demanded and then stepped back, deferring to Treven.

"By the oaths I have declared before the king, I will hear you fairly," Treven told them. "Eldred, you stand charged of brutal murder. Your wife Cate died five days past and you stand accused of her killing. I ask you, how do you plead?"

"I will swear and have brought as decreed twelve good men to help my oath, that I laid no hand on my wife that led to her death. And further, I accuse Hugh de Vries of being the one that took her life. Unto that end, I do demand justice."

Treven surveyed the twelve men Eldred had brought with him. "Hugh de Vries has no oath helpers to stand beside him," he said, "instead he has chosen judgment of Almighty God. He will endure the ordeal of fire and iron. Have you more to say on this matter?"

"I have said all the words I must," Eldred told him. "If Hugh de Vries chooses this path, then I will not disclaim his right, but I do believe that the good Lord will find him guilty as my heart knows him to be."

"You must not pre-judge," Kendryk told him gently. "Eldred, this is now taken from your hands. Have your oath helpers step forward and name themselves and then declare their oaths and may the Lord ensure that they believe in their hearts what they swear with their lips."

Treven was aware of the ripple of anxiety that passed through those gathered. This was no small thing that Eldred asked them to do. A man's oath was made not just with the mouth but with the heart and soul and if a man should make a false declaration . . . Treven felt his belly grow cold at the thought of it. He looked again at Hugh, so calm and so composed and could scarcely believe that his friend was about to make just such a false declaration before both man and God. How could he hope to survive? A small part of Treven's consciousness asked if this could ever be a true testing. Wasn't it more a matter of will and fitness and strength than purity of soul or of intent? But Treven had seen younger, stronger men than Hugh die when their wounds festered. Men who had declared their innocence yet who had confessed as they died that the accusations against them had been true.

He turned his attention back to the dozen men lined up beside Eldred preparing for the *forathe*. "If any should have doubt, however small, or simply be in ignorance, then let none hinder his leaving and none later question his intent," he said softly. "It is better to depart now, an honest man, than to swear false out of loyalty or misjudgement. Look now into your hearts and listen to what they tell you. Is your kinsman innocent? Can you truly swear to this?"

Though there were uneasy glances and foot shuffling, no one moved. In truth, Treven had expected nothing else. Eldred would only have chosen those men filled with conviction of his righteousness. "Then let the first step forward and so swear," Treven commanded.

Somewhat to his surprise, Edmund moved from the end of the row and came to stand beside his brother facing Treven.

Eldred took a deep breath. "By the lord I do swear that I am guiltless of either deed or instigation of this crime. I neither killed my wife nor wished another to do so. I am innocent of the charge brought against me."

"And I do swear by the Lord that this oath is pure and that Eldred is not false in the swearing of it. I, Edmund Scrivener, do assert and attest this."

Edmund stepped back with a fierce look cast in Treven's direction, pride in his eyes and his mouth set in a tight line. The next strode forward to take his place and Treven did not move or blink as the *athas* were one by one sworn by the oath helpers. Only when the *Compurgation* was over and Eldred stood before him a man declared innocent of all crime, did Treven turn slowly to face his comrade in arms.

He had been dreading this moment and was almost selfishly glad that the administration of the ordeal was a matter for churchman and not Thegn.

"Hugh. How do you plead?"

"As I have always done. I swear by the Almighty that I did not by word or deed cause the death of Cate Scrivener, neither did I wish her death. I swear my innocence and, by God's will, I will prove it now."

It seemed to Treven that the speaking of the oath had unfrozen him. The rigidity vanished from his limbs and the pallor of his skin was replaced by a rush of blood. Hugh's cheeks burned and his eyes brightened as though with fever. Treven almost moved to stop what would happen next. He must have taken a step because Osric lay a hand upon his arm. Kendryk's stern look brooked no argument and reminded him that this was no longer his concern.

"Let the matter commence," Treven managed, his voice raven- harsh. He nodded to the smith that they were ready and forced himself to watch as Hugh stepped forward.

Treven had never had reason to doubt Hugh's courage, but the exercise of that courage had always before been in battle. If you know that you will kill or be killed, then choices are limited and often men not cut from warrior cloth will perform great deeds simply because they must. But this was different. This was unlike anything Treven had seen in battle and, though he had seen such ordeals three or four times in his life before, he still had no stomach for this deliberate wounding, so cold and so contrived.

With long tongs, the smith drew the iron bar he had heated from the flames. In the cold light it glowed with such fierce redness it was almost painful to look at. Two of Kendryk's men had taken position either side of Hugh. Should he change his mind and try to run, they would be there to see this trial went ahead.

"You have one last chance to tell your guilt," Kendryk informed him. "Plea now and we will hear you fairly and judge you according to your words."

"I have made my plea," Hugh told him angrily. He drew a deep breath and stepped forward, taking the glowing metal from the tongs with his own bare hand.

Treven gasped as Hugh's hand closed about it. It was clear from the fierce contortion of Hugh's face that he had not, even in his wildest imaginings, been prepared for such pain as the red-hot brand welded itself to his palm and fingers, the heat constricting the tendons and tightening his grip against the bar. The stink of burning flesh, born on the clear cold air, filled the open space. Around him, Treven could hear the gasps and sighs of those who watched, most of whom would never have seen such a sight before.

Hugh took the first faltering step. He held his hand away from his body, holding it before his own eyes as though it pointed the direction he must take. The second step, the stink of flesh grown stronger now that it had reached bone.

Treven was certain he could catch that acrid stench. The third step, Hugh cried out for the first time, head thrown back as he roared his pain to the clear blue sky. The fourth step and the fifth, he almost stumbled. Treven knew he could not release the bar now even if he'd a wish to. It would have forged itself to his flesh as tightly as the smith forged metal to metal. The sixth step and his hand dropped almost to his side. He was faltering now, his feet stumbling on the path and his cry failed to just a childish whimper.

The seventh step was taken, but he had almost lost his footing. "Sweet Lord," Treven heard him cry. "Help me."

Treven groaned. Drawn towards Hugh he reached out to help him make those final steps. He was close enough to feel the heat of the bar wrapped so tightly in Hugh's hand. The colour was fading now to that of straw, heat passed into flesh and bone.

"For pity's sake," Treven whispered fiercely as Kendryk took his arm and ordered him to stay.

"He must take all nine paces alone, King's Thegn. You cannot help him."

Treven fixed his eyes on Hugh's face, willing him on. He could see that Hugh was sick with pain. The eighth step taken, then the ninth, one stubborn foot forced before the other, Hugh fell to the ground and Kendryk gave the signal. The smith came forward with a leather bucket filled with water. He tipped this over Hugh's burning hand, the flesh smouldering and black from palm to fingertip. Then he bent down and dragged the metal bar from the clawed and welded grip. Hugh screamed as what was left of his flesh ripped from his palm. Treven could only watch as the monks lifted him and carried him away. The hand would be bandaged and left. If after three days Hugh had not died and the wound showed signs of healing, he would be declared innocent of all crimes and they could treat his injuries and give him poppy to kill the pain. Treven closed his eyes, then opened them again, aware that Kendryk was speaking to the smith, though it took a moment for his words to make sense.

The smith turned away and returned to his forge carrying the now cooling bar.

"*What* did you say to him?" Treven did not think he'd heard right.

"I told him to forge a new sword, to weave that metal into the heart of it. It should hold great power, King's Thegn."

Treven stared at him. "Sometimes I doubt you follow the Christ," he said. "Your thoughts are more like those of my heathen grandsire."

"And I have told you, the land does not forget and neither does the metal torn from the womb of the earth. Better the sword be made and be presented to me for safekeeping than let it loose into the world. Treven, I have no more liking for this display than have you. I would prevent the effects from spilling further into this land." He smiled, then: "and, besides, does not that *Heliand* Gospel of yours teach that the Christ was a great warrior, worthy of a woven sword?"

He followed after his men and Hugh and left Treven open- mouthed and gawping like an ill-mannered child. The crowd began to disperse, their interest no longer held now that Hugh was gone and nothing would be known for three more days. Treven listened to their gossip as they went, aware that this incident would be told and retold with much enrichment in the months and winters to come. Aware too, that he had done himself no harm in permitting it. He felt sickened. After a moment of hesitation, wondering if he should accompany Kendryk, he decided he could take no more. He called for his horse and servants and returned to his own Hall.

CHAPTER 27

Clara Buranou sat in the interview room with her coat pulled tight round her skinny body and stared, her face stony and drawn, at the coffee Rozlyn had placed on the table. The room was bare but for a red-topped table, four wooden chairs and a tape player fixed onto the wall. The scuffed floor showed the marks of chair legs and years of restless feet. The walls had not been repainted in the decade and more Rozlyn had known it. She found their industrial flecked grey utterly depressing.

"Where were you going?"

"Anywhere."

"You'd bought a ticket?"

"Yes. To Scotland."

"Why Scotland?"

"It is far away." Clara sighed and shifted in her seat, reached for the coffee and drank the scalding liquid in one go.

"Would you like some more? Are you hungry?"

Clara weighed Rozlyn with tired blue eyes, studying her face as though to catch the double meaning behind the words. The tape in the machine hummed softly and Jenny crossed her legs, the skim of fabric on fabric unnaturally loud in the quiet room.

Finally, Clara nodded.

"OK, I'll send for more coffee and some sandwiches. Will that do? Is there anything you don't eat?"

Clara shrugged and then shook her head. "I am not fussy," she said. Then, "Thank you."

Rozlyn regarded the young woman thoughtfully. "Charlie Higgins cleaned for the man who brings people like you into the country," she said. "Is that how you met him?"

Clara hesitated and then sighed again, nodding her head. "You will send me back?"

"That's not up to me. I'm just a police officer."

"But I will be sent back?"

"Perhaps. I don't know. Where is 'back'?"

"Kosovo. A little village."

"And what made you leave?"

"There was no one to make me stay. No one left."

Rozlyn hesitated. There was so much here she'd like to know, but if it did not directly concern Charlie's murder, then this wasn't the time to be asking.

Brook came into the room followed by an officer carrying coffee and sandwiches. Brook took them from him and then placed them on the table in front of Clara. "DCI Brook has entered the room," he announced for the tape. "The time is two fifty-eight p.m. on the afternoon of October fourth." Brook grabbed the spare chair and turned it around, sitting astride. "If you want to take a break now, you can, or you can eat and talk, that's up to you."

"I can talk," she told him. She studied him as closely as she had Rozlyn and then turned her attention back to the coffee and food.

"What have you been doing since you left your flat?" Rozlyn asked.

"I walked. I think about what to do. I walk some more. Last night, I sleep outside."

"It was very cold last night."

She nodded. "So today, I decide to catch a bus."

"When you met Charlie, was it at one of the houses?"

She took a bite of sandwich and nodded, chewing fast so she could answer. "I arrived with others, they all went away. I did not know where to go. I came back to the house, they had told me not to, but I had nowhere else to go. I come back to the house to ask where should I go; what should I do? No one is there but Charlie. I sit on the steps and I tell him. He takes me to his home but I cannot stay there. People will see. Charlie finds me a place to live and work. I see him sometimes, but not often. People will see and Charlie will be in trouble. Charlie Higgins is a good man."

"These others that came into the country with you, where did they go to?"

She shook her head violently. "I do not know. Some left in another car before we reach here. Others, two women, they leave with a man. I do not go with them. He promise work in a restaurant, but . . ." She shook her head. "I have seen this kind of man. He say, if I do not go, then I will find my own work and place to stay and I must go away from that place. So, I go, but two days later, I go back. No one is there except Charlie."

"And when was this. When did you arrive?"

"It is May the fourth when I get here. May of last year."

"Do you think anyone saw you with Charlie?" Brook asked her.

She shook her head but then nodded. "I did not think so, but Charlie did. He is frightened."

"And when was this?"

"Two weeks ago. Charlie say I should be ready to leave. Soon he will have big money and we can go to Scotland."

"Why Scotland?"

"I do not know. Charlie wanted to go there. He had never been."

"And this money. Where was it going to come from?"

She shrugged helplessly. "He say he has something to sell. Something of value that is very old. He does not tell me more."

"Did you have a relationship with Charlie Higgins?" Brook asked her.

She looked away and took another large bite of sandwich, and then finally she shook her head. "Charlie was my friend, but if he asked me to, I would have had relationship with him," she said simply. "He is a good man. I like him. I am sorry he is dead."

Brook rose and beckoned Rozlyn to the door. Jenny announced their departure for the tape and the entry of the watch officer.

"Well. That's that then," Brook announced as he stood with Rozlyn in the corridor.

"That's what?"

"Oh, don't be so bloody obtuse. Someone saw Charlie with Clara and realised he'd got curious, so they shut him up before he decided to do anything about it. End of story."

"No. Not quite. What about the spear and the place his body was dumped, to say nothing of not knowing where he was killed. And what about this valuable something that Clara Buranou talked about?"

"What about it? Look, once we get our mystery landlord, you'll have all that sorted too. Let immigration do the legwork for us. Could be someone's idea of a joke, for all I know. Most likely someone fed Charlie a line and he swallowed it. It's nothing. Forget it. We know *why* Charlie Higgins died and the rest is someone else's pigeon. He stuck his nose in where it wasn't wanted, and he paid for it. Simple as that."

"Not so simple. Look, you may have the result you want, but that's not the end of things. For one thing, we're no closer to Thomas Thompson."

Brook waved her objections aside. "If I can spare the manpower, I'll keep obs on the houses and on the office we turned up from that number you found in Charlie's book. Frankly, I'm more than prepared to leave that one to immigration too. They've got the bodies, let them handle it."

"And you're satisfied with that?"

Brook shrugged. "He's off our patch; someone else's problem. Drop it, be satisfied."

"Time was, you'd never have said that. You'd have worried at it like a dog with a rag until every last drop had been wrung out."

"Aye, well, maybe I've learned. You don't get any more applause for chasing what no one's interested in. Charlie Higgins is dead. We found the cause, and we've got ourselves a nice line in people smuggling into the bargain. It's up to someone else to find who stabbed him with that fancy bit of ironwork. Frankly, I'm happy to let them have the glory."

"I'm not," Rozlyn told him, heat in her voice. "And as to the other business, we've got a driver and a receiver. Sweet F.A."

"And, like I said: immigration will take it from there. That's their business. We've bloody well done our bit. I'll make sure you get credit due if that's what's bothering you and, speaking of which, I've arranged a nice little press briefing for you tomorrow morning."

"Oh, good of you to tell me."

"I'm telling you now, aren't I? Take my advice and let the rest drop. When immigration find our Mr T. Thompson, I'll make sure you get to ask him where he got his sense of the theatrical from." He winked and strode off, leaving Rozlyn feeling frustrated and oddly sullied by his comments.

"Hey," Rozlyn shouted after him. "What about Mouse Man. Someone damn near killed him. You going to dismiss that too?"

"Probably just couldn't stand the stink," Brook called back.

CHAPTER 28

It was the first chance Rozlyn had to see Mouse since that first morning. She'd arranged for clothes and the other items on the nurse's ad hoc list to be taken in, but circumstances had militated against her own visit.

Mouse was pleased to see her. He looked better, not so pale, and the bruises were now mostly yellow edged, with the blackest reduced to a mere deep violet. Now the swelling had subsided, the ruined eye had a hollow look, the half-closed lid sunk back against the blood-red void. Rozlyn was surprised to find it exposed like this. The heavy bandages, she could cope with, but being faced with the emptiness where Mouse Man's eye had once been was unsettling and nauseating.

Mouse saw her look. "The doc's coming to examine it again," he said, "so they took the dressing off." He smiled. "You're my second visitor today."

"Oh?"

"Yes, that pretty blonde girl, Jenny, she called in to bring me another magazine. Found out I like mice, she did. Look."

So, Rozlyn thought. There *were* magazines for mouse fanciers. "That's good of her," she said.

"Yes, she's a lovely girl. She brought in all those things you got for me yesterday just at dinnertime and stayed for a chat. I let her eat my jelly. I've never been a big one for jelly, but she liked it. Raspberry, she said. She told me you were *investigating*, so you couldn't come yourself." He imbued the word with an almost religious awe.

Good on you, Jenny, Rozlyn thought. The thought drifted unbidden that Mouse did not think of *her* as pretty. She told herself not to be so stupid. "You look a lot better," she said.

"Didn't think I'd make it, did you?" Mouse said. "They told me you stopped half the night, then came back again early in the morning. I appreciate that."

Rozlyn smiled tightly, uncomfortable with the role in which Mouse Man had cast her. "I fed the mice," she said.

"Not many of them left, were there?"

"No. I'm sorry."

"That's all right. Jenny told me. She said they must have escaped into the street because I'd not shut the door properly. They'll be all right."

Silently, Rozlyn blessed Jenny again. It would never have occurred to her to lie, but she was glad Jenny had. Mouse shouldn't know the cruelty that had been meted out to his little pets.

"She told me a few of them died," Mouse went on. "He knocked the cages over, you see and some probably got trampled when we fought." He shook his head. "He's a cruel sort, whoever he was. He didn't need to knock the cages down. The little folk couldn't do anything to hurt him or to defend themselves. I'm glad most of them managed to run away."

"I'm glad too," Rozlyn said. "Mouse, can you remember any more about what happened?"

He shook his head. "I let myself in and I put the shopping down. Then I heard a noise. I heard them squeaking and someone moving about. Then he was all over me. Punching and kicking and shouting about Charlie stealing and hiding something."

Mouse closed his eyes.

"He gave you no clue to what it was?"

"I've been thinking about it, Inspector Priest. Truly I have. I think . . . I'm almost sure, he was shouting something about a box. Charlie taking something from a box or a cabinet or something." He shook his head again. "I'm sorry, it all happened so fast and he was kicking and hitting me all the time. I couldn't think straight."

The ward sister arrived then with a doctor in tow and Rozlyn, telling Mouse to rest and get well, thought it time to leave. She drove home, the problems surrounding Charlie's death nagging her.

When she'd gone to visit Mouse Man she'd left her coat in the boot of the car and lifting it out now, she felt the weight of the spearhead still in the pocket.

"Damn." She'd meant to return that to the evidence locker. She considered her options. Should she take it back tonight? Would anyone notice it was gone before morning? She decided not and that, even if they did, they'd find it had been signed out to her. It wasn't as if it had walked. She went inside, pausing only to check for messages before going through to the kitchen.

She laid the spearhead on the kitchen table, glancing at it from time to time while she made tea and cobbled together a sandwich of cheese, smoked ham, salad and mayonnaise, thinking about that strange sensation she'd got, those weird impressions, when she'd taken the thing from Ethan's hand.

Her head ached. She took a couple of paracetamol and went up to shower, leaving the spearhead in her bedroom. She didn't want it out of her sight, not when she was the one who had not checked it back in. That night she slept but found it hard to settle down. The object on the bedside table loomed large in her consciousness and, when she turned in her bed to look at it, it seemed larger in the darkness than it had any right to be.

Serves you right, she told herself, for bringing a murder weapon home to bed. She turned away from it again, but its presence at her back unnerved her and finally she picked it up and locked it in the wardrobe.

Rozlyn stepped back and observed the tightly locked cupboard. She'd swear she could still feel the presence of the thing even through the locked and heavy wooden door.

"You're a fool, Rozlyn Priest. Get yourself to bed."

She lay down, switched off the bedside lamp and then, almost at once, switched it back on, regretting for once that she had neither television nor radio in the bedroom. This was one occasion she'd overcome her dislike and have it on.

Finally, she closed her eyes and forced herself to breathe slowly, relaxing consciously from her toes towards her head. She'd read somewhere that this could help calm a mind ready for sleep.

Something must have worked because finally Rozlyn slept and when she slept, she dreamed of Ethan.

CHAPTER 29

Rozlyn woke feeling as though she'd been beaten. Her body ached and her throat felt sore. At first she put the symptoms down to a poor night's sleep but by the time she'd choked through the press conference — pausing every few words for cold water to lubricate a burning throat — she knew it was something more.

"You look like shit," Jenny told her when she arrived back at the police station.

"Thanks a lot."

"Welcome. Why don't you get off home? You're not going to be able to think straight and I've no wish to catch whatever it is you've got."

"Oh, pure self-interest, then?" It was good advice but when Rozlyn studied the stack of paperwork on her desk and caught a glimpse of the number of emails and messages awaiting a response, she figured she just couldn't walk away. She'd have to deal with some of it at least.

One email caught her attention immediately. It was from Stevens, her friend in Art and Antiques and the title in the subject line was Dr Donovan Baker.

Rozlyn opened it and read.

Rozlyn,

Sorry to take time getting back to you. Truth is, we're very interested in this Donovan. If my guess is right, his full name is Dr Donovan Baker, which explains why your search, if it was by last name, wouldn't have got you anywhere. Donovan Baker is something of a mystery man. Respectable background — an academic, in fact, in the field of archaeology. Problem with our Donovan Baker is that he's a greedy bastard; a question of much wants more, as they say. Got himself involved in some very dodgy insurance deals.

Look, give me a call this afternoon and I'll fill in the gaps.

Cheers.

Jack.

So, Rozlyn thought, he was real, not some bogeyman created by Charlie and reinvented by Mouse Man. It felt both better, having this confirmation of Donovan's solidity, and worse. Stevens was not someone who issued warnings without considering need.

Rozlyn thought about Mouse Man's injuries and shuddered.

"I said you should get off home. You're shivering."

"No, I'm all right. We've got something on Donovan."

"I'm guessing *not* the folk singer . . . anyway, he was skiffle. My dad told me." She leaned over her shoulder to read the email. "Interesting. Certainly fits, doesn't it."

Rozlyn nodded. "I'll ring Jack Stevens later. Meantime—"

"You're going home to bed?"

"I'm going to have another word with Mark Richards."

"Spreading your germs."

"I couldn't give them to a worthier recipient." She hauled herself out of the chair, body protesting and the dull ache spreading from between her shoulder blades and into the lower back. Her head throbbed. "You got any aspirin?"

Jenny went over to her desk. From the drawer she produced a shiny box containing something that described itself as "Max Strength". She gave Rozlyn two with water, then handed her the box. "Just go home."

"After I've seen Richards."

"Promise?"

"Maybe. I'll see how I feel."

How she felt was truly dreadful. Her eyes bulged in their sockets — or, at least, they felt as though they did, displaced by a pain like toothache in her sinuses. She knew Jenny was right and she should give it a rest and head for home but somehow, the news about Donovan had galvanised her and she knew that she would not be able to relax anyway.

Rozlyn eased herself carefully into the car, wondering how long the tablets would take to work. It had started to rain, a steady downpour that blurred the windscreen even with the wipers on and the drive seemed infinitely longer because of it, but by the time she'd reached the wall running around the estate perimeter, Rozlyn was feeling somewhat better. The painkillers hadn't quite lived up to their name but at least the ache and cramp in her lower back had subsided, even if she was left with dulled sinuses and the fist-sized lump of discomfort between her shoulders that refused to shift.

When she reached Mark Richards' house, having been kept waiting for some time at the gates, Albert stood guard in the shelter of the ostentatious porch with his arms folded and a facial lividity that had Rozlyn wondering about his heart.

"I thought you'd completed your enquiries."

Rozlyn shook her head. "I did tell you I'd be back." Albert's position atop the steps left Rozlyn with no alternative than to pause, one step down, exactly where the rain dripped from the elaborate pediment. She had no doubt that this was deliberate. Irritated, she stepped around the guard dog in grey trousers and walked ahead of him into the house. "In his office, is he? I can find my way."

There followed a comic turn as Albert sought to get ahead of Rozlyn before she reached the stairs and then pushed her in ungentlemanly fashion out of the way so that he could precede her. Rozlyn almost laughed out loud, but the thought of laughing set her sinuses off again and manifested a spasm of such pain between her shoulders that it threatened to crease the rest of her back.

Mark Richards was seated at his desk. Rozlyn wondered if he'd moved since his last visit or if this office was the heart of his home, much as the kitchen had been in her grandparents' place, their entire lives seeming to revolve about that warm, welcoming hub.

There was nothing either warm or welcoming about Mark Richards or his office.

"What do you want, Inspector? I've already told you everything I know — and that's nothing."

"Have you? Y'know, I'm still not convinced it wasn't you that lost that spear and I wondered if, seeing what a fine collection you have, you could have overlooked it, somehow. Do you have an inventory for your collection, for instance? For insurance purposes and the like. You could show it to me and me and Al here could have a check through. See what else might have gone for a walk."

Albert gasped at the insult of having his name shortened. "I think you should leave."

"Hmm. I can see how you would like that. But I've another question for you and this one, you'll be glad to know, is new. You ever hear of someone called Dr Donovan Baker?"

"Of course."

His reply took the wind out of Rozlyn's sails and, for a moment, she floundered.

Mark Richards smiled. He got up from his desk, crossed to one of the bookcases that lined the wall opposite the window and withdrew two books. He brought them over for Rozlyn's inspection. "Before he retired, Donovan Baker was one of the foremost field archaeologists working on late Anglo-Saxon sites in this area."

"Oh?" Rozlyn pulled the books towards her. They were fat volumes, packed with coloured plates and comparative tables. "He retired, you say? Old man, is he?"

Mark Richards laughed. "No, just well off enough to make choices."

"Money to be made in this archaeology lark, is there?"

"There can be, but I believe that Dr Baker had a private income. Inheritance from his mother's side."

"Oh, you know him well, then, this Donovan Baker."

"I didn't say that."

"No? You seem well appraised of his financial situation."

"I met him on odd occasions when we attended the same functions." Richards scowled. "In fact he did some work for me here. On the chantry."

Rozlyn got the impression that Richards regretted saying that almost as soon as the words fell from his mouth. "Chantry? That's some kind of chapel, isn't it? Where's that then?"

Richards' involuntary flick of the head took her over to the window. The rain had eased, though glowering skies promised much more. Across the vast expanse of lawn, and to the side, between the line of trees that marked the road and a more formal clipped yew hedge, Rozlyn could see the remnants of a building, the top of a wall and a high arched window. The yew hedge would have hidden it from the drive and she'd not looked out of that particular window on her last visit. "How old is it?" she asked, pure curiosity taking the place of police-type questions.

Mark Richards sighed. "What you can see is twelfth century," he said, "but it's built on a much earlier foundation. Records suggest that it was founded by the abbey out at Storton, about ten miles away, some time in the late ninth century. Now, if you've satisfied your curiosity, I'd be glad if you went."

"What kind of work did he do, this Donovan Baker? Was it a private commission?"

"What business is it of yours?"

"Mr Richards, we're conducting a murder investigation. Anything that might impinge upon that is business of mine."

"I still fail to see . . ."

"Mr Donovan Baker's name has come up in relation to some dodgy dealings in the antiquities market and a predisposition towards violence. Personally, I think that's enough to make him of legitimate interest."

Mark Richards shrugged this aside, but Rozlyn knew from the way he left his desk and began to pace the room that he was shaken. Or maybe it was just that he really didn't like Rozlyn.

"He did a preliminary excavation, that's all. As I say, the records indicated earlier foundations; I wanted to know."

"Find anything to add to that personal museum of yours?"

"That's enough, Inspector. This is my home and I insist that you leave."

Rozlyn shrugged. She made a meal of writing down the titles of the two books she'd been shown and checking the flyleaf for other books Donovan Baker might have authored. Then she took her leave. "See you again, Mr Richards."

"Only if you have a search warrant and a bloody good reason."

"Oh, don't fret, I'm working on it."

"I have friends, you know."

Rozlyn had been wondering when that would come up. "I'm sure you do, but you know something? It's always amazed me how those kinds of friends tend to vanish back into the woodwork when they think their own reputation might be affected. I can see myself out."

Albert escorted her to the door and watched as she got into her car. Rozlyn drove off round the sweep of drive and onto the straight avenue that led to the gates and then she pulled over. She guessed that the chantry was about level with her present position and wondered if she could reach it through the trees. Quite why she wanted to look, she didn't know but the place drew her with an insistence that felt like more than just idle curiosity? Or was it simply the opportunity, not to be missed, of winding up Mark Richards just that little bit further.

The verge was muddy and the heavy fall of leaves damply fragrant beneath her tread. Rozlyn inhaled deeply of the summer ghosts and was refreshed by the warm pungency of the rain-washed, wet-leaf scent. Once past the line of trees she could see the chantry. Two walls remained, one around eight feet in height, then the end wall that she had glimpsed from the house, towering much higher. An arched window had been set into the wall at this tallest end and she tried to recall what little she knew about ecclesiastical building. She assumed that this portion must be the church and, from what scatter of low, ruined walls she could pick out in the long grass, that there had been other buildings surrounding and supporting this.

The highest wall leaned at an alarming angle and Rozlyn moved round to the outside of it to get a better view. Its final fall had been delayed by one of the ugliest constructions Rozlyn had ever seen. A cruel frame, arched and welded out of box section, had been wedged tightly against the wall, tracking around the windows, cross bracing the main wall and with its base firmly set against the ground. That, in turn, was propped by a metal column, set at a forty-five-degree angle, pushing back against the metal frame and preventing the entire structure from crashing earthward.

Rozlyn stared at it, shocked by the brutality of the metal work and struck by the thought that it might be better to allow the ruin to fall, to be reclaimed by the nature that had provided stone and mortar and was now encroaching across its structure, whether Mark Richards would have it or not. Tiny plants clung to the stonework, some winter-browned and decayed, others still fresh and vibrant against the grey.

She was aware that Albert had begun to cross from the house even before she saw him, as though the knowledge that he and Richards would soon realise she had not passed through the gates had alerted and sharpened her senses. She moved back to what would once have been the interior of the building, and discerned deep russet tiles on the ancient floor that gleamed like river-smoothed pebbles amongst the grass and dying nettles. A rough stone block suggested an altar, although its position seemed odd. She'd read somewhere that in early churches the altar was placed somewhere else than she would have expected in a modern church, but she couldn't think where. Near the entrance? This didn't look to be aligned with anything, though, and she examined the stone and its position with increased interest. It was carved with a pattern of intertwined animals and plants. The shadow cast by the walls and the heavy clouds darkened the day and made it hard for her to see but, as she dragged her fingers across the surface and as they helped her eyes to pick out the shapes, she understood that this was a complex and beautiful work and that it deserved better than to be standing here in this unsheltered spot, torn from its roots and abandoned to the weather and the years.

"You were told to leave. I've called the local constabulary."

"Really, that's nice. Many hands make light work, as they say."

"What do you mean?"

"I mean that they'll send a patrol car around and when they realise your intruder is a detective inspector who outranks them, then they'll either take themselves off or they'll be asking me what they can do to be helpful." She turned with a pleasant smile. "Albert, where did this stone originally stand? It was the altar, wasn't it?"

"I wouldn't know," Albert told her frostily.

"You couldn't move it far. It must weigh a ton." She circled it, looking not at the altar stone but around it. Two feet away, almost hidden by the overgrowth of grass and bramble and nettles, she saw it, the stone base on which the altar must have been placed and, as she glanced again at the altar, she saw that the great block was carved on only four of the sides that she could see. "Three sides and the top, then. Probably the fourth side too. This here . . ." she bent and examined the unadorned section more closely. "This here, must have been the base." She looked curiously at Albert. "It was rolled," she said. "Just turfed sideways and here, I can see where the crow bar was rammed beneath it." She stood and went to look at the plinth. Beneath the level at which the altar must have rested was a hollow, only ten or twelve inches deep, but lined with dressed stone broad enough to support the weight of the great slab. "Find anything?"

"Did I find anything where?"

Rozlyn laughed. "Oh, Albert, you're a bad liar," she said. "You get many trespassers here, do you?"

"I'm not sure what you mean."

"Or maybe undesirables wanting to see your boss?"

He frowned. "We have security, as you are well aware."

"Sure you do, but you've also got a lot of unguarded wall. The reality is, anyone could get in, couldn't they, Albert. So, do you get many unwelcome visitors? Like, for instance, a little man with short grey hair and wearing a pinstriped suit?"

It was there, Rozlyn thought, that slight twitch of recognition. Albert knew who she meant.

She walked slowly back to the car, Albert watching her as she left. Only when she had turned the ignition on did she look at the tiny fragment of cloth she held now in her left hand. It had been caught on a bramble close to the altar and she would have missed it if she'd not bent closer to look at the carving and caught her own sleeve on the thorns. Suiting, cheap and synthetic, black with a hint of paler stripe. It could have come from anywhere at any time — but it looked to Rozlyn like the stuff that made up Charlie's cheap pinstripe suits.

Not enough to prove a damn thing, she knew, and if there'd been traces of violence or blood, she would have seen them. She doubted he had been killed in that place but she was convinced now that Charlie had been there.

CHAPTER 30

Rozlyn took more painkillers and then drove back towards work. On the way she called in at the university bookshop and asked if they had any of Donovan Baker's work. She was surprised to find that one volume was a set text on the Archeology degree. The book was one of those Rozlyn had seen earlier that day.

"And there's this," The assistant told her. "He did a lot of work locally and a small press put out this book based on his excavations. He didn't write it, but he did a foreword for them."

Rozlyn flicked through the pages. There were a number of photographs including two that she recognised; a photograph of the chantry, pre-grotesque ironwork, and also an image of the cross she had seen depicted on Ethan Merrill's wall. "The small press that published this . . . um . . . Birch Wood. You know if it's still going?"

The assistant shook her head. "I've not heard from them in a little while. We get reprints of this from one of those print-on-demand places. To be honest, we only sell a handful, though I think the museum does a bit better. I think the address should be . . . yes. Here." She pointed and Rozlyn caught her breath. The address for Birch Wood was Ethan Merill's place out at Stamford.

* * *

Reaching the police station Rozlyn got straight onto the phone to her colleague in Art and Antiques. Stevens had been waiting for her call.

"I'm told he was first rate at his job, directed several really significant excavations, did international lecture tours, published books . . . he was even called as an expert witness by the Met. Then the shit hit the fan big time. Baker was implicated in an insurance scam and, even though nothing was proved, there was enough of a stink hanging around to make him persona non grata in certain respectable circles. Donovan Baker retired from academia and we've been trying to pin something on him ever since. Best we've got so far is assault and that was dropped 'cause the bloke he hit refused to testify. We couldn't prove it, but we figure Baker got to him and he didn't want to risk another beating . . . or worse."

"What would you prefer to have him on?"

Stevens laughed. "OK, the game is played like this. Donovan Baker has the contacts, both legit and not so kosher and he knows who owns what, makes it his business to know who could do with a little cash injection. Lo and behold, they get turned over, usually a range of artworks lifted, sometimes antiquities, but not always. They claim on the insurance and Baker, who has the art or antiques stashed somewhere, arranges the sale. He takes a hefty commission, but even so, said previous owner gets insurance cash and part of the proceeds from the sale. Two payouts in one."

"Nice arrangement."

"Exit Donovan Baker, considerably better off. We know it goes on — know he's at the heart of it — but no one, so far, is willing to testify. After all, they've been on the take too."

"You can't cut a deal?"

Steven's groaned. "Don't think we haven't tried but the collectors in question are usually wealthy society types for whom reputation is everything and they'll move hell and high water to keep us plebs of police officers at bay."

"People who don't need the money, then? So why risk it?"

"Because some of them are in hock up to their eyeballs. Sell the normal way and the tax man gets his share, or the government refuses an export licence and, believe me, that's happened more than once. Someone's got all upset at the idea of a national treasure being sold off, export licence is delayed to give some UK museum or other the chance to get the cash and, suddenly, the item in question is part of a general haul snatched by picky thieves. Sure, it looks suspicious, but in one case — and I can't name names, we're still investigating — the claim was that all the media coverage alerted thieves to the presence of said valuable object."

"And you're certain Donovan Baker is involved?"

"Certain as we can be without actually catching him in the act. Like I say, we believe he has full cooperation from the owners, but to act as a cover, we know he sometimes involves domestic staff — the lowest paid and most easily disaffected. One let him down. Our GBH recipient. Seems he should have let Donovan know about changes to the security system. Instead, he went to his boss, who, we figure was in on the game. Baker beat seven shades out of him and he confessed all to a junior doctor at the hospital that night. Of course, he then withdrew his statement before we could make it official and any good defence brief would tear his testimony apart because of when and where it was given. CPS decided it wasn't in the public interest to pursue. End of story."

Rozlyn thought about Mouse Man. Would he even recognise Donovan Baker again? Never mind agree to testify. "How did he get from professor to bruiser?" she asked.

"He had a record from age sixteen," Stevens told him. "Seemed to get himself straightened out when he went to live with an uncle up north somewhere. Got him back into school and then university, but it seems that was just a veneer. I've interviewed several people who knew him from those days and they all recall him as having a short fuse and a liking for his own way. He was making a decent living. I guess it just wasn't enough quickly enough. Look, I've got to go. You watch yourself, you hear? He's a vicious bugger."

"Already figured that," Rozlyn muttered as she replaced the receiver. She picked up the books she had bought and flicked through them again, pausing from time to time to read an extract. Far from being dry and technical, the book authored by Baker shone with the man's enthusiasm for his subject. The pages were enlivened by small asides and witty footnotes and the style of writing was easy and surprisingly accessible.

She turned back to the slimmer volume published by Ethan Merrill. There was no reason at all that Merrill should have mentioned Donovan; Rozlyn had not asked about him, but . . . the doubt set in. Did Merrill know something about Donovan's activities? Was he even a party to them?

Rozlyn shook her head, dismissing that idea, then reminding herself that she'd not even met Ethan Merrill until a few days before and the man could in fact be capable of anything.

Her thoughts were interrupted by the ringing of her mobile phone. It was the hospital. Mouse Man had disappeared.

CHAPTER 31

"It was visiting time," the ward sister told her. "There were people coming and going all the time and we'd encouraged him to get out of bed and go to the day room, so I don't know how long he'd been gone before we noticed. It was only when we did the drugs rounds and couldn't track him down that we realised and then a visitor came back to look for her coat . . ."

"He took a coat?"

"A raincoat, yes. He even left a note. Here, at the nurse's station. Apologising and promising to bring it back as soon as he'd finished with it."

"Can I see this note?"

"Oh yes, sorry. I should have given it to you straight away." The paper was crumpled and had someone's shopping list written on the other side. Mouse must have scrounged it from a bin. He'd written in small but clear letters, cramped together so he could get it all in and had obviously been planning his escape since earlier that day.

Dear Inspector Priest, I been thinking hard about what we talked about and I think I know where to find that Donovan man but I have to find him today or he'll be gone from the place. I decided I would borrow someones coat when they came visiting and get off into town some people goes out to smoke so noone will notice if im in my pijamas.

"A raincoat, you said?"

"Yes, trench-coat type with a belt. Dark blue, the woman said."

"So he's walking the streets in striped pyjamas and plaid slippers and a dark blue trench coat." Rozlyn sighed. "He's gonna freeze. Was his head still bandaged?"

"No, we'd just taped a gauze pad over the wound. Doctor wanted it to dry out. The woman was tall, that he took the coat from. It'll probably reach his ankles. I'm so sorry." She fretted. "This just shouldn't have happened. It never occurred to me . . . and this Donovan, he mentioned?"

"We think it might be the man who attacked him," Rozlyn told her.

Shock and horror spread across the sister's face and drained the colour from her already pale skin. "Oh, dear God. You think he went to find him? That's . . ."

Rozlyn nodded. Something she'd never have expected Mouse to do. "You've got my mobile number just in case he gets brought back here?"

She nodded. "You're going to look for him."

"Of course. I'll get a call put out, that way we've eyes and ears all over the town."

The ward sister nodded. She looked so stricken that Rozlyn felt she had to reassure her. "Look, how hard can it be to spot a man in a trench coat and striped pyjamas? I'll find him and I'll bring him back."

* * *

It was a question Rozlyn was still asking herself two hours later. She'd driven to all the places she thought Mouse might go. His house was boarded up and secure. The little chapel he attended on Sunday? Locked on a weekday, with no obvious way inside. The pubs he sometimes frequented; others he'd mentioned in passing. She drove, she walked, she asked questions and finally arrived at the Queen's at six-fifteen, a scant quarter hour after it had opened. Big Frank was already in residence in his favourite corner. He nodded almost amiably at Rozlyn and pointed at the bar. Rozlyn duly ordered him a pint and orange juice for herself, hoping the sugars and vitamins might help to counteract the weariness and deep bone ache that suffused her entire body.

"Fruit juice?" Big Frank was not impressed. "Going soft on me?" He scrutinised Rozlyn closely, leaning across the table to peer into her eyes. He grinned. "You look pale," he said, then laughed at his own joke. Frank's boys joined in. "You going down with something?"

"Feels like it." Rozlyn's voice croaked.

Frank pursed his little cupids bow of a mouth. "You should be home in bed," he affirmed. "Not spreading your germs amongst decent folk."

Rozlyn thought of telling him that if she met any decent folk, she'd be sure to follow that advice, but she didn't know if Frank's sense of humour stretched to subtle. "So I've been told," she said. "I'm looking for Mouse Man. Once I find him, I will be going home to bed."

"Tried the hospital?" Big Frank laughed again.

"He took off from there. Seems to think he can find this Donovan Baker. He . . . borrowed a coat but he's only got his slippers and pyjamas between him and the weather and it's bitter out there already."

"Donovan," Big Frank said. He narrowed his already tiny eyes and squinted at Rozlyn as through seeing her through bright sunlight. "Get the lass a brandy," he barked. One of his boys moved to obey. "I'll have my people keep a look out for him, that's what you want?"

Rozlyn hadn't actually thought this through. Her head was packed too full of painful cotton wool for that, but she croaked that it would be good to have extra eyes and ears on the job.

Big Frank nodded sagely. “I know how shorthanded you lot are,” he said, then roared again, the room erupting, this time, with genuine amusement. The brandy arrived and Rozlyn drank it, the fiery liquid warming her throat and momentarily cancelling out the burning, fevered sensation that had been her companion throughout the afternoon. She dug in her pocket for the last two of Jenny’s Max Strength tablets and swallowed them with a swig of orange juice, earning herself a look of disapproval from her drinking companion.

“You shouldn’t mix tablets and alcohol,” Big Frank told her sternly. “They can mix funny like.”

“It’s only paracetamol, or something.” Truthfully, she hadn’t looked to see what it was that Jenny had dosed her with.

“That’s what a lot of people think but let me tell you they can interact in ways you don’t know about until you’re swerving off the road and into a ditch. I won’t let any of my boys touch drink and drugs together. I saw a documentary on the dangers of over-the-counter medicine and alcohol. Opened my eyes, I can tell you. Maybe I should get someone to drive you home.”

It wasn’t the sort of conversation police training taught you to react to, Rozlyn thought. “I’ll be careful,” she promised with utmost seriousness.

“You let us find Mouse. I’ll get in touch and you take my advice. Now. Get yourself off home.”

Rozlyn nodded and thanked him. She left the pub wondering if accepting a brandy from Big Frank was against regulations and if so, what the hell was accepting his help because they were shorthanded. Her relationship with the Mastermind of Marfitt Street had taken some strange turns in the past few days, she thought. Her dealings with Big Frank had previously all been at arm’s length — preferably someone else’s arms — and she was still trying to figure out how this sudden camaraderie had come about and where it was all going to end.

Then she gave up trying to figure it out. Big Frank was right, she wasn't fit to be out unsupervised, never mind in charge of a car. Her head was throbbing and her eyes and throat felt raw. The brandy — had it been a double? Was she still legal to drive? — had gone to her head and the painful wadding was now swimming in a sea of loose brain. She could swear she could hear it sloshing about inside her head.

She phoned Jenny to tell her what was going on, then headed for home, just making it upstairs before collapsing, fully clothed, onto the bed and falling into a heavy, troubled sleep.

CHAPTER 32

Treven had never known three days pass so slowly. He had kept away from Theading, knowing that he must be seen to accept the conditions of the trial and not interfere. Osric gathered news for him. The comings and goings of serving men excited little interest or comment and from this he knew that Hugh was in great pain and had not slept more than odd half hours since the ordeal. There was no fever, Osric told him, although they would not know if the hand showed signs of putrefaction until the dressing was removed.

"He does not stink," was all the comment Osric could make and Treven had to accept that. Osric knew as well as Treven himself the sweet, choking stench of rotting flesh.

The morning of the third day dawned as clear and cold as that morning of the trial. Pearl-pink clouds blemished the brilliant blue of the sky, churning and moiling on the horizon in a manner that caused Treven to expect snow before nightfall. He pulled his cloak tight about his shoulders, tugged his winter sleeves down to cover his hands and donned his gloves, noticing how worn they were and wondering how long since they had been new. Treven had no love of the cold. Too many nights spent lying on ice-chilled mud, his bones aching and his joints too stiff to move had stolen any joy he might have had at the sight of snow. He welcomed winter only as a time when men were less inclined to war and he still took pleasure in the feasting and celebration of Yule and, before that, the celebration of All Souls and the night of heroes that followed eleven days after. A time for fresh beginnings and remembrance of those lost, it was, by turns, both joyful and solemn. This year, though, he was among neither family nor comrades and when the festivals came, he wondered if he'd have the heart to celebrate.

Treven rode ahead of his little company, a borrowed wagon trundling and creaking behind. Its use, either to convey Hugh alive to Theadingford and to receive due care and treatment for his wounds, or to carry him bound and trussed to the gallows on the hill.

Kendryk waited for him. He too had been absent these last days but had left five of his monks in charge of Hugh: burly men, trained in use of the quarterstaff and sword. Kendryk had chosen them for his own bodyguard when he travelled and upon their heads the tonsure sat somewhat oddly. Kendryk, wrapped in his travelling cloak, had only just arrived when Treven and his modest entourage clopped and clattered into the open space before the Hall

"Let us go now," he said. "I've no stomach for the food Edmund has provided until I know what is to follow."

"You believe him guilty." Treven stated.

"But guilty of what? The trial was for the murder of Cate, nothing more or less. God will have judged him solely on that score."

Treven snorted, wishing in his heart that God could be a little more comprehensive in his judgement.

Hugh had been confined in one of the ancillary buildings belonging to the Scriveners and used for storage. A pallet had been provided, with a straw mattress and blankets, food and water given to him twice daily. That apart, he had been left alone to contemplate.

Hugh was not a man used to confinement and Treven had expected to find him chafing with impatience for whatever the outcome should be. Instead, as his eyes became accustomed to the dim light inside, he saw that Hugh lay motionless on his bed, his good hand resting on his chest and the wounded one lying beside him almost as though he disowned it.

He's dead, Treven thought and felt a guilty stab of relief. Then he saw the slight rise of his chest as he breathed.

"Hugh," Kendryk commanded.

Painfully, Hugh opened his eyes and then sat. As Kendryk brought the rush light closer, Treven could see that he looked green and sick, but his eyes were not brightened by fever and, as Treven sniffed the air, he caught only the hog-grease smell of the oil lamp, the fragrance of fresh bread and the stink of a man left in the same clothing for too long without means of washing.

"Stand," Kendryk ordered and Hugh rose wearily to his feet. He did not lift his eyes to face either of them, but instead, he extended the wounded hand for Kendryk to see.

They had been unable to prise open the fingers; the hot bar had been dragged from his fist, taking palm flesh with it. The hand was still closed and Treven, who had seen such wounds before, knew that he would never have the use of it again. It seemed wasteful, Treven thought, that such a warrior as Hugh was brought down by . . . by what? By a woman? By love or lust or some combination of both. Had he truly had such feelings for Cate Scrivener? Or by pride or conviction or something else that Treven could not name. Whatever the cause, Treven counted it waste. Better to have respected his father's wishes and entered the monastery than come to this.

Kendryk himself began to unwind the bandages. The hand had been bound with clean linen and no attempt had been made to open it flat: the fingers had simply been wrapped as they lay, cramped against the palm bones. Kendryk paused as the first layer was pulled free. He fingered the wrapping, then called Treven to his side. "I feel oil on this," he said, "and there is a scent too that I cannot identify."

"I knocked the grease lamp while I slept," Hugh told him. "It was out but the grease still warm."

Treven frowned. He bent his head to catch the scent Kendryk had mentioned. It was familiar, but he couldn't name the herb, though he knew one who could. Osric, he thought, and his throat clamped closed with fear.

Kendryk looked at him, expecting an opinion but when none came he shrugged and continued with his work. Hugh was in great pain now, as the inner layers of bandaging pulled and tore the still open wound.

Slowly the layers were undone and Kendryk leaned close to sniff and examine the wound. "The fingers are fused and the hand will not unbend," he said. "But I see no pus and there is no smell of putrefaction." He inclined his head towards one of his servant monks. "Bring him outside, we will examine him properly in God's own light."

Outside a crowd had gathered, smaller than that which had come to watch Hugh maimed. "If you had choice and could go back, would you do this thing again?" Treven asked him softly.

Hugh did not reply direct. Instead he said. "I did not kill her." Then, more quietly. "But I can name the man that did."

"What?!"

Treven's shock was loud enough to have others turn and stare. He recovered himself and murmured some excuse, then stepped back to allow Kendryk to complete his work. He was aware that Kendryk had also heard Hugh's words.

Kendryk turned the hand this way and that in the daylight, ignoring Hugh's cries of pain. In the end he pronounced himself satisfied. Though there was little sign as yet of healing, the burns were dry and clean.

"God in his wisdom has spoken," he declared.

He sounds disappointed, Treven thought.

"The man accused is declared innocent of the crime of murder and stands free to leave this place."

The crowd murmured but Treven was unsure if they approved or were still aggrieved.

"If you've words to say," Kendryk told Hugh sternly. "Then speak them now or keep your silence."

Hugh cradled his wounded hand across his body and remained silent for so long that Treven began to feel that he'd thought better of his quiet accusation, but he was wrong. Slowly, Hugh lifted his head and he surveyed those gathered, Treven and the villagers and Kendryk and the brothers.

"Cate told me a secret thing," he said, his voice strong with conviction. "She told me that on the night her sister left, she saw another leave after her. When he returned, there was blood on his tunic and on his hands. Cate herself helped to wash them clean."

"What?" Eldred's expression of shock only echoed Treven's own. Sound erupted from those gathered; wordless questions and expressions of dismay both at the thought this might be true and also outrage that this man should dare make such claims.

Kendryk lifted a hand for silence. He waited until he had it, then he asked, "And whom now do you accuse? Cate's husband, Eldred, or his brother Edmund, perhaps. Hugh, I am loath . . ."

"Neither." Hugh told him. "There is one man only Cate would protect and that only out of a habit born of lifelong regard. The secret tore at her heart. She could tell no one."

"And yet, she told you. A stranger?" Eldred's fury broke him from the group and he stepped closer to Hugh.

"Who else, but a stranger," Hugh told him seriously. "Could she tell a kinsman that the one she accused—"

"Was her father," Treven said. He could see Hugh's enjoyment in this and he hated him for it. This time, the shock of Treven's words caused silence to fall.

"You accuse one not capable of his own defence," Eldred spat at Hugh. "You disgust me more each time I come into your presence. If you are the measure of man the king chooses, then I for one do foreswear the King."

"Such words are treason!" Treven exclaimed. He stepped forward, sword unsheathed from its scabbard.

Kendryk laid a hand upon his arm. "And we did not hear them spoken," he said firmly. "Hugh, why say this now. If you knew before, why not tell your lord, or even me of this claim?"

"Cate made me swear to silence. Now she is gone, I no longer consider myself bound by that vow."

"And Cate was dead when you took the trial. Why wait until now?"

"I waited because I stood accused of murder. I wished to clear my name before I condemned another. Who would have heard my words or chosen to believe?"

"What is this leading to, Hugh?" Treven demanded. Then the realisation. "You claim that this sick old man also took the life of his second child?"

Slowly, Hugh nodded.

"On what grounds?" Eldred demanded. "Abbot, this is madness. Take the man away, we do not want him here."

"He has won his right to be heard," Kendryk said mildly. "But tell us, Hugh, how is it you know of this. Did Cate's father come and make confession to you?"

"He's been nowhere near this man," Edmund argued. "And should he have declared to all and sundry that he murdered his children, well, you have seen him, lord, would you believe his word?"

Treven was cautious in his reply. "I have seen him with the madness on him and his mind befuddled by too much drink," he said. "But I know that such men can still have moments when their minds clear and they can speak truth."

"So, you join this accusation? You are no better than . . ."

"I caution you, Eldred, watch your words." Treven warned. "I do not accuse your kinsman. I wonder though, if he knew what his daughter did and followed her and there met with trouble. Perhaps the *Waelas* man she left with fought with the father. Perhaps Cate knew this and that is why she defended and protected him? Blood does not always speak of murder."

"He killed them both," Hugh said steadily. "I do so swear. I had this knowledge from Cate herself and then . . . from the evidence of my own eyes."

Treven turned on him. "You saw him kill Cate?"

Hugh nodded, but would no longer meet Treven's gaze

"You saw and you did nothing to defend her?"

"A failing I will live with lifelong! Treven, I swear, by the time I reached her side, the deed was done. He struck her twice and then ran. I thought her dead and I let her lie. In the darkness . . . truly, I thought her already dead and gone."

Treven moved closer and thrust his fist beneath Hugh's chin forcing him to raise his head. "You've seen death often enough, Hugh de Vries. You and I have stood knee deep in blood and killing. You know if a woman breathes or not even in the dark and that night, there was moon enough to see. You may not have struck the blow, but you left her there to die and in my heart I still see you as murderer for that act of cowardice."

Hugh held his gaze then raised his mutilated hand. "*You* cannot accuse me now," he said softly. "When God himself has acquitted me. I blamed myself when I knew she had lived until morning and because of that, I took this test. I wounded myself so deep I may never heal and yet, I am not dead. God looked into my heart and saw that the guilt was not mine. Now, I can declare what I know. Had I spoken of this before, who would have held the truth of it?"

Treven, lost for words, stepped away, releasing his hold on his one-time friend. He felt sick to the stomach, his body pained in every fibre. He could not believe that God would allow anyone to argue right and wrong on such a fine line and yet . . . and yet . . . here was Hugh. Hurting, but whole and so certain of his rights that Treven could find no argument.

"You presume to know the heart and mind of God?" Kendryk's voice was soft but dangerous.

"No, Lord Abbott, only to be thankful for his mercies."

Kendryk nodded slowly but said nothing more. Treven could see the hardness in his eyes and realised with shock that

Kendryk looked for other solutions even as he did himself. That the Abbott, this man of God, no more accepted the simplicity of Hugh's claim, than did Treven himself, Treven who spoke of the Christ with his lips but whose heart was still partly in thrall to his mother's gods. What was the answer here?

"You saw the father strike that fateful blow?" Treven confirmed.

"I saw it, yes. I stood in the shadow of the birch trees and saw her run across the rough grass and onto the path. She turned and then he came from the withy-stand behind her. He must have called her name or made some sound because she wheeled to face him. He struck her once and then again as she tried to run. Then he left her."

Treven was thinking fast. "When she left you, she was not headed towards home?"

Hugh looked confused, then shook his head. "I did not think of it," he said, "but it seemed to me that she went the other way along the path. Towards the cottage of the one that found her." He shrugged. "Perhaps she intended to visit."

"So late at night?"

"How should I know what hours she kept? She had some errand, perhaps."

"Strange that you did not ask nor she tell you, since she told you so much else. Or that you failed to see her safe home or to whatever destination she chose? You claimed to have feelings for this woman, Hugh. I am beginning to doubt that. Already, you told me that you spent the night with another."

"And she confirmed that."

"We spoke with her, yes. She said you arrived some time in the middle of the night. She could not guess the hour. You spent the remainder of the night rutting with another man's wife while your cast-off love lay dying in the mud."

Hugh flinched. "I told you, I thought her dead."

"Even so, you spent little time grieving."

"I thought . . . I thought to be elsewhere should any ask. Cate had promised Eldred that she would see no more of me. I would not have her foresworn, not even in death."

"Unless it would be to convict her father." Treven let out a slow, despairing breath. Battle, he understood. In that art he was master. Not this. His hopes for peace and a new life seemed suddenly to be an empty wish.

"Why did she run from you?"

"I did not say that she ran from me."

"You frightened her, Hugh. I saw the marks on her neck and if the father killed her with a blow to the head, why place his hands at her throat? The bruises were caused by your fingers and not his. Did you think to kill her then?"

Hugh's colour had been lifted by the fresh air but he paled again now.

"I remember another time." Treven asserted. "I came back to our lodging and found you with a woman. You played rough with her, hands about her throat until she bruised because in some way she had displeased you. You made excuse that she'd been stealing and that you acted in anger. I believed you and took your word that you meant only to put the fear of God back into her soul, but I know what happened that night with Cate, Hugh de Vries. She told you that she planned to return faithfully to her husband or, perhaps, she threatened you by saying that the child she carried was yours and wanted provision for him? Whatever the cause, you sought to frighten her, maybe even to take her life."

"I sought . . . I sought nothing. Yes, I was angry. Yes, I behaved as no man should. Anyway, that other one was nothing but a common whore . . ."

"She was still a living woman . . ."

"Maybe so, but when I realised what I had done to Cate . . . believe me Treven, I went too far without meaning anything. I released her and she ran. I did not follow. I would have confessed to my assault of her . . ."

"But then her father struck the fatal blow and you assumed all would think her killer sought to choke her first."

He turned from Hugh and spoke angrily to Kendryk. "Your laws tried him, I'll leave it to you to give him passage home. I'll have no more of this."

"You cannot send me away," Hugh reminded him. "The King appointed me. I go or stay upon *his* word, not yours."

"And I will send word to the King and plead my case with him. You think he'll want a lawgiver that the people despise?"

"A lawgiver that dared to give himself up to justice and was victorious," Hugh retorted.

Treven gave him one last look before striding away. "I thought once that I knew your heart," he said. "You were impulsive, sometimes foolish and your liking for women was ever wont to lead to trouble, but at least I knew you to be loyal and honest. I look now at your heart and see it rotten, eaten by maggots. Keep from my doors, Hugh. You are not welcome in my hall."

CHAPTER 33

Osric followed as Treven rode back to Theadingford, though keeping a respectful distance from his master. Treven was in no mood for either conversation or observation on what had passed.

As they dismounted, Osric reached to take the reins from Treven's hand and said, "I've done a wrong thing."

"I know it. Osric, did you think none would notice the scent of herbs or the feel of the oil you'd brewed them in? Kendryk is too sharp for that to go by."

"You'll punish me?"

"I should have you flogged but, truthfully, I've no stomach for it. If Kendryk had wished to challenge he would have done so back there. No, he'll save that knowledge for some other time when it might be of use to him . . . as will Hugh?"

Osric looked puzzled. "He can't tell on us without impugning himself," he objected.

"Hugh is subtler then either you or I. If there is a way then he will find it. This is not the man I knew in battle, this is someone I do not understand. A man who looks, as I suppose do we all, to get the most from the king's peace, but Osric, should I ever dishonour myself as deep as Hugh has done, cut my throat while I sleep and bury my body face down in the earth."

Osric looked away, choosing not to hear. Instead, he led the horses to be groomed and stabled.

"Osric," Treven called after him, "I will walk for a while. I've no mood to be confined. If any come to ask for me, you will not know where I have gone or how long."

Osric nodded, though his face was creased with concern. Treven, unable to offer words of comfort, turned away from his home and walked back to the ford, crossing carefully on the larger rocks to keep his feet dry. The skies, heavy with snow, began to loose the first flakes and they drifted down to settle in his fox-red hair. He drew the hood over his head and pulled the cloak closer, even though the day had warmed somewhat since morning, and as he walked swiftly up the rise towards that place with the wooden cross, Treven felt less chill in his bones though the lump of ice still sat hard in his belly.

As he reached the crossroads where the cross and gibbet faced each other and the three roads to Storton, to Theadingford and back towards Winchester met, a flock of black battle crows flew overhead, their harsh cries causing him to pause and look skyward. They and he were the only things moving in this quiet landscape, the muffling of snow clouds even deadened sound. Treven stood and listened to the silence.

The body had long since fallen from the rope onto the hard ground below, flesh and sinew rotted through, left to be dragged away by those creatures hungry enough to feed on putrefying flesh. In spring, someone would gather what was left and bury it at the crossing of the roads. Too few would come here in the winter months to worry about the walking of restless spirits and besides, it would soon be All Souls. Such walkers were expected and it might be that his kinsmen would still lay a place for him at their table and even hope that he would return.

Treven wondered what kind of a man he had been. None in the village could name him, but those in Theading were not the only locals to hang their guilty here and, he guessed, they most likely chose not to remember his name even had it been known to them. It came to his mind that he should have brought Hugh here this day, placed the noose about his neck and driven the cart from beneath his feet. He closed his eyes, imagining the hairy texture of rough rope between his hands. Treven himself would have placed the rope about Hugh's neck; it was not a task he could in conscience have passed to another. He asked himself, could he have done it?

He closed his eyes tighter, recalling the marks on Cate's neck and knew that he could, though to kill in such cold blood was not something he would willingly have chosen, even though he believed the crime deserving of it.

He turned away from the remains of the man and walked on past the cross. Kendryk had spoken of an ancient grove that he wished destroyed. Treven searched for it now, seeking solace in a place that was not of Christian mind.

The track was overgrown, though in no place had the undergrowth encroached enough to make it impassable. Someone still used this place then. Here and there he noted where saplings and brambles had been chopped back to keep them in control and the woodland was coppiced between the taller oaks and white-skinned birch. Thickets of hazel rustled with the life of small birds and rodents disturbed by his presence and the coppiced trees showed two or three winters' worth of growth. It would be ready for cutting back again this next spring. Beyond the coppiced woodland rose a circle of grey-skinned ash, crowning a slight rise. Treven paused. Snow was falling heavily now, muffling his footsteps and crusting his long-suffering cloak with a rime of white. He glanced back over his shoulder, suddenly afraid that Kendryk might have guessed his destination and be watching him.

"Fool," he told himself. "Kendryk has more sense than to be traipsing abroad in this." He took a deep breath of chilled air and stepped through the curtain of falling snow and into the sacred grove.

Within the grove was silence. Treven walked to the heart of it and turned slowly, gazing up at the leafless canopy and the heavy sky.

"What do I do? Lord, I have spent my life since childhood in battle and war; in blood and death. I came here hoping to have left that life but it has followed after me. Death comes to my door and even justice is blinded by one man's misuse of faith.

"God, Christ, Wotan, whatever I should call you, whatever name you bear, guide me now. Tell me, show me what I should do?"

His words stumbled, blocked, it seemed cushioned by soft falling snow and lowering clouds. Treven closed his eyes and for a moment, gave himself up to anger and despair.

* * *

"Are you all right?"

The woman's voice was strange, the words seemed familiar and yet said with an accent that Treven could not truly understand. He frowned and turned towards the speaker and as he did so the sounds resolved themselves inside his head into words that he could comprehend. The woman stood at the edge of the grove, her posture stiff and uncertain as though finding herself in an unfamiliar and private place and not sure of her welcome.

"You!" Treven took a step towards her and then two back, gripped by unreasoning fear. He felt he should speak, hide his dread. "I have seen you, walking with the hooded one. Are you a spirit?"

The woman or woman shaped thing stepped further into the circle.

"A spirit? No, I mean, I guess everyone has a spirit or at least I like to think so. But unless I died and no one thought to tell me, then I think I'm still alive."

Treven stared at her, wondering if this woman thing were at the very least mad. Her clothes were strange. She wore a long dark coat just a shade or so darker than her skin. The fabric — no, leather so soft it draped like cloth — fell almost to her ankles and her head was bare, the black waves of her hair tied back in a bright red band.

Strangest and most fearful of all, the snow fell all about her but not a single flake fell upon her clothes or skin. Treven stared harder and his throat closed on the cry of alarm that rose when he saw the way the snow refused to touch this woman. As if his realisation brought the same fact home to the stranger, she held out her hands as though to catch the flakes.

"Well, will you look at that," she commented. She laughed. "Will you look at that?"

Treven watched as she wandered over to the largest of the trees and sat down with her back to the smooth trunk. She seemed untroubled by the frozen ground.

Slowly, Treven followed her and seated himself on a large root, sweeping away the gathered snow. "You must be a spirit," he informed the stranger. "The snow falls all about you and yet . . ."

The woman shrugged. "Maybe I'm just dreaming," she said.

"You dream?" Treven shook his head. "*I* am not sleeping. This is not *my* dream."

"No, I'm the one dreaming." She frowned, puzzled. "Who knows? I'm not sure it really matters anyway." She extended a hand towards Treven. "I'm Rozlyn, by the way. Rozlyn Priest."

"A priest?" Treven stared at the hand, unsure of what to do. If he reached to clasp it, would it be there or would he, like the snow, be cast aside?

"No, I'm not a priest, it's my surname."

"Your father was a priest?" Treven had to know. He reached out and touched the other's hand. "You're warm!"

"Um, yes. So are you."

"You are a woman, then. Or a spirit taken woman's form."

"Or a dream. Who knows? Look, like I said, I'm not sure it matters anyway. What's your name?"

Treven frowned. To tell a name was to give another power over it. True, this woman had told her name, but Treven had no means of knowing if it was real. He took a deep breath. "I am Treven," he said. "King's Thegn."

"Oh. Pleased to meet you, Treven. Which king?"

"I serve Aelfred." A new suspicion arose in Treven's mind. "You are Guthrum's man?"

"Who? I'm sorry, I've no idea what you're talking about."

"Why are you here? What brought you?"

The stranger shrugged. "I don't know," she said. "I fell asleep. I woke up here. I think, before that, I was looking for someone, but . . ." she turned deep dark eyes on Treven, so deep and dark that Treven felt like drowning when he gazed into their depths. He tore his gaze away.

"When I got here," Rozlyn Priest said. "You looked upset, kind of lost. I must be here for a reason, so I may as well be useful. Is there anything I can do?"

Treven had come here to ask for help but that the help should be offered in such a strange and mysterious way was beyond his expectation. "What can you know of justice," he asked. "I came here looking for answers. I asked the gods to help me; the old gods and the Christ and any powers that rule the Wyrd." He laughed shortly. "I did not look for such as you to come to my aid."

"And I didn't ask to come here, but as my grandfather used to say, if you're truly lost, maybe it doesn't matter who you follow. Everyone's going somewhere." She laughed at Treven's expression. "No, it probably never made a lot of sense, but I guess what I mean is, it's often easier to tell your problems to a stranger and, like I said, I must be here for a reason?"

When Treven still did not reply she added, "and as for what I know about justice, well, I guess I spend my life dealing with what I hope is justice."

"You are a law giver?"

"Um, no. I don't *make* laws. I just try to see that people keep them."

Treven nodded. So there was, after all, a kindred spirit here. "I too seek to keep the king's law," he said. He sighed heavily. "I've come to realise that I am ill equipped for the task he gave me."

"We all feel like that sometimes. Look, I don't know how long I'm going to be here. I have this feeling that it's time limited some way or another, so tell me and we'll see if two heads are better than one."

Treven nodded. Suddenly, it seemed correct and right that he should do so. "I came here as King's Thegn," he said

"Thegn? No, never mind, I can ask Ethan. Go on."

"Ethan?"

"A friend."

"Oh." Treven frowned, puzzled. "I came here and brought with me a man called Hugh de Vries who the king had promised would be Shire Reeve in this place. I . . . blame myself. I knew what Hugh was, that he liked women and had little concern for discretion, and I should have spoken when he first took Cate Scrivener to his bed. But I did not and when she was found dead and Hugh was blamed . . ."

"Why would Hugh want to kill his lover?"

"She told him she would see him no more. He was angry, he confessed to having laid hands on her, to strangling her until she feared for her life. Then, he says he realised what he did and let her go. She ran from him and, so he claims, another came and felled her with a blow and then a second."

"He witnessed this?"

Treven nodded. "It was dark, he says he thought her dead, but she did not die then. She lived until the coming day and when they found her, she spoke his name."

"You think she accused him? Or that she knew he'd left her to die?"

"Either, perhaps both."

"And did he see who hit her?"

"He claims so, though he stood some distance away."

"So, and I'm assuming from what you've said that this is night, but that if there was enough light for him to see who did it, there was also enough for him to see that she was still alive."

Treven had not put this so clearly to himself. He nodded. "He knew she lived, but likely knew also she could not long survive."

"Even so, she might have stood some chance if he'd raised the alarm. Why didn't he?"

"He claimed fear that he would be accused anyway and that the marks on her neck were clear. He would have . . . he thought to blame those also on her killer."

Rozlyn nodded. "So, what happened?"

Treven told her in few words about the trial. That the law of God had found Hugh innocent of murder because he had not struck that final blow.

"Wow," Rozlyn breathed. "You know, I've heard about that sort of stuff, but I never really thought about it happening for real. You know, I never reckoned on God being someone who would split hairs like that." She laughed, but there was no humour in it. "This Hugh'd make a good defence lawyer or make a fortune in litigation."

"A what?"

Rozlyn frowned. "I don't know that I could explain," she said. "So, what are you going to do about it? In my book, he killed her or least he denied her the chance she might have had if she'd seen a doctor. That's manslaughter at the very least."

"Manslaughter," Treven considered. His mind felt clearer now. "You are right, Rozlyn Who is Not a Priest. Manslaughter." He stood. "I know what I must do." It occurred to him that he had always known; his mind had just refused to see.

Rozlyn also got to her feet.

Treven's cloak was weighed with a heavy stratum of crisp white snow. He shook it off and stamped his feet to free them of the ice caked on the soles. Rozlyn, by contrast, remained untouched. She tilted her head as though listening to something and, somewhere in the distance, Treven heard the sound of bells.

"What is that sound?"

"Oh," Rozlyn told him. "I think that's the sign for me to go." She smiled. "Good luck, Treven, you'll do OK, I'm sure of it."

Treven watched in wonder as the stranger began to fade. Rozlyn too stared at her own hands and laughed. "Oh, will you look at that. I can see right through me."

Her laughter, dying softly on the windless air, was the last thing that remained.

Treven shook himself. He should, he thought, have been afraid, but he was not. Instead, he felt calm and filled with purpose. Murmuring a prayer of thanks to whatever form of god or Wyrd had given him aid, he left the grove and, pausing only to cut from the coppiced ash a staff as high as his head and thick around as he could grip, he headed back towards his home.

CHAPTER 34

Rozlyn stumbled down the stairs reaching the phone just as Jenny finished her message.

"Hello. I'm here."

"You sure? You sound like death."

She managed a laugh but Jenny's words brought the dream back so vividly that Rozlyn had to ask her to repeat her next comments.

"I said, they've found Mouse Man. He's OK."

"Oh, thank Christ for that. Who found him? Where is he?"

"Your friend — and I use the word advisedly — has him holed up at the Queen's. He's been fed and watered and they're giving him a bed for the night. The hospital wants to check him over in the morning but they're being sniffy about taking him back as an inpatient after he discharged himself so dramatically. I thought we could sort that out tomorrow."

"He's seen a doctor?"

"Apparently," Jenny said, cautiously.

"Don't tell me. We'll be getting a bill from Big Frank."

Jenny laughed. "I'll leave you to tell Brook all about it in the morning. I know nothing!"

Rozlyn groaned. "I'll get over there and see he's OK. Where the hell did he get to?"

"He's not saying. Won't tell anyone but you. Look, I'm knackered. I'll be off home and see you tomorrow."

Rozlyn went back upstairs and studied herself in the bathroom mirror. The reflected face was creased and grubby. She'd fallen asleep fully clothed, not even having managed to shed her coat. Turning from the reflection, she shrugged out of the leather and hung it in the bedroom, shaking and patting it critically, worrying at the creased skin. Then she peeled off the sweat-soaked shirt and washed herself, splashing her puffy face with cold water in an effort both to wake up and to ease the wrinkles from her eyes.

A second check in the mirror revealed partial success and a rummage in the bathroom cabinet found a new supply of painkillers. She dragged a plain T-shirt from her drawer and completed the look with a weekend shirt of dog-toothed check. It was eleven-fifteen on Friday night.

Putting the much-abused leather coat back on she prepared to leave, then did an about-turn and unlocked the wardrobe, removed the spearhead, wrapped it in an old scarf and slipped it into her pocket.

She wondered at this, telling herself it was so she didn't forget to return it to the evidence locker in the morning, but it was really the effects of the dream, still so powerfully there in her mind that she could taste the chill, snowy air even in the warmth of her centrally heated room.

* * *

Mouse Man sat in Big Frank's corner ploughing his way through a plate of sandwiches. A second, scattered with crumbs, betrayed the fact that this was a repeat performance. In his left hand was a large blue mug, gripped tight as though he worried someone might take it away and alongside that a tray with a family-sized tea pot and a milk jug and sugar bowl.

The pub was closed and the main lights off. One of Frank's boys sat in an opposite corner chatting to the barman and playing what looked like Texas hold 'em. Rozlyn felt a pang. It was years since she had played. She pointedly ignored the stack of coins lined up beside each player.

Mouse beamed at her from across the room and beckoned with his sandwich. The borrowed raincoat hung over the back of a chair and his pyjamas were spattered with mud, the hems caked in it. Soaked slippers steamed on the radiator and his feet were clad in a pair of thick fisherman's socks. Borrowed from the barman, Rozlyn guessed. Frank's boys subscribed to the sort of sartorial elegance that didn't call for heavyweight socks.

"Mouse, just what do you think you were doing? You should be in the hospital, not traipsing the streets in your PJs. What the hell were you playing at?"

Mouse's sandwich waved the objections aside. "I found him, Inspector Priest. I seen Donovan."

"You what! Mouse, what were you thinking? What do you mean you've seen him?"

"I seen him," Mouse repeated. "At his office place."

"His office . . . Mouse, start at the beginning and tell me what the hell you're on about."

Mouse looked somewhat offended by her tone. He took another large bite of sandwich and swig of tea before he continued. "I remembered what Charlie told me," he said. "Charlie said Mr Donovan collected his messages on a Friday because he was in town doing something else. I don't know what the something else was, but he told me Mr Donovan came and got his messages and his letters and any letters or anything Charlie found when he cleaned he had to leave at Donovan's office on Fridays so he could fetch them."

"Donovan. You're saying Donovan was connected to Thomas Thompson and the houses Charlie cleaned?"

Mouse nodded. "I told you that," he asserted proudly.

"No, Mouse, you didn't tell me."

"Yes I did, I told you just now."

Rozlyn sighed. "OK, Mouse, you get on with the story and I'll ask questions at the end."

"His office place is behind a shop. I went there with Charlie one day. I wasn't supposed to but it was early and Charlie knew he wouldn't be there that early so he said it was all right but today I sat on the fire escape back of the other shop and I watched for him and he came. I wanted to know, see, if it was him that came to my house and killed my little pets and hurt me before I told you about him. I didn't want to go accusing the wrong man, did I? That wouldn't be right, Inspector Priest, not right at all. And it was him," he added triumphantly. "It was that Mr Donovan."

"Mouse," Rozlyn forgot she'd promised not to interrupt. "What the hell were you thinking? He'd half killed you already. You want him to finish the job?"

"I was all right," Mouse told her earnestly. "That big man was hanging about. Donovan didn't see me but if he had the big man would have sorted him."

"Big man? What big man?"

"The big man I saw waiting outside of the Queen's one night. I told you about him. I was scared of him then, but this time I knew he was all right."

"How did you know? Mouse. What does he look like? Who is he?"

Mouse shrugged and reached for the tea pot. "I just knew," he said. "He's a big man with long red hair."

"Red hair?" Rozlyn shook her head, the image of Treven in that circle of snowy trees suddenly impinging. She thrust it aside and focused back on Mouse. "This office, we're talking about the building back side of the shops on Thurlmere Road, right?"

Mouse nodded. "That's the one."

"Right. Charlie had the number in one of his books. We're supposed to be keeping obs."

"He wasn't supposed to write the number down," Mouse said solemnly. "He told me so, but he said it was untidy just to keep things in your brain and not write them down proper like."

Rozlyn smiled. That was so Charlie. But that tidy streak might also have contributed to his death. And where the hell were the officers on watch if both Mouse and Donovan Baker could sneak past them? "Mouse, what did this Donovan do at the office?"

Mouse looked relieved now that Rozlyn was asking for actual information. "He put things in bags," he said. "I could see some of it through the window, but not everything. He put the telephone in a bag and then he went away. He dumped the bag in a skip just up the street. I seen him."

"You followed him!"

"No, I ain't quite that stupid. I waited 'til he'd gone out of the place at the back of the shops and then I went to the place where the alley opens onto the road and I looked. He dumped the bag in a skip, so . . ." He paused and smiled broadly.

Rozlyn could guess what was coming. "You went and got it."

Mouse beamed. He got up and shuffled round to where the borrowed coat was hanging. On the chair was a black dustbin bag. Puzzled, Rozlyn opened the neck and peered in.

"Careful!" Mouse warned. "Don't you touch the bag inside, there might be fingerprints." He nodded to emphasis the point.

"Fingerprints?"

"He carried the bag and he didn't wear no gloves. I asked at the greengrocer's shop for a dustbin bag. They looked at me like I was a down and out, but they gave me a bag and asked me if I wanted holes cut for my head and arms. I told them no, then I put the bag over the other one and took it away."

Rozlyn was impressed. "You did well, Mouse, but I'd still rather you hadn't been there at all. I'm scared to think what he'd have done to you."

Mouse shrugged, trying to look nonchalant, but it was clear Rozlyn's praise and concern had gone right to his heart. "I'm safe now," he said. "Big Frank tells me I can stay here until my house is all right and they make good tea. He says it's the best place for me."

He was probably right, Rozlyn thought. She couldn't offhand think of a more secure place to stash Mouse than the Queen's.

She was about to ask another question but Mouse Man seemed distracted. He was peering beneath the table and then glancing anxiously across at the barman.

"Mouse?"

"Shh, you'll frighten her."

Mouse dropped to his knees and scrabbled about beneath the table. Looking down, Rozlyn saw a mouse hiding in a crack in the skirting. "Jesus, Mouse, what the hell?"

Mouse Man was on his knees. Softly, almost under his breath, he made a series of soft clicking, crooning noises, interspersed with almost inaudible squeaks. Rozlyn watched in fascination as the tiny creature poked first its twitching, bewhiskered nose out of the crack and then the rest of its head. Mouse Man lowered his hand slowly to the floor. In his palm were a few crumbs from his sandwich. He made that squeaking, crooning noise again. The mouse detached itself from its place of safety and scrabbled over to the waiting hand.

"Mouse! You can't!" Rozlyn glanced across to where the men sat still playing cards. They seemed oblivious to the rodent charming taking place across the room. Mouse hauled himself back onto his seat and tucked his new friend into the pocket of his pyjama jacket.

"She'll be all right now," he said.

"How do you know it's a she?"

Mouse awarded her a withering look.

"OK, OK, I'll take your word for it. Mouse, did Charlie ever mention cleaning or working for anyone else? Or did he say he'd ever met the Mr Thompson that owned the houses?"

Mouse thought about it for a while then nodded slowly. "He must have seen him or met him," he said, "because he knows what he looks like. He saw his picture in the newspaper and he cut it out and put it in his drawer. He said he had a different name in the picture and a big house."

"In his drawer?" In the sideboard. Rozlyn remembered that she'd left before the search had been completed. She didn't recall seeing any news clippings, but Jenny would know.

"OK, I'd better go." She got to her feet. "You get a good night's sleep and I'll drop back to see you. And please, don't go wandering off on your own again."

"I won't," Mouse told her. "I already promised Big Frank that." He looked troubled all of a sudden and Rozlyn wondered why. Mouse enlightened her. "He says I should go to court and tell that it was Donovan that took my eye away," he said.

Rozlyn sat down again. "And how do you feel about that?"

Mouse nodded. "I know I got to," he said. "I feel scared, but I'll do it, Inspector Priest. If he's the one killed Charlie, then he ought to go to prison for ever."

"He should go to prison anyway for what he did to you," Rozlyn told him quietly. "Mouse, it's very brave of you. I promise we'll keep you safe."

Mouse nodded across in the direction of the card players. "I'll be fine," he said. "Big Frank says he'll take care of me. Don't you worry. You just go and catch that Donovan man."

* * *

Jenny was not best pleased to get a call just after she'd fallen asleep.

"Anyone but you and I'd have ignored the phone," she told Rozlyn.

"OK, what can I do you for?"

Rozlyn grinned. "You know when you searched Charlie's flat? Did you find any newspaper clippings?"

"God, yes. Piles of them all neatly filed in plastic pockets. I put them back in the drawer. You onto something?"

She told Jenny what Mouse had said.

"You want me to come over? I mean, being you, you're not going to wait until morning, are you?"

"Wasn't planning on it."

"Well, you're going to have to contact the key holder. The place has been secured on behalf of the council. You'll have to get the shutter people to come out and unlock and I think they're in Bedford or somewhere."

"I'll bear that in mind." Rozlyn rang off and took two more of her tablets, remembering belatedly that she had no water to swallow them with. One stuck in her throat. She swallowed urgently, trying to get it down but it seemed as though it had wedged there. She had begun to feel rough again for, while the sleep had helped, its benefit was fast wearing off. Rozlyn stopped off at the police station, leaving the dustbin bag with the duty sergeant together with a note explaining what it was and that it should be sent to forensics. Then, armed with the number for the key holder, she drove to Charlie's flat, to wait in her car for the man to arrive. It was just after one in the morning. Charlie had been dead for fourteen days.

By the light from the glove compartment she glanced at the booklet she'd bought on local history, reading about the chantry she had seen on Mark Richards' land.

It was haunted, apparently — Rozlyn would have been disappointed to find otherwise — and had been excavated twice, once in the 1920s and again only three years ago by Dr Donovan Baker. From the sound of it, the 1920s excavation had been a casual affair, more of a treasure hunt to entertain guests at an elaborate house party. They'd turned up an eighteenth-century brooch shaped like a bird and a load of pottery, the earliest dating from the medieval rebuild, but rumours and legends of a hoard of gold being hidden there had come to nothing. The writer of the book commented that it was hard to find an historical site in the county that didn't bear such a legend and they were only relieved that the house guests had quickly bored of their game and gone back to their charades.

Rozlyn thought back to the altar stone so carelessly removed from its mount. It compared so strangely to the careful and considered excavation she had seen at the Theadingford dig. No one there would have cast an artifact aside with so little concern. She'd willingly bet that the 1920s lot would never have troubled to move such a weight, but had Donovan Baker? He was at that time still a professional, the excavation being dated when Donovan Baker was at the height of his career, before his status as expert witness or conscientious professional had been challenged. What had been so important that he'd cast his training and his expertise aside? Was Donovan Baker also a would-be treasure hunter? Did he know some truth behind these all-too-common rumours?

Rozlyn needed to know more about Donovan's fall from grace. He must have fallen fast and he must have fallen hard.

Headlights rounding the corner told her that the key holder had arrived, none too pleased at having his weekend interrupted.

Rozlyn calmed him down, promised to lock up herself and assured him that this was too important to wait — the very murder case could pivot on his cooperation. Then she made her way up to Charlie's landing.

Only two weeks and yet so much had changed. Charlie had been removed from his small corner and his world collapsed behind him. The tubs of plants had gone, not just from his door but outside his neighbours' too and the steel doors that prevented vandals from entering his little flat had been sprayed with graffiti. Rozlyn knew that it was fresh; the tag a familiar one, "byo" being a local with the facility for marking his domain that the average tomcat would have envied.

The landing stank of drink and piss.

Rozlyn let herself in, glad that the power was still connected. She shut Charlie's door, careful to pull the metal shutter closed before she did so, not wanting to advertise her presence inside, then made her way swiftly to the sideboard and withdrew the drawer that Jenny had searched. The flat already had that faint smell about it that indicated damp and neglect. Rozlyn thought about Mrs Chinowski. She had no one now. Charlie was gone and so was Clara Buranou. What would she do? Rozlyn sighed, knowing that she would have to ensure that Charlie's dependents had someone to take his place. She couldn't just walk away.

Rozlyn sifted through the neatly arranged bills and papers. Jenny had put things back as close to Charlie's order as she could and the cuttings, because of their size in their plastic folders, had been put back beneath the rest. There were about twenty of these clear wallets, their edges pierced so that they could be fastened in a ring binder. Charlie had filed roughly two clippings in each, back to back, cut precisely and, where the clipping had removed them, the date and newspaper recorded carefully in Charlie's neat round hand. Most were meaningless to Rozlyn, though she found one which talked about the new crime initiative on the estate and another which advertised Rozlyn coming to talk to the residents. The clipping she wanted was easily identified.

Mark Richards posed for a picture at the top of the steps leading to his grand front door. He'd had a garden party to raise money for a local charity and some of the more prestigious guests stood with him, dressed in their summer finery.

"Are you our Mr Thomas Thompson?" Rozlyn asked the photograph of Mark Richards. "Did our Charlie realise this, confront you with it? Though, why should he, you provided him with the cash he needed. Why would Charlie care that you bought houses under an assumed name? Or was it because of what Clara told him? I can't see Charlie wanting any part of that."

Rozlyn scanned the names beneath the picture. Most meant nothing, though she could recall having heard them in other connections. "Or did he clip this out because of you?" One other name stood out. On the right of Mark Richards, chatting affably to a female guest, was Donovan Baker.

One more thing to look at. Rozlyn went through to Charlie's bedroom and opened the small wooden wardrobe. Two identical pinstripe suits. He'd been wearing his third when his body had been found. At first she thought she must be mistaken. No sign of a tear or a snag that might account for her find in the chantry, that little scrap of fabric that she had tucked into a plastic bag and kept in her pocket. Rozlyn sighed. So much for that idea. She was suddenly horribly deflated.

And then she saw it. The tiny rip in the sleeve, now carefully mended in black and pale cream thread using a technique her grandmother had called invisible darning. She doubted Charlie had done this; Charlie was always clean, but frayed sleeves and little snags were part of his standard uniform. She placed the fragment of fabric against the now camouflaged hole. It matched. "My God, Charlie, what did you think you were doing, going there?"

Was it enough for a search warrant?

Rozlyn shook her head. Not on its own. But it was a start.

She found a black bin bag in Charlie's kitchen and packed the suit inside, then left, locking the door carefully behind her.

CHAPTER 35

Rozlyn drove out to Mark Richards' place and climbed the wall. She knew it was stupid, she wasn't even sure what she was looking for, but despite the way her body ached and her head thumped she couldn't even think of going back to bed. The answer lay in that house or in the chantry.

Answer to what? The reason Charlie had been murdered? She couldn't quite get to grips with the logic of it or see the full picture, but the answer had to be yes.

She ran through everything in her mind. Charlie had worked for Mark Richards — Richards' alias was Thomas Thompson. Donovan knew both Charlie and Richards. Question, how did he get to know Charlie? Ah, that was right — Mouse said he'd met him at one of the houses, that he organised work for those people Richards brought into the country. Or was that speculation? He knew that Charlie took any items found at the houses to Donovan's office — with the exception, presumably, of the little radio he had given to Mouse. Did Mark Richards know of this arrangement? And what did Donovan want, anyway, with those sad little items the migrant workers had left behind?

Yet whether or not Mark Richards and Donovan had continued with what had been a superficially friendly relationship was irrelevant, really. The important thing was that she now knew Charlie had been at Richards' place.

So, why had he gone there? Did Mark Richards have something Donovan wanted? Was Charlie going to warn Richards of that? Was Charlie threatening to tell what he knew about Richards' alias, as Thomas Thompson, a man who brought illegal immigrants into the country?

Had Charlie stolen something from Mark Richards' place? Rozlyn's best guess was that Donovan had stolen from Richards and had used Charlie to carry out the theft. Charlie had then kept something for himself, something he hoped to sell to help Clara Buranou, and Donovan had killed him because of it — except, of course, Rozlyn couldn't even prove there'd been a robbery and Charlie couldn't have returned whatever it was before he died because otherwise Donovan would not still be looking for it and his attack on Mouse clearly showed that he was.

So, had Charlie simply refused to tell where he'd hidden the object and Donovan murdered him because of that? Seeing what he'd done to Mouse Man, Rozlyn would have expected Donovan Baker to try and beat the information out of Charlie rather than killing him immediately, but there'd been no other significant marks on Charlie's body. The thrust of the spear spoke of a single impulsive act, not a systematic attempt to extract information, so, not Donovan Baker, then? Mark Richards, perhaps?

Had he caught Charlie returning to collect whatever it was he had stolen? Rozlyn was more than half convinced Charlie would have concealed the object in the grounds, rather than risk Donovan searching him later and discovering it — and Rozlyn did not for one minute believe that Donovan would put trust in his associates. So, it would have to be something small, something Charlie could slip into a pocket and hide easily and, also, something Charlie would have immediately recognised as valuable.

Something like that missing brooch — which might not be missing at all, but simply, as Alfred had told her, sent for restoration or whatever he'd said. Had she any sense, she'd talk it over with Brook in the morning and, should Brook agree with her, demand that Mark Richards produce the missing brooch or give the address of the conservator and, Rozlyn supposed, that would knock her theory of the robbery fair and square on the head especially if Mark Richards then produced his inventory. An inventory which would not, anyway, include the supposed stolen objects because he'd not declared them in the first place. Rozlyn's head swirled. Her fever had returned, accompanied by the thumping head and dryness in her throat that no amount of fluids or soothing pastilles could shift.

Simplify your story, she told herself sternly. Charlie had been in the chantry. Had he also been in Mark Richards' house? Had he gone there to tell Richards he knew exactly what he was up to and maybe try and blackmail him? Maybe while there he had stolen something on impulse. The cabinets in the room that housed the collection were not locked. Maybe Charlie took something valuable and Donovan got wind of it after Charlie was dead, assumed Mouse must know where it was.

She tried again to order her thoughts. She had been thinking in terms of the insurance scam that her colleague at Art and Antiques had told her about, but if the chantry treasure — the probably *mythical* chantry treasure — had been found, then Mark Richards hadn't declared it so it wouldn't be insured, so there'd be no money to be made from such an enterprise even had he declared the robbery. Had he intended to sell it and promised Donovan a cut from the profits? And, if so, why wait three years? Had he reneged on that agreement?

Rozlyn sat, perched at the top of the wall surrounding the estate and told herself that this was stupid. Not only did she not know what she was looking for; she didn't even know if there was anything *to* look for.

Then, she decided that she'd never know unless she tried to find out and, feverish fuzzy logic taking precedence, she swung her second leg over the wall and dropped down on the other side.

She kept a small Maglite in the car and she used that now. She kept it low to the ground to minimise the chance of anyone seeing from the house. In her fever-fuddled brain, Albert had assumed almost superhuman faculties for observation and Rozlyn thought of him as a latter-day Argos, one eye always open while the others slept.

The distance to the chantry was further than she had expected, her expectation based on just that few minutes' drive. Walking was different. For one thing the ground was boggy after the rain and the grass long, concealing holes and hollows that opened without warning beneath her feet. Twice, Rozlyn stumbled. She risked an upward flash of the light in order to orient herself and realised that she'd swung too far to the left. Much further and she'd have ended up on the lawn in full view of the house. A flick of the light to the right revealed the outline of the chantry, a darker shadow against a black sky. Rozlyn stared at it. Her feet were wet and she was cold and shivery and had a head that hurt worse than the most acute hangover she'd ever had. Just what did she think she was playing at?

Sighing, feeling that she'd committed herself now, she stumbled the final fifty yards towards the ruined wall and flopped down wearily upon the discarded altar stone and stared down at her wet shoes and soaking, freezing feet.

Somewhere off in the distance she heard dogs bark. Rozlyn frowned. She'd heard none the last time she was here. She hauled herself back to her feet and began to search, swinging the torch back and forth across the space. But the beam of light, though bright, was skinny compared to the area she had to search. She had to be more systematic about this.

Rozlyn chose a wall and, starting at the one end, began to search again, using torch and fingers to probe for gaps in the stone walls.

How high could Charlie reach? Not as high as Rozlyn. He was a good eight inches shorter. Rozlyn restricted her attention to the lower wall, nothing much above shoulder height. She figured that if Charlie had hidden anything here and done it in a hurry, it would have to be in a place that a casual observer would never see.

The grass was long against the wall and climbing, clinging vegetation covered a good third of the exposed stone.

Rozlyn played the light on the thick tendrils of ivy level with her head. There. What was that? A bird's nest?

The dogs were barking again and, to Rozlyn's alarm, they sounded closer. Peering round the safe haven of the wall, Rozlyn could see a light moving from the side of the house and round onto the drive. As they passed the newly bright window at the side, Rozlyn could discern a man, then another, the second moving as though something tugged at his arm. The barking was louder now.

"Shit!"

She hesitated, wanting to go back and investigate that bird's nest. If she did, if she delayed, she'd never reach the wall before the dogs reached her. Rozlyn hesitated no longer; she turned and ran, holding the torch so that the beam lit the ground ahead, not caring now that she could easily be seen. A shout went up telling her that she had indeed been spotted. Would they loose the dogs?

The thought that they might cleared her head and gave speed to aching limbs. She tried to recall what little she knew about dealing with dog attacks . . . about how fast a dog could run. She wished she'd brought a bigger torch; maybe one she could use to whack the dogs with.

The wall was just ahead. She could see it looming, dark but comforting in its proximity. Rozlyn leapt for the top, the Maglite falling from her hand as she scrabbled with both hands for purchase on the coping stones.

"Damn!" She heaved her body onto the ridge and looked back down. The torch gleamed in the grass, pointing back towards the pursuers. Rozlyn spared them only the swiftest of looks, appalled at just how close they were. Two men, two dogs. A voice that shouted, "Stop where you are or I'll bloody shoot." Rozlyn rolled off the wall, praying for a soft landing. Praying she had climbed close to where she'd parked her car. She landed on a bush, bounced and rolled onto the road, regained her feet and made a dash for the car, praying again that she'd make it before they climbed the wall.

Her keys were in her coat pocket. She pressed the pad to unlock the doors. The beep and little flash of lights as it responded were the most welcome sight and sound Rozlyn could imagine. She hauled on the door and fell inside, slamming and locking it then fumbling for the ignition. In her rear-view mirror she saw that one man at least had scaled the wall and was pounding along the narrow road. The engine fired and she crashed the car into gear, redlining as her foot clamped the pedal to the floor. The engine screamed . . . and so did Rozlyn. In her rear-view she saw the man halt and raise his arm. The flash, then the shattered screen as the bullet hit.

CHAPTER 36

If Ethan was surprised to have Rozlyn show up at his home at six in the morning, he didn't show it. He took one look and then took charge. "You're burning. Come on, get into bed and I'll bring you something cool to drink."

"Bed?"

"I've a spare room. You never know when people will arrive, so I keep it made up. Come along now."

He sounded like a bossy nanny, Rozlyn thought. She wondered about the "never know when people will arrive". Used to folk landing on your doorstep unannounced, are you? She asked, or at least she thought she did. She might only have posed the question in the confines of her own head.

Ethan had directed her through the door from his living room and up the narrow, enclosed stairs. Rozlyn suddenly sat down, legs giving way and a cold sweat momentarily replacing the fever and chilling along her spine.

"Christ, Ethan, someone shot at me."

"Shot at you?"

She nodded. "I feel nauseous," she confessed, taking deep controlling breaths.

"The bathroom is the first door to your right," Ethan informed her, "and your bedroom next door to that. I'll wait for you in there."

Rozlyn didn't manage to reply. She struggled to her feet and surged through the door Ethan had indicated, just making it to the toilet bowl before throwing up so violently she felt herself almost pulled inside out.

"Feel better?" Ethan asked from the doorway.

Rozlyn nodded pathetically, sat back on her heels and watched the water flush around the bowl.

"There's a new toothbrush in the cabinet. I always keep a couple extra. You never know."

"Thanks," Rozlyn managed. "You often have unexpected guests throwing up in your bathroom?"

"I generally find it's the best place to do it."

"Yeah, right." She closed her eyes and stopped wondering about Ethan's guests. All that mattered at the moment was that she was one of them and Ethan had a bed, a spare toothbrush and a cool drink. She managed to get to her feet despite the fact that the room shifted beneath them, then she brushed her teeth until her gums tingled. Ethan, as promised, was waiting in the little guest room. There was space for a single bed and a narrow wooden wardrobe set against a background of rosy wallpaper, the closet dark oak and wonderfully carved. The corner near the door was occupied by a low, bow-legged, pink upholstered chair. Curtains had been drawn and a red shaded lamp glowed on the tiny round table set between the chair and the inviting bed.

"Who shot at you?" Ethan asked.

Rozlyn shook her head. "I was where I shouldn't have been. Mark Richards' place. One of his security men shot my rear window out."

Ethan frowned. "Where did you leave your car?"

Rozlyn tried to remember. "I usually park near The George," she said. "I think it must have been there. I'm sorry, Ethan, I don't seem to recall." She smiled weakly. "I feel bloody lousy."

"You look it," Ethan told her frankly. "There's a bug going around. Looks to me like you've caught a dose of it. Now, give me your keys and get yourself into bed. I'll get you a drink and then go and move your car."

"Move it?"

"I don't imagine you were in a fit state to pay your parking fee," Ethan said practically. "You don't want to be clamped, do you? Besides, if your rear window's been shot out it will attract the wrong kind of interest, don't you think? There's a little side road at the back of here and I've a friend with a place to park off-road. Don't worry. It'll be quite safe there."

"You know," Rozlyn said, "anyone else would be having hysterics and wanting to call the police if I was to tell them I'd been shot at."

"I'm not given to hysterics," Ethan told her. "And, frankly, I've never found the police much use. Now, get into bed and let me sort things out."

Rozlyn closed her eyes. Her body was shaking and the chill had returned. She didn't know if she had the strength to get undressed. She wondered at the fact that she'd had the strength to run and climb the wall but figured two slavering big-toothed dogs and a couple of armed men were probably the ideal motivating factor. Dimly, she was aware that Ethan was easing her out of her coat.

"Come along now."

Ah, nanny was back again. Rozlyn surrendered. She let Ethan help her with the rest, feeling oddly unconcerned that this man she barely knew was helping her remove her jeans and shirt. Ethan covered her with warm blankets and cool linen sheets. Helpless as a child and quite happy to be so, Rozlyn was asleep in minutes.

CHAPTER 37

A visitor awaited Treven on his return home. One of Kendryk's brother monks, a heavy set, squat faced man with a scar that ran the length of his cheek. They called him Aiken — the Oak. Treven had noted him before; he was rarely far from Kendryk's side.

"Father Abbot wishes you to return with me."

"For what reason?"

"When you had gone, he sent out men to search for the sister of the dead woman. And the one she fled with. He thought it best to test the words of Hugh de Vries."

"Have they found anything?"

"Not when I left but I have waited an hour before your hearth. We should return now. The Lord Abbot said to tell you that I ride well. Horses would save time spent walking."

"You can ride Hugh's horse," Treven told him. "But have a care, his mouth is like leather and he's as headstrong as his master."

Snow fell heavily as they returned the two miles to Theading. It had come early this year, Treven thought — it was still a few days before the year's end at All Hallows. Not a good omen for the winter to come. Aiken handled his mount with ease and, looking at his hands, Treven noted they were broad and calloused. He wondered what the monk had been before he took his vows; what work he did for Kendryk now.

Kendryk was waiting for them in the open space before the Scriveners' home. Snow fell about him but he stood bare headed and seemed not to notice the cold. Treven was reminded of the stranger he had seen in the ash grove. Aiken, of course, had not enquired as to where he'd been, but Treven knew that Kendryk would and he wondered if he could lie . . . or if he should.

"The searchers are returning," Kendryk told him.

"And has aught been found?"

"No and in this white mirk I doubt it could be."

"Then why send them out?"

Kendryk sighed and regarded him steadily with those cool grey eyes deep set in the death mask of a face. "I sent them in your name, Treven of Theadingford. A claim was made. You, as Thegn, must be *seen* to do your duty as regard that claim and to act immediately. You should not allow time for folk to question your intent or your reasoning."

Treven's anger surged, the more piquant because he knew there was truth in what Kendryk had just said. "When will you cease instructing me in the rule of my affairs?" he demanded under his breath.

"When you learn to see what must be done without my guidance," Kendryk returned. "Treven, in war, I doubt you have equal. In this time of so-called peace you have no practice and as yet, little skill. Though," he smiled and the death's head grimaced, skin tightening over bone so Treven thought almost that it might split, "I have high hopes of you King's Thegn."

Treven glowered at him, but his planned retort was interrupted by a cry from across the field that lay between the homestead and the wood.

"They have found something?"

A small knot of searchers broke from the woodland and struggled through the snow that now lay ankle deep. Their leader held something in his hands. Fabric, Treven saw as they drew closer. Woolen cloth that had once been deepest blue but which now was half black with mud and torn and mired.

"Aliss Scrivener wove this cloth two winters since," the man told Treven and the Abbott.

"You are certain?"

"I am certain. She taught my children the art. The Scrivener women wove fine cloth, the mother and the two girls. Cate was the better spinner of yarn, but her sister wove with a tight weft and this pattern on the hem . . ." He thrust it forward for Treven to see. A band three fingers deep had been created in a pattern that twisted the weaving into a checkerboard design. Treven, no weaver himself, could not guess how it was done, but the tightness and skill were obvious even to an unskilled eye. "This was a pattern of her own making," the man told him.

"So, if the cloak is there, so might be the owner."

Treven looked upward at the sky. Snow-filled and dense, he could not see higher than a house roof before his vision became blocked by the swirl and dance of heavy flakes.

"Be that as it may," he said. "I'll not send any out in this." He reached out to take the cloth from the searcher. "You've done well." He said. "When the weather clears, lead me to the place you found this. If the woman lies in the woods, we will find her and bring her body back for decent burial."

"And the *Waelas* man she ran with?" Kendryk asked him, and Treven knew this was yet another of the abbot's tests. Impatience and anger battled but he held them back. "The man and woman fell into sin through too much love," he said quietly. "I'll not expect Edmund to have him here, but I'll see him buried on my own lands. It seems to me they have paid penalty enough for such misjudgment." The man with the cloak nodded and handed Treven the sorry bundle of blue cloth.

"I'll get to my home. My wife will be watching for me."

"That was well done," Kendryk told him when the men had left.

"I do not seek your approval."

"No, but you will get it or otherwise. Treven, make no mistake, I would rather claim this land for my Abbey and for the glory of the Christ, but since my earthly lord decrees otherwise, I would at least see his servant keep it well, whether that servant enjoys my words or not."

Treven scowled and strode off towards the Scriveners' homestead. Inside, he ordered the trestle table lifted from the wall and spread out the cloak. The shape was simple; a long rectangle of cloth meant to wrap around the body and (if necessary) be drawn over the head. He could see the signs of wear at the point where the brooch would usually have fastened. The fabric next to that had been ripped as though the cloak had been torn from the body while the brooch was fastened. Streaks of black mud showed, Treven fancied, where the fabric had folded and creased and been most exposed.

"The cloak was torn from her body some time after death," he told Kendryk.

The Abbott nodded. "Wild animals could have done that. See, here, tears from teeth or tusks. There are boar in these woods and a body lying on the ground would attract scavengers."

Treven nodded. "I doubt there'll be much to bury," he said "unless we find her before winter really sets hard. This, I believe, is blood. It looks like rust against the blue, though the whole is so caked in mud and filth it is impossible to tell."

"It seems that Hugh's claim may be genuine," Kendryk observed.

"And if we find the older sister and her lover, what to do with the father?"

"Unless another can be found with more reason to kill, and, I do not believe, Treven, that either brother struck the blow that killed their wives, then the father is guilty and such guilt cannot be left unpunished."

"The man has lost his mind."

"But did he lose it and then strike his children down? Or lose it after through grief and guilt."

Treven shook his head. "I find it hard to think that a man with full reason would want his child dead because she loved unwisely."

"Fathers have killed for less."

"Then they are not fathers." Treven drew a deep breath. "I find it hard, no, impossible, to think of a reason or an act that would lead me to want to strike my own child dead." He folded the cloth, then changed his mind and laid it by the fire to dry. "Where is Hugh? For that matter, where are the brothers?"

"The brothers have gone to Storton with the girls' father. You were not here to consult. I thought it best to have him moved before more damage could be done."

"Consult? What damage?"

"You think a mad man will stop with two deaths?" Kendryk questioned. "Treven, we can debate *when* he might have lost his reason but simple observation will tell you that however it was lost it is most definitely gone. I have seen men sick like this. They devise in their minds a sly cunning that those of us who still, God willing, retain our faculties are hard pressed to read. Two women came to me and reported attacks upon them and their children. Both times their husbands were at hand, but as time passes, we can only expect the old man to become more unthinking in his actions. At Storton, we have a hospice. He can be confined and cared for and watched closely. It seemed to me a solution you could only approve."

Treven was forced to admit that he was right. He nodded. "Thank you for your wisdom," he said. "I will send alms to care for his needs."

"And if you did, I would soon be returning them to you. Treven, when your land can support such pledges, then I will accept them. I shall expect your tithing, with the rest, but beyond that I will not ask until you have riches to spare. Only then will I be more demanding. Hugh," he added, "waits for you in the place he was confined. I made it plain he was not welcome in my presence, though I've ensured he has food and fire. He'll neither starve nor freeze. Oh, and tell Osric, from me, that I should like to know what herbs and oils he used in his potion. I could make use of them in the infirmary."

* * *

Hugh lay on his back, a blanket thrown across his legs. The hut was warm. A brazier set up in the middle of the room burned with a smoky light. When Treven opened the door, the sudden draft caused the wood to roar and the smoke to billow. Treven waited for the blaze to die down and watched the vapours rise again and drift up towards the roof. When he cast his eyes down again, Hugh was looking at him.

"Do you still damn me, Treven?"

"I do." Treven paused, crossed the room and stood over the prone figure of his one-time comrade. Hugh sat, he cradled the wounded hand across his body, though his face was no longer creased with the agony it had caused him and his speech, slightly slurred, told Treven that wine laced with poppy had taken most of his pain. Treven pulled a wooden stool close to the pallet bed and sat down, studying Hugh carefully

"When you have healed sufficiently, I will have you escorted home," Treven told him.

"And I have said I will not go."

"The King will command it."

"Will he? Treven, I come from a family of powerful men and well-connected women. They have wealth and land and the king's ear. He needs his allies and they have been his and his brothers before him. You think he will offend them by sending me home under the cloud of an imagined disgrace? Treven, you have nothing to offer him but your honour and your courage. Ask yourself. In this time of peace, when playing politics is more valued than that game of spear and sword, who will our lord most cherish?"

"Aelfred gave me land."

"Aelfred gave you a border territory to defend. You have a ruined hall and fields that will need clearing before they are again put beneath the plough. It will take many years and many men giving their tithing before you make any profit from your precious earth. Many more before it becomes a place where men of quality could feast or *Scops* sing their tales of glory." He sat forward, leaning close to Treven. "I have wealth, I have influence. Put this matter aside and look to the future. Think of all the hopes and dreams we had when first we came here. You have need of me. Would you throw all away because of some scrap of a girl?"

For a long moment Treven considered his words. He could see the truth of them. He thought of all the times he and Hugh had fought, slept, eaten side by side, shared all manner of hardships, grumbled and scolded and celebrated victory. They had shared a closeness that he had not even known with Hild and it hurt all the more to know that someone he had known so well should now have changed beyond all recognition.

"I have no need of your wealth," he said softly. "I will wait for the profit from my fields."

"And when your people go hungry and look to you for bread?" Hugh demanded. "Will you tell them they must wait? Or would you use my wealth to trade for what they need?"

"And I have no regard for influence," Treven continued, ignoring Hugh's question. "I believe, and you *know* I believe that a man should be judged by his own deeds and not those of his brothers or his forebears. The poet tells us that all men must die. All things die and pass away. All that remains is the memory of our deeds and that memory should be glorious and honourable. Hugh, if the only legacy I have is that I am remembered as an honourable man, then I call that riches enough."

"Tell me that when you go hungry and watch as others starve."

"The people now in my demesne have managed their own lands and filled their own bellies in the years before I came. My being here will not diminish their skill, neither will it add to their burdens."

"They will look to you for leadership."

"And I will learn to lead them."

"You expect Kendryk's help in this? If so, then you're a fool, Treven, and remember also, that this land is given under the King's deed. Aelfred can take away what he has given. Don't forget, my family have the ear of the king and should I have them whisper in that ear that Treven betrayed a comrade and cast him aside? A comrade in arms that the King himself appointed to serve, how long then will you keep this precious place?"

Treven rose from his stool and stared at Hugh with a mixture of incomprehension and pain. Hugh returned his gaze, looking upon Treven's puzzlement and misreading it. He spoke with a quiet urgency, leaning still closer to his one-time friend. "Treven, I will do none of that, I swear. You only have to let me stay."

"So you may wait and bide your time and then one day take it from me?" Treven asked him.

He took a deep breath, ignoring Hugh's protests and then he stepped away towards the door. "Come to me tomorrow, if you can ride. Or the day following if not. I have things to show you. Plans I have made that I would share with you."

He heard Hugh's sigh of relief and was glad that the smoke and heat between them, together with the twilight, hid his face. Treven knew that he could never lie without it showing in his eyes.

CHAPTER 38

Rozlyn lost a full day. It passed in a fevered haze. The doctor came, gave her pills and went. Sometimes Ethan sat beside her and read aloud. The words permeated Rozlyn's dreams, seeped down into her memories so that she was a child again and her grandfather's voice imparted tales of great adventure.

"Call me Ishmael . . .

"Leave this place and don't look back. Keep playing and keep your eyes looking forward, Euridice will follow you . . .

". . . Sir Knight, your honour doth enjoin . . ."

"Treven was a man who knew how to touch the earth and read what was written there . . ."

Most of all, she remembered the day of her parents' funeral. After, she and her grandfather had walked together in the cemetery and the realisation had dawned, more poignantly than ever, that the two of them were alone and that death had torn from them a whole lifetime of promise. Rozlyn's parents had divorced when she was nine. Life between nine and sixteen had been lived between two countries. Term time, she had lived her mother's life and gone to school, first in an English village and then, from eleven, joined the throng of uniformed children in the nearest town. Oakham, almost drowning in history and tradition, with its castle that looked nothing like a castle, but that had, to the child Rozlyn's eyes, more in common with a large barn and the collection of upside-down horseshoes, the rows of tiny shops and the formal school that took up half the town, filled with kids in blue uniforms.

In the summer she had travelled stateside to her grandparents. New York sweltered in the heat and dust of traffic. Buildings blocked the sky, their tops shimmering in a haze that made them seem unreal. Manhattan was loud with a capital L. Loud and bright and brash and, in her grandfather's neighbourhood, she went from being one of only a handful of black kids in her school to being one that was counted among the handful of almost white. Her accent was all wrong, the things she learned in school different from those of her peers. Life in a tiny English village and school in a small English town separating her culturally in ways that as a child she found hard to define and even harder to bridge. That as an adult still seemed to set her apart. In both worlds she had been a liminal being and that liminality had not diminished as she had grown to adulthood.

She had friends in both places, often kids that, for one reason or another, shared that sense of being just a little outside of things. A little awkward, a little different. Though as the years passed and lives had gone in different directions those friendships had drifted. In her dreams Rozlyn thought now of those friends, most now settled with families and jobs that absorbed their time. The sense of regret, rarely acknowledged, that she had not accepted invitations to visit, responded to suggestions that they should speak more regularly or, for those old friends who lived more locally, that they should meet up for a drink now struck her forcefully.

"Loneliness is not something we should seek out as if it were a vocation. Friendships matter."

Was that her grandfather's voice or was it Ethan's? Either way she both resented the insight and acknowledged the truth of it.

She missed so many English summers that when she had turned sixteen and spent her first full season there, she had been shocked by the soft rain that fell so often in the evenings and the sudden cold that could blow up before a storm and the high blue skies with no tall apartment buildings to block the view.

The Christmas before her sixteenth birthday, her grandmother had died. She went back for the funeral, grieving for the soft-eyed lady who had loved her so well and so intently. Who taught her to cook, whose little book of recipes Rozlyn still used. Who told her stories and, from one year to the next, kept Rozlyn's artwork and hesitant attempts at poems pinned to the corkboard on the kitchen wall and who only took the pictures and the poems down when she had new treasures to replace them.

For her parents, this time had been a revelation. Rozlyn's mother and her father's parents had always remained friends, even after the divorce. Grief drew her parents together once again and they rediscovered what had brought them close in the first place. For Rozlyn, watching their love rekindle had been at once wonderful and embarrassing. She caught them kissing in the kitchen, her mother pushed back against the table so that her buttocks pressed and deformed against its edge, her father's hand fumbling at her mother's breast. Rozlyn had been both shamed and exultant. She closed the door, hoping they would not know that she had seen. Later, she found it hard to sit at that place at the kitchen table where her mother's body had been pressed. It seemed at the one time soiled and intimate and . . . she didn't know what words to use, only that to touch that place discomforted her beyond any words.

And then, she had been late home, not been with them in the car when it crashed on that wet road. And the dream was ended almost as soon as it had been restored to life.

"There's just you and me now, girl."

"I know. What do we do?"

"We carry on. What else is there to do? You've got to go back and finish this year of school, then in the summer, we'll decide if you carry on over there or come and study here."

"Will you come back with me, Gramps? I don't want to be alone."

And so, finally, the worlds had begun to collide. Her grandfather living in her mother's house and walking through the village street to the tiny post-office-cu-shop a couple of times a day, just because he liked to talk to the owners and then in the autumn, returning to the high towers and hazy skies to finish school in New York.

And all through her memories and dreams Ethan's words wove and wandered, the language strange and sonorous resolving itself slowly into words that she could understand . . .

"I placed his treasure beneath the altar stone and gave orders that, when I too had fled my body, I should be placed beside these things as guardian. A Pagan thought of which Treven, child of ancient gods, would no doubt have approved. A sword, a spear and a brooch like a shield boss, enriched with red enamel . . ."

* * *

Rozlyn thought she dreamed, but this time she was in another place. She had returned to Mark Richards' house and this time she knew exactly where to look. She stood beside the chantry wall and turned the object she had found so that the moonlight struck its gleaming surface. It rested in her palm, round and heavy and precious, though surely not so precious that it should have cost a man his life. She had been right in her guess. Charlie had hidden something here. Though not in the bird's nest but in a chink between the stones, right next to that, where the mortar had been pulled free by the clinging roots of ivy. The bird's nest had fallen away as soon as she had touched it and as she examined it in the light of her torch, she had realised at once that it had never belonged in that position. It had been shoved among the ivy, settled into place between the roots and leaves. Of course, Rozlyn thought,

Charlie would have seen the bird's nest, used it as a marker. He would not have hidden such a precious object where it could so easily be found. Instead, he had found that little gap between the stones, and pushed the brooch, wrapped in cloth, into it and placed the old nest into position. Such a simple deception, neat and precise. So Charlie.

In the distance, she could hear the barking of the dogs. One let out a howl that chilled her blood and a man's voice shouted.

In her dream, Rozlyn turned and ran, the grass, wet with rain that was freezing fast now the clouds had been blown away and the night sky opened to draw heat from the sodden ground. Her feet slid and she stumbled, falling to her knees. The cold and damp seeped through her trousers and the hand she put out to slow her fall dug deep into the earth. She scrambled to her feet and ran again, aware that the dogs were gaining.

And then the challenge. A man shouted, a dog appeared from nowhere, teeth bared, snarling and growling, its entire body one mass of sprung muscle waiting to attack.

A second man appeared beside it, with the second dog. Rozlyn stood still, knowing that dogs and men wanted her to move, wanted the excuse to attack. Then a familiar voice.

"Inspector Priest. Well, this is a surprise. When the alarm sounded and Albert told me we had an intruder, I never expected it to be you."

Rozlyn drew a deep breath. Eyes still on the dogs, she forced herself to reply as calmly as possible. "No, well, you knew it wouldn't be Charlie Higgins come back. He's dead, isn't he."

"Charlie who? I'm sorry Inspector, but I've no idea who that might be."

"Really. I'd have thought you might remember the man who stole from you. A brooch, wasn't it, from the cabinet beside the window."

She noted the slight frown, knew she had hit her mark but his reply was smooth. "I have nothing missing, Inspector.

As Albert told you, that item has gone for some conservation work to be done. I like to keep my collection pristine."

Rozlyn shifted position. Her back and her head ached abominably, the world swam. She could feel the sweat break out on her forehead and her whole body was slick with it. She swayed slightly where she stood. What was going to happen now? She felt too ill to care. Besides, she was dreaming, wasn't she? When did dreams ever make sense?

"You don't look too well, Inspector."

She could hear the distaste in his voice.

"My people will escort you back to the house. I think that's best."

"So you can do to me what you did to Charlie? Though I'm forgetting. You can't. You lost that weapon back at the dig site, didn't you. That pretty spearhead. You'd have to make use of something else from your collection."

The dogs were snarling, their handlers allowing them to close the gap. She could feel hot breath and spittle on her hand.

"No, Inspector," Richards said steadily, though she could hear the anger in his tone. "I'm taking you back to the house so I can call your colleagues in the police and report you. As I told you before, I have some friends in some very high places. You'll be out of a job before you can say . . ." he paused, drew a little closer, leaned in, "Charlie Higgins."

It was as though everything suddenly became very clear. She knew beyond doubt that once he had her inside the house that would be it. She'd turn up later, dead in a ditch somewhere, stabbed in the back or with a bullet hole in her head. The two men with the dogs stood stony faced. They'd say nothing.

Richards was smiling now and Rozlyn's first thought was that she had to get away. Her second that she wanted to wipe that smile from that arrogant face. She hit out with the torch, catching him beneath the chin. He stumbled back.

In the split second of confusion that followed, she turned and ran, knowing she could not outpace the dogs, but knowing that she had to try — or she would be as dead as Charlie Higgins.

Behind her, she could hear Richards cursing. She could also hear the shouts of the handlers and . . . the howling of the dogs. What was going on? She dared not look back but it was clear that something wasn't right. The dogs no longer snarled — they yelped and whined as though something scared them far more than the shouts and threats of Richards or his men. She ran harder, her muscles screaming and her breath rasping in her lungs and throat. This time, Rozlyn was not alone. Running beside her was a man, tall and strong and battle hardened. A man that turned as the dogs and handlers made up ground and threatened to surround them once again.

What the hell? Rozlyn leaped for the wall, scrambled to the top and paused briefly to look back. She saw a shadowy figure fighting with a sword, his hair and cloak streaming out behind him and a cry of victory on his lips as he laid into both dogs and men. The man she had seen, or thought she had seen, standing by the half-imagined watchtower back at the dig. She was certain it was him.

Rozlyn dreamed that she dropped from the wall and ran, as she had run the night before, back towards the car, the familiar weight of the spearhead in one pocket of her coat. The round brooch, enamelled in red and set with a crimson stone, rested heavily in the other.

CHAPTER 39

It was well past midnight when DCI Brook hammered on Ethan's door and was duly admitted. On being told that Rozlyn was asleep upstairs he asked for no permission but opened the door and stomped up the enclosed staircase and then stood at the top of the stairs wondering which room to try. Two uniformed officers had followed him and, by the time Ethan had arrived, his tiny landing was somewhat overcrowded. Ethan pointed to the door.

"She's not well," he said tetchily. "And I don't like people bursting into my home."

"I didn't burst in, you invited me," Brook told him acerbically.

"I didn't invite you upstairs." He took a deep breath. "She's in there, but you'll clear out as soon as you've satisfied yourself. I'm expecting the doctor."

A door further along the corridor opened and Cassie looked out, rubbing her eyes.

"What's going on, Ethan?"

"Nothing. It's all right. These are colleagues of Rozlyn's. They want to see her."

"What's up with her?" Brook asked, ignoring Cassie.

"The doctor says it's some kind of flu, but she's been very bad. How did you know she was here, anyway?"

"Call it an educated guess," Brook sneered. "Mark Richards reported an intruder last night, reckoned they came back tonight and assaulted his security guards. Beat one of them badly enough to need hospital. His place is only five miles from here and Rozlyn didn't go home last night."

"Oh? Well, take a look, but I think you'll agree that Rozlyn isn't in a fit state to get out of bed, never mind assault anyone."

"According to Richard's people, the intruder wasn't alone." Brook said.

* * *

The sound of their voices had permeated Rozlyn's consciousness. She felt cold again, though she knew that she was hotter than ever, her body burning with a dry heat that had Ethan worried and determined, despite Rozlyn's hoarse protests, to call the doctor out again.

She turned her head as the door opened and Brook flicked the light switch, filling the room with an unbearable brightness. Rozlyn groaned and hid her eyes.

Brook sniffed. "You stink, you know that?" He approached the bed and lowered his head over Rozlyn, his body blocking out sufficiently enough of the glare for Rozlyn to try and focus on him.

"What the hell's going on?"

"Been on a little trip, have we? Small excursion to see Mr Mark Richards?"

"Don't know what you mean."

"No? Well he can't prove it was you last night, but we've got a pretty good description from tonight's little escapade. Who's your friend, eh? The red-haired bloke with the fancy sword."

"The what?"

"I thought," Ethan said mildly, "that you said they'd been beaten. Surely, if someone had a sword . . ."

He let the query hang upon the air and Brook swore, then cast himself into the low chair beside the bed. "What the hell's going on? I've had the bloody Chief Super on my back because someone higher up is biting at his bum."

Rozlyn smiled weakly. "Richards reckoned he had friends in high places when I disturbed him the other day."

"Aye, well fuck 'em." Brook frowned. "My office, tomorrow. You can't drive, I'll arrange a car." He struggled out of the nursing chair. Standing, he seemed to fill the room, broad shoulders and height obscuring the door. "Tread on some interesting toes, don't you? You got something against the rich and famous."

"Oh, not in particular. I just don't like assholes."

Brook considered. "Wondered why you were never my number one fan," he said. "Tomorrow, then, and I want the full story, no political omissions."

"Would anyone like some tea," Cassie asked from the doorway. "We've got biscuits."

"That's a good idea," Ethan approved. The doorbell rang again. "I'll get that, Cassie, it's probably the doctor."

"I'd better tell the Chief Super it wasn't you, then," Brook sneered as Ethan left.

"Not me what?"

"Traipsing about the countryside with a bloke carrying a sword?"

Rozlyn's heart beat an odd rhythm, but she managed to shake her head and keep her voice steady. "Sorry, can't help." She frowned. "What the hell time is it?"

Footsteps on the stairs heralded the arrival of the doctor. He glanced at the uniformed officers and Brook and ordered them from the room. Brook hovered in the doorway. "Really sick, is she?" He sounded disappointed, Rozlyn thought.

"It's not life threatening," the doctor said cheerfully, "Actually, I think the fever's beginning to break. Your skin's damp. Better than yesterday afternoon." He turned his attention to Brook and it was clear that he must have been briefed by Ethan. "Better, but certainly not fit enough to be anywhere she shouldn't. She's barely capable of making it to the bathroom on her own and that's just next door."

Rozlyn watched as the doctor ushered her visitors out of the door. She could hear Brook talking to Ethan, could catch the odd word but that was all. Rozlyn closed her eyes. She heard the shop door open and then close, the bell jangling until Ethan reached to still the sound. She wondered if Brook and co. had passed Jasper the guard cat unscathed and found herself hoping not. The doctor hemmed and hummed as, Rozlyn had found, doctors seemed to do, then told her he was pleased with her progress and went on his way.

Rozlyn could not help but wonder at the strangeness of a doctor making house calls in this day and age and at this time of night and she wondered if that was a favour to Ethan — she vaguely recalled that he had said this man was a good friend — or if she'd be presented with the bill later.

Brook had left the main light on and the only way to switch it off was to cross the room. Slowly, head throbbing like it had the shop bell inside of it, Rozlyn sat up in bed and swung her legs over the side. Something bothered her. She lifted the fingers of her right hand to her face and looked closely at them. Mud caked beneath the fingernails and smeared across the palm. She remembered falling . . . reaching out, her hand breaking the fall and sliding in the mud.

Her coat hung on the back of the door, but her clothes . . . she was sure that Ethan had hung her shirt and trousers on a hanger and suspended that on the wardrobe door. Cassie had lent her a nightshirt and she wore that now, no sign of mud on that at least.

Rozlyn stumbled across the room and fumbled in the pocket of her leather coat. The spear. God, she still had the spear. Brook would go spare.

Then in the other pocket. She had a terrible premonition of what she would find even before her fingers touched that cold surface. She was sitting on the bed with the disk of bright metal resting in her palm when Ethan returned.

"Ah," said Ethan. "So, that's what you found."

"You knew?"

"Not exactly. I went out for a while so I missed you leaving. Clever of you to find your car; you were hardly fit to pay attention when I told you where I'd parked it. Cassie took your clothes to be washed, by the way. They were soaked through and caked with mud. Red mud. I guess from Mark Richards' land."

"I thought I dreamed all that."

Ethan smiled. "Apparently not. What your boss said about a man being with you . . . ?"

"No. No one. I mean who?" she broke off, recalling the image of the red-haired sword-wielding man who had run beside her. "I dreamed of someone," she said. "And maybe I hit out with my torch, injured someone."

"My torch," Ethan said.

"Your torch? I took your torch?"

"We had a major power outage last winter. Cassandra does not like the dark. Since then we've kept torches in the bedrooms and on the landing."

"Oh." Rozlyn didn't know what to make of it all. She looked more closely at the brooch. "It's beautiful," she said.

"It is. Do you know how you found it?"

She shook her head and then said, "in my dream, which turns out not to have been a dream, I was trying to think how Charlie would have thought."

"You think your friend stole this from Mark Richards?"

"I don't know. I mean . . . Look, we know there have been a series of thefts and that our Art and Antiques division think Donovan Baker was responsible. I found out earlier this evening that Mark Richards and Donovan Baker know one another. And I found evidence that Charlie had been there."

Ethan looked unsurprised. "Baker and Richards move in the same circles," he said. "Both are collectors and they belong, or should I say belonged, to the same organisations. Donovan has not been as prominent of late, not since his little problems."

"Well, Charlie told Mouse that he knew something about stolen antiquities, that this Donovan was involved. Charlie had, I suspect, also figured out what game this Thomas Thompson was playing and had almost certainly worked out that Thomas Thompson and Richards were one and the same person. I figure he went to Richards' place, confronted him, maybe. Stole the brooch but for whatever reason hid it in the chantry."

"Well, you have it now," Ethan said quietly. "Get some sleep. You've got to conserve your strength for seeing your boss tomorrow."

Down to earth with a crash, Rozlyn thought. "Yes, that is going to be fun," she said.

CHAPTER 40

Rozlyn woke mid-afternoon the following day. She felt better, oddly refreshed and clear headed. She showered and then, dressed in the now clean clothes, went downstairs taking the brooch with her.

Ethan had heard her moving about and made tea. He smiled warmly as Rozlyn entered the room and indicated a chair beside the fire. Cassie was curled up on the other side, reading *Alice Through the Looking Glass*, her pretty face creased by a frown as she concentrated. She glanced up at Rozlyn, grinned at her, then went back to her book.

"I should say thanks," Rozlyn told Ethan. "I'm embarrassed. I turn up here at some ungodly hour and you take me in and then I bring trouble to your door. I don't know what I was thinking."

Ethan handed her a mug of tea. It was hot and strong and slightly sweet when Rozlyn sipped at it. It tasted like nectar.

"You're looking better," Ethan told her, "and as for looking after you, what else should I do? Anyway, my belief is that these things happen for a reason. Part of the interconnectedness of life. For you to come walking through my door was not without its purpose."

"The Web of Wyrd," Rozlyn laughed. "You read to me about that. No one's read to me since I was a little kid."

"Ah, well I thought it might be appropriate under the circumstances," Ethan said.

Cassie looked up, bright blue eyes gleaming with interest. "Did you read Kendryk's letters to her?"

Ethan nodded. "Some of them. Would you get them for me please, Cassie? I left them in my room, on the dresser."

Cassie leapt to her feet and trotted off up the stairs. Rozlyn watched her, wondering and saddened at this woman with the body language of a child. "Who's Kendryk?" she asked. "And," taking the brooch from her pocket, "what the hell is this?"

Ethan picked it up and weighed the object thoughtfully in his hand. "In nineteen twenty-two my father was staying at what is now Mark Richards' place. It was then called Albermy and belonged to a man called . . ."

"Frederick Greer. A banker of some sort. I read the book you published. Donovan Baker wrote the foreword."

"Oh. You found that, did you?" Ethan nodded thoughtfully. "In those days we were still . . . we'll I'd never have said we were friends, but we rubbed along well enough. Both experts in the same field, though I was already retired of course but it was inevitable we should work together from time to time, I suppose. Anyway, the quickest way to give you the story, is if you let me tell it from the start."

Cassie returned, carrying a polished wooden box. Ethan took it from her and sat it, closed, on the floor at his feet.

"In nineteen twenty-two, my parents were house guests and, if you read the book, you'll know that a so-called excavation took place one Sunday afternoon in the middle of July."

"A treasure hunt, Donovan called it."

"And a treasure hunt it was. Imagine it, ladies in their silks and gentlemen in waistcoats and shirt sleeves wielding shovels and spades borrowed from the outdoor staff, digging away there in the ruins. There was more of it then, the chantry I mean. A wall fell not long after and another section was removed as a precaution. The stone went into building a rockery in the 1950s, when that sort of thing became something of a fad and I've no doubt close inspection of the rest of the estate would reveal pillars and cornices recycled as birdbath stands or some such."

"I didn't think they found anything?" Rozlyn said.

Ethan smiled. "My father was an amateur historian. He was also interested in what was then the developing science of archaeology. Techniques were still primitive, by today's standards, but some albeit patchy methodology was starting to be applied and my father was an avid reader about such stuff. It was his influence, I suppose, that led me to where I am now. His and my mother's rather unusual skills."

"Unusual?"

Ethan hesitated, but Cassie giggled. "She could see things like Ethan does," she said. "Ethan says you can too, but you don't like to do it yet."

"See things? You mean she was psychic or something?" Rozlyn's laugh was derisive. "I'm sorry, Ethan, but I don't do with that sort of stuff. It's about as real as Alice in that book Cassie's reading."

"And yet, when you took the spearhead from me, you *saw*," Ethan said softly.

"I saw nothing. I just . . . imagined it because of the stuff we'd been talking about, that's all."

"And Treven?"

"Treven?"

"You talked about him in your sleep. That's when I knew you should be told about all of this," he indicated the box and the brooch.

"All of what? Look, I've got one man dead and another beaten so badly he lost an eye. I've got a racket bringing illegal workers into the country and a bloody psycho who, though he might well be an educated man, is little more than a thug, as far as I can see. If you have anything to help me with that, then Ethan, I'll listen gratefully enough. But I don't have time to sit here and let you ramble. You've been great and I don't mean to be rude, but I think it's time I went."

Ethan let her finish and when Rozlyn stood, he did not move. Instead he sat regarding her thoughtfully with his hands steepled beneath his chin. "You can spare me an hour, no more." He said. "Call it a return for hospitality. Then I'll drive you over for your appointment with Brook."

"I don't need that. I've got my own car."

"Which is missing a rear screen and has a bullet hole in the front dash."

"What?" Rozlyn sat down, the strength suddenly going from her legs. "He shot at me, didn't he? Christ." She wiped her hands across her face as though to clear the cobwebs from her thoughts. So much had happened over the last two or three days that they had taken on a dreamlike quality. She was no longer certain she could sort clearly what had actually happened from what she had only imagined. She reached across and took the brooch from the little table where Ethan had placed it.

He poured more tea into her mug. This time, he added milk but no sugar. "Cassie, darling — could you bring those sandwiches through and I think we might have some cake? Can you manage?"

"Sure. You like cherry cake, Rozlyn?"

She nodded, wondering if *they* had gone mad or if it was just her. So many threads but she still wasn't certain how any of them tied up.

"So," Ethan continued. "Nineteen twenty-two."

Rozlyn stared, then came to a decision. She reached for her tea and sat back in the leather chair. "Ok," she agreed. "An hour, then you drive me to town and I see Brook and tell him . . ." She paused and took another deep breath. "Whatever there is to tell."

"Some of it he knows already," Ethan informed her. "I thought it best to mention the car. I told him I'd moved it for you and that you'd been rambling about shots being fired.

Of course," he continued airily, "I'm not *au fait* with such incidents and assumed it was the fever talking."

"Oh sure. Not *au fait*. Right."

"He came back this morning to take a look. They removed the car about an hour ago but there've been people in white overalls crawling over it most of the day. They recovered the bullet, I believe. Brook wasn't impressed by the idea that Mr Richards might have armed men on his property, even if they did happen to be shooting at trespassers. I think it offended him even more that the trespasser in question was one of Brook's own."

"One of Brook's . . . Don't make me laugh."

"Oh, I think he takes this very seriously. I think he takes *you* very seriously. I told him I'd bring you back to town when you woke."

"Happy with that, was he?"

"He didn't have a choice. Ah, thank you, Cassie. Rozlyn, would you move the tea tray? I'll go and make some more, I think."

He left Cassie fussing over Rozlyn's choice of sandwich and disappeared into the kitchen. Rozlyn suspected Ethan was enjoying her impatience.

"Now, where was I?" Ethan asked as he returned.

"Nineteen twenty-two," Rozlyn muttered darkly.

"Ah, yes. You know that there had been rumours about a treasure hidden in the chantry ruins."

"Oh sure. I hear it has a ghost too."

"I imagine it has several. Anyway, the digging didn't last very long. They found a few trinkets and the odd coin, but nothing of any age or worth and so, once boredom set in, off they went, satisfied at having got their hands dirty and carried out more manual labour than ever before in their spoiled little lives. But my parents went back. My mother had *felt* something, you see. She sensed that there was something to be found. Oh, if you don't like that explanation you can settle for the one that says my father knew enough to suspect that the legend was not without foundation. These things rarely are. So they hung around after the others had gone and, beneath the altar stone, buried in a lead casket still sealed with wax, they found these."

He lifted the box from the floor and set it on his lap. Opening it, he removed what Rozlyn thought at first were smaller wooden boxes. As Ethan handed her the first, it dawned that this was a book, the pages thick and oddly textured between wooden covers carved with twining leaves and words she could not read.

Letters chased across the pages, crammed together so that there was little break to define them. The lines ruled by the scribe were still visible and the ink remained black and bold. The writing had been formed in a rounded almost childish hand and the whole was written as though right justified on a modern printer, the margins equal all around. Looking at it, Rozlyn could *almost* make out words. Trying to shape them, to discern where one ended and a second began, she felt a soft jolt of recognition in the pit of her stomach and a shiver that began at the base of her spine and raised hairs on her neck and arms, but she could not immediately place the source of that recognition.

"How old is this?"

"As old, almost, as the brooch. A little younger than the spear."

Rozlyn stared, disbelieving. "It must be worth a fortune? Are you sure it's genuine?"

"Oh, yes, as genuine as it was the day my father stole it from the chantry."

"Stole it? I don't quite understand."

"What is there to understand? He found it and he took it. They replaced the altar stone and disguised what they had done by rubbing the scuffed stone with moss and mud."

Rozlyn shook her head. "I've seen that thing. It's lying toppled on the ground and I'll bet it weighs a quarter ton if it weighs a pound. One man, even a man and a woman together, couldn't move it."

"No, I don't believe they did. My father told me he paid a couple of the gardeners to help. You've got to remember, Rozlyn, even between the wars a house like that would have retained most of the staff it had from when Victoria was queen, so there was help to be had. You've also got to remember that pay was poor and that the demarcation lines were still fully drawn between the indoor and the outdoor staff. In an establishment like Albermy, the outdoor labourers were the lowest of the low. For a few shillings, they'd have kept quiet, at least for a time and, besides, who would have believed them? My father was a respected man. A fine surgeon and a pillar of the community . . . he was, in this case, also a thief."

"But why? What was he, a treasure hunter? He must have been pretty pissed off to find the box contained a couple of books and not the fabled chantry treasure." Even as she said it, she knew that was a stupid statement. These books must be so rare as to be worth more than any gold to a man like Ethan and, probably, to a man like Ethan's father. "How come they've survived so well?" she wondered, turning the precious object in her hands and stroking the heavy cover.

"The pages are vellum. Prepared animal skin. Hence the wooden covers. It has a tendency to curl if it's not weighted down. And they were buried with the intent that they should be preserved, inside a sealed reliquary alongside fragments of bone. The bone served to absorb moisture and the casket was lined with lead and sealed with pitch and wax. Even so there is a touch of the miraculous in their survival. My father was, of course, certain that these would not be the only things concealed beneath the altar. But he never had the opportunity to search again. Albermy was sold the following year and it's been through many changes since.

"In the second war it was taken over as a convalescent home. After that, a school for orphaned children. It went to rack and ruin through lack of money and everyone lost interest in the pile of stones and broken walls that stood in the grounds. I expect children climbed the walls and jumped off the altar stone. I imagine it must have made a wonderful playground. I saw Albermy just before it was sold to Richards. The stucco falling from the stonework let the damp through. The panelling was rotting on the walls and the place stank of mildew and neglect.

"As for the chantry, I could barely reach it. Brambles and birch had invaded and the place run wild. The altar stone itself was invisible behind a stand of nettles higher than my shoulder. I blistered my hands trying to tear them down. Then Mark Richards bought the place and began the restoration. And to give him credit, he's brought the old house back to life."

"And the Donovan Baker excavation? Were you there?"

Ethan was silent as he poured fresh tea. "At first," he said. "Please, eat, you need to build strength. Mark Richards knew nothing of the legends until Donovan and I approached him. Donovan had done the initial research, as he mentions in the book — incidentally, the version you must have is the updated one, published after the second excavation. There was still a demand for it and I allowed the revised version to be printed, though I had little to do with the actual production by then.

"Anyway, Donovan was certain, as was I, that the foundations were earlier than the walls. I'd found an obscure reference to the building of a chantry by the Abbott Kendryk, of Storton Abbey. We've lost the location of Storton, but the chantry . . . Donovan and I believed that this could be the window we searched for, having a view directly onto those past clues to the mother Abbey, perhaps. And, of course, for me there was the incentive of my father's story. Beyond that stupid little treasure hunt back in the twenties, we knew it to be a virgin site. On private land so long that no one had ever touched it. No ploughing, no disturbance to speak of. It was a wonderful opportunity."

"And, of course, you knew what had already been found."

"And was stupid enough to tell Donovan." Ethan fell silent for a while and stirred his tea. It was a meaningless act as he'd added no sugar, and Rozlyn realised, it was merely to give him space to collect his thoughts.

"I let slip to Donovan that something else had been buried beneath the altar. Oh, I didn't tell him about the books. I said I'd found a paper in the library and that it looked like a copied inventory — one list in the original Old English and a second written in translation. In truth, I'd had one of my old students mock this up for me." He smiled, "we are deceivers all when curiosity or greed gets the better of us. My father went to his grave frustrated with the need to know what else lay beneath that stone. It gnawed at him and I never truly understood why. Then, when the opportunity arose for me to find out, it began to gnaw at me in much the same way and for a month or so, I suppose I would have sacrificed anything, moved heaven and earth, never mind a block of stone, to know, to discover what was there.

"Kendryk was right, you see, as was Treven. What lay beneath the altar stone should never have been disturbed. The monks that buried him, didn't fully understand his wishes, so they buried these books with their Abbot and with the other things, believing they had carried out his wishes. I think that he wanted these writings to be known. To serve as a warning."

"Back up a bit," Rozlyn told him. "The library. You're talking about the library at Albermy?"

"Odd, isn't it? But you've got to remember that houses like Albermy were often sold with their contents and furnishings more or less intact. The banker who owned it in 1922 lost almost everything a few years later. Killed himself, I believe. He was an American you see, and even before the famous Wall Street Crash he was making rather bad investments. Selling Albermy was the first of his attempts to . . . downsize, I suppose you'd say now. When Richards bought the place, the library had been locked for years, all through its time as a hospital and a children's home. At the time of the excavation there were conservators in Richards' pay going through it and rescuing what they could, but he knew my work and allowed me free rein. Donovan soon realised we would have to go to Richards with this 'find'. We could hardly move the altar stone without him noticing and, understand, Rozlyn — Mark Richards is an educated man with a genuine interest in his subject. He spent a part of every day on the site."

Rozlyn frowned. There had been something else in Ethan's account that puzzled her. "You believe this Kendryk fellow had been buried beneath the altar too? You know, there's only a small gap, about a foot depth, I'd have said. Is that enough room for a body?"

"Probably, but it's more likely they'd have simply buried his bones there, possibly in a reliquary of some sort. Anyway, I never had the opportunity to find out. I agreed we should go to Mark Richards. He was as excited as we were, but over the next days I began to feel as though I was being sidelined in some way and I also became aware of rumours concerning Donovan Baker . . . there are always rumours, of course. The academic world breeds jealousies and rivalries much as any other, but these came from a source I had to take note of."

"Oh?"

"I had a visit from the police. A Detective Chief Inspector, would you believe? All the way from the Metropolitan Police. The evidence they showed me, combined with odd things Donovan had said convinced me that they may have a case and slowly I began to understand that Donovan was using his position to steal."

"As your father had done," Rozlyn stated softly.

Ethan closed his eyes. He nodded. "My father justified his acquisition and maintenance of these items by saying that he saw the value of them when others — the rightful owners included — would not have done. That was nonsense, of course. Between the wars there was a flowering of Anglo-Saxonism that has since largely withered. Later I began to realise that, for my father at least, this was not the point. He owned a secret and, as I soon discovered, this was not the only thing he owned that rightly belonged elsewhere.

My father was, in his own way, as much a thief as Donovan Baker, the only difference being that my father never sought to profit financially from his thefts. I came to understand also, that, to the very end of his life, my father was consumed by the wish to see what else had been concealed within the chantry."

"What else was there?

Ethan took the second book from the box. Leaning forward Rozlyn could see that the cover on this volume had been faced with enamelled metal. It gleamed in the light from Ethan's small fire, gold and red and vivid blue figured into the shape of a cross. Hanged upon that cross was a one-eyed man, a spear thrust deep into his side. Rozlyn glanced up at the image above the fireplace. "It's the same!"

"There are some differences, but essentially, yes."

"My God, that's magnificent." She reached across and drew her fingers reverently across the gleaming surface. "I can understand why he didn't want to give it up. Though of course," she added quickly, "I can't condone it."

Ethan smiled, his lips thin and pained. He opened the book a few pages from the back and began to read. Rozlyn didn't understand the words, but it was evidently some kind of list. Ethan paused and translated, his words dropping softly into the breathless silence of the room. "Two swords, one with a gold and granulated hilt; a spear head, woven from fine metals and with a long socket; coin to the value of fifty shillings of silver and some twenty more in gold. Harness fittings, gold and silver both, with an ornament like a bear's head and . . ." he paused and looked Rozlyn in the eye. "A brooch, like to a shield boss made in gold and with a trim of red enamel. Let these things lie for all eternity, bought in blood as they were and carried in sin. As Treven wished, these objects shall not be passed on to taint a second generation. Let men yet to come with more wisdom than I lay claim to, do as they please with them, but for me, I am content to give them to the blessings of time and the weaving of the web."

"This brooch? You found this brooch?"

"*I* found nothing," Ethan said. "I made a second mistake. I felt that Donovan deserved the right to answer the charges that were being laid at his door and I told him what I knew. I have never seen such a rage. If a man was ever possessed by evil then that man was Donovan Baker on that afternoon. He ordered me from the site and I left, certain now that the story the police had given me was true. I called Mark Richards, but it became clear that he was more interested in acquiring the chantry treasure than he was in anything Donovan Baker might have done. I realised then that I'd been a fool to trust either of them. I came home and put the matter aside. Until the day you came."

They were silent for a while, listening to the crackling of the fire and their own thoughts, then Rozlyn asked. "This Kendryk, he believed the objects were tainted in some way. That they carried something evil with them?"

Ethan nodded. He tapped the cover of the book he held. "It's all in here," he said. "But I think we have more pressing concerns. I began to realise on the day he threatened me, just what violence was contained within Donovan Baker. He needs to be stopped, before he damages anyone else. This Mouse Man of yours, you think he'll testify?"

Rozlyn was surprised. "I don't recall telling you about him."

"You mentioned him and you talked in your sleep. Besides, I read the papers, you know."

"Mouse can identify Donovan Baker as the man who attacked him. And I believe he'll testify. He's scared out of his wits, but he's shown a good deal more steel than I'd ever have given him credit for."

"That's good," Ethan approved, "and if Donovan implicates Mark Richards . . ."

Rozlyn shook her head. "I've a feeling that's going to be down to Art and Antiques," she said. "They've got facilities for following the paper chase that we ordinary plods don't have." She paused, feeling the need to reprise what she knew. "Richards we know to be involved in people smuggling and

Donovan Baker is at the very least aware of that fact. We've still got to prove it definitively, but I'm certain that Richards is also known as Thomas Thompson, although I don't have any proof as yet. He owns a number of properties that the people he's trafficked are brought to until they're dispersed. Charlie used to clean those houses for him. That's how he became involved."

"And so, presumably, how he became a threat if he found out Richards' real identity."

Rozlyn nodded. "And now Charlie's dead."

"But there was the shooting. Richards' man could have killed you."

Rozlyn nodded. "And that's enough for us to bring him in for questioning at least. Friends in high places or not." She dug in her pocket and produced the clipping Charlie had saved. She showed it to Ethan.

Ethan smiled. "Charity events were always something Mark Richards enjoyed, I believe. Public generosity covering private greed. I wonder if he decided to cut Donovan out of the deal, you know. Once the treasure was found, he'd have to sit on it for a while, at least so long as the excavation was in the news. Or maybe he didn't want to sell in the end. Maybe the pull of what he found was too strong to resist. He stroked the cover of the book with long, strong fingers. "I think I'd be willing to kill to keep these and I'm not a man given to such unconsidered passions."

CHAPTER 41

Events had moved at such a pace that Rozlyn felt she had been absent for weeks rather than under two days. Brook nodded briefly to Ethan then ordered them both into his office. On his desk lay two small evidence bags. Brook picked up the first and passed it over. "Bullet taken from the dash of your car. Nine-millimetre round. And this," picking up the second bag, "bullet recovered from the verge outside of Mark Richards' place. Nine-millimetre round and ballistics are positive for a match. I don't want to know why you were there or what you were bloody playing at. We'll call it following up on information received and call you a stupid fool for not getting back up first. Whatever, I take a very dim view of people firing at coppers, so I've got a nice little warrant here and a couple of armed response units to give that extra puissance to the proceedings."

"Puissance?" Rozlyn didn't think Brook knew words like that.

Brook cast an apologetic look in Ethan's direction. "The younger generation has no feel for the complexity of the English language," he said.

Rozlyn scowled. "Anything on Donovan Baker?"

"My opinion is that he's skipped. The Met have had someone watching his London place for the past two days.

Nada. They went in last night, took his stuff for analysis. If he wants his computer and his papers and his little trinkets back he'll have to go to them and ask nicely. It'll hit the news tomorrow. Donovan Baker's face will be all over the shop. Not," he added bitterly, "that it'll do us any good. Bugger's long gone. Took himself off the same day your Mouse Man saw him leave his office."

"Pity we didn't have anyone available to see him go," Rozlyn couldn't resist the dig.

"Point made and taken," Brook told her irritably. "But he'll turn up. Bad pennies always do. Just give him time and enough rope."

Rozlyn decided it was wiser not to comment on the mixed metaphor. "So, we go when?"

Brook glanced at his watch. "*You* weren't actually factored into this."

"Tough. I want to see his face when we turn up mob handed."

Brook tutted. "Still got it in for the moneyed classes," he said. "Get yourself organised then. Jenny will brief you no doubt. Have to leave your friend here though," he added, nodding at Ethan.

Ethan smiled. "I think I'll be getting off home," he said. He rose and reached across the table to shake Brook's hand. Brook looked as startled as if he'd slapped him in the face.

"Oh, right," he said and shook the proffered hand. He watched thoughtfully as Ethan left the office. "Brothel creepers?"

Rozlyn smiled. "Don't be tempted," she told Brook. "On Ethan, they work. You'd just look even more of a . . ." She left Brook to fill in the missing word and went off to find Jenny Harper.

* * *

They had waited until dark so that the security camera at the gate would be of minimal use and as it would be less likely that

Mark Richards' security people would be in place. Two ARVs parked in the lane on either side of the gates. Their occupants, armed and clad in full safety gear, waited with their vehicles. Rozlyn figured there had to be some additional security system, either by the wall or the chantry ruins. She had done something to trigger a security alert last time and she didn't think it was simply the light from her torch. That knowledge in hand, it had been decided that all units would use the main drive.

Rozlyn watched as a 4x4 was hitched to the gate. It drove slowly forward. The gate creaked and protested, then gave way with a sharp crack that echoed through the stillness like a rifle shot.

"If that didn't wake the buggers I don't know what will," Brook observed. "All right, let's move."

Sandwiched between two armed-response vehicles, Rozlyn — in the passenger seat of Brooks car, flak jacket digging into her thighs — felt dislocated, as though this was something happening to another version of herself. The threads were being pulled tighter, drawing Mark Richards further into the web and, she had no doubt, it would eventually entangle Donovan Baker.

"Quite a place he's got," Brook commented as they crunched onto the gravel in front of the house and the colonnaded facade came into view. Lights blazed in the downstairs widows and in one upper room. Did Mark Richards never leave his study, Rozlyn wondered?

"You reckon we'll find anything? Chances are they'll have dumped the gun and you know his solicitor will be there as fast as Richards can make the call. He'll probably be back home and snug in his bed by morning."

Brook shrugged. "But it'll scare the shit out of him," he opined. "And scared men turn into stupid men." He opened his door and got out. Rozlyn followed. "And knowing Mr Donovan Baker is out there somewhere and looking for revenge on the man that brought his little scams to public notice will mean however soft his bed, he won't sleep easy in it."

Rozlyn frowned. "But Mark Richards hasn't told us anything yet, never mind dumped Donovan in it."

Brook shrugged. "Funny how those bloody journalists get the wrong end of the stick, isn't it?" he said. "Even if our friend Donovan doesn't see tomorrow's papers, you can bet your bottom dollar Mark Richards will and he'll find out a lot of things about himself he didn't know."

He glanced around. The armed officers were in place. The double doors opened with a bang as they made use of a ram in place of a front door key. From inside shouts could be heard. "Armed police. Flat on the floor."

A shadow moved against the lighted window of Mark Richard's room.

CHAPTER 42

Another cold dawn. Frost lay upon the grass and the snow glittered beneath it. Treven recalled that other dawn when he stood and gazed upon the be-webbed jewelled grass as the early dew turned it to a maze of silvered threads.

The web guided them all, wove their lives into a single cloth and there was no escaping it.

Hugh came alone. Breath fogging in the cold air, his horse snorting at the chill and skittering impatiently at the slow pace its master had set.

With an effort of will, Treven greeted him with a smile.

"Stay mounted," he said. "I have something to show you and we would be better riding."

"It takes effort, Treven. I hope you do not plan for a long journey." He spoke lightly, but his face was pale and his eyes creased with pain.

"A scant mile," Treven told him. "Back to the crossroads, no further."

"A spear?" Hugh looked curiously. Treven had blackened the heirloom with soot. A casual glance would not reveal its true identity.

"Osric warned me there are boar sighted near the crossroads. They are hungry. It seemed best to be careful, especially as you are not yet fit for battle, even against a wild pig."

Hugh laughed. "Give me time," he said. "I will find a way."

"Given time, I've no doubt of that."

They spoke little and when they did it was of plans for improving the land, reinforcing the banks close to the ford, and the rebuilding of the hall. When Treven drew off the main path and led Hugh to the sacred grove, he was curious and a little disparaging.

"I confess I am of a mind with Kendryk on this," Hugh said. "Such places hold such fascination for you that it cannot be counted healthy. Given my way, I would raze this place and use the timber for building. The trees are wide and strong. Any woodworker would give them a welcome."

Treven shook his head. He dismounted at the entrance to the grove and helped Hugh to do the same and led him to its very heart.

"I came here hoping for a vision," he said. "Asking for guidance. The snow fell and I could barely see across the circle, so dense was the fall."

"And did you get your vision in the dancing snow?" Hugh mocked gently.

"I received my answer," Treven told him. Softly, he hefted the spear in his hand, finding the point of balance. "Run, Hugh," he said. "Escape the circle and you will go free."

For a stupid moment Hugh stood and stared. He smiled. "You would never . . ." then he looked at Treven's face and the smile faded. "Is this your definition of an honourable act?" he asked harshly.

"When you left the girl to die, you denied yourself all claim on honour," Treven told him coldly. "Now run. Break the circle and I will let you go."

Hugh backed away from him. His gaze swept the snow-covered grass, as he sought the swiftest exit. Then he turned and began to run, knowing that the cause was lost to him even as he took the first steps.

Treven drew back his arm. His aim was straight and true. Hugh fell and lay very still and Treven waited, watching the blood flow from the wound and then cease. When at last he knelt and pulled the weapon free, the ground beneath Hugh's body had sucked the final life from him. He imagined that it left his imprint on bare ground, earth reddened and nourished by his blood.

Treven lifted the body of his one-time friend and tied it across the saddle bow of Hugh's mount. He then broke the shaft from the spear, casting it aside. The spearhead itself he cleaned with freshly fallen snow, wiping blood and soot away from the twining patterns that brought the blade to life and gleamed like dulled sunlight against the silver winter.

* * *

From the writings of Abbot Kendryk of Storton Abbey, Year of Grace 878.

That day he came to me, with the precious heirloom of his house wrapped in red cloth. He knelt, this man who knelt before none but his King and laid it at my feet.

"It is best you keep this for me," he said. No explanation or excuse. He laid the instrument of his judgement at my feet and then left me to make mine. I knew when I unwrapped this weapon, so beautifully wrought, so precious and so deadly, what he had done.

Should I have called him to account for this? I will let those who come after me make their own judgement on that score. But I will say this. I have never had cause to regret my decision, to take this thing from his hands and then to take it to my grave with me. I have ordered that this is to be so and the other things beside, those things of Hugh de Vries that Treven kept and from time to time sold to relieve the suffering of his people. The rest, he gave also into my care. It was his belief that no good could come of handing them down to his sons and to their children and I believe that, at least, was a sound judgement.

For the other, God will examine the hearts of each one of us come that great day when we stand before him and, for my part, I would give more for the heart of Treven of Theadingford than that of Hugh de Vries.

EPILOGUE

Rozlyn arrived home after the raid on Mark Richards' house to find a message on her phone. Her grandfather had fallen ill. There was little hope of him surviving. Could Rozlyn come at once? It made everything else seem wholly unimportant.

It was three in the morning but by five she had arranged her flight and it seemed the most natural thing in the world for her to call Ethan and ask for a lift to the airport.

Her flight left at nine and, gazing out of the window, glimpsing the patchwork of land below the high, wispy cloud, Rozlyn prayed that she would be in time to say goodbye to this old man that was the last of her family. To wish him safe journey and Godspeed to whatever destination he might be headed.

From up here, Rozlyn thought, it was easy to imagine the web of life and fate stretching across the world and linking all things living and . . . whatever the opposite might be. The web that had brought her into Ethan's life and Ethan into hers and Mrs Chinowsky and the old man at The Larks. And Donovan Baker. Rozlyn wouldn't rest until Baker had been found. Silently, she promised the ghost of Charlie Higgins and the living spirit of the Mouse Man that she would find Donovan Baker and see that he paid for what he'd done.

I've always lived life from the sidelines, she thought. Never stepped off the edge. Sometime or other, she told herself sternly, you've got to commit. *Loneliness should not be a vocation*. She had friends and she should value them. Some, she knew, would come to the funeral and Rozlyn made up her mind that she should see her grandfather's end, desperately sad though that was, as a chance for fresh beginnings.

She had new friends too, now, she thought, and she should and would cultivate those as well.

The cloud cover thickened and the view of the ground went from patchy to nothing. For a few minutes she watched the sunlight bouncing off the clouds. Gold and pink and rosy hued and then she turned her attention to the envelope Ethan had given her just before she'd boarded. Inside were notes Ethan had made on the Kendryk scripts. Some he had translated. Others were in their original, incomprehensible form. He'd given Rozlyn what he called a glossary. It appeared to be a dictionary of sorts, though a quick glance told Rozlyn it was all a bit more complicated than that. There seemed to be a half dozen ways of saying 'I' for goodness sake. Just as well it was a long flight.

She riffled through until she found an entry that Ethan had already worked on and began to read. "*Treven*," Kendryk said, "*was a man who knew how to read the land . . .*"

And there had been a second phone call. This one on her mobile as they drove to the airport, from Emlyn Reece at the dig site. He'd been trying to reach Rozlyn since the day before.

"We've found another murder," he said. "Only I think you're a bit late to investigate this one. It was beneath where that poor man's body was found."

"You're kidding me?"

"Oh no, our forensic archaeologist is very excited. The poor chap had been stabbed in the back and then buried face down. That's usually a sign that he'd committed some crime or other and been shunned by his community. But you know what's really strange?"

"I couldn't begin to guess."

"No. I don't suppose you could," Emlyn told her. "But it looks like he'd been killed with a spear."

THE END

ALSO BY JANE ADAMS

MERROW & CLARKE
Book 1: SAFE

DETECTIVE MIKE CROFT SERIES
Book 1: THE GREENWAY
Book 2: THE SECRETS
Book 3: THEIR FINAL MOMENTS
Book 4: THE LIAR

DETECTIVE RAY FLOWERS SERIES
Book 1: THE APOTHECARY'S DAUGHTER
Book 2: THE UNWILLING SON
Book 3: THE DROWNING MEN
Book 4: THE SISTER'S TWIN

DETECTIVE ROZLYN PRIEST SERIES
Book 1: BURY ME DEEP

Thank you for reading this book.

If you enjoyed it please leave feedback on Amazon or Goodreads, and if there is anything we missed or you have a question about, then please get in touch. We appreciate you choosing our book.

Founded in 2014 in Shoreditch, London, we at Joffe Books pride ourselves on our history of innovative publishing. We were thrilled to be shortlisted for Independent Publisher of the Year at the British Book Awards.

www.joffebooks.com

We're very grateful to eagle-eyed readers who take the time to contact us. Please send any errors you find to corrections@joffebooks.com. We'll get them fixed ASAP.

Printed in Great Britain
by Amazon

61509082R00203